To Anne

REJUVENATION I

Book 1 of The Rejuvenation Trilogy

Byddi Lee

It's been great getting to know you at #SHISS23

Byddi Lee

Cover designed by The Gilded Quill

Byddi Lee
Visit my website www.byddilee.com

First Printing: April 2020
Castrum Press

Print Edition ISBN: 9780990769552

DEDICATION

For Mummy

Byddi Lee

ACKNOWLEDGMENTS

Thank you to Castrum Press for first publishing this story and giving it wings. My heartfelt gratitude to Dr. Kate Evans who did a wonderful job with the first round of edits and for teaching me so much about writing in the process.

When I started the *Rejuvenation* trilogy, the amount of research it needed was almost overwhelming. People who were already over-stretched in their busy lives and hectic jobs willingly gave up their precious time to coach me through medical conditions and jargon. To the nurses in my life, your enthusiasm for your work and willingness to share your expertise truly left me humbled and full of gratitude. Do you ever switch off? Thank you to Mickey Moen for advice on fixing broken wrists and fractured skulls, to Tracey McGuigan for advice on hair regrowth, and to Paula Toner, Prudence Vincent, Deidre McCory, Frances Moen, my Godmother -Teresa Kelly, and my Mum - Bernadette Grimley for fielding my stream of medical questions. Thank you also to Dr. Orna Hananel-McCusker and Dr. Dana McManus for their advice and encouragement. I'm also grateful to my old university buddy, GP Carlo, who gave me great suggestions with regards to the future world of pharmaceuticals. Dr. Adam Mellor, thank you for our chats on rising sea levels, marine temperatures, and other stuff *we* think is important!

Dan Bourque, thank you for unraveling the tech and helping me 'invent' the ONIV. Your expertise was invaluable, and your enthusiasm for this project so very much appreciated. Thank you for reading Book one and for giving me your inspiring feedback.

Thank you to Lindsey Williams for sharing her knowledge of police procedure with me, as a new mum back then I appreciate how precious your time was, and how generous you were to share it with me.

For brainstorming the names to use in the trilogy, thank you, Robert Sposili.

If writing a short story is a sprint and a novel is a marathon, then writing a trilogy is the triathlon. It takes a dedicated writing group to get you through a trilogy, so my heartfelt thanks go to the members of the Potluck Publishers in San Jose: Cathy Thrush, Shannon Hemphill, Lucy Geever-Conroy, Eva Smith Glynn, and Anne Geever

Riconosciuto, for seeing me through to the end despite me moving to two different countries during that time – we were more tech savvy that we realized. Thanks are also due to Martha Engber and the Monday Night writers in San Jose for their critiques of book one while I lived there, and especially to Doug Stillinger, who helped me craft the first plot outline. When I moved to Paris, Sonya Moore, Omaya Nasser, and Nina Francus bravely started at book two and stayed for book three also sticking with me when I left the country. Thanks for the encouragement, the friendship and the reason to return often to Paris (as if anyone needed a reason to visit Paris!) And a special thank you to Paulette Boudreaux, a friend and writing mentor who has taught me so much – I look forward to more long chats with you.

Thanks are also due to Jo Zebebede for providing an excellent local platform for Sci-Fi writers with Otherworlds NI. I met Jo through Women Aloud NI and want to thank the women there for their camaraderie and providing a wonderfully supportive writing community and platform for local women writers, especially my dear friend Karen Mooney for promoting local authors so brilliantly. I'm also extremely grateful to the Arts Council NI for the National Lottery funding for mentoring by the amazing Bernie McGill which helped me finish the trilogy.

To Allan Lee, my wonderful husband, thank you for the tech advice, and the unconditional support – I could not have written this without you. Thank you to my family and friends for listening to my story ideas, encouraging me, and believing in me.

REJUVENATION

CHAPTER 1

JUNE 10, 2034

A worm flew up against the kitchen window. It stuck for a moment then peeled off, dropping into the rose bushes beneath, leaving a bleary smudge on the glass. The toddler, Joy cackled on the lawn. Her hand star-fished above her head from flinging the creature. Her other hand, curled into a fist around another worm, and drifted toward her mouth. Strands of Joy's black hair tangled with the worm and stuck to the mix of snot and muck smeared across her flush chubby cheeks.

The sight turned Bobbie's stomach.

"Joy, let go!" Bobbie grabbed the child's coiled fingers, aware that anger made her rougher than she should be and added a sharp edge to her voice.

Joy dropped to her knees and arched her back, flinging her head back into Bobbie's stomach, causing the older sibling to release a gasp. Bobbie held on and pried the worm loose. One end of the creature was a bleeding mush, the other writhed, tickling the palm of Bobbie's hand. Torn between disgust and pity, she stepped away from the toddler who rolled on the ground, pounding her dismay into the grass with clenched fists and kicking feet.

Bobbie ignored Joy's screams and stared at the mess of worm. Should she put the creature out of its misery or tend to its wounds? At sixteen, Bobbie had her heart set on being a doctor, but that didn't include administering to worms. *Kinder to kill it and put it out of its misery.*

Cringing, she dropped the worm to the ground before pressing the grub beneath her shoe, thankful that the sturdy sole did not transmit the sensation of a soft body squishing. Her imagination was not so considerate.

Joy pushed herself to her feet and tore off toward the daffodils.

Exhausted after twenty minutes left in charge of the little terror, Bobbie reached her sister a second too late. Joy sheared the tops off three flowers and shoved them into her mouth. Petals fluttered and stuck to the slime around the child's face. Her lips bulged, unable to close around the ragged yellow flower heads.

"Stop, you brat!" Bobbie grabbed Joy's arms wanting to dig her fingers in hard but stopped herself. Joy was only two. Bobbie wrestled the crushed blossoms from the child's mouth. *How can someone so small be so strong?*

Joy threw her head back and discharged an ear-shattering squeal, tattered daffodil petals sputtering from her mouth in a furious yellow fountain.

"Shut up!" Bobbie said, letting the words drip with the bitterness that exploded inside her. When Bobbie's twin sister, Gracie died three years ago from a rare genetic disease, the government had permitted her parents another pregnancy to replace their lost child. But this creature was no substitute for the sister Bobbie mourned.

The back door slid open. Bobbie's stomach dropped as she looked up into the taunt face of her mother.

"Girls–get into the house right away," her mother said in a voice Bobbie would never have dared defy.

We're both in trouble now.

Bracing for a lecture, Bobbie grabbed a much-subdued Joy by the hand. Together they followed their mother through the house and into the living room. Father strode the length of the room, speaking into his headset in urgent tones, twisting his neck to keep the TV in his line of vision as he paced. Bobbie's eyes followed her mother who was also staring at the TV, her hands raised to cover her open mouth.

Bobbie's head turned to the screen and Joy's hand slipped from her own as her complete attention became focused on the broadcast: explosions and blasts of steam climbed high into the sky. *Has there been a huge volcanic eruption? Are we in danger?*

Bobbie tuned out her father's voice as she tried to make out what was being said on the TV. "The Antarctic icecap is melting... unidentified source of heat energy... vast tracks of land have flooded, populated, unpopulated..." The studio returned to the news anchor, sitting behind his desk struggling to keep his face business like while the plume of steam rose high into the air on the image behind him. A sheen of moisture broke through the make-up on his forehead. He ignored the drop of sweat rolling down his temple in a pale rivulet to his jaw and continued his report.

"There are now reports that this spike in global temperatures is melting glaciers in the Rockies, the Alps, and the Himalayas, inundating inland areas in smothering mud-washes and causing landslides, laying waste to prime farmland and desert alike."

The image behind him switched to show boiling torrents of gray-brown water surging between houses. A grainy, momentary close-up of a swept-away car showed the driver and one passenger with faces pressed against the windscreen. Mouths opened in soundless yells. Fists pounded the glass. The car swung around, struck the corner of a building, and flipped over, before sliding under the swirling, muddy water.

"News just in," the news anchor stated urgently, ratcheting Bobbie's heart rate. "More high energy blasts have hit London, Dubai, Mumbai, Hong Kong, and New York. Over to our US correspondent..."

On the screen, something that looked like a green candle was melting, wax dripping down its sides. With a fresh rush of horror, Bobbie realized the candle was the Statue of Liberty.

"... There's no hope for Manhattan now. No-one could have survived that blast. The melting point of bronze is about 950°C." Behind him, surging waves broke against the feet of the melted statue.

Manhattan!

Bobbie turned to face her father who had stopped his pacing, completely enthralled by the developments on screen. "What's happening?" Bobbie asked, her chest tight.

"A high-energy beam originating from outside the earth's orbit... started with Antarctica," her father said without taking his eyes off the screen. "Maureen," he said, managing to tear his eyes from the TV and step over to Bobbie's mother, taking her hand in his. "The US Air Force, Indo-Asian-Pacific Allied Front, and Euro-Alliance are calling in all pilots, anyone with aviation experience. I have to go to Shannon Airport. Right away!"

"Oh, God!" Maureen put her hand to her throat.

"No! Daddy, you can't," Bobbie cried, grabbing his free hand. "Please. We need you here."

The hug he pulled her into didn't ground her like the gesture should have.

"I have to help, Bobbie." He kissed her head. "I have to go for you and Joy, for all our sakes."

As her arms wound around his waist, she inhaled in his scent: spicy, woody, clean, the smell of safety, of family.

"... we estimate the worldwide death toll to be approaching one billion as people get trapped in flooding coastal cities..." The anchor's voice broke with emotion. Bobbie had never seen a journalist cry before. Somehow that alarmed her more than the horrific footage.

Her clasp on her father tightened. Gently, he unwrapped her arms, dropping to one knee, his face now level with hers. His dark almond-shaped eyes, brimming with a mix of concern and fear, bored into hers. "I love you. I'm so proud of you. You were so brave and strong after Gracie died. I know you can do this." He folded her into another hug, crushing her face to his chest, the woolen sweater he wore scratchy against her cheeks, sensitive and raw from tears.

Her first sob fed into another then another. She pushed him back, hiccupping as she fought for enough control to speak. "Isn't Shannon by the sea? Won't the Air Force base there be underwater? How high are we here?" She broke free of his arms and ran to the window. Outside nothing had changed - yet. But was their house in Armagh high enough? Ireland was a tiny island. Would they all drown? Would one of those high-energy beams come crashing out of the sky and blast them, just like Manhattan?

"Come back from the windows," her mother said, balancing a wide-eyed Joy on one hip. She placed Bobbie beside her father and reached around to embrace them both, drawing them closer. Bobbie clung to her family. Terror clawed at her chest.

Her father pulled away from the huddle first. Bobbie trailed behind him out into the hall where he grabbed a suitcase from the cupboard and raced upstairs. Standing with one foot on the bottom stairs, Bobbie was torn between following him and staying with her mother. She jumped when her mother's phone rang.

"Yes, we're okay," Bobbie's mother said.

Thumps on the floor above made Bobbie look up at the ceiling. *What was he doing up there?*

Bobbie took Joy into her arms, flattening herself against the wall as her mother squeezed past her and tore up the stairs. Bobbie followed behind her mother as she burst into the bedroom talking so fast into the phone that Bobbie couldn't make out what she was saying. Clutching Joy to her, Bobbie watched in disbelief, her eyes blurring with eyes, as the suitcase, open on the bed, filled with her father's clothes and essentials.

"I'll see you in a minute then, Mum." Maureen finished the call and focused on Bobbie's father. "Mum and Dad are on their way. He's going with you."

"What?" Bobbie jolted from her stunned silence. She set Joy on the bed and the whimpering child scrambled toward her mother.

"What can Granda do? He's seventy-five!" Bobbie cried.

"The United Nations has called up anyone fit enough to work a consol." Her father closed the clasps on the suitcase with a snap. "Thank God, your mother can work from here. Granny Gloria will be here for you too. She'll keep you right." He lifted the case and marched downstairs into the living room, his family trailing behind him.

"No, please, Daddy. Don't go." Bobbie ran to him sobbing.

He took her face in his hands and said, "It's alright, sweetheart. I'll be back before you know it." He bent and kissed the top of her head.

The urgent sound of the TV broke the moment. "It's just been confirmed." The TV anchor's voice shook, sending a swoop of terror through Bobbie. She twisted around in her father's arms to look at the screen. Tears flowed down the man's face as he continued, "The energy beam is extra-terrestrial. We are under attack!"

The television screen went blank.

* * *

SEPTEMBER 2053

A striped mackerel swam past the window. The shimmer of its silvery scales mesmerized Doctor Bobbie Chan as she watched it through the thick glass that spanned the entire length of the ward, Pelagic 1 North. The hospital took up thirty floors of the sixty story Belfast Subscraper One, with the upper twenty floors rising above sea level. Bobbie's worked in the geriatric wards of the Pelagic Levels, located on floors six through forty. Residential homes for the elderly comprised the Bethnic levels which ran from floor one, seabed level, to floor five. Bobbie, at twenty-five meters down, had good visibility today. She could make out the remnants of Belfast City Hall nearby. Decades of submersion had draped the city hall in a rainbow of color as corals and algae made the once pristine Portland stone brickwork their home while the green copper tops of the four corner towers were visible among the blue shadows of water. A tourist submarine chugged past emblazoned with neon advertising for underwater tourism franchises in London, New York, and Sydney.

More mackerel streamed past in a lazy upwards spiral. Bobbie wondered if her mother could see them from her hospital bed a few floors above. A forlorn smile tugged at the edges of Bobbie's lips as she remembered how she used to get a kick out of saying, 'Holy mackerel,' and pointing at them when they'd swim past her window when she'd first been admitted.

Was mum doing that now? Bobbie wondered. Unlikely. Her mother might not survive the night.

Grief hung like a wet, woolen cloak around Bobbie's shoulders. She sucked in a deep breath, pulled her doctor face on, and continued down the ward. Twelve cubicles housed the patients she shared with Doctor Hicks. Each compartment, separated from the others by intepanels, contained a bed, a locker, and a chair.

Outside, light flickering in yellowed glints off a cluster of sand-like grains drifting toward the ocean floor caught her eye–the underwater equivalent of dust motes gentle descent had a soothing quality on Bobbie's mood.

Holy mackerel shit thought Bobbie, giving herself a mental shake. *Back to work. Concentrate.*

Bobbie stopped at the first cubicle and stood, so her elbow touched the wall to avoid the swell of nausea she suffered if she read her ONIV while walking. Eight years ago, when she'd had her Optic Nerve Intercept Visualization inserted, the biotech practitioner assured Bobbie she would get used to it. No chance. The communication chip, implanted along the optic nerve between her eye and her visual cortex, tricked her brain into seeing images as if they were floating in front of her, but it didn't fool her stomach into believing it was a natural occurrence.

Numbers clicked past, delivering her patient's biochemistry status, along with temperature, heart rate, blood pressure, oxygen saturation levels, and respiration rate. In the top right corner of her field of vision, the icon for her blink application hung dull and lifeless–no calls or text messages about her mother yet. No blinks at all.

A lock of hair fell over her face and swung behind the display in a distracting blaze of ginger. She tucked her hair behind her ear. Directing her gaze, she selected from the drop-down menu and pressed the electrode embedded in the pad of her little finger against the one in her thumb.

The technology was antiquated, but she had avoided moving over entirely to mind-controlled devices. She found it difficult enough to put a filter on her mouth without needing one on her thoughts too.

Bobbie directed the intepanels that sectioned off the cubicle to turn opaque on either side of her. Another selection allowed her to bring up the data on the intewall above the patient's bed. Bobbie preferred to view the data on the intescreen where there was more room to see everything at once and it left her vision free to work and interact with the patients.

Aayushi Dhawan, lay propped up and dozing. Her silver hair hung in strands over one shoulder, flowing down onto her pale pink sensorfabrik tunic that kept her body temperature constant. Aayushi's choice of color lent a warm hue to her skin; it looked like rich toffee, warm and soft, etched with fine gray-brown wrinkles.

She scanned the information listed in scrolling columns. Aayushi's calcium levels were abnormally high. Bobbie arched an eyebrow. Had she detected a parathyroid tumor? But that couldn't be, or else she would see a rise in the parathyroid hormone levels, but conversely, those hormone levels had dropped.

Interesting, and very unusual, but how concerned should she be? Curiosity zoomed Bobbie's thoughts to focus like a lens. *Okay, let's work this problem through.* Parathyroid hormone levels elevated with age, contributing to osteoporosis, but in Aayushi, both the calcium levels and the parathyroid levels suggested values more commonly found in a thirty-year-old, not someone who was 112.

Bobbie's hands were pale against her patient's arm as she felt for the pulse. Aayushi opened her eyes, the lids disappearing into a swath of wrinkles that reached down into her cheeks. The old lady's face folded into a smile as she spoke, "It's good to feel the human touch. The scanner is so impersonal."

Bobbie kept her hand on Aayushi's wrist, remembering her small hand in a less wrinkled version of this one–back thirty years to her first day at school and the first time she'd touched this woman who'd taught three generations of Bobbie's family.

"Okay, you caught me," Bobbie said, smiling back. Technology often alienated the elderly, leaving them lonely. "How do you feel today?"

"Much better." Aayushi pushed herself up in the bed. "The swelling in my joints seems to have gone down. I'm not in as much pain. In fact, I think I missed a pill last night, and I haven't been able to do that in ten years." She nodded to her bedside table.

An unopened medipatch lay in a tray. Bobbie picked up the medicine, smiling at Aayushi's description of the medipatch as a 'pill' though it resembled an old-fashioned Band-Aid. Last week Aayushi had been moved into the ward from the Benthic levels where she lived, twenty-five stories below because she had needed help with pain management.

"This is great, Aayushi. And you're comfortable? Pain free?" Bobbie studied her patient's face, noting with a lift to her heart the relaxed expression and twinkle that had returned to her old teacher's eyes.

Aayushi nodded, grinning, her implanted teeth too new for her face. "I feel great."

As a geriatrician, Bobbie didn't experience her patients' 'recovering' often. The symptoms Aayushi was displaying were strange and most likely temporary, but preferable to the permanent relief that her patients ultimately received. She made a mental note to discuss Aayushi's improvement with Doctor Hicks.

Bobbie cleared the intepanel of data and replaced it with a woodland scene she knew Aayushi liked. She turned to the old lady and caught her staring at her hands.

"What is it?" Bobbie asked gently.

"It makes my decision harder now." Aayushi kept her head bowed, her eyes down.

"Your decision?" Bobbie's scalp prickled.

Aayushi waved a hand. "Nothing, never mind."

"You're not thinking of–" Bobbie didn't want to trigger the blink audio by saying the words Elective Passing.

Aayushi turned her head away.

"Did you have a nice visit with your granddaughter yesterday?" Bobbie brightened her tone, but her pulse pounded in her ears.

Aayushi nodded.

Bobbie's heart plunged to her stomach. She looked around. The ward was quiet. No carebots, no staff nearby. She wasn't allowed to turn off her blink while on duty, but if she were careful, her conversation would go unnoticed.

"Your granddaughter must have been thrilled to hear you were feeling better," Bobbie said. Silence descended on the room.

Aayushi turned to face her. Tears quivered in her brown eyes. Her lips pressed into a thin line.

Careful, careful. Bobbie narrowed her eyes in warning.

"It's alright for you," Aayushi said. "By my count, you and your sister have two Rights to Birth now. Am I right?"

Sadness puckered Bobbie's brow. Her father and grandfather's deaths in the war each translated into a Right to Birth.

And another on the way...

She tore her thoughts from her mother and nodded, searching for impossible words. How could Bobbie urge this lovely woman to stay alive if she wanted to go because she couldn't bear the pain any longer? But, how could Aayushi's granddaughter push her toward Elective Passing? Medical advances had smashed the biological clock, yet some people were just too impatient, too selfish. Was it selfish of Bobbie to want to keep her patients alive? With the right pain management, the right resources, everyone could live a good life right to the end, a natural end.

"It makes sense." Aayushi's fingers toyed with a button on the cuff of her nightgown.

Biting her tongue, Bobbie smoothed down the sheets and straightened Aayushi's pillows.

"I voted against the Dependency Law you know," Aayushi said.

Was she inviting Bobbie to voice an argument for rejecting Elective Passing?

"You don't have to–" Bobbie began.

Aayushi cut in, "Boy, those government ads; they were rough."

Belus Corp had portrayed a future world of old folks rotting away in unstaffed care facilities, with the streets full of wild-eyed, starving street urchins who had no parental supervision. The ads had seemed to Bobbie to be less about population age structure and more about scaring folks into supporting euthanasia. As far as Bobbie was concerned, Elective Passing was the thin edge of the wedge.

"There are medical breakthroughs every day," Bobbie said.

"I don't need to live forever."

"That's not what I mean." Bobbie never knew how to explain her stance. Sure, Elective Passing would release a suffering elder from pain with dignity, but death was such a full stop. Dammit, why had she chosen geriatrics? It was the ultimate dead-end job. But back when she'd had to pick her specialty, Bobbie had no other choice. She did it for Gracie and offered every day up for Gracie.

Bobbie scrolled through Aayushi's biometrics on her blink screen. Steady. Calm. Professional.

"And you should be caring for children, not geriatrics." Aayushi sighed. "I'm a dead weight here..."

Bobbie closed her hand around Aayushi's fingertips and gave them a gentle squeeze. "One out, one in doesn't work anymore." Bobbie picked up the unopened medipatch beside Aayushi's bed. "You have been feeling better, haven't you?"

"Yes, but it might be too late," Aayushi said, her voice a shade darker.

Bobbie resisted the urge to turn and face her old teacher in case her sudden action attracted attention. "You haven't signed anything, have you?" Bobbie's pulse sped up as she opened the dialogue box on the pharma-streamer to view Aayushi's medication history.

Aayushi huffed out a laugh. "Who signs anything now?"

"Electronically, I mean. Did you make any agreement?" Bobbie urged, impatient for the answer but trying not to bully a woman who was already so vulnerable.

"Maybe," Aayushi said, a haunted quality to her eyes.

A chill shivered up Bobbie's spine.

Aayushi closed her eyes, her head falling back onto the pillow.

Bobbie waited. Time ticked out a pulse at her ear.

"I told my granddaughter I'd consider it." A tear formed in the inner hollow of Aayushi's eye and slid along the side of her nose.

"Let me talk to her," Bobbie said. "Please. Especially now, you are making progress."

"She'll not take kindly to you talking to her. She'll get you disciplined you know. She's like that." Aayushi sighed. "Besides, I'm in the way. It's a fact. This is not me feeling sorry for myself."

Her words broke Bobbie's heart to hear such a wonderful woman talk this way. As a teacher, Aayushi would make up a song on the spot about a child, making them feel like the star of their own musical. She had given so much of herself to so many people over the years, was it too much for her to ask for something in return? But Bobbie knew Aayushi wouldn't want to take–she was one of life's givers.

Bobbie stopped laying out the new medipatches dispensed from the pharma-streamer and faced her patient, "We have so much to learn from you."

"Good Lord, I have nothing new to say," Aayushi said.

"I love hearing your stories, all about the old days before the Melters War..."

"Back then, there was nothing but war. At least the Melters War brought us peace. Nothing like an alien threat to unify us," she said ruefully. "The young ones don't need to know about people shooting other people, nor about us blowing each other up over differences like skin color, religion, water shortages." Aayushi's dark eyes lost focus as they gazed out from her furrowed face. "We were worse than animals back then."

"Those are the stories we need," Bobbie said, "to remind us not to go back, and to show us how far we've come. Besides," Bobbie winked, "who'd be there to scold us and tell us the same story dozens of times over?"

"Oh, Doctor Chan." Aayushi reached up to touch Bobbie's chin. "My little Bobbie. Even as a small child, your heart was big. Your grandmother and mother were the same." She lifted her head a little and looked to Bobbie. "How is your mother?"

"Not great." Bobbie's chest constricted. "She's receiving palliative care now."

"Hard to believe there are cancers we still can't cure," Aayushi said. "It hardly seems fair. Here I am, 112, and waiting to go."

Bobbie swallowed the scorch of sorrow as she pictured her mother a few floors above them, dying. "I'll tell Mum you were asking about her." Bobbie kept the choking flood of emotion from her voice.

Don't cry–be strong for them... make them laugh... Bobbie's twin sister's words floated to her from another era.

"Don't cry, Bobbie," Gracie had said, thirteen years old and dying. "Be strong for them. Mummy and Daddy will need you to pull them through after I go. Make them laugh, not cry." Curled together on Gracie's hospital bed, cuddling as they'd done since conception, Bobbie had clamped down on her sobs and vowed to live up to her sister's last words. She hadn't honored her promise to Gracie each and every day of the twenty-two years since then. Making them laugh was tough, but Bobbie had the don't cry thing under control.

Bobbie checked Aayushi's calcium and endocrine levels again. They continued to register abnormally high for someone her age. *A software malfunction?* She sent a blink to the unit's manufacturers, Succor Tech, to report the glitch.

She patted Aayushi's arm. "You're doing well but take your patch if you need it. We don't give out medals here for those who can stand the most pain."

"I will. I will." Aayushi placed her hand on top of Bobbie's. The skin on the palm of Aayushi's hand felt smooth, not soft, just firm and well-worn, like a pebble from a riverbed.

"When Mum..." Bobbie cleared her throat. "I wanted to let you know that there will be a replacement doctor taking care of you for a while when..." Bobbie found the words too hard to say. "When the time comes."

"Okay, dear, I understand." Aayushi fingers squeezed Bobbie's hand.

"Do you want the screens open?" Bobbie asked, stepping back from the bed.

Aayushi nodded drowsy-eyed.

Bobbie set the intepanels to transparent and activated her ONIV in ticker-stream mode so the words from incoming messages or data would trickle along the bottom of her field of view, appearing to float six feet in front of her. She hated walking with the full screen on. Bobbie had an irrational fear of bumping into it, never mind overcoming the nausea. Hicks had laughed at her when she first got ONIV because her left hand would defensively rise as she moved.

A closed eye icon popped on to the screen. A new message. Panic bubbled in her chest. News about her mother? How long did she have? Months? Days? Perhaps... only hours...? Using the trembling fingertips of her clammy hands she opened the blink. It was the hospital personnel department; a sigh escaped her lips. *Replacement doctors are in shortage at this time. Therefore, a locum will not be assigned to you until the hospice ward confirms the necessity.*

Relief transformed to frustration and Bobbie swore under her breath as she walked halfway down the ward to the staff station. A squat scourbot, humming like a swarm of bees as it cleaned the floors, scooted beneath a patient's bed as if it were hiding from her mood.

Necessity! How much dying was dying enough? She knew how short-staffed they were, how short-staffed everyone was, everywhere, with a planet full of elderly people, but that didn't make it any easier to keep it together for the next hour until her shift ended. She wanted to be with her mother. Hold her hand. Stroke her hair. Smell her skin. Tuck every memory away somewhere sacred, instead, she was tending to other people while strangers nursed her mother.

At the staff station, Nurse Phillips nodded to Bobbie as she approached before his gaze zoned back to the space directly in front of him, his right hand making a palm-down stroke as he resumed flicking through files on his ONIV.

The sound of low voices caused Bobbie to look toward the far end of the ward where Doctor Ryan Hicks was chatting with a patient. The old woman grinned at something Hicks said then shook a finger at him as though scandalized. All the female patients were besotted with him. At six-foot-three, he towered over his patients like a giant in a fairy tale. Their beds always needed to be raised for him.

Bobbie and Hicks had grown up together, and he'd always been big, as kids he had taken up so much space at the doll's tea parties that Gracie insisted he attend. Now, his large hands had trouble fitting into surgical gloves, and hospital-issue scrubs stretched taut across his back and chest. The matching pants skimmed his ankles and rode up his legs when he bent his knees to walk. Hicks was put together all wrong for a doctor. Bobbie could picture him out working the land, swinging bales of hay onto his shoulders, and striding across the fields.

Hicks's strode up the ward toward Bobbie, his five-o'clock shadow made his skin appear sallow below his high cheekbones and the brown bristles echoed the brown crew cut of his hair. The residue of a smile lingered in the creases around his gray eyes.

Phillips rose to greet him, "I'll get those meds for Ms. Wattson now."

"Thanks," Hicks said. "I've just sent you the new dosages."

Phillips's eyes lost focus as he read his blink, then his vision seemed to reignite as he looked at both Hicks and Bobbie and said, "Thanks."

Hicks gaze followed Phillip's receding back for a moment before turning to Bobbie, his face beaming.

"You're early for your shift," she said, feeling warmed by his smile.

"I wanted to discuss some case notes with you," Hicks said, joining her at the staff station and leaning against it on one elbow.

"Oh, really? Funny, I'd like to discuss one of my patients with you, Aayushi Dhawan." She faced him, mirroring his pose with her elbow on the countertop.

"Your old teacher?" Hicks peered down into Bobbie's face. "You're upset. Too close? Want me to take her on?"

Bobbie looked around to check on Phillips's whereabouts before saying, "She's talking about... you know."

Hicks narrowed his eyes.

Bobbie drew a line along her neck with her finger and stuck her tongue out the side of her mouth.

"Oh, I see," Hicks said in a rush. "I hope you didn't say anything. You're on thin ice already."

Ironic that he kept telling her that, in a world that pretty much had no ice.

"No, I'm not stupid," Bobbie said. "Can you take a look at her notes or not?"

"All right, all right. Send me her case notes. In return, could you look at Michaela Wattson for me? I'll blink her notes to you now."

"Okay. Got it," Bobbie said, opening the Wattson file immediately it appeared on her ONIV and scanned the notes. "Yes, I see. Sats improving, BP down to normal, and increased mental acuity." Bobbie paused at an entry and looked up at Hicks. "She recognized her daughter yesterday? That must've been nice for her." She wondered if her own mother would ever recognize her again. Her heart skipped a beat, but she shoved the sadness away before Hicks saw it.

"I checked other wards." Hicks lowered his voice. "Three of my patients have a high incidence of non-compliance with BP medication. Yet the BP normalized without treatment."

"Are you sure they didn't start taking their BP meds again?"

"Positive."

"Have I missed a new medication? Have you changed their prescriptions?" Bobbie scrolled through the notes trying to answer her own questions.

"No. I wondered the same," Hicks ran his hands through his hair, leaving it in untidy spikes, "but we use the same nanopharm company, so I checked the scripts for all my patients. Nothing has changed."

"We've only observed these symptoms in a few patients, but if it were a pharmaceutical issue, wouldn't they all be improving?" Bobbie closed Wattson's notes and opened those of her own patients looking for comparable changes in medication. "Less pain relief requested in two arthritis patients."

"I have another three patients with the same thing. Their pain points are lower. It's great but very unusual," Hicks said.

"I'd like to go see them," Bobbie said, standing up straight. "Which ward are they in?"

"Pelagic 1 North and South only. Nothing unusual in P1 East and West." Hicks straightened up too. Bobbie turned on her heel and trotted through the ward.

The intepanels glowed white as Bobbie and Hicks made a brisk pace along the corridor that ran, like one of many spokes of a wheel, through the center of the subscraper to Pelagic 1 South, on the opposite side of the building. Pelagic 1 South was where the male geriatric patients were treated.

"How's your mum?" Hicks asked as they walked.

She stared ahead and swallowed. Her voice dried up.

"That bad, eh?" Hicks said.

"Worse but not bad enough to give me time off."

"I'm sorry."

"I know."

Hicks had been there, a solid rock every time she'd lost someone. He'd been lucky. His parents were still alive, and he was an only child, though she and Gracie had been like sisters to him.

"If there's any –" he began.

"I... no... please don't," she said.

"Bobbie, it's okay to show your feelings." He glanced sideways at her as they continued to walk.

Bobbie shrugged. Hicks was all about getting her to talk, but she wanted to stuff these horrible feelings into some dark corner.

"Emotions are like a cowpat," Bobbie said, making her voice sound jaunty as she stole a glance at him.

"Cowpat? What?" His expression questioned her sanity.

She couldn't blame him.

"Yes, cowpats–when they are fresh, they stink the most. Older cowpats are gooey inside, but with the crust over the top, they stop smelling so bad," she said. The banter helped her hide the pain.

"Oh, I see, and when they get old enough, you can pick them up and throw them away like a Frisbee?" Hicks flicked his hand.

"Exactly!" She felt a rush of warmth toward him for playing along and allowing her this emotional distraction.

"Hmmm. Nice analogy."

"No," Bobbie said, trying hard to keep her lips from twitching. "It's a crap analogy!"

Hicks rolled his eyes and groaned.

Bobbie smiled. Gracie was right. Laughter was better.

"Are you going to see your mum after your shift?" Hicks asked.

She nodded, feeling her smile fade. She'd sleep on the hard bench beside her mother's bed. It might be enough to fool her biosensors into thinking she'd gotten real rest.

"I'll look in after work," he said.

"There's no need..."

"For me, Bobbie. Not for you. I've known her all my life remember."

"Sure, sure. Okay, then..." She turned but kept her face away from Hicks as they continued walking toward Pelagic 1 South.

"What about Davitt?" Hicks asked, changing the subject. "Is he home from India yet?"

"No. One more week." Bobbie didn't mind that her boyfriend had to be away right now. It gave her space to concentrate on her mother. Sharing her sorrow with Davitt felt too intimate.

Their pace slowed as they entered the ward. Bobbie hauled in her emotions and stashed them far away from her professional persona. The ward was identical to the one they'd left, except all the patients were men.

"What's up, Docs?" Gomez Lantana called from his bed in the first cubicle.

"How are you today, Gomez?" Bobbie walked closer to him, waiting for her proximity to him to trigger his medical notes to her ONIV display.

"I feel so good; I could watch a marathon." Gomez's lips stretched and caved inwards, where his teeth should have supported them. His eyes, though watery to the point of gummy, still carried a spark. He'd have been cute in a baby-faced way in his prime. Now at 112-years-old, he was bald and wrinkled.

Hicks stood beside her and picked up an unused patch from Gomez's bedside table. Bobbie and Hicks shared a glance.

"You haven't accessed pain relief today, Gomez. Why not?" Bobbie asked. This guy was one of the easy patients.

"Don't need 'em, Doc. Might start training for that marathon." Gomez reached forward in the bed as if to touch his toes.

Bobbie noticed a patch of dark fuzz on the back of his head. It looked like the downy hair on a new baby. *How curious.*

"Can you sit forward again, please?" she said, switching on her Eye-cam-di and snapping a couple of photos. As she leaned in closer to Gomez, she caught his scent, milky yet earthy, normal for him.

She blinked a message to Hicks. *You need to see this.*

She moved aside to make room for Hicks, who leaned forward and scrutinized the new hair growth. They switched places again, and she fluffed up Gomez's pillow. "There. That should be more comfortable now."

Gomez lay back, thanking her as she made her goodbyes. She followed Hicks back to the staff station in the middle of the ward in silence. When they reached it, he turned and scratched his bristled chin.

"Is his hair growing back?" Hicks asked, his eyebrows pulled together. "How extraordinary!"

"Odd, and his parathyroid levels are abnormal, just like Aayushi Dhawan. I'm thinking endocrine imbalance?" Bobbie loved a challenge, but this one seemed to have no loose thread where she could begin to unravel the knots.

Hicks stared off into the distance as he read the data in his ONIV. He shook his head, equally stumped.

"I'll check the biosensors," Bobbie said.

Hicks nodded. "We might have some technical issues. Let's find out, but if not, then what? We need to consider all angles. Are we seeing a pathogen? Must we contain it?"

"Haz-mat suits to protect against hair regrowth?" Bobbie said. "Disease Control would laugh at us."

"I hear you." Hicks rubbed his chin. "Unless this condition was harmful to everyone..."

He had no need to finish his thought. Disease Control's lack of concern with saving the lives of the ultra-elderly already angered Bobbie, but if these symptoms proved contagious, or harmful, to the general population, they would have to act.

A buzz at the base of her skull alerted her to an incoming message. Panic beat in her chest. The words floated off to her left field of vision, and she couldn't catch her breath.

"Oh, God," Bobbie stammered and leaned against the desk. "I've got permission to call the locum."

CHAPTER 2

The elevator traveled in an ear-popping ascent from the geriatrics ward on Pelagic 1 to Pelagic 3, the hospice level, taking Bobbie closer to but not quite at the surface of the ocean. These sixty-story glass cylinders were like giant test-tubes shoved down onto the ocean floor. Topped off with roof gardens, from a distance, they looked like they had frothy green tops.

Subscrapers had become a necessity now that dryer, more arable land was in such short supply. But few people wanted to live in the submerged parts of buildings hundreds of feet below the surface of the ocean. Rumors of potential structural malfunctions leading to flooding and collapse had abounded even though no such disasters had taken place. 'The Buckets' had become the colloquial term used to describe the buildings, all ready to spring a leak. However, the lack of disasters had not stopped the real-estate value of subscrapers plummeting. Seeing their investment in trouble, Belus Corp had tapped into the ever-growing medical care market, converting subscrapers around the world into facilities to house the global aging population. Hospices and geriatric residential units were below sea-level while above sea-level, the subscraper housed general hospital wards, labs, and administration.

The elevator doors opened. A four-foot-tall, cylindrical carebot glided up on rollers, blocking Bobbie's way. From a panel in its side, a mechanical appendage provided a handle for its patient, a salt-and-pepper-haired woman with translucent skin and defeated eyes. Her hospice dressing gown had no color-code program leaving it the lifeless color of the default gray.

"Thank you, doctor," she said as Bobbie flattened herself against the side of the elevator to allow the woman and carebot to move in.

"You're welcome," Bobbie muttered, wishing they'd hurry up. Eventually, she could squeeze past without knocking carebot or human over and sprinted to the first door along the corridor.

At least up here, closer to the sea's surface, her mother had a room to herself rather than in the crowded wards below. Her mother's bed hung from the ceiling, suspended on a thick-jointed arm with a channel for fluids and meds. Alongside the bed, benches hung from the ceiling on retractable cables that allowed machines to clean the room more efficiently. The medical staff must have decided turquoise was soothing and set the three intewalls of the room to glow that color. Natural light from the wide window on the fourth wall competed against the turquoise.

Bobbie approached the bed. Sorrow made her limbs heavy. She wrapped her arms around her waist as if pulling herself in, holding herself together.

Her mother had fought off the first bout of cancer in her late forties, a short time after Joy was born. Even then, medicine performed miracles, but the cancer immunizations had failed. The following year her mother had developed ovarian cancer. A year later, tumors took her uterus, and now cancer had returned for her life.

To the untrained eye, the woman in the bed appeared to be sleeping, in reality Bobbie knew that her mother was adrift between life and death. Above the bed, an intepanel displayed data from the tiny biosensors embedded in her organs. The numbers added up to a reality Bobbie couldn't accept. She stopped by the bedside and buried her face in her hands, forcing the tears away. Granny and Joy, her younger sister, would hopefully be here soon. *Don't fall apart Bobbie. Not yet.* She drew a deep breath, pivoted, and forced her lethargic legs to pace the dozen steps of the length of the room.

Bobbie focused on her ONIV and thought about what she wanted to say to Joy, the words springing up in her field of vision, G*et here now. Mum is fading.*

She massaged the hard pellet under the skin of her pinkie finger with the one embedded in the pad of her thumb. The message sounded curt, and she chewed her bottom lip as she reread the words. *Should I say more? No, this would do for now.* She pressed the tip of her little finger to her thumb, engaged the electrodes, and the message blinked to Joy's ONIV. This was the fifth blink she'd sent Joy in two weeks. So far, her sister had not responded. When would Joy rejoin the real world instead of spending all her time neuro gaming or using recreational viruses?

A message icon popped up. Joy at last. But when Bobbie inspected the message header, she saw it was from Davitt. Dammit, she couldn't deal with his sympathy right now. Maybe she was a bitch, but she'd make it up to him in time, always later, always promising to be kinder to him. Irritated, she put a hold on the message, so she'd not forget to read it when she had more time and fewer distractions.

Her pacing brought her back across the room to her mother's bedside. Bobbie quashed her anger at her younger sister and focused on the bed in front of her. Her mother's skeletal frame and prominent bones made a mockery of her elegant figure and fine facial structure she'd once had as a healthy woman. Lying on the bed, struggling for breath, her poise and dignity hung like a veil over a woman who had borne many painful moments in her life with grace.

Turning, Bobbie walked back toward the window where she stopped and stared out through the glass into the water. Rather than contemplate a future without her mother, she tried to take her own advice to patients who suffered from stress. Meditation might help Bobbie control the adrenalin she felt surging right now. She cleared her mind and inhaled and exhaled deeply while gazing through the glass. Underwater guidance lights blinked on the next subscraper–a dark blob in the distant gloom. She was too high to see the Belfast City Hall from here, but the neon of the tourist submarine penetrated the water as it passed by, returning to shore.

Reflected light seared across the glass as the door behind her opened. The blue-green hues of the room lifted as white light from the hallway spilled in and, reflected in the glass, a hunched figure leaning on a carebot entered the room.

Bobbie's eyes focused on her own reflection. She looked like shit. With one hand she tucked a strand of orange hair behind her ear. It didn't help. With her complexion and red hair, she didn't do sleepless well. Green tinged her peachy-tan skin. Dark rings shadowed her hazel eyes, heavy-lidded and sleepy looking at the best of times. The reflection faded as the light behind her snapped off with the closing door.

The shuffling of feet accompanied the soft burr of the carebot. Bobbie abandoned any attempt to make herself presentable and turned to find Granny perched on a small seat jutting from the side of the machine. She shared this carebot with her neighbor, stating to anyone who'd listen that she was not incapacitated enough to need one full time.

Bobbie greeted Granny with a hug and kissed her cheek, inhaling her familiar lavender scent. Nodding, Granny patted her arm. She stood up, dismounted the carebot, and let Bobbie walk her to the bench beside her mother's bed. Bobbie helped Granny get comfortable. Done with her pacing, heartsore and exhausted, Bobbie sat across the bed from her Grandmother and took her mother's hand. The thin bones of her mother's hand felt so fragile that Bobbie was afraid to give them as much as a gentle squeeze.

"Mum," Bobbie whispered, "Granny's here."

A faint rasp of air from her mother's lungs was the only response.

Granny shook her head and sighed. "It should be me lying there."

"No!" Bobbie swallowed the sob that rose in her throat. The thought of losing either of them pierced her. "You're healthy and not that old."

"By today's standards," Granny replied. "Ninety-three. Yes, I'm a regular spring chicken! But we can't live forever, darling. Death is just the next step." She sighed and shook her head. "But my Maureen, only sixty-two... so young..."

Bobbie looked across at her grandmother. Granny wore her thin white hair pulled up to the top of her head in a little bun. Soft fluffs of hair framed her pale and wrinkled face. Her blue eyes glistened with tears yet crackled with energy.

"Gloria, is there anything else you need?" the carebot asked from the center of the room.

"A cigar and a line of coke."

The carebot's lights blinked red.

Granny waved her bony hand. "Never mind." The carebot's lights returned to green as the machine rolled toward the door.

"Ach, Granny, don't tease them," Bobbie said. "Remember Protocol 57. If you get cited for abusing the carebot, you'll have it taken away."

"Sorry," Granny called after the machine.

The carebot left, closing the door behind it.

"Lobotomized Daleks, you know," Granny said.

Bobbie smiled at her grandmother's reference to the evil half machine, half alien life-forms from a children's TV program that had not aired in decades.

"That darn machine got me up and out so fast that I thought The Buckets had sprung a leak." Granny looked over her shoulder at the window.

"Don't say that, Granny." Bobbie shuddered. As a once spritely middle-aged woman before her cancer, her mother had been allowed to live in the higher levels of the subscrapers. Poor Granny was a bottom dweller. She lived in the residential home in the lowest Bethnic levels of the subscraper where it was claimed there was the biggest risk of springing a leak.

"Maureen loved living underwater," Granny said. "She always loved water, swimming, diving anything like that. I'll bet that's where you got it from. Not like your father. He hated water. But he gave you those beautiful eyes." She smiled. "We knew you'd be beautiful children when Maureen married your father. The auburn is from me." Granny clucked with pride.

Nope, both my parents gave me red hair–a recessive gene on chromosome 16 that mutated the MC1R protein. Bobbie struggled to keep a straight face, Granny had always taken credit for the color of her granddaughters hair and even though Bobbie had learned all there was to know about hereditary traits in medical school she had never had the heart to contradict her.

"You look nice today, Granny," Bobbie said, wanting to move the conversation to a less emotive topic. "I love that color on you. Do you like the fabric better?"

Granny lifted a thin arm and let the sleeve of her top hang in the light. "It's called 'Ashes of Roses.' The fabric's okay. I'm not sure what all the fuss is about." Granny wore old-fashioned denim jeans, but her top was made from sensorfabrik, the same self-regulating fibers as the bed linens and Bobbie's own clothes.

"I don't know how you can wear something as uncomfortable and archaic as denim," Bobbie said.

"I've worn denim all my life," Granny said. "I suppose it's like me not understanding how my grandmother wore woolen tweed skirts and nylon tights all the time."

They both pulled a face, united in their opinion.

Silence settled between them. The machines hummed.

Bobbie could only look on as Granny's fingers wrapped around Bobbie's mother's hand. Both their hands were covered in paper-thin skin blotched with liver spots. It was impossible to separate one from the other. Bobbie looked down at her own hand cradling her mother's. When she was a child, she had stressed about every blemish, every blotch, worried that she had the same aging disease that had taken her twin sister. Now, at thirty-five, she noticed freckles blooming on the backs of her hands. Looking again at her grandmother and mother's skin she knew age would eventually claim her too.

Bobbie concentrated on her mother's breathing; each breath shallower than the one before.

"Let go, my darling," Granny said in a voice barely above a whisper as she stroked her daughter's face.

Bobbie sucked in a mouthful of air. Despite the horror of watching her mother suffer, she could not give her mother permission to leave them. She struggled with the concept of death, even with her ultra-elderly patients. Hicks considered his role as a doctor was to ease pain and offer dignity to his patients in their final days. Whereas Bobbie battled with her first instinct–where there was life, there was hope. Bobbie had become a geriatrician because Gracie had died of a rapid aging disease that had shown Bobbie the fragility of the elderly, had made Bobbie intuitive of their needs. But that last step, from this world to the next—if there was a 'next' — presented a dilemma for Bobbie. Her sister and her father had left this world, and she suffered from their absence. It was the 'forever' nature of dying that pained her so.

Her mother's eyelids flickered open, a flash of soft gray as her eyes focused on Bobbie. The shadow of a smile creased the corners of her mother's mouth. The sudden strength in her mother's hand gripped Bobbie's, startling her.

"... Gather... Joy... anew..." The words were no louder than a husky whisper. Her mother's eyes locked onto hers as if pleading for understanding as she gasped again, "... tether... thing..."

"I'm here, Mum," Bobbie said, as she struggled to make out her mother's words. It stung that her last words were about Joy, the sister who broke all the rules, who took no responsibility, who danced with danger.

And here I am, invisible as usual. Bobbie closed her eyes as she banished her jealous and juvenile thoughts. Now wasn't the time.

"It's okay. Just try to relax, Mum." Bobbie used these soothing words on her patients all the time but trying to comfort her own mother was a different story. A tear trickled down the side of Bobbie's nose and plopped onto the cream bedspread, forming a near-perfect circle before fading. She felt hopeless, had done for the last six months since her mother's cancer had been diagnosed as untreatable.

Her mother's hand went flaccid. Bobbie's eyes flew to the numbers on the intepanel which showed oxygen saturation levels dropping, pulse rate thready. Bobbie jumped up and thumped the call button mounted on the wall.

"Nurse Wilks–"

Bobbie cut the woman off. "Get the doctor in here now. We need a cardiac team. Now!" Adrenalin pumped through her.

"Bobbie, don't," Granny said. "Your mother is ready to go."

Bobbie flopped back down, sucking in gulps of air, fighting back panic.

No, no, no!

"It won't be long now, darling," Granny whispered to her daughter. "Say hello to Gracie for me."

Bobbie's chest tightened. She screwed up her face to keep her chin from wobbling.

"Ah Bobbie, death is a part of life," Granny said.

Grief swelled behind Bobbie's ribcage. She wanted to throw back her head and howl. She'd lost her twin sister, Gracie, at thirteen, her father and grandfather at sixteen in the war with the Melters. And now her mother. Death stole everything important. Tears ran down her cheeks falling onto her mother's lifeless hand that she still held in her own.

"Doctor Chan?"

Bobbie looked up and through her blurred vision she saw the nurse standing beside her.

"Doctor Chan, I'm sorry. There's nothing more we can do," she said in a gentle yet practical tone. "They've switched off her biosensors."

Bobbie heaved in a sob. The hospice had cut the power to her mother's life support. They would not maintain dependents with no hope of survival any longer than necessary. Grief growled within her, but she answered, "I know."

"When does your sister get here?" the nurse asked.

Bobbie stiffened. Sweat prickled the small of her back despite her sensorfabrik clothing. "I don't know. She's not answering her blinks."

Granny snorted from the other side of the bed. Bobbie glared at her, silently pleading with her to say nothing. Did Granny suspect, as she did, that Joy was neuro gaming or using recreational viruses? Bobbie wasn't sure which, but if Joy got caught, she'd be sent to the PARC, the Personality Augmentation and Rehabilitation Center.

"Her ONIV software might be malfunctioning," Bobbie continued. "But I've left a message with her, um, co-worker."

Granny raised an eyebrow.

Bobbie bent her head and let ginger hair fall over her face to hide the rising heat. Releasing her mother's hand, Bobbie wiped at her damp cheeks. She resented Joy more than usual for making her lie at her mother's death bed, telling lies to cover up her absence when most people would be praying. That said, Bobbie had discovered something about both prayers and lies a long time ago - neither worked.

"Call Davitt," Granny said.

Bobbie shook her head. "He's in Ladakh, at the genetics conference. I–I–I don't want him to worry." Another lie, but Bobbie didn't have the energy to explain right now–she couldn't find the right words.

"Wouldn't he want to know?" Granny asked. She peered at Bobbie, squinting as if trying to probe her thoughts. "At least send him a blink."

"I already did." Bobbie looked away.

The now zero numbers on the intepanel's screen above the bed flashed in silence. Pain roared through Bobbie's chest as she watched the face she loved relax. Like a feather on a breeze, her mother slipped away. Bobbie held her breath waiting for her mother to breathe again–one more inhalation, just one–but she was gone, far beyond Bobbie's reach.

Just then, Bobbie's ONIV screen fired up with Joy's name.

She pressed her fingertip, selecting voice and said with icy anger, "Joy, you're too late."

CHAPTER 3

Granny sobbed at the other side of the bed, grasping her daughter's hand. Bobbie fought her anguish. She'd never wept at the hospital, and she wasn't going to now. If she had control over this one thing... by not crying, she'd get through this awfulness. She needed a clear head to lay her mother to rest.

Later, she decided. *I will fall apart later when people aren't depending on me*. She inhaled for the count of three, leaned forward, and kissed her mother's forehead. The skin was already waxy.

"Granny," Bobbie said, standing up, walking around the bed, and placing an arm around her grandmother's thin shoulders. "We should have the wake at my place. Okay?"

Granny nodded and smoothed her hands along her thighs, but she didn't seem able to talk yet.

"The staff need to sort things out with Mum now," Bobbie continued. She found it unbearable to think of the dreadful sterilization techniques they'd perform on her mother's body before releasing it to the family. Bobbie couldn't escape that knowledge. As a doctor, she knew too much about the process – how every organ was removed and incinerated; How her mother's emptied body would pass through a radiation field to kill off microbes or viruses; How Bobbie's family would be given a waxen husk of skin and bones to take back to their home for the old tradition of the Irish wake.

On the surface, Belus Corp respected cultural differences among the various regions of the planet, but right now, Bobbie felt only desecration. Cold logic told her that hygiene came first, and what the average person didn't know wouldn't hurt them. But she wasn't the average person.

"We should go now and prepare the room. The hospital will send the remains..." Bobbie faltered. "I'll ask Hicks to bring Mum's... her personal..." Her voice gave out.

Granny reached up and patted Bobbie's hand. Bobbie helped Granny to her feet and linked her arm. Granny was thin and frail, but Bobbie felt her strength in the gentle squeeze on her arm, a rod of steel wrapped in silk.

"It will be okay, darling. She's in a better place now," Granny said in a brittle voice.

Granny believed that with all her heart, Bobbie realized and envied the comfort such faith gave her. Bobbie summoned the carebot with a blink. By the time they'd shuffled across the room and opened the door, the carebot was waiting for them. Granny's face looked pale and her breathing came in ragged breaths. The simple task of walking across a room had left her exhausted. Bobbie helped her onto the carebot's seat. Grief was grueling. They'd both been here before.

Evening was falling and the intewalls of the corridor adjusted their luminosity to counteract the increasing gloom. By the time Bobbie and Granny reached the inner circles of the subscraper and they moved closer to the core of the building the walls had no windows since they were folded inside the structure of the building. Here, the intewalls were the only source of light regardless of the time of day.

The day shift was ending so the elevators at the heart of the building were a never-ending series of opening and closing doors that either spat out a throng of people or filled to the brim as soon as the doors opened. Bobbie maneuvered herself and the carebot carrying Granny before an elevator that the display showed was going up. As the doors opened with a soft *ping* a mass of bodies confronted her. The elevator already filled to near capacity.

No point in waiting for the next one, thought Bobbie. That elevator would most likely fill up, too. Despite the crowd there was enough room for Bobbie, the carebot, and Granny to squeeze in. Bobbie felt relieved to be escaping the crush in the elevator as they exited into the carport at Sea Level 2 – the Sea Levels being all floors above the surface of the ocean where traffic could access the building.

As Bobbie and Granny made their way to Bobbie's hovercar on the outer edge of the building, condensation dripped from the ceiling. The plop of water drops landing on bare concrete echoed throughout the cavernous structure.

Bobbie helped Granny navigate the carebot around the puddles. The distance between Bobbie's parking space and the elevator illustrating the low rank of geriatricians in the hospital.

A warm, damp breeze blew in from the carport openings and the large rectangular apertures that lined the outer walls. The smell of the ocean and the flap of her hair against her cheeks lifted her heart until she saw Granny wipe her cheek.

"This wind, you know..." Granny said.

"We're nearly at the car now." Bobbie nodded, indicating a row of squat pillars, some with cars hooked up to suck electricity. Bobbie was forced to stop to allow a vehicle in a seemingly endless flood pass to join a long line of vehicles virtually parked at the exit to leave the carport. As the next car in line reached the lip of the wide opening, its engine tempo rose and with a sudden downward thrust propelled the vehicle up and out. The normality of it all angered Bobbie. She wanted to stop the traffic, tear her clothes, and scream. M*y mother is dead, Goddammit, dead! And you have to care!* Instead Bobbie plodded toward her car with Granny, on her carebot, alongside.

Bobbie's blue F-Class Mercedes had the aerodynamic shape of a fat, flat-bellied dolphin made from graphene-infused photovoltaic glass. Bobbie called up the cars control system in her ONIV, which identified her and released the door locks allowing the door to slide open for Granny. Inside, Bobbie had left the four seats up, facing toward the center of the vehicle in a social configuration. There was no point in lying down. The quick hop from the Belfast Buckets to her apartment in Armagh, not forty miles away, took about fifteen minutes – most of the time spent taking off, slowing down, and getting into the parking booth.

"Once I'm inside, I can never figure out which way faces forward," Granny said, sitting in one seat then moving to another. The muted cream interior glowed with violet light as the interface switched on. Bright lights danced out from the screen on a section of the car's wall as adverts jangled on about full-immersion, virtual reality dream vacations to the lost wonders of the world. Her parents had taken Bobbie and Gracie to see the leaning Tower of Pisa when she was eight. But Gracie's deteriorating health had prevented them from going anywhere else and then the Melters had destroyed so much of the planet that these virtual reality holidays have become popular. Now in the bitter wake of her mother's death, the adverts seemed sad and senseless, piercing her heart with jagged nostalgia. When Bobbie touched her pinky finger to a pad near the door, the screen snapped off, leaving the only sound in the vehicle, the low hum of the motors.

"You're good there, Granny," she said as she blinked to the car's interface, *Home.*

A second blink command sent the waiting carebot around to the rear of the vehicle where the trunk opened, and a small ramp extended to allow the carebot to maneuver itself into its traveling position. The cars systems checked the carebot was secure before closing the trunk.

"These self-drivers freak me out with their Melter technology," Granny grumbled.

"It gives me time to relax," Bobbie said as she settled back into her seat beside Granny. She understood Granny's fear of new technology. The wave of innovation resulting from the Melter's War unsettled most people. Bobbie was sure the self-drive component of the hovercar was not Melter, but human in origin. Either way, self-drive was far safer than having Earth's growing number of elderly people behind the wheel.

"I need to let people know," Granny said, clicking her fingers in frustration.

Bobbie reached across and cupped Granny's fingers in her hand. "Let me help," she said. "Have you got the message on the screen in your ONIV?"

"Yes," Granny said, staring straight ahead and holding her head stiffly as if the words would drop from view if she moved.

"You don't click your fingers; you press them like this." Bobbie helped manipulate Granny's finger to the action – pinkie-finger against thumb.

"So why is it called a 'blink' if you don't send it by blinking?" Granny asked.

"I don't know," Bobbie said with a chuckle. "It just is."

It wasn't the first time Granny had asked her this question, nor the last, Bobbie suspected. "So, do you want the light on, or shall we look outside?" she asked. Bobbie noted in her ONIV that the car's route-planner had selected a flight path that would skim them across the water until they reached land then hug the ground at an altitude of ten meters until they reached their destination.

"Let's look outside." Granny leaned forward as if she already had a view.

Bobbie blinked her setting selection, and the top half of the F-Class turned transparent.

"I'm glad the floor doesn't do that," Granny mumbled, looking over first one shoulder then the other.

Conversation with Granny was always the same in the car, but Bobbie wallowed in the familiarity of it, like reciting a well-loved poem or childhood storybook, especially today as sorrow numbed her.

The car lifted then maneuvered itself out of its parking space, moving to join the exit line behind a sizeable box-shaped vehicle. Bobbie hated not being able to see past the van as they approached the exit, but she wasn't driving, so it didn't matter. She'd been in flying vehicles for fifteen years, but it still made her dizzy to watch the van in front move to the edge of the carport, pause as its motors spun up power then move forward clear of the buildings structure, dropping a couple of inches before the downward thrust from its motors halted its fall and carried the van off over the grey, rolling sea.

As they reached the front of the line, the car paused, and the noise level grew to a robust buzz. Moments later the powerful motors on the F-Class shot them forward. Granny clutched her armrest, eyes on the horizon as the cars onboard systems controlled their descent to the desired height and brought them onto the correct heading.

Bobbie sank into her seat and drank in the westerly view of the Cave Hill a stark, black mound rising from the sea against the indigo sky. Stars winked above and behind in the east, and the low hanging clouds shone silver, highlighted by the rising moon.

Off to the right, Bobbie barely made out the unnaturally straight lines of the water-covered M1 superhighway and train tracks – the route home from Belfast when Bobbie was a child and her mother took her shopping to the 'big city.' But that was before the war – before the Melter's attack had raised the level of the world's oceans. Now everything had changed except the worn-down mountains.

A retro car shaped like an old Porsche 911 whizzed past them. Bobbie had a fleeting memory of this brand of car zipping along the M1 highway and marveling at its aerodynamic contours. This one, however, was manufactured from a carbon-fiber skin molded over the standard hovercar with fake wheels and a faux steering wheel.

They came with speed upgrades too, though, Bobbie never understood why anyone would pay more for software that allowed vehicles to travel faster than was legal. What was the point when Belus Corp delivered instant fines as soon as their global RadarNet picked out a speeding offender?

Watching the sham Porsche 911's navigation lights disappear into the distance, Bobbie stretched out her legs and sighed, contented with her F-Class. A comfortable model, great for the short trips between her home in Armagh and work, and with a range of a thousand miles, could transport her from her home to Zurich, the Belus Corp global headquarters, in four hours.

White Mountain Island loomed ahead. The car swept over the land-rise, hugging the earth's contours. Then they were back over water again, Greater Lough Neagh feeding into the Portadown Pond. Portadown – a whole town with a population of 22 thousand, gone. Bobbie felt as though much of her life was about remembering what was gone.

After the Melters attack, very few people were okay. Governments scrambled to respond to the attack but didn't know who or what they were fighting. Bobbie didn't think she could cry any harder when she kissed her father and grandfather goodbye the day they left to 'save the planet.'

The summer that year was unbearably hot, especially for Irish weather. She helped her mother hang damp towels from the open windows to try to cool down the house. They didn't work very well in the humid air.

"Swamp coolers," her mother called them. "My uncle told me about them when I was about your age. But I guess you need dry heat."

They had just taken them all down when they got the phone call from the War Department to inform them of her father and grandfather's deaths. There were no bodies to bury, but the family held a joint funeral for Bobbie's grandfather and father anyway.

After the funeral, her mother had gathered Bobbie and Joy in her arms and told them, "We have each other. Together we'll get through this."

It was the same thing she had said after Gracie died. Bobbie had refused to eat. Her mother had coaxed her, forkful by forkful, like a baby, though she was thirteen years old. "Both of us, together," she'd say as she cradled Bobbie in her arms. "So long as we're together, we'll be okay."

...Gather...Joy...anew...tether...thing...

Her mother's dying words – Together Joy and you, together, you can do anything!

Together...

Bobbie and Joy and their mother would never be together again.

A closed eye icon, superimposed on a headshot of Davitt, swam in her vision. Bobbie considered ignoring his blink message. She'd rather talk to Granny, sit with Granny, and remember even though the memories flayed her.

"Is it Davitt?" Granny asked. She could always tell when Bobbie received blinks. Bobbie reckoned it was the way her body stiffened and her eyes lost focus – but Granny claimed that she could sense Bobbie's brain ticking over – Granny liked to tease. "Take the call. Don't mind me. I won't listen. Promise." She placed her hands over her ears and winked. The ridiculously out of place gesture made Bobbie want to laugh. Bobbie frowned. She didn't want to talk to Davitt, but perhaps it was better to get it over with. Bobbie took a deep breath and opened the blink in talk mode.

"Davitt, hi, you got the message," she said.

"Yes, Sweetie, I did. I'm so sorry."

"She went peacefully." Bobbie was grateful that her voice didn't wobble.

"Did Joy make it?"

Bobbie felt the suppressed anger well up in her at the mention of her sister's name, instead, she steadied her voice. "No, she's on her way to my place now for the wake."

"Oh, you're going through with a wake after all?"

Bobbie shook off a ripple of irritation. She knew that sticking to the wake tradition raised eyebrows among people who hadn't grown up locally, but she didn't think she should have to defend holding a wake to Davitt – a tradition that went back centuries. Families and friends sat up with their deceased for two days before they buried them. Bobbie believed it a healthy approach to death that helped provide acceptance of the death of a loved one before the final goodbye.

She changed the subject, "How's Ladakh? They say there's snow starting to form on the tops of the Himalayas. Can you see any?" Davitt was a guy who enjoyed being first with anything; perhaps his ego would sidetrack his inquisition into her holding a wake.

"Eh, well, you know the conference has kept me busy, not much time for sightseeing. My presentation on genetic virology went well. The panel looked engaged. I think Belus Corp are interested in my findings. They hardly paid Jinko any attention, he was pissed and that was funny!"

Davitt's taunting of Jinko annoyed her, Doctor Jinko, a researcher at Boulder University was a nice chap, in her view, and in the few brief times they'd crossed paths, she discovered she and Jinko shared a deep respect for the privacy rights of the ultra-elderly. Jinko was one of life's good guys.

"But, hon, this is nothing. Wait till you see what I'm working on next. My research will change lives, more than anyone realizes," Davitt said making no attempt to hide his enthusiasm.

"That's great," Bobbie murmured.

"Yes, it is great, and it's just the start. I've so much more to tell you, but..." the line went silent.

Bobbie straightened in her seat. "Davitt, you still there?" She hoped he wasn't, that she could put a swift end to this conversation.

"Yes, yes, still here. Sorry."

Bobbie was glad Davitt could not see her glum face. "Okay, so I'm glad it went well then." Bobbie said, at a loss for anything more to say.

"Thanks, sweetie. Look, I'll get home as soon as I can. I gotta go. Give my condolences to Granny for me, and to Joy."

"Will do..." The connection dropped.

Bobbie turned her head away from Granny's gaze and stared out of the window. The hovercar was on the home stretch, over solid ground now, trees and fields flashed past mere shadows in the near darkness that cloaked the land.

In the distance, lights twinkled in the Armagh skyline bookended by the silhouette of twin spires on one hill and a church tower on another hill. The original ancient cathedrals now nestled inside gigantic church-shaped skyscrapers encapsulating the two old buildings that had defined the city skyline for the best part of three centuries.

Once the water levels had stabilized Armagh had been the last remaining city, north or south, left relatively intact on the island of Ireland. Armagh became the capitol city of a united Ireland, something that many on either side of the argument had fought either for or against for decades. Now, nobody cared, they were just happy to have survived the Melters War.

"I love this view of Armagh nearly as much as I loved the original," Granny said with a sigh and dragged Bobbie back to the present. "Back when we used roads, and it took three hours to get to Dublin. I loved when we'd come down the Newtownhamilton Road and see the twin spires in the distance. You knew you were almost home."

"I remember that, too." Bobbie marveled at the woman who found beauty in this world just hours after her child had died. One glance and Bobbie saw the pain in Granny's faded green irises. Bobbie pushed back her surging emotions, just as Granny did.

The F-Class settled down on the carport next to the balcony of Bobbie's apartment, its engines winding down until they became still. They were eighteen stories up in the Markets complex, a monolith of glass and steel, a marvel of modern construction methods in contrast to the century and a half old Saint Patrick's Cathedral it had been built beside. A power cable extended from the wall and plugged into the car readying it for its next journey. Safety protocols satisfied, the cars systems allowed the doors to unlock and slide open. Bobbie stepped out and turned to help Granny. By the time she had the woman out of the car the carebot had extricated itself from its storage rack in the trunk and was waiting patiently. Once Granny was settled on the carebots seat, the machine spun in place and trundled toward the balcony door of Bobbie's apartment. The apartments security system recognized the carebot and its passenger as they approached and opened the door allowing the carebot to trundle through with Granny.

Bobbie took a moment to look out over the night-wrapped landscape. She couldn't see much beyond a twinkle of lights that outlined the buildings around her, but a warm breeze carried the smell of fresh-turned earth. Building upwards on land already built upon left the surrounding area free for agriculture. Crops grew less than a mile from the city center, but then again, Armagh had always been a tiny city. With a sigh, Bobbie turned and headed after Granny.

Inside, the apartment looked the same as when Bobbie had left for her shift yesterday. The intewalls set to app code 'Mountain Cottage' displayed sunny yellow walls and windows that looked out onto tranquil alpine scenes complete with floral curtains fluttering in the mountain breeze. Her mother loved the view so much she'd bought the décor-app for Bobbie. When Bobbie had entered the code and first shown it to her mother she grinned with delight.

'The hills are alive!' her mother had declared and swung around; arms outstretched reminding Bobbie of an ancient movie that was old even when she'd been young.

"Let's get a wee cup of tea going," Granny said, motoring the carebot into the kitchen area. "And maybe a different wall setting. One with a cozy fire and no views?"

Bobbie nodded but didn't move.

"So, Davitt can't make it home?" Granny called from the kitchen. Able to manage on her feet for short bursts of time, Granny liked to 'make tea' which meant lifting the cups of tea from the matter stream, place them on a tray on the carebot, remount the carebot and transport the tea to the living room.

Bobbie emotions threatened to overwhelm her as she looked around the room her mother would never visit again. She turned to meet Granny's eyes and noticed the red at the edges of her eyelids. Poor Granny had buried so many people.

How did she remain so damn strong?

The damn broke and Bobbie burst into tears.

"Ach darling, don't worry. He'll be here for you when all the fuss has died down. You'll see. I'm sure he tried his best to get away." Granny navigated the carebot to Bobbie and pulled her into a hug. "There. There."

Bobbie dropped to her knees and laid her head against Granny's lap. Bobbie wasn't crying about Davitt at all, but she let Granny think what she liked. Her grandmother's warm hand rubbed Bobbie's back, soothing her a little, but at that moment, Bobbie would have given anything to feel her mother's arms around her.

"A good cry is what you need," Granny said, stroking Bobbie's hair the same way her mother had done in this very room not so long ago.

Bobbie clung to Granny and sobbed, panicking for a moment that if she didn't catch herself now, she'd cry forever. Like sliding down a hill, she gained momentum with each bubble of sorrow that burst over her. She pushed Granny away and gulped in air. Using her sleeve to dry her face, Bobbie hauled herself to her feet and stood by the carebot, placing her arms around Granny's shoulders.

"Ach, Bobbie," Granny said softly into her ear, "you don't have to be strong for me. It's normal to be sad, and it's okay to need people. You're not weak because you'd like Davitt to be here when you are grieving for your mother."

Bobbie sniffed and shook her head. "It's not that, Granny, really it isn't. I just want..." she swallowed a sob. "Not Davitt–I want Mum, and Dad, and Gracie. And Granda." She stopped when she heard Granny expel a deep sigh.

"Me too, darling, but they're all with God now. Their pain is over. They're at their journey's end. Try to be happy for them." Bobbie straightened her back and allowed Granny to guide her to the couch.

"But what about us?" Bobbie heard the desperation in her voice. "Sorry, I don't mean to be selfish, but..." What could she say? Maybe she was selfish but, oh God, losing them hurt. Would she feel differently if she believed in Granny's god as much as she did?

Bobbie sat down on the couch. Granny climbed off the carebot and snuggled in beside her.

"Bobbie, it's worse for you. I know that, sweetheart."

"No, no, – you lost your daughter..." Bobbie hurt physically, a wash of fire spreading up from her sternum.

"Yes – no parent should ever go through losing their child, but at least I know it won't be long before I see my dear little girl again."

Flames of pain licked up through Bobbie's neck. Unable to make her voice work, she shook her head and hugged Granny.

"Have faith, my darling. God will give you what you need." Granny's grip tightened on her like silken steel.

CHAPTER 4

A good cry and a cup of tea later, Bobbie felt up to preparing the apartment for her mother's wake with Granny's guidance. The yellow intewalls had to go. She touched her thumb to her little finger and blinked a simple command to the house system. *Pastels.* Swatches of colors appeared on the wall, Bobbie scrolled through the house computer's suggestions and with a second command she selected. *Matt oyster peach.* Soft tones, more appropriate for a wake, flooded the walls of her four-room- apartment.

Bobbie heard the whirr of hovercraft engines on the carport beside the balcony of her apartment. Heart heavy, she went to the door. She thought she was prepared to receive her mother's remains, but she felt kicked in the stomach at the sight of the black lozenge-shaped hovercar Belus Corp hospitals used as hearses. A hatch opened at the end of the hearse closest to Bobbie. A mechanized silver casket glided out of the hearse and settled onto a squat transport bot in matching silver. Bobbie stepped back into the apartment to give it room and blinked a floorplan of the apartment to the transport bot, indicating she wanted it to take the casket to her bedroom. She watched the casket slide past her through the living room until a polite cough made her look in the balcony's direction.

Hicks could not get away from the ward, so the on-duty Belus Corp priest had accompanied her mother on her journey from the hospital to Bobbie's home.

Bobbie greeted him with a tight smile and showed him through to the bedroom where the transport bot had laid the casket on the bed. The transport bot powered down and took on the shape and function of a little side table while the casket lid opened and folded into the side of the casket to reveal Bobbie's mother.

Bobbie swallowed hard at the sight of her mother's face, beautiful with the gold sensorfabrik cover pulled up to her chin. Her body barely presented any contours on the bed. The makeup artist had done a fantastic job, her mother looked younger, her face fuller, just like she had done before the cancer had eaten away at her. But then again, they got plenty of practice.

Father Paul smiled his approval as Bobbie laid out her mother's bible and lit an electronic candle and set it on the transport bot's tabletop.

Bobbie called up a selection of pictures in her ONIV, choosing an image of a golden cross, she blinked *Buy and display*. The cross shone from the wall at the head of the bed. More pictures of windows scrolled past, complete with beautiful scenes of the countryside, fields, forests, and beaches, but she didn't want to see any more water. Then she remembered, windows were not appropriate for wakes. In olden days, they covered the windows with curtains during a wake, some nonsense about keeping evil spirits out.

Bobbie selected a new file that contained pictures of her mother as a young woman. She tapped her thumb to her fingertip, and a photo of her mother on a gondola in Venice, ice cream dripping down her hand, appeared on the intewall beside the cross. She raised her hand parallel to the wall, tapped the connectors together again, and swept it with a wave of her arm, to the wall across the room from the crucifix.

Word of her mother's death had spread via ONIV instant feed between the Buckets in Old Belfast to where Bobbie lived in Armagh. As the day went on her apartment filled with people, their low voices a melody against the harmony of the whirr from their carebots. Granny sat in the corner of the living room with a few friends. Gray heads slowly bobbed and shook as they conversed. Granny stared off into space, pressing her lips together.

As Bobbie approached, Jimmy Wilson, Granny's friend, looked up and made eye contact. His bushy white mustache twitched as his mouth worked, lips pressed together, chin crumpled.

"I'm sorry for your loss," he said, adjusting his carebot so he could stand, strapped to the machine for support.

She liked his old-fashioned sense of etiquette. Her face softened as she smiled and shook his hand, his skin dry and smooth against her fingertips.

"Thanks for coming," she said. "I appreciate it, and so does Granny."

Granny shot her a narrow-eyed glare from behind Jimmy's back. Her reaction heartened Bobbie. At least grief hadn't completely shut Granny down. Bobbie thought it adorable that Jimmy was sweet on Granny.

"You must excuse me for not staying longer. There are three wakes tonight."

"Three!"

"All oldies," he added hastily.

"Who?" she asked.

"Noel Hughes, Michaela Wattson, and Gomez Lantana." Jimmy counted them off on his fingers.

"Are you sure?" Bobbie asked, confused. She'd spoken to Hicks about Michaela Wattson, and Gomez Lantan before her mother had died. They'd all been doing so well. Noel Hughes was also one of their patients.

"Aye, 'twas sudden, too."

"Do you know the cause?"

He peered at her as if she were dim-witted before continuing in his country accent. "Old age? They were well over a hun'red, so the' were. Noel was my supervisor when I first joined the Belus Corp Engineering Division."

Ice washed over her. *They had all been too old for resuscitation. What could have happened?* She tried to remember if any of their symptoms had showed deterioration. *What had I missed?* Was that why Hicks hadn't been able to accompany her mother's remains? She wanted to blink him, and normally she would, but the room was full, and the ultra-elderly were extra-sensitive when they saw folks zoning out, reading blinks, and composing messages. Unlike younger people, such as her sister Joy who had lived with this tech all their lives, Bobbie couldn't manage an incoming feed, blinks, and flesh-chat simultaneously. She needed to get back to the hospital.

"Bobbie, now don't you be getting all in a fluster," Granny said as if reading her mind. "They have plenty of doctors and nurses there. If God wants to call them home..." she faltered, cleared her throat, and continued, "Darling, you won't be able to stop Him. It's okay for old people to die."

Jimmy gave her a look. "Speak fer yerself!"

"Ach, you know what I mean." Granny gave him a nudge with her elbow. "Our Bobbie beats herself up every time she loses a patient."

"Granny, maybe you should stay here overnight?" Bobbie said. She wanted Granny close by. What if whatever had killed Jimmy's three friends was something contagious after all? She should have called Disease Control. Now that these patients with shared symptoms had died, Hicks would have to.

"Ach, howl yer wheesht!" Granny told her to quieten down, "You know I can't stay here."

Bobbie opened her mouth to argue, but Granny kept talking.

"Once Joy gets here, my friends will give her their condolences, and then they'll go visit the other wakes. Sure, you know how they love a good wake."

The silvery white heads bobbed in agreement. To them, a good wake was one that celebrated the life of a very old person, a reunion of sorts. Bobbie knew that this wake – the wake for Granny's daughter – was not considered a good wake.

"Then Jimmy will call back here for me, and we can share a ride back to the Buckets." Granny gestured for Jimmy to sit his carebot back down.

Bobbie hadn't the strength to argue. Granny was right – focus on the wake. She couldn't bring back the dead. A sudden coffee craving hit Bobbie hard, but if her caffeine levels spiked again, her bio-monitors would alert Belus Corp. Belus Corp didn't care if her adrenalin levels spiked – they couldn't outlaw stress – but overindulging in alcohol, sugar, stimulants, or recreational drugs was another matter. She had already received an official warning about her caffeine consumption and this time she could be looking at a stint in the rehab center.

Thoughts of the rehab center only caused Bobbie's exasperation with her sister, Joy, to soar. Joy thought her addiction was untraceable because biosensors could not detect neuro-gaming. Not that Joy would admit to being addicted. She claimed she wasn't neuro-gaming, but when Bobbie had asked her if it was recreational viruses – the only other thing that would take people away from real life for days at a time, Joy had laughed in her face.

I don't need to be infected with Belus Corp's sanctioned diseases to feel good, Joy would say.

Bobbie believed her. Belus allowed prescribed use of recreational viruses that delivered endorphins directly to the target cells in the brain without the side effects that had plagued the population with addiction until thirty years ago. The Succor tech biosensors monitored the viral delivery of the endorphins. Overuse triggered a report to Belus, who issued sanctions where necessary. Bobbie had checked up on her little sister. Joy had not had a visit of any kind to the PARC. Bobbie wanted to keep it that way. She knew how the PARC worked, as a medical student she had done her time there and had seen things she wished she hadn't.

The therapies on offer at the PARC meant that the prison systems of the past were no longer needed. Able-bodied people could be treated for their anti-social behaviors and sent forth to be model citizens. Therapy at the PARC worked for the most part, but she shuddered at memories of men who after treatment for being cruel and abusive had opened their eyes and seemed to have no personality left. They could not connect at all and while they never again harmed another person they may as well have been dead such was the living shell of a being left behind. Bobbie had witnessed the other extreme also – one young woman who had suffered from kleptomania regained consciousness after surgery screaming and raging, attacking a nurse, and then gouged out her own eyes with her fingers. There was still so much they didn't know about the brain, and every so often a treatment took an unpredictable turn. Yet no-one could present a better alternative. The doctors who had to work there shouldered the brunt of the population's frustration.

Bobbie shook off the dark thoughts of the PARC, and finding herself in the kitchen, touched her little finger to the sensor on the matter-streamer. A glass of water materialized behind a mesh screen. The mesh slid back when the water was ready. She gulped it down and dropped the glass into the recycler, before making her way back to the bedroom.

Bobbie was passing the front door of the apartment when it swooshed open. Joy entered, arriving like a bird, landing from flight, in a burst of air, and a flurry of color. Her straight black hair, tipped with electric blue, hung in a sheet over her shoulders. Black eyes, lined with blue pencil, sung from a heart-shaped face. Carrying herself with a combination of sorrow and drama, Joy wore a sheath dress in midnight navy. Dark enough for mourning, yet vibrant. Bobbie, dressed in evening-dove-grey, felt dull as she joined her sister at the door.

"Bobbie!" Joy reached out to her sister. "I got here as soon as I could." She wrapped Bobbie up in a hug and began to weep.

Bobbie submitted to the embrace for a few seconds then disentangled herself.

Joy wiped away her tears with the back of her hand. "I want you to meet John." She pulled a tall, dark-haired man in from the hallway. He needed a haircut and a shave.

"This is my sister Bobbie."

"Ni't'you," John said.

Bobbie struggled to still her features, hating the way the younger ones cut sentences down to words, if not letters. It sounded like he'd said, 'Nichew.' More like a sneeze.

"Nice to meet you too, John," Bobbie said with deliberate slowness.

"John's in my class." Joy said, turning to him. "Bobbie works for the government."

"Actually, I'm a doctor," Bobbie said coolly, but her blood boiled. People these days did not understand a doctor's role. She interpreted and communicated what the sensors told her, but she didn't insert them. That was all carried out by Belus Corp Commissioned Practitioners. Sometimes the way Joy talked about Bobbie's work made her job seem like nothing more than an instrument in some overbearing state. But then again, Joy couldn't remember the war. She didn't appreciate what Belus Corp and its Chief Executive Officer, Lisette Fox, had done and continued to do for the planet.

"Been down to the PARC lately?" John asked, the disdain in his voice obvious.

Bobbie's skin prickled. She would not lower herself by answering him. Instead, she forced herself to be civil.

"Go on through, John, help yourself to refreshments." Bobbie waved him toward the matter-streamer. "Joy, we need to talk. In private."

"I'll be right back, John," Joy said as she fell into step beside her sister.

Escaping the burble of chat from the wake, Bobbie grabbed Joy's hand and dragged her out the door of the apartment and into an elevator that carried them down to the atrium on level 10.

The elevator door opened, and they exited onto a balcony that looked over an internal womb-like atrium. The city planners for Armagh City refurbishments had wanted to preserve the two cathedrals built on neighboring hills, so they encapsulated each of the cathedrals in an atrium around which they built twin high-rise blocks a hundred stories tall at their highest point. The exterior of each building comprised photovoltaic cells that mimicked the look of original brickwork of each cathedral while absorbing the sun's energy and shading the building within. That the city planners had learned the lessons of their predecessors and avoided using reflective glass that confused and killed birds, heartened Bobbie. So many species had been made extinct during the Melters attack that Belus Corp had taken every precaution to prevent more loss of life.

Bobbie and Joy followed the curve of the building until they came to a bench with a breathtaking view over the old cathedral. She came here when she needed to cast off technology and look at something real.

Bobbie and Joy sat down and gazed out over the Old Protestant Cathedral. Two little boys, laughing and shrieking, chased each other around the gravestones.

"That one could be yours," Joy said, nodding toward the smaller kid whose loose red curls were visible from ten stories high.

"Or yours...You could carry the red hair gene too. Like Dad," Bobbie said, reaching out to adjust a lock of Joy's hair that had fallen in front of her face. "You're beautiful. So like Dad... I wish you'd known him."

Silence settled between them.

"Did she go peacefully?" Joy asked. Bobbie could always rely on her to fill the quiet moments.

"Her last words were about you," Bobbie said and heard Joy gasp, in pain? Or guilt?

"What did she say?"

You'd know if you'd been there. Bobbie pushed the bitter words away and instead said, "It was hard to hear her. She was so weak."

...Gather Joy anew, tether thing... What had she meant?

She'd nearly said, gibberish, but how could she describe her mother's last words as gibberish?

"She said your name clearly," Bobbie continued.

Joy swallowed hard.

The moment settled between them.

"I can't believe she's gone," Joy said softly.

Bobbie let silence land like a loose cobweb floating from the ceiling. She reached for her sister's hand. "Where were you, Joy? We needed you. Mum needed you." The pain felt raw all over again.

"I-I can't tell you."

"She was so proud of you. She had such big dreams for you. So do I."

"Bobbie, please…"

"No, honey, you have to stop the games."

"I'm not playing games."

"Really? Really? Then why the false nails?" Bobbie asked, holding up Joy's hand. The electrode connections to the fingers for neurogaming damaged the nails and were often an indicator that a person was addicted to escaping into the other world.

Joy pulled her hand away and curled them into fists. "You won't understand."

"Well, help me understand," Bobbie said. "I can get you help. You have it all. You're a fabulous musician, a top-tech student with a brilliant career map, yet you are willing to risk everything. You're so talented. More talented than me, or …Gracie."

"Wow," Joy leaned back and held up both arms, "that's an accolade. Better than *Saint Gracie*."

Blood rushed to Bobbie's cheeks. "Don't you dare! You're not fit to–"

"Fit to what?" Joy cut her off. "Replace Gracie?"

"I didn't say that."

"Yes, but you think it. You always have."

"Don't do that," Bobbie said. "I just want what's best for you. Can't you see you're addicted? Your fingernails have burnt off, and what's next? What if you're caught?"

"I won't. I have a hack," Joy said, turning to face Bobbie. Her dark eyes blazed. "It's not like you'd miss me anyway."

"Don't be ridiculous!" Bobbie wondered how a twenty-one and thirty-five-year-old could bicker like thirteen-year-olds.

"You have to stop," Bobbie breathed.

"You're not my mother."

"No. Your mother's dead, and you weren't there for her because you were playing neuro-games." Bobbie stopped when she heard the quiet sobs beside her. An urge tugged at Bobbie to hug her sister, to tell her it would be okay, to let her into that secret place that she'd kept Gracie in. But Joy would wreck everything. Joy would let her down. Bobbie could not bear to feel as empty and bereft as she had after losing Gracie ever again. She couldn't let anyone in, not Joy, not Davitt.

"So, who is John anyway?" Bobbie asked, changing the subject while struggling to keep her tone steady. She wanted to be friends with her sister, not constantly at odds with her. Maybe if Joy had a boyfriend, she would settle down, abandon her wild ways. But John didn't seem like the steadying influence Bobbie thought Joy needed.

Joy sniffed and dabbed at her cheeks. "He's an engineer," she said. "At Belus Corp. That's where I'm doing my social value hours now."

Bobbie let out a low whistle. "That's sailing close to the wind, isn't it? Doing mandatory social care for the elderly alongside the very people who would see you sent to a PARC."

Joy shrugged.

"I thought John was your hacker." Bobbie searched Joy's face, watching for the flare of her nostrils, the 'tell' that Joy was lying.

"Please! I do my own hacking." Joy met Bobbie's gaze. "I am careful, you know. And besides," she said, batting her blue eyelashes, "I'm smart as well as talented."

"And modest." Bobbie nudged Joy playfully with her elbow. "So, are you and John more than just co-workers?"

"God, no!"

"That's a relief."

"Ha! You know I'm saving myself for Ryan," Joy said.

Bobbie felt a mix of envy and warmth for Joy, remembering her as a four-year-old who had followed them around. Hicks had had the patience with Joy that Bobbie couldn't muster. He'd set her upon his shoulders, hitting six feet, at least, at seventeen-years-old. Joy had idolized him and had sworn to marry him when she grew up. By the time Joy reached the 'yuk boys' stage a few years later, Bobbie was parceling up her own crush on Hicks and hiding it as far from the world as she could.

"Yeah, well, you could do worse," Bobbie said, feeling empty.

"Like you?" Joy said. "Where is Melter-face, anyways?"

Joy always could turn the mood sour in a flash.

"Working." Bobbie felt her hackles rise at Joy's childish name for Davitt and gave in to it a little. "Contributing a damn sight more to society than you have ever done."

"Nanotechnology!" Joy snorted. "Tiny little Melter-bots."

"Please! You don't know what you're talking about," Bobbie said, standing up. "I don't need to defend him to you."

"No, you don't," Joy said, crossing her legs and stretching her arm along the back of the seat. "But you need to watch him. He's just... I dunno...trust me; you need to watch him."

Trust Joy? Bobbie pictured the fourteen-year-old Joy she'd found drunk and naked racing through the fields with her chums the night before they'd been due to have their biosensors implanted.

'One last party!' Joy had said laughing, but it would have been no party for the adult in charge of her health. Their mother would have been in big trouble if Belus Corp had found Joy first.

"You know what?" Bobbie said, throwing her hands up, "I don't care how you treat Davitt. And I'm used to how you treat me. But the way you treated Mum. That's what gets me."

In a red haze of anger, Bobbie strode off, leaving Joy sitting there. No point arguing. What did Joy know? She spent too much time hooked into virtual reality. Her neurons were scrambled.

CHAPTER 5

It had been three days since Bobbie's mother's death. Three long days of organizing the wake, receiving people's condolences, making small talk that never quite distracted from the pain in her heart, and then the hardest part, sending her mother's body off to be recycled. Bobbie knew her mother wholeheartedly agreed with having her body made into fertilizer. She had believed it more useful than the old ways of burial or cremation. Belus Corp gave them no choice in the matter now but Bobbie took comfort in knowing her mother's wishes would be granted. Her mother would be contributing to the land reclamation of the scorch zones, turning the barren land, burned by the Melters high energy beams, into something useful.

Belus Corp allowed only three days for mourning, but truthfully, Bobbie gladly went back to work despite feeling she could melt with weariness.

Hicks met her as she entered the ward, his expression grim.

"Gomez had been feeling so well. What happened?" Bobbie asked.

"Tachycardia leading to ventricular fibrillation."

"Shit." Bobbie sighed. She understood why they were not allowed to prolong lives over 100-years-old medically, but she didn't have to like it. She had campaigned against the Do Not Resuscitate, or DNR, Law as a first-year student in medical school, back when she fought to have a say in her world.

'Every Human Life is Precious!' Bobbie's placard had proclaimed in big red letters as she had stood with about fifty other students on the steps of the Queen's University of Armagh, an ancient limestone building that had been a hospital back when Granny was a young woman.

She'd not had a chance to sand the placard's wooden handle; splinters dug into her hands, especially when the wind caught the cardboard banner and twisted it.

Other signs read 'NO DNR after 100!' or displayed the outline of a heart surrounding a silhouette of an elderly person bent over a walking stick.

Bobbie raised her loudspeaker and called for quiet, handing her placard to Hicks, who always stood with her. Tall and gangly, he hadn't yet grown into his body.

The crowd gathered before her was smaller than she had hoped for but better than nothing. Clearing her throat, she took command of her jangling nerves.

"Six years ago, the global population was out of hand. We'd reached ten billion... ten billion people!" She paused and let that sink in. People nodded. Heart palpitating, she continued, "Sure, the Melter War reduced the world's population to three billion, but between losing land to the rising ocean and the scorch zone—the planet has only one-third of its former capacity. Yes, we have a problem."

The crowd muttered.

"Yes, most of the population is either too young or too old to work. The Dependency Law..." Bobbie stopped as the crowd booed—at her words, not at her. Her pulse pounded. She waited while her audience settled down before continuing.

"The Dependency Law was meant to fix the situation. By forbidding people to have children until a family member died, we were supposed to make sure there was enough for all. We made that sacrifice."

The crowd grew restless. Bobbie needed to get to her point.

"But now the government is attacking our grandparents," she said, raising her voice. "They want to deprive the old of their basic right to healthcare. Men and women who fought for our world against the Melters are being cast aside and deemed worthless. They're told they have to die because saving them is a waste of time and money."

The crowd booed and shouted.

"It's not fair! The Dependency Ratio may suggest that there are more dependents than able-bodied people to take care of them. But..." she raised a finger in the air. "That's no excuse for disposing of an entire generation, especially of people who have given so much."

The crowd murmured agreement.

Buoyed by the crowd and heart hammering, she continued, "Centenarians still have a lot to offer. Using an arbitrary number is wrong. Letting people die because they're old because it's convenient, is wrong! Mahatma Gandhi once said, '*A nation's greatness is measured by how it treats its weakest members*.' I, for one, am ready to fight for a great nation. One global nation, united under Belus Corp. If we have to sacrifice, we'll sacrifice together. There is enough for all if we are all willing to share. No to DNR at 100—every human life is precious! No to DNR! No to DNR!"

The crowd cheered and began to chant, "No to DNR!"

Hope infused Bobbie, and Gracie's spirit warmed her with a faint whisper in her head. *Good work, sister.*

But Bobbie's protesting had gotten her nowhere and Belus had imposed strict regulations around resuscitation on the elderly. As a fully qualified geriatrician, Bobbie still did not agree with setting age limits on DNR. Sure, she agreed it was necessary when people had a poor quality of life, but these days people stayed fitter longer. Being a centenarian, or older did not necessarily mean a patient could not recover from ventricular fibrillation and go on to enjoy more healthy years with a minimum of care.

The morgue didn't smell. That bothered Bobbie the most; losing a key sense to help her with diagnostics. It smelled of nothing. Not even disinfectant. Some deodorizer for foul smells left the room a blank slate.

A bank of shiny stainless-steel drawers along one wall held the bodies. Counters and smaller drawers for utensils lined another wall. A variety of microscopes sat on the counters. A glass cabinet held racks of bottles filled with formaldehyde, solvents, and diagnostic dyes. Three dissection tables occupied the center of the morgue. Above each one hung a long mechanical arm housing the cutting lasers.

The temperature in the room was cold enough to make her shiver as she and Hicks located the three bodies they had come to see by using their ONIV to scan the info-gem crystals mounted on the center of each drawer that stored the details on the drawer's contents.

"I've got Noel Hughes," Hicks said, heaving open the drawer. Inside, a plastic membrane clung to the body's skin like the shrink-wrapped meat that they used to buy at the supermarket before the invention of matter-streamers. By the head, a tube ran from the membrane and hooked into a valve on the inside of the drawer door. Hicks pressed a blue button beside the valve. With a swoosh, the membrane inflated. He unzipped the bag along the sides of the body and rolled back the plastic.

Hicks bent to look at the Hughes' head then jerked back to standing, pointing to the man's hairline, "See that? Pigmentation of the hair follicles had changed in the days before death."

Bobbie moved closer and could make out a couple of millimeters of brown at the bottom of each white hair.

"His hair color returned?" she said in disbelief.

"And that's not all. Check out his eyes."

She lifted the eyelid. The iris blazed bright orange.

"Liver problems?" she queried.

"Liver function biosensors came back normal."

"Endocrine?"

"Normal."

"What about the others?" she asked, moving along the drawers to the ones highlighted by her ONIV. "Here's Gomez." She opened the drawer. "He had dark brown eyes."

Bobbie repeated the procedure Hicks had carried out to open the vacuum wrap.

"Jesus! Have you seen this?" she asked, shocked.

Gomez's eyes stared at the ceiling, bright orange too.

Behind her, she heard Hicks unzipping the body bag containing Michaela Wattson.

"Yea, and it's the same here," he said.

Bobbie didn't look up from examining Gomez's body, but raised her voice so Hicks would hear her. "So, they all showed signs of improvement before–" she began.

"Signs of getting younger," Hicks interrupted, "if that's possible,"

She nodded, absorbing that thought. "They all suffered a massive heart attack and died. And the biosensors read normal?"

"Normal, until the tachycardia started. The biosensors recorded the abnormal ventricular rhythm," Hick said.

"And the eyes? Did they turn orange post-mortem?" She glanced at Hicks.

"No, the patients' irises changed color about twenty-four hours before they died," Hicks said, staring over her shoulder, seemingly checking the data displayed in his ONIV.

"Why didn't you contact me as soon as possible?" she snapped.

"Your mother had just died." He reminded her. "Besides, they seemed healthier than ever. And the pigmentation had no impact on their vision." A line creased Hicks forehead as he frowned. "By the time they indicated any deterioration, it was too late."

"I want a closer look at the irises," Bobbie said, moving to the counter along the wall. Her hands found the sanitizer by themselves. She held her hands in the specialized matter streamer that laid a protective flexible film over them until the telltale went from red to green.

"Alright, so no detectable symptoms, other than the visual cues... hmmm," she continued as she gathered up a microlaser-pen, sample pots, and slides from the cabinets along the wall.

"Do you want Gomez's body on the table?" Hicks asked as he set up the 3D microcam above a small raised platform on the counter.

"No need. I can examine it here." Bobbie set out her instruments beside Gomez's body, pausing to examine his face. He'd been such a nice old guy. She'd miss him on the ward. Thoughts of how she'd miss her mother poked through the cracks. She pushed them back. Work was all that mattered now, and it allowed her to hide from her loss.

Lifting the microlaser-pen, she cut through about two-thirds of the way around the circumference of the cornea of Gomez's eye.

"Careful," Hicks said, "Don't lose your sense of humor!"

She grunted a half laugh as the aqueous humor behind the cornea oozed through the incision.

"What about the bio-sensors—I reported a possible malfunction when I first noticed the changes in Aayushi Dhawan?" Bobbie asked, as she extracted a sliver of the iris and placed the sample on the microscope slide.

"They tested okay," Hicks said. "The tech at Succor Tech is double-checking the software now, but so far, nothing unusual." He swung around to face the intewall, where a large white three-foot square glowed. "Ready for the slide."

She placed the slide on the platform, and a row of pink-knobbed columns filled the square on the intewall. It took Bobbie a moment to get a fix on what she saw, the iris pigment epithelium reminding her of a coral formation.

"There seems to be a vast number of melanosomes," she said, pointing to spherical organelles within the cuboidal cells.

"So, if these extra melanosomes are all producing melanin, wouldn't the eyes be dark brown?" Hicks asked.

"Yeah, they should look nearly black," she replied.

"So, where is the orange coloration coming from?"

"It has to be from here... so... the molecular structure of the melanin has changed? Let's get these samples up to the lab for molecular analysis," Bobbie said, grabbing a few more sample pots from the shelf.

They worked in silence, gathering samples from Hughes and Wattson. Concentrating on the task at hand, Bobbie pushed her questions aside until they were done.

Samples collected and marked, Bobbie peeled off the protective film covering her hands and dropped it into a micro incinerator as she spoke over her shoulder. "Is this the same condition that Aayushi Dhawan has?" A knot tightened in her stomach, thinking about her gentle kindergarten teacher. "Three dead..."

"We've already isolated patients reporting any symptoms," Hicks assured her.

Bobbie turned and leaned back against the edge of the counter. "Basically, anyone who's feeling better?" she said, thinking out loud. "Have you contacted Disease Control?"

"Yes." Hicks cast his eyes as if she'd asked him a stupid question. "But DC practically laughed at me."

"Sorry, I'm playing catch-up here." She helped him pack away the bodies.

"It's the same old geriatric thing," Hicks said. "No-one under the age of 110 has the symptoms. You know Belus Corp doesn't give a damn about the ultra-elderly."

Moving from drawer to drawer they resealed each body bag and reconnected the tube, the membrane tightening around the body with a slurpy suck.

As they left, the door clanged shut, echoing off the walls. A man in his seventies, sporting a bad hair implant, sat at the desk in the morgue foyer and nodded to them as they passed.

"Thanks, Donald," Hicks said, waving a salute as they passed.

"Why do they need to waste staff guarding a morgue?" Bobbie asked Hicks in a low voice.

"People are dying to get in there."

"Oh, that's bad!" Bobbie said, shaking her head.

"He doesn't look like he's fit for much else. He must be filling his quota for social contribution hours."

"Poor old guy," Bobbie said. Belus Corp was so rigid. Bobbie would prefer to let Donald choose a volunteer post rather than waste his time at the morgue.

"So, if the melanin molecule has changed," said Hicks, getting back to business, "that would suggest a change at the DNA level?"

"Right. If the gene code changes or mutates, a different protein is produced. Perhaps one with a different shape absorbs a different spectrum of light?" Bobbie said, keeping pace with Hicks's long legs as they walked to the elevators.

"What does that? What changes the DNA and gets expressed in the genes within twenty-four hours?" Hicks scratched at his stubbled chin.

"Well, it's not twenty-four hours," Bobbie said. "The eyes were orange for twenty-four hours but in the run-up to that–"

"¬–the patients were getting better," Hicks said, completing her thought.

"Yes, so how long did that take? They could have been developing symptoms for weeks," she said.

"I'd need to check the patients' notes. But that wouldn't necessarily tell us the cause of the condition."

"Something viral?"

Hicks shook his head. "Viruses never showed up in the biosensors. No pathogens at all."

"Radiation?" she asked.

"If it were radiation, surely the patients would feel ill first, with radiation poisoning, nausea, rash, blisters," Hicks said. They stopped at the elevators, and he turned to face her.

The fact they couldn't explain the problem made Bobbie sticky with panic.

"Oh, God, Hicks," she said. "No earthly origin. Something turning up unexplained. Alien, like the Melters."

"You're stretching it." Hicks's face darkened.

"Didn't you see the news report last week?" Hicks looked at her blankly. "Belus Corp destroyed what they identified as a Melter scout beyond the moon's orbit. We might have beaten them back, but they're still out there somewhere." Bobbie's chest tightened.

"I can't see them attacking us at the microscopic level." Hicks pressed the button to summon the elevator.

"But who's to say what form the next invasion will take? No one ever saw a Melter. We only saw their weapons. What if these symptoms are the result of another weapon? One we've never seen before." She heard her voice rise in pitch and knew she had to calm down, but the thought of Melters returning was terrifying.

"Why would the patients' health improve first?" Hicks asked. "Why would someone kill only the ultra-elderly? If it's a concerted effort to take over the planet, it's not a very good one." Hicks folded his arms and leaned against the wall as they waited for the elevator.

Bobbie liked his argument. She was desperate to be wrong. If the cause were alien, then surely DC and Belus Corp would be investigating, and so far, they didn't seem to care.

"You're right. Of course." She nodded slowly. "And judging by DC's response, I think we're on our own with this disease... for now."

* * *

Aayushi Dhawan lay dozing, her face relaxed, a soft snore purring from her lips as she exhaled. Bobbie had her ONIV displaying the woman's bio readouts in one corner of her vision. She and Hicks had agreed to communicate only via blink so he could help her with the examination without having to interrupt her conversation with the patient. He sat on the bench beside Aayushi and nodded at Bobbie—ready to start.

From her notes Bobbie saw that the old woman had not taken any pain medication since Bobbie had last seen her. She had taken a walk, unaided, and visited with another patient on the ward. All things which would have been impossible for her to accomplish only days before.

Aayushi closed her mouth and swallowed, then licked her lips as they curled into a smile. She stretched her arms and legs longer in the bed as she opened her eyes and turned her head to face Bobbie.

Bobbie stifled a gasp. Aayushi's once soft brown eyes now glowed a bright orange. Twenty-four hours, Bobbie thought. Her old teacher had only twenty-four hours before she too would have a heart attack and die.

"Hi." Bobbie kept her voice calmer than she felt. "How are you feeling?"

"Hungry," Aayushi said, sitting up and rubbing her stomach.

"Okay, hungry, good." Bobbie kept her tone chirpy. "I need to do a quick check of your eyesight."

Aayushi nodded.

"So, can you read that line on the intepanel?" A line of letters and numbers appeared on the screen that divided the cubicles.

Aayushi identified them all correctly.

"Brilliant, everything normal there," Bobbie said, the lie flowed easily off her tongue. "And when did you last eat?"

"Only a couple of hours ago," Aayushi said, glancing across at Hicks before returning her now wary gaze to Bobbie. "Why the random eye test?"

"What did you eat?" Bobbie asked, ignoring her question while her mind raced. *How could she best treat Aayushi?*

"Bread and soup, mushroom soup. It was lovely."

"What do you feel like eating now?"

"Anything–why all the questions?" Aayushi asked, sitting up straighter.

Her appetite had been poor, but now it had returned. It was usually a good sign, but now? Bobbie's gaze flicked to Hicks. Their eyes connected, but he kept his face expressionless. She guessed Hicks's mind was working overtime too. Bobbie concentrated on keeping her voice calm as she said, "Aayushi, your eyes have changed color."

Aayushi pulled her eyelids open wide and blinked as if she were attempting to see her own irises. "Let me see."

Bobbie projected the live image captured on her ONIV onto the intepanel.

"Oh... my... goodness..." Aayushi stared at the image, maneuvering her head around as if a better angle would give a different result. "What is it?"

"We aren't sure, but we are working on finding out," Bobbie continued, placing her hand softly on Aayushi's arm. "I want to make sure your eyesight is not affected. Let's check your peripheral vision." She held her hand out to the side of Aayushi's head. "Focus on the screen but tell me how many fingers I'm holding up."

"Three."

"Good." Bobbie carried out a couple more checks. "Everything seems fine. But if you feel any different call staff immediately: shortness of breath, pain of any kind, anything, okay?"

"Please, turn off the mirror b-app. I can't handle any more staring at myself with these weird eyes. But apart from that, honestly, I feel fine, great actually." Aayushi smiled as if reassuring Bobbie. At that moment, Bobbie caught a glimpse of the younger Aayushi peeping through a hidden veil.

Bobbie turned off the b-app and smiled at her old teacher with affection. "I'll call back later," she said and patted her hand one more time.

Bobbie and Hicks left the cubicle.

"She's running out of time," Hicks said in hushed tones as they walked down the corridor.

"Time..." Bobbie said, thinking aloud. "That's what we need—more time to let the good symptoms unfold." She paced to the window and looked out at the underwater world. "We need to meet with the Medical Board right away."

"They won't be interested, Bobbie, you know that."

A green frond of seaweed ripped from its mooring, hung suspended, wafting hypnotically back and forth about ten feet away. As the water moved, the frond rotated in one direction, paused, then revolved back with the ebb of the water. Bobbie let her eyes follow the frond, her heartbeat seeming too slow to its pace.

Pace... pace the heart... if we can keep the patient's heartbeat regular... stop the tachycardia...

"I have an idea," she said, turning to Hicks, her own heartbeat much faster now. "I don't know if the Medical Board will buy it, but if they do, I might just be able to save Aayushi."

CHAPTER 6

Bobbie entered the conference room on the thirty-fifth floor of the subscraper. The floor to ceiling windows that ran along one entire wall overlooked restless gray-blue waves. No-one else had arrived yet. Good. She had time to ground herself, to direct her thoughts toward the task at hand. If she didn't argue her case right, Aayushi would die.

Bobbie sat in a chair midway along a large oval touch-surface table. Pressing against the cushioned seat, the small of her back felt cold, her sensorfabrik tunic losing the wick-away battle with her nervous sweat. Her mouth felt dry. She touched the table's surface and ordered a drink of water from the built-in matter streamer. A clink and a gurgle sounded from the dispenser before the mesh screen slid back.

"Dammit," Bobbie muttered as she noticed the bubbles. She had accidentally ordered sparkling water. Plain water would be better. Less chance of burping in front of the top medics in Europe, but she'd feel stupid sitting with what would look like two glasses of water in front of her. Bobbie brought up the time in her ONIV. The meeting would start momentarily. She reined in her thoughts.

Focus! Rehearse your pitch...

A holographic image of a person appeared sitting in the chair beside her, making her jump, so she slopped some water onto her lap. The damp patch spread, then shrunk nearly as fast as the sensorfabrik did its job.

"Ah, Doctor Chan. It's very nice to see you again." Doctor Octavio Coughlin's image came through strong and vibrant. His white hair grew in a crescent-shaped tuft around the back of his head, matching a trim white beard that contrasted well with his tan. Bobbie felt like if she reached out, she would feel a solid person, but she refrained from this poor display of etiquette. His warm brown eyes helped Bobbie to relax. He'd been her mentor at medical school, and she held a deep-seated respect for the man.

"I'm glad you could come," Bobbie said.

"Ha, well, I haven't actually traveled anywhere," he replied, looking around the room, similar to the one she sat in and ten stories above her. Management had their own executive conference room.

She gave a nervous, fractured little laugh, "True, but thanks for taking the time."

"I'm happy to help my star pupil," he replied with a wink.

Her laugh this time was a little more relaxed. Doctor Coughlin referred to all his past pupils as his 'star' pupils.

Four more images visualized around Bobbie at the table: Doctor Jarret, the meeting chair, a man in his mid-forties with ebony skin, short black hair curled tight against his scalp and dark, serious eyes. The other three doctors on the medical board were unknown to Bobbie. Two were women, both in their fifties, both with brown hair pulled back into a ponytail at the nape of their necks, and another man, older again, but with dark brown hair, that looked to Bobbie suspiciously like it may have been dyed. Everyone around the table bobbed heads in acknowledgment of each other, and then all eyes turned to Doctor Jarret.

"We are waiting on one more. Perhaps we can begin with introductions," Doctor Jarret said. "I am Doctor Jarret, Chair of the European Medical Board based in Zurich. We're meeting upon the request of Doctor Bobbie Chan from the Belfast Geriatrics Unit. She works in the geriatrics ward in Belfast Subscraper One. Let me introduce Doctor Kiara Avignon, from Turin."

One of the women nodded her head at Bobbie and smiled.

"And Doctor Maria Cabera, from Andorra la Vella."

Another nod, another smile exchanged.

"Doctor Theodore Lichtenberg, from Munich."

The man with the dyed hair cleared his throat as he nodded.

Doctor Jarret continued, "You already know Doctor Octavio Coughlin based in the Belfast Subscraper One as well."

"I do," Bobbie said and smiled at her old mentor, trying not to be distracted as another holograph materialized across the table from her.

Orinda Slade's black, bobbed hair swung around her ears as she turned her pointy face and scanned up and down the table.

"Perhaps I'll start again," Doctor Jarret said. "Doctor Orinda Slade..."

"No need, no need," Slade interrupted. "I know Doctor Chan already." She didn't smile or look in Bobbie's direction. "Let's get this over with." She spoke through her nose, making her sound more condescending than she perhaps intended to be. Bobbie gave her the benefit of the doubt, but the woman's voice raised Bobbie's hackles. Slade insisted on the title of Doctor. She had a Ph.D. in Social Science, not medicine, and as Director of the

Medical Board, Slade was the top administrative official in the health system in Europe, the liaison between the Medical Board and Belus Corp.

"Please, Doctor Chan." Doctor Jarret waved his hand to go-ahead.

Bobbie tucked a short breath into her chest and began by outlining the symptoms she and Hicks had noticed in their patients from the onset. Out of the corner of her eye she noted Slade fidgeting in her seat. Something at her location was attracting her interest. Bobbie needed to get to the point of her request before she lost the attention of the rest of the board.

"My patients appear to be getting younger," she said.

Slade's interest condensed on Bobbie again.

"Getting younger? What exactly do you mean?" Slade asked.

Heartened, she plowed on. "The symptoms they suffered due to old age are clearing up," said Bobbie. "An examination of their skin tissue indicates the same amount of collagen of someone three decades younger. A significant reduction in wrinkles has been documented. Age spots are disappearing, and gray hair is returning to its original color in these patients."

"The symptoms sound too good to be true," Doctor Jarret said.

"They are. A number of patients exhibiting the symptoms have died. But there's more." Bobbie went on. "There is an improvement in vision, especially in patients with macular degeneration. As if the retina has repaired itself."

"Impossible!" Slade interrupted.

"Patients with chronic lung disease can mobilize normally without feeling breathless," Bobbie said, ignoring the impatient sigh from Slade. "Dementia patients are more lucid. A patient with weakness due to stroke can move all limbs freely today. One patient with debilitating osteoporosis was able to stand tall again. I know it sounds unbelievable however, I invite you to come see for yourself."

"How many patients are we talking about?" Doctor Coughlin asked.

"Twelve so far, but whatever is rejuvenating the patients is also causing ventricular tachyarrhythmia leading to cardiac arrest. So far, there have been three fatalities." Bobbie paused, scanning the faces of the attendees. "Three preventable deaths... If we could use cardiac resuscitation on these patients, it might be possible to allow the effects of rejuvenation to progress further..."

"Are you suggesting we experiment with these patients?" Doctor Jarret said.

"No. Absolutely not," Bobbie said. "I'd like to use the approved medical treatment for cardiac arrest that is used all the time on younger patients. I am only asking that the protocol for resuscitation be extended to these patients."

"Doctor Chan," Slade said, her close-set dark eyes crowded against her thin nose as they bored into Bobbie, "I remember we discussed the DNR Law when it was introduced."

Bobbie's heart dropped, but she kept her features bland, concealing her hatred of Slade behind a carefully constructed mask. The 'discussion' had taken place after the rally outside Armagh University fifteen years ago.

The crowd Bobbie had addressed had been composed mostly of student doctors, too busy to give Bobbie more than their lunch hour, but she'd had to try. Gracie had taught her that every life was precious. No matter how sick or how old you were, you were a worthwhile human being.

Slade had summoned Bobbie to her office. Originally from New York, Slade had been appointed the Dean of the School of Medicine during the education reorganization following the Melter war. She had been a personal friend of Lisette Fox's from their college days. Bobbie couldn't understand how someone as philanthropic as Lisette Fox could tolerate being friends with a mean-spirited person such as Slade. Her office was large and furnished with a big oak desk, sporting only a computer monitor, a sheaf of paper, and a ceramic jar bunged with an assortment of pens. A single landscape painting hung on the otherwise bare, cream walls.

Slade had looked more like a mid-level executive than a dean of a school with her black skirt-suit with a fitted jacket. The collars of her blouse sat crisp and white over the lapels. Her black hair skimmed her shoulders. She leaned back against the desk, perched on the edge, balanced on her high heels.

When Slade had nodded at a chair, Bobbie sat, hopeful that she could get some traction now that she had the Dean of the School of Medicine's attention.

"Belus Corp has introduced this law. Simply put, people over the age of 100 cannot be resuscitated," Slade began.

"I just want to say..." Bobbie interrupted.

"No discussion," Slade said. "It is a law now! You cannot change that, especially..." Slade looked sideways at Bobbie, "Especially if you have no clear argument against the order other than every life is precious. Every life is precious, but we all have to die sometime, and we should be allowed to die with dignity. Now, get back to your studies and make yourselves useful to your society! Demonstrations like this are not helpful. I will hear no more about it, and if you value your future career as a doctor, you will do well to remember that. That is all. You may go."

Bobbie had left the office speechless, frightened, and humiliated.

Bobbie stared across the conference room table at Slade. Was she threatening her now—ten years later — with this oblique reference to that 'discussion'?

"Resuscitating patients after the age of 100 is against the law as outlined in the DNR statutes," Doctor Jarret said as if explaining to a very young child.

Bobbie's heart sank, but she had to keep trying. "Unless foul play is suspected," she countered.

"Foul play in the case of attempted murder, yes, but how does that apply here?" Doctor Jarret asked.

"Poisoning," Bobbie said. She had discussed the possibility of radiation exposure with Hicks. "We are not sure, and we need more evidence, more time." She pulled her hands into fists to stop them from trembling, digging her nails into the palms of her hands. "I'm asking to invoke the exception. Just for these patients. If they continue to improve at this rate, we might be able to discover the mechanism for the positive symptoms they are displaying. Just think how such rejuvenation could help society." The expressions on all but one of the faces before her told her that she was getting nowhere. Her crystal of hope dissolved. Doctor Coughlin met her eyes and nodded. Was he looking at her, agreeing with her, or was he interacting with someone out of view at his location?

"How do you think rejuvenation might help society, Doctor Chan?" he asked.

Coughlin had thrown her a lifeline. This was her chance. "Right now, we have a problem with the dependency ratio, too many young people looking after the elderly. But think where we could go with something that alleviates age-related diseases. Fewer human resources would be required to look after a healthy, robust aged population. Our global population density is nowhere as high as before the war, so material resources are not yet an issue. We could build a healthy population base, decrease the dependency ratio, and possibly eradicate the Dependency Law altogether. People could have children when they wanted to."

Slade puffed out a long sigh.

Bobbie ignored her and pressed on. "If we can discover the components that ease pain, reverse the effects of arthritis, osteoporosis, prevent high blood pressure from being an issue, and treat dementia, Belus Corp can save money on healthcare by not having to treat so many people for age-related diseases. Repercussions exist in the cosmetic industry too: skincare, no more dying gray hair, a cure for pattern baldness."

Slade snorted a laugh. She put one hand over her mouth and waved the other as if she were too speechless with mirth to talk. Bobbie suppressed her anger. That woman had shut her down once before, Bobbie couldn't let her do it again.

"Fitter people mean less work for the able-bodied. Ultimately increased fitness among the elderly will mean less use of human resources, robotic relief, medication..." Bobbie continued.

Slade snorted again, her cheeks pink.

"Have you something to say, Doctor Slade?" Doctor Jarret asked.

"Doctor Chan, do you think that these patients are going to recover from old age?" Contempt edged Slade's words.

Bobbie looked straight at her and tried to calm her thoughts. "Right now, we don't know where this dis–" She stopped herself. "... these symptoms are going. But if we can buy some time to let them run their course, then we'll know more."

"So really, you are asking for more treatment for the ultra-elderly. Putting more strain on already stretched resources. I cannot fathom how that will help society," Slade said in her pinched nasal tone.

"One patient," Bobbie said. "Let me use cardiac paddles and epinephrine once—on one patient. I don't know what's going on here, but I want to get to the bottom of the cause of this condition." *Do I sound like I'm begging?* Her pulse raced.

Coughlin cleared his throat. "How would you choose that patient?"

Bobbie had already chosen her patient, but she couldn't tell the board that. She'd be accused of being unprofessional. She decided to hedge her bets. "Treat the next patient that goes into cardiac arrest."

"Wouldn't the patient have to have some say in the matter?" Doctor Jarret asked.

"Yes, of course." *Maybe they were changing their minds.* Bobbie allowed herself to hope again.

"I think this needs more discussion," Slade said, her nasal whine plucking at Bobbie's nerves like a lousy banjo player. "I say we let this phenomenon run its course a little while longer. If we do nothing, it may help improve the dependency ratio."

Bobbie could not believe what she was hearing. "We can't let people die because it's convenient! What if this condition starts to affect children?" Bobbie asked. "Or the able-bodied?"

"So far, there are no reports of this disease affecting children or the able-bodied in the other reported cases..." Doctor Jarret began.

"There are other cases?" Bobbie said. Alarm spiked through her. *Why the hell hadn't they shared this information?* "Where? How many?"

"Ten cases in the Canadian Rockies, twelve in Geneva, eight in Tibet, eleven in Reykjavik, Southern Chile has seven, South Africa somewhere in the Drakensberg, I believe, has reported ten as well." Slade said. "None of them have spread to any other sector of the population. It's obviously an age-related disease. None of the medical practitioners in those countries have requested to repeal the DNR Law."

So, Slade had cross-examined her about the symptoms but had known about the other cases all along. *Was she hoping I would make a mistake? Were they testing me?*

"The other cases — are the symptoms the same?" Bobbie asked. "Will you share the data with us?"

"If you mean getting younger," Slade made a tittering little laugh, "then yes. Disease Control is gathering data now."

"In fact, we'd like you to contact DC and prepare an information pack for your patients and the Benthic Level residents," Doctor Jarret said.

That made sense thought Bobbie through her annoyance; the residents living in the bottom levels of the Belfast subscraper, being predominately centenarians, were most at risk.

"But wouldn't it be better to offer them hope? Tell them treatment is available if they arrest?" Bobbie said.

"Hope?" Slade said. "Don't be ridiculous. What do the ultra-elderly have to hope for, other than a peaceful death?"

"Now, now, Orinda, that's a bit harsh," Coughlin interjected.

Slade held up her hands, surrendering, but pulled an innocent face.

"I think if Doctor Chan had the full picture, she might feel differently," Slade said.

Full picture? What did she mean? What else were they keeping from the world?

"I would like the full picture, Doctor, please enlighten me," Bobbie said, scanning the assembled faces. No-one would meet her eyes, except Slade. The woman had a sly smile on her face.

"You have the full picture, Doctor Chan. I believe Doctor Slade is using a figure of speech." Doctor Jarret cleared his throat and moved on quickly. "You said you have a quarantine in place. There is no evidence of pathogens or disease vectors," Doctor Jarret continued. "So, I agree, these symptoms seem to be age-related. What is the age range of the victims so far?"

"110 to 115," Bobbie said. She looked at Doctor Coughlin. He refused to meet her eyes, instead staring down at his hands.

"Yes, I see. The condition may be telomere related. I'll contact the genetics team with your findings. Send me cell and tissue samples too, please," Doctor Jarret said.

"If I can resuscitate the next patient, we'd have a comparative study," Bobbie said.

Come on - help me out here, dammit!

"I propose we vote on allowing Doctor Chan to take action now..." Coughlin began.

"Or postpone the decision for a month," Slade interrupted. "Until we have more information."

"A month!" Bobbie cried. "That's too long. We need a decision now."

"No, Doctor Chan," Slade said. "We need time to gather more data."

"One week, then?" countered Bobbie.

"Three," Slade replied.

"I agree with Doctor Slade. What say you?" Doctor Jarret said, looking at his other three colleagues.

"Postpone," Doctor Avignon and Doctor Cabera said in unison.

"Yes. Postpone for three weeks," Doctor Theodore Lichtenberg said, nodding.

Doctor Coughlin was the only one who sided with Bobbie. She felt weighed down.

"Doctor Chan, the decision to vote on your request has been postponed. We'll meet again in three weeks to review the case." Doctor Jarret stood up. "Thank you for attending. Good day." His image disappeared. The rest of the committee followed suit, leaving Bobbie alone with her defeat sitting like a hard, heavy rock in her gut. After a few moments, she rose from her seat and headed for the door.

Hicks was waiting for her outside the conference room.

"Well?" he asked.

She shook her head.

"So that's it? They won't let you try?" He looked as crushed as she felt.

"Slade," she hissed.

"That bitch! I forgot she's on the board now." He punched his fist into his palm. "What did she do?"

"Made the board postpone for three weeks," Bobbie said.

"Well, that's something, better than a straight no."

"I suppose, but I'll have to present my case all over again, and by then, it might very well be too late for Aayushi Dhawan."

"I'm sorry, Bobbie."

She stopped walking, alarmed by his tone, and spun to face him.

"It's already too late for Aayushi," he said.

"Oh, no," she whispered, leaning back against the wall. "When?"

"She arrested while you were in the meeting. She died quickly." Hicks's forehead furrowed over sad eyes.

Swallowing back a sob, Bobbie centered her energy. She wouldn't cry at work.

"There are more cases all over the world." Bobbie said, her throat tight, "And we're not being told the full picture."

CHAPTER 7

Bobbie scanned the faces of her patients sitting in front of her in the dayroom of Benthic levels: wrinkled, liver-spotted, and capped with white hair—if they had any hair. Warm yellow lighting augmented green-blue tones that managed to filter down through a hundred feet of water and in through the window. Her audience numbered 120 people, very few of them born within the last 100 years. While some attended without the aid of a carebot, most needed some kind of support. Vacant eyes stared from many a furrowed face where, besides stealing their youth, time had also flushed out their coherence. Her heart ached for these untethered minds. Dementia treatments had improved in the last couple of decades, but some minds still slipped through the cracks.

Along the edge of the crowd, a kerfuffle drew everyone's interest until the more compos mentis residents realized the commotion was an old man arguing with the empty space beside him. The majority of the audience returned their attention to Bobbie. She scanned their eyes, alert for any hint of iridescent orange. Rumors and misinformation were rife within the tight-knit community of the elderly in regard to the unexplained deaths on the levels above. These residents needed reassurance. Bobbie wasn't sure she could provide that, but she was willing to try.

Following the medical board meeting, the local communicable disease specialist, Doctor Ross Hatchet, had called and updated Bobbie on the other reported cases around the globe. When she'd told him she was giving an info-seminar at their weekly social, his reply had been, "Benthic 3? Oh, public speaking on the seabed—the pressure!"

He had blinked back within the hour and included as much information on the new disease as he had, a small file.

Bobbie cleared her throat and began her address to those gathered by outlining the initial symptoms.

"Should you develop any of these symptoms, please tell a member of staff straight away," she said, raising her voice to be heard over the growing murmur of conversation that traveled through the crowd.

"I'll be calling my barber!" said a bald man at the front with liver-spots on his scalp.

Mirth rippled through the audience.

"This is a serious condition!" Bobbie said. "Six people have died so far."

"Honey, we're ancient. What else we going to do?" yelled a tiny little lady near the back.

Everyone laughed, except Bobbie. Frustration was giving her a headache.

Granny's friend, Jimmy Wilson, a tall thin man with a huge white mustache and a light fuzz of white hair, stood up. "This lady is looking out for us, folks. I think we ought to give her some respect and at least listen to her," he said.

Several heads nodded.

"Go ahead, dear," Jimmy continued.

"Thank you, Mr. Wilson."

"It's Jimmy to you, Doc," Jimmy said with a grin and sat down again.

Bobbie took a calming breath as she tried to put herself in their shoes. They'd been alive a long time, sure, but didn't they want to keep going, especially if they felt well enough? But how well was well enough? Gracie had surrendered in the end, and Bobbie's anger at the tiny coffin carrying her sister still haunted her.

She addressed the crowd again in a commanding voice. "So, we've established that whatever causes this syndrome cannot be transferred from person to person by touch, nor is its cause airborne."

"I heard they got it from carebots," a lady called from the crowd.

"No, it was the matter-streamers," said another.

Bobbie shook her head. "Both of those scenarios are highly unlikely."

"Maybe it's Belus Corp? Perhaps they've had enough of looking after us?" another voice added.

"There's always bogus anti-aging remedies! It's probably just too many acacia berries or something!" said another.

"Well, I don't mind going. My great-granddaughter wants a family, and she can't start one till I kick the bucket. Perhaps Belus Corp is right about that too," chimed another.

Bobbie marveled at their altruism. Their love for their descendants never failed to touch something primitive in her.

"Wait!" Bobbie yelled above the rising fracas.

"Let her finish!" Jimmy stood up again.

Bobbie flashed him a grateful smile.

A hush fell over the crowd.

"I think you are giving Belus Corp too much credit." She looked around her at their faces, lined with the stories of their lives, their bodies invaded and crumpled by time. "You deserve better treatment. We all do. We can learn from you. You fought the Melters;

many of you lived through wars before that, just as terrible. Teach us. Show us how to do better. You looked after us for so long, now it's our turn—my turn. Let me help you." She paused, scanning the audience before her one more time. "Please, think about what I said. Look out for each other. If you see anyone develop orange coloration in their eyes, please tell your staff-member-in-charge."

The audience nodded and shuffled in their seats. There was nothing more she could tell them, so she wrapped up her presentation. "I'll be here for another fifteen minutes or so," a weak smile creased her lips as she nodded toward the back of the room, "to help you with the sandwiches, tea, and cakes of course." Her smile widened as a chorus of laughter rose from the residents. "So, please feel free to ask me questions."

As soon as she stepped away from the podium, a group gathered around her.

"My knee hurt last week, but this week it's okay," a frail woman said in a quivering voice as she reached down and pulled up her skirt to mid-thigh. "Do I have the disease?"

"Doctor, what about..." came a gravelly voice from her left.

Bobbie held up a hand. "One at a time, be patient, please." She kneeled to examine the proffered knee and saw a yellowed bruise on the skin below the knee cap.

"Did you bang this last week?" Bobbie asked.

The woman squinted and chewed her lip as if remembering was a physical effort.

"Yes, yes, I did," she said after a long second.

Bobbie heard a grumbled, "F'God sakes," but kept her attention focused on the knee as she turned the leg one way then another.

"You'll be fine," Bobbie said gently. "It's just healing. It's perfectly normal."

"Thank you, doctor." Relief flushed the worry from her face.

"Doctor?"

"Doctor?"

Bobbie chose another question, answered, and repeated the process until she'd satisfied the group's concerns.

Eventually, Bobbie was able to make her way toward the exit only to be halted by a thin voice saying, "Doctor?"

Bobbie turned to the see Miley McGregor sitting on the extended seat of her carebot. Miley's sweet and gentle nature coupled with her devotion for Justin, her husband, made her one of Bobbie's favorite patients.

"Yes, Miley?" Bobbie said with a warm smile. "What can I do for you?"

"This candy has no more taste," Miley stuck her fingers in her mouth and fished out a flattened hard disc, concave on one side but convex on the other.

"I'll take that for you." Bobbie held her hand out as Miley tipped hers, letting the offending object topple off. The 'candy' felt hard in Bobbie's hand. She stared at its glassy white surface and flipped it over to reveal a black target-like spot surrounded by a gray circle.

"Justin McGregor," Bobbie said in a raised voice that was a very good imitation of her mother when she was looking to scold her children, "have you taken out your glass eye again?" Looking around she quickly spotted his shock of white hair atop a leathery face. A smile spread across the wrinkles like an accordion waking up. One gray eye looked up and focused on Bobbie, the other eyelid drooped, half-closed, revealing a fold of pink flesh.

"I left it on my carebot tray," he said, looking around him, the picture of innocence. "Oh, Miley!"

"Did I do that again?" Miley shook her finger at her husband. "Jeez, Justin, can't you keep your eye in its socket?"

Laughter swam in Miley's eyes as she seemed to emerge from the mists of confusion that threatened to engulf her.

"Here's your glass eye," Bobbie said. "Just let me clean it."

Bobbie touched a control on the side of the carebot and a clear plastic tray popped out from below the machine's flat screen display. She placed the glass eye in a drawer before tapping a command into the display. A flash of green light filled the compartment before the drawer slid out again. Lifting the eye with a tissue, Bobbie handed it to Justin. He pulled his eyelid up with one hand and popped the glass eye in with the other.

"You know you could get a new, functioning eye 3D printed," Bobbie said as she placed her hands under the sanitizer by the door for a few seconds until the telltale light turned green.

"I've had this here eye since I got hit in the face with a rubber bullet during the 2030 climate riots. Don't really fancy a bout of surgery now. Besides," he said with a wink, "It's all I can get Miley to suck these days!"

Miley swatted the back of her husband's head with a thin, gnarled hand. Justin cowered, face down as he raised his hands for mock protection.

"See," he went on, his voice muffled, "Husband abuse!"

Miley took one more swipe at him but gave a throaty chuckle. Justin joined in with a wheezy laugh.

Bobbie couldn't stop her grin. Her grin which froze in place as she noticed from Justin's one good eye a glint of orange.

"Justin." Bobbie reverted to her doctor face to mask her unease and said, "Do you mind if I have a look at your eye?"

How could the iris have changed color so quickly?

"Sure, knock yourself out," He raised his eyebrow, deepening the wrinkles on his forehead and the orange iris shone out at Bobbie.

"Don't be alarmed," Bobbie said. "But..."

"Oh, my God, Justin! Your eye!" Miley shrieked in Bobbie's ear.

Some people milling around the food table looked up but went back to procuring food, unfazed by what they must have taken to be another senile outburst. A nursing assistant looked over and mouthed, 'Okay?'

Bobbie beckoned him over with a nod. Directing her attention to the distressed old lady, Bobbie took Miley's hand and placed it in the nursing assistant's hand. "It's okay, I'll look after Justin. And this nice man will take you to your room and make sure you have everything you need."

"What? Why?" Justin asked, fear creeping into his voice.

"Justin, it's important you stay calm," Bobbie said.

"Last time someone told me to stay calm, we were under attack by the Melters!" Justin said.

The Nursing Assistant wrapped his hand around Miley's elbow while accessing her carebot via his ONIV and began to guide her away. Miley shifted in the carebot's seat as she attempted to stand, the action caused the machine to come to an immediate standstill. The old woman twisted her body to stare back at her husband with sad, confused eyes.

A thought struck Bobbie. Justin was younger than his wife. He was only on this ward because of Miley. "How old are you, Justin?"

"Ninety-five."

Miley had already turned 100. "Good. That's really good," Bobbie said.

"How's that good? What the hell is going on?"

"Justin, your eye has turned orange—like I was describing in my talk," Bobbie patted his hand. "But you don't have to worry. We can treat you. I just need to get you up to my ward."

"But I feel fine! I want to stay with Miley."

"No, go with her," said Miley. She trembled more than her usual old lady shakes, but Bobbie could sense Miley gathering her lucidity and clinging to it. "Please look after him for me."

"I will." Bobbie wished she could keep them together, but Justin had to go into quarantine. Bobbie couldn't risk her catching whatever the hell this disease was. The DNR rules did not apply to Justin, so she was free to resuscitate him if his heart stopped.

Miley made to stand, to reach her husband, but Bobbie moved to block her.

"I'm sorry, Miley," Bobbie said. "It's not safe. You have to stay here on your floor, and I'll take him upstairs."

"But I want to go with him." Bewilderment gathered in her eyes. Already she seemed to have forgotten her sensible words uttered moments ago as the fog gathered in her brain. "What will I do without him?"

"Sleep, watch TV..." Justin said. Bobbie heard the crack in the cheeky tone. "I'll be okay; Doctor Chan knows what she's doing."

Oh, God, do I? Bobbie thought Justin couldn't be further from the truth.

"Oh, alright then," Miley said. "Enjoy the ballgame, honey, I love you." The mists of her dementia had completely clouded her mind as she blew a kiss from her trembling hand.

Justin patted his cheek, as if he'd felt the kiss landing, "I love you too. I'll be back soon."

* * *

Two more patients arrested in the time it took to admit Justin to Pelagic 1 South. Due to the patients' ages, the staff had no choice but to obey the DNR law. When Bobbie heard of the deaths, she struggled to control her renewed anger at the medical board's decision not to waive the rules for patients showing symptoms of this new disease. She glanced across at Justin as the staff settled him in his new room. He was making no secret of the fact that he was unhappy at being separated from his wife.

You might not be happy being here, Bobbie thought, *but least we'll be able to intervene if the worst happens.*

The clearing of a throat behind her broke into her thoughts and she turned to find Hicks standing there.

"You've been working without a break for hours," Hicks said. "I'll watch him. You go eat."

Bobbie was going to object when a rumbling in her stomach made Bobbie realize how hungry she was. "Seems like my belly agrees with your diagnosis, doctor."

"I'll call you if anything changes," Hicks assured her.

With a nod, Bobbie headed for the staffroom that was shared between the duty personnel of Pelagic 1 and 2

In the staffroom, Bobbie settled at a table with a steaming bowl of soup from the matter-streamer. Activating her ONIV, she scanned through the news. During her mother's last days, Bobbie had lost interest in keeping track of current affairs. Returning to it, she felt like she'd been cut off from the world for months.

The news anchor spouted, "Twelve men and twelve women died today in a geriatric unit in India. The shocking twist - they all reportedly got younger before they died! Conan Coulter reports live from Manali, Himachal Pradesh, India."

Bobbie's ears pricked up and the spoonful of soup stopped halfway to her mouth. Davitt was in Ladakh. That wasn't too far from Manali.

A plastic-perfect male stood surrounded by beautiful gardens. Mountain tops peeked over his shoulders as he gave his report, listing the same symptoms Bobbie had observed in her patients and concluding with, "After their irises turned orange, they enjoyed four days of rejuvenated life before all suffered a fatal heart attack. The coroner is still investigating."

Four days? Had Bobbie heard the reporter correctly? That was longer than her patients had survived. Had the disease mutated already? Or was it a different strain from the outbreak they were suffering here?

If you had the full picture... Slade's sneering voice echoed in her head, making Bobbie flush with anger. *How much more was there to this picture?*

Bobbie wondered if Davitt was aware what was going on in a hospital so close to him. The disease must be a topic of discussion at his bionanotech conference. Bobbie composed a message on her ONIV. As she thought of what she wanted to say, the words appeared before her eyes seemingly hanging in midair.

Morning, sweetheart. I'm still at work. Her blink read.

Good morning, honey. Just finished giving a great Q and A session. I rocked it. Only one more week. Can't wait to see you. Sorry I ump missed the funeral.

Bobbie smiled while recognizing the letter combination that Davitt's neuro-network interface always inserted after "I." This 'thinko', as the techies called it, was distinct to him, though she'd seen variations of thinkos where the letter 'h' was always inserted before vowels, or random consonants doubled up where they shouldn't. The presence of a thinko seemed to be associated with an individual and never made much sense. A tech glitch that was annoying but accepted.

She wished his apology didn't irritate her so much, she felt guilty but didn't know why. Davitt was a good guy, so why react to him like this? Was he too eager to please her? Had she lost her respect for him? His six-week trip was nearly over, and Bobbie knew that she should have missed him more than she had—something that she had avoided thinking about, using the excuse of her mother's illness to explain it away.

Bobbie simply blinked. *We already talked about that. Your project is too important.*

Thanks. I ump love you.

Bobbie cringed at his reply, she never used the 'love' word, she wondered how Davitt failed to notice that, but backed into a corner she answered as best she could. *You too xo. Saw a report from a hospital in Manali. Have you heard?*

Yes, yes, I ump heard something. Are you on the research team?

Bobbie's forehead creased in confusion and she blinked back. *What research team? What have you heard? Do you know anything about the unexpected deaths among the elderly?*

A need to know clawed at her. She pushed back from the table, lunch forgotten as she crossed her left leg over her right and pressed one knee into the back of the other.

Nothing. No more than the news reports.

Dammit Bobbie was forced to erase the involuntary cuss from her reply. Tapping her right foot and jiggling her stacked legs, she concentrated her thoughts, while wishing she'd been blessed with patience. *Let's talk later.*

OK. Sorry for not being there.

Bobbie clenched the muscles in her right leg, stilling its motion, and enjoyed the burn in her calf as she pressed down with her toe, keeping her heel lifted. God almighty! Yes, yes, he was sorry. He felt guilty for leaving her alone in her mother's final days. Davitt's discovery of how to control and stop genetic cancers, though still in the testing stage, was a harsh irony in the face of her mother's death.

Bobbie gave up on her lunch deciding that work would be a perfect distraction from her feelings—or lack of them—for Davitt. Accessing her ONIV, she attempted to call up data on any fresh admission displaying symptoms similar to the disease only to get a repeated error message as she tried to access the data. Frustrated, she uncrossed her legs and stamped her feet, pushing herself back, so her chair scraped against the tiles.

Adrenalin again, more dangerous than too much caffeine.

She tried to blink message Hick's but wasn't really surprised when he failed to answer. He didn't like blinking when he was with his patients.

The staffroom door opened, and a carebot entered with a large plastic tub filled with stock which it proceeded to use to refill the matter streamer.

"Give me an admissions update," Bobbie said to the carebot as it completed its task.

Red lights flickered along the top of the machine. "Sorry, you cannot access this information."

"Why the hell not?"

"Please remember protocol Fifty-Seven," the carebot said.

"Damn Protocol Fifty-Seven."

"You are directly contravening Protocol Fifty-Seven. I cannot proceed."

Bobbie sighed. "Please forgive me." She tried to sound pleasant through her clenched jaw. "Explain why I cannot access an admissions update, thank you very much."

"Familial proximity Protocol Twenty-Three."

"What!" Protocol Twenty-Three covered close family members being admitted to the emergency unit. "Dammit!"

"Please remember Protocol Fifty-Seven."

"Oh, fuck off!" Bobbie yelled as she raced for the door and barreled down the hallway toward the admissions ward.

Hicks must have seen her coming, as he intercepted her at the entrance to the ward. The concern evident in his gray eyes sent a flash of cold fear down Bobbie's spine.

"Who is it?" she asked, barely able to breathe.

"Your grandmother," he said.

"What happened?" Her heart pounded.

"She's okay right now, but..."

"What? What's wrong?" Bobbie felt like shaking him, but she was already in trouble for abusing the damn carebot.

"Come see for yourself."

Bobbie felt his hand guide her by the elbow, the same way that she'd escort a patient who she was afraid might faint. They walked into the ward and up to a cubicle. Granny lay on the bed with her eyes closed, her hands folded on her chest.

"Granny?" Bobbie could hardly breathe.

Granny stirred. Her face awakened from the chin up, as a smile spread across her face, and she said in a husky voice, "Darling, don't worry, I'm fine, just fine."

Granny opened her eyes, and her irises were two shining discs of orange.

CHAPTER 8

A wave of nausea watered Bobbie's mouth. She swallowed hard and stood mute while inside she fought a frantic battle to compose herself as she leaned her hip against Granny's bed.

"Her vitals are good," Hicks said. He stood close beside Bobbie, their elbows touching, forearms brushing, and the nearness of him helped settle her a little.

She swallowed again and cleared her throat with a polite cough.

"I'll do everything I can for her, you know that," he said.

"She knows that," Granny said. "I know that. I'm fine. Stop fussing."

Bobbie nodded, taking Granny's hand, and holding it tight for the several minutes it took before she trusted herself to speak.

"Let me patch into her biometrics, please?" Bobbie asked.

"No!" Granny sat up straighter in the bed. "You are my granddaughter, not my doctor. I have a perfectly good doctor here." She patted Hicks's shoulder. "I need you to be my granddaughter, darling."

"I agree," Hicks said. "I've got this. She's under strict supervision with access to the best medical resources."

At least the DNR law didn't apply, thought Bobbie. Granny wasn't yet 100 years old. Bobbie eased her weight off the leg, leaning on the bed and balanced on both feet.

"I want to stay with her," Bobbie said to Hicks.

To his credit, he looked to Granny for permission and, with a weak smile and a nod, she consented.

"I'll get a nurse to sort something out," he said, turning to leave only for Bobbie to reach for his arm and stop him.

"Thank you, Hicks," Bobbie said.

Hicks nodded and left without another word. He didn't need to say anything. They both knew what was inevitable.

* * *

Hicks allowed Bobbie to set up a cot by Granny's bed, but after the third night, Granny protested and sent Bobbie home to get a decent night's sleep. But Bobbie had lain in her own bed with her mind whirling through the events of the past few weeks. She'd dipped in and out of fitful dreams, jumping awake in a sweaty panic so often that she longed for the cot by Granny's bed.

When Bobbie returned to work the following morning, Hicks met her at the door to Granny's ward.

"Sleep didn't happen did it?" Hicks asked with a frown.

Bobbie glared at him. "Nope." She sighed. No point being angry at Hicks, she needed him on her side now more than ever. "I have to find out what's going on with Granny before–"

"Look, I understand. I want to get to the bottom of this too, but–" Hicks began.

"But what?" Bobbie interrupted.

Hicks shifted in the doorway giving Bobbie a view of Granny's bed lying empty. Panic rocketed through her.

"Granny!" Bobbie cried. "Did she arrest?" The air felt sucked from Bobbie's lungs.

"No, Bobbie, Granny's fine. Listen to me." Hicks placed his hands on Bobbie's shoulders and turned her to look into his face. "They've discharged her."

"But why? She could arrest at any moment." Bobbie shrugged off his hands.

"Calm down," Hicks said touching Bobbie's elbow and guiding her into the ward. "Look they've sent all the residential patients with orange irises home."

More residents had developed the same odd symptoms as Granny since Bobbie had talked to the residents. The hospital was struggling at the best of times and Bobbie understood that. She looked around the ward at the fleet of carebots changing beds and setting up for the next patient.

"Belus don't care about them, do they?" she said working to keep the tears from her voice.

"I know how you feel," Hicks said. "I'm worried too but after extensive testing Disease Control determined that the disease was not transmitted from person to person. All those infected, including Granny, reported feeling well so, rather than eating up limited hospital resources Disease Control ordered them discharged."

"So she's home now on her own?" Bobbie asked.

"Joy said she'd drop by." Hicks shrugged and arched an eyebrow.

Fat lot of use that is!

But there was nothing Bobbie could do until her shift ended. She saw the sense in their decision but that did not stop her disagreeing with it. She wanted her grandmother under the watchful eye of a doctor and close to emergency treatment should her heart stop. Bobbie decided she'd have to be that doctor and provide that treatment, if possible, despite Granny's protests. Bobbie would need to be discrete about it.

* * *

Bobbie wished she had a key to Granny's apartment as she knocked on the door, but Granny valued her privacy as much as her independence and had never shared the ONIV access code to her apartment with Bobbie. Granny didn't even like to be alerted by ONIV that someone was at her door. She liked her guest to knock but recently her hearing had meant that Bobbie could be banging on the door for a while before the door was answered. But today she'd only rapped the door once before Bobbie heard the hiss of its mechanism moving.

As the door opened Bobbie held up a carton of ice cream with a flourish. "Ta-da!"

Granny's face lit up; an effect heightened by the brilliance of her glowing orange eyes. Bobbie forced herself to keep eye contact, belying how much the color freaked her out.

"Oh, darling, thank you," Granny said, hugging her granddaughter before she noticed the large bag resting at Bobbie's feet. "My goodness, are you moving in?" Granny asked.

"No, just some things from work," Bobbie said. Granny had orange eyes for nearly two weeks now without any arrhythmia or any other heart conditions, but the thought of having to use the defibrillator she carried in the bag on Granny turned Bobbie's stomach to water. Bobbie forced a smile onto her face. "But let's not forget about the ice-cream."

"My favorite!"

Of course, Bobbie knew that, having listened her whole life to Granny tell her that the locally made Macari's ice-cream was 'homemade to the same recipe since she was a little girl.' Bobbie hugged Granny, inhaling her lavender scent. The smell comforted her, made her feel like she'd arrived home despite home being in a glass tube at the bottom of the ocean.

"You're welcome," Bobbie said, grinning at Granny's pleasure.

"Macari's homemade. Matter-streamer-free!" Granny said, reading the small print from the carton. "Must have cost you a fortune." Granny ushered Bobbie in the door.

"So, you've augmented your vision now?" Bobbie asked.

"No, why do you ask?"

"You were able to read the small print on the carton," Bobbie said, tapping the side of the ice cream.

"Oh, yes!" Granny said, holding up the carton. "I can read the small print and all that nutritional information too. Sugar content per portion..."

Bobbie squinted, straining to pick out the words herself. *Damn, her eyesight is better than mine.*

"Will I get two spoons?" Granny said, skipping across to the kitchen area.

Bobbie swung between being happy to see the amazing changes in Granny to being freaked out at the same time. Bobbie's shook her head and brought herself back to the moment. "No, none for me, thanks. My Succor Tech gauge on sugar intake today is nearly at its maximum."

Granny retrieved a spoon then sat down on her brown and cream patterned sofa modeled on a retro theme from the last century. "One of the joys of old age," she said, digging into the softened ice cream. "Belus Corp doesn't care if we oldies die of sugar overload."

Bobbie spotted a bunch of roses on the side table, too perfect to be natural, but even matter-streamer flowers were lovely. She inhaled and caught their perfume, a strong chemical undertow but close enough to the real thing to send Bobbie back in time to her mother's garden. Bobbie pictured her mother, secateurs in hand, selecting blossoms in the glow if a summer evening and her heart ached.

"Who got you those?" she asked.

"Joy brought them earlier," Granny said, looking over at them. "You just missed her. She's away to do community hours."

For Granny's sake, Bobbie bit back the snide comments. Community hours? And why Joy's sudden interest in being part of the family? These could be Bobbie's last moments with Granny. She intended to make those moments beautiful, not filled with bitching about how selfish Joy was.

"I wish you girls got on better," Granny said.

Who needs thought control blinks with Granny around? Heat rose in Bobbie's cheeks.

"You have to stick together. You are all you have left for each other." Granny placed ice-cream cold fingers over Bobbie's. "I'd go easier to my grave knowing you girls were friends."

"You're not going to any grave," Bobbie said. "But I'll try harder with Joy." She slipped her forefinger to the soft spot below the base of Granny's thumb.

Granny snatched her hand away and jumped up. "You're trying to read my pulse!" She cocked her head and raised an eyebrow: 'The look' her grandchildren had called it growing up. The orange pupils gave Granny a shocked bug-eyed appearance.

"Sorry, sorry, I'm worried about you," Bobbie said. Her grandmother was a hard woman to fool. "Please sit down, I'm sorry, okay."

"I swear to God, I feel fine. Would you stop making such a fuss?" Granny said. "Bobbie, you are not my doctor. I'm not giving you access to my biometrics. That's my business. And I need my privacy. You have enough patients to worry about. Doctor Hicks is more than capable of looking after me." Bobbie sensed, more than saw, a youthful shadow passing over Granny's countenance. "And besides, I live in the same building as the hospital! It's only an elevator ride. What's going to happen?" Granny continued. "I feel far better than I have in a very long time."

Bobbie looked at her again. Really looked, as if resetting the image that her brain was receiving to see the refreshed picture sent from her eyes rather than the old jaded image her brain expected. Granny's skin glowed and seemed to fit the contours of her face better. She stood tall and walked fluidly. Considering she was in mourning for her daughter, Granny looked better than Bobbie could remember her looking for a long time. But Bobbie knew that others had gone down this very same road. Granny's eyes had changed color six days ago, she had survived longer than anyone had to date, but her heart could stop at any time.

Granny sat back down on the couch. Bobbie tried to will away the tension strung between her shoulders. The intewalls were set to some historic, mid-twentieth century-themed brown, purple, and orange floral pattern that Granny seemed to love, but which threatened to give Bobbie a migraine. In the corner of the room, a little ornate cherry-wood table matched the one in the other corner where Granny had placed Joy's flowers, but both looked out of place against the glare of the intewall. On the tabletop, Granny kept photographs in old fashioned photo-frames. Most people did not display pictures this way anymore. Printing photographs or finding any place that sold frames was nearly impossible. After the Melter war, everyone used intewalls to post images of their lives.

Bobbie knew the faces in Granny's pictures by heart. There was the photo that had always filled Bobbie with wonder, the black and white of Granny and Grandpa's wedding, Granny radiant and Grandpa, heart-achingly handsome. And her own parents' wedding—her mother's peaches-and-cream complexion, dewy and glowing, contrasting with her father's blue-black hair. The thought of her mother brought a raw feeling to the base of Bobbie's throat.

There were the pictures that hollowed her out with sadness, pictures of Gracie and Bobbie as babies, snuggled together sleeping, and then older, holding hands, wearing matching dresses. There was the photo that always provoked a sour feeling in Bobbie's gut, of teenaged Bobbie, sunken eyed from unhealed mourning, holding the newborn Joy, a red-faced monkey with a tuft of black hair framed against Bobbie's bright orange hair.

The remaining wall was made from reinforced glass looking out over the sandy ocean floor. At this depth it took an exterior floodlight to light up the perpetual gloom beyond the window, penetrating outwards about twenty yards in a weakening glow.

Grandmother and granddaughter sat together on the sofa and watched the deep-sea garden eels poke their heads out of the sand. The eels would retract at the slightest flicker of movement from inside the glass. Bobbie and Granny settled comfortably into a little game they often played. Whoever moved enough to cause the eels to retract lost, so both women sat ramrod stiff watching the eels extend and hook their necks until they looked like a field of brown candy canes that faded off into gray-green gloom.

As they sat there stock still, playing the eel game together, Bobbie read the blinks scrolling by on her ONIV… Twenty more fatalities in London, ten each, male and female… twelve men and eleven women in Newest Delhi had died in the same geriatric camp… fifteen men and the same number of women in Durban… Something about the numbers bothered her. This disease wasn't playing out like a typical epidemic with first one victim, then the infected numbers rising exponentially. The numbers were consistent, but the pattern of the locations seemed random. What did these blocks of data remind Bobbie of? The answer hung beyond her reach, wafting in the back of her mind.

"In fact," Granny said, breaking the silence they had been sitting in. "I'd go so far as to say that I feel better than I've felt in a very long time."

The eels swayed in hypnotic unison, but their calming qualities didn't ease Bobbie's mind. Granny didn't seem to care if she dropped dead. In four days, the medical board would decide on the appeal of the DNR Law.

As for a cure, the government was indifferent, tepid at best. Dead dependents were a windfall for the able-bodied: less work, access to new resources, and, most importantly, the freedom to reproduce. Bobbie had applied for access to the coroner's reports in her hospital and had blink messaged with international colleagues about exchanging information, but the data was slow in arriving. Hicks seemed the only one as concerned as she. Without him in her corner, she'd have thought she was going crazy, being paranoid.

"My hair is growing back auburn again. I'll show you when you lose this round," Granny said.

Bobbie's mother wasn't dead a month yet. Now she might lose Granny, and the woman didn't seem to care. Bobbie was still having difficulty sleeping. Her biosensors were pinging. She'd already had a call from Succor Tech to find out why. Succor Techs job was to keep people productive, well past traditional retirement age, by making sure they stayed at optimum health for as long as possible. As a doctor, Bobbie agreed with the sentiment, but as a citizen, she wanted her privacy and a stiff drink! Succor Tech had issued her with a bereavement pass for the two weeks following her mother's death, but no pass was going to prevent her from feeling wrung out and exhausted.

"So," Granny said in a tone of voice that made Bobbie dread her next question, "Is Davitt home yet?"

"No. He was delayed in Ladak. Something about new data that needed to be analyzed." Bobbie had been relieved that he had been held up.

Why were they talking about Davitt?

"He should be here with you at a time like this. Call me old-fashioned but–"

"You're old-fashioned."

"I'm just saying," Granny continued, "How long have you two been going out?"

Bobbie kept her eyes fixed out the window. Not feeling defensive, not arguing her case with Granny, proved difficult. They weren't having the 'beautiful memories' conversation she had been pitching for.

"Well?" Granny asked.

"Really?" Bobbie said. "You want me to talk about my relationship with Davitt now?"

"Yes. Definitely." Granny managed to sigh without moving a muscle. She was well-practiced at the eel game. "Life-altering decisions should only be made at times of extreme stress in your life," she proclaimed. "That way, if it all goes pear-shaped, you have something to blame."

Bobbie squinted and caught Granny's reflection in the window.

"Don't give me the stink eye, young lady. How long?"

"Six years."

"Holy mother of God, is it that long already? Why aren't you two married? Please tell me that you are at least living in sin."

"No, we are not living in sin. He has his own apartment nearby."

"Wales is hardly nearby!" Granny gave a muted snort. "In my day, that was a whole other country!"

"The world has shrunk, Granny dear. We can go door to door in less than an hour. The same length of time Granda had to travel to visit you when you two were courting."

"That was nearly a hundred years ago. Back when I was a girl."

"Only seventy-five years, Granny. Don't exaggerate."

"Well, it's not a kick in the arse off a hundred, is it? Anyway, stop side-tracking me with details. Seriously, you should be married," Granny went on.

"I'm just not ready." It was more than that. The thought of a lifetime with Davitt made Bobbie feel claustrophobic. She didn't love him; it was that simple. She looked to the ceiling and sighed.

"Don't cast your eyes at me. I've seen you keep people at arm's length your whole life since..." Granny paused, her voice softened, "since Gracie died. Let people in, Bobbie. You need them. You can't get through life on your own."

"Ach, Granny, I'm not trying to get through my life on my own," Bobbie said. "I do like Davitt, but he's just... just..." How could she tell Granny that, yes, Davitt was a hottie, the sex was great, but she didn't feel like she needed him enough? He never meant as much to her as Hicks, yet if she'd told Hicks how she'd felt about him way back in her teens, they would never have made it this far as friends. Romantic relationships were too fragile. Friendship with Hicks was better than no Hicks at all. *Was she using Davitt?* The thought made her uncomfortable. Navel-gazing like this served no-one.

"If he's not the one, you should move on," Granny said.

"I really can't deal with how I feel about him now," Bobbie said. "Please, Granny, let's not discuss Davitt."

"Well, you need to figure out your feelings, or Joy will get to have all the kids to replace your parents and grandparents."

"Oh, Granny, don't say that. There's years left in you yet."

"Stop being such a pain in the arse, Bobbie. If I die, I die!"

"What?" Bobbie turned to stare at Granny. The eels disappeared into the sand outside.

"Ha, you lose!" Granny said. "Now, what shall I make you do for your forfeit? Hmmm." She propped her chin in her hand and drummed her fingers over her lips.

"Granny, aren't you worried?" Bobbie asked. She shuffled in her seat now that she could move again.

"What? Worried? No," Granny said. "My options are feel better then die, or just die. I like the first one better. You should be happy for me."

"I don't want you to die." Bobbie heard herself sound like a stupid kid, like she was thirteen again, begging Gracie not to die, not to leave her all alone. Her eyes felt hot with tears.

Granny tucked her chin, raised her eyebrow, and glared at Bobbie from those strange orange eyes. "God, Bobbie! You're a fucking doctor!"

"Granny!" Bobbie wasn't so much shocked by Granny swearing but by her savage tone. Granny was the one person who understood the pain death had delivered to Bobbie's life.

"Oh, get over yourself. Don't you think you've wallowed in grief long enough? So, your twin sister up and died on you. Oh, boo hoo, a big swing of the Mickey. That was twenty-two bloody years ago. Get the fuck over it already. It's not always about you."

Bobbie stared open mouthed. Her hands shook. Her limbs loosened as if the glue that held her together had become unstuck. Granny spoke so viciously. This cruelty could be the last thing she said if Bobbie didn't calm her down. Granny's pulse must be pumping, and her blood pressure skyrocketing.

"Why are you being like this?" Bobbie asked, trying to stop her chin from wobbling.

Was Granny drunk? High? Is this a symptom? Bobbie pulled her sleeve into the palm of her hand and swiped at her eyes.

"Like what, darling?" Granny's eyebrows creased together. "What's the matter, dear? I said I feel better than I've done in ages. Aren't you happy for me?"

Bobbie stared at her, dazed. With a smiling face of concern, Granny reached over to clasp Bobbie's hand. Had the last few moments been a hallucination? Maybe the lack of sleep was playing tricks on her mind.

"Davitt's getting back today, isn't he? Are you looking forward to seeing him?" Granny asked, seemingly oblivious to her outburst. "Some tea, Darling?" Granny loosened her hold on Bobbie's hand and tapped the top of it before letting go completely.

Hadn't they just had this discussion?

Granny went over to the matter-streamer and touched the menu sensor. Nothing happened. She touched the sensor again. Still nothing.

"Fucking cunty-hole fuck!" Granny slammed her hand down on the machine.

Bobbie jumped. After a few stunned seconds, she stood and moved over to the machine, tapping into her professional reserve, keeping her outward movements measured and calm despite her shock at Granny's behavior.

Granny smiled sweetly, folded her hands, and sat back down again.

Keeping one wary eye on Granny, Bobbie touched her finger to the machine's sensor, connecting to its diagnostic software via her ONIV.

Status report. She blinked.

"No ceramic molecules," the machine chimed.

"Have you been keeping the cups again?" Bobbie asked as breezily as she could, not wishing to rile her again. Her bizarre mood swings had to be another symptom. *Had I missed seeing altered dispositions in other patients? Perhaps only those close to someone would register these behavioral changes.* Some of her patients acted up as a matter of course. But not Granny, not so far.

Bobbie opened the cupboard door and saw stacked cups filling the shelf. Taking a calming breath, she turned to face her grandmother. "These need to go into the recycler so the matter-streamer system can break the molecules down for reassembly."

"I'm sorry. I keep forgetting." Granny's face turned pink. "I can't get used to throwing crockery in the bin."

"Ach, Granny, it's not a bin. It's a recycler. Nothing is wasted. Besides, your carebot should be tidying up. You'll exhaust yourself."

"I usually do let the machines clear up, but I've been feeling so good lately, I overrode the clean-up mode." Granny pursed her lips. "The old memory is not so good. My brain doesn't seem to be improving as well as my muscle tone. Sorry, dear." She shrugged. "Looks like we've found a forfeit for you losing the eel game."

Bobbie walked across to the couch and gave Granny a hug. "Not to worry. I'll clean up… as my forfeit, but you did cheat." She gave Granny a fake scowl and received a stuck-out tongue in return.

Bobbie moved cups into a chute. The matter streamer made a low grinding sound like a giant cat purring.

"I think putting all the stuff in the same chute is not good. How does the machine know what's what? How come the matter streamer doesn't feed us the broken cups by mistake?" Granny asked.

"The recycler breaks the molecules down into their basic components, and the matter streamer puts them back together–like when you eat. All the food and drink go in one hole but gets digested and built up by the body to make the necessary tissues and organs," Bobbie said. "Granny, remember, the more you recycle, the cheaper running costs are. You don't have to pay for the raw materials." Bobbie fumbled a cup, and it dropped and smashed into a clatter of pieces on the floor.

"Shit!" Bobbie picked up the fragments and threw them into the recycler.

"Goodness, Bobbie," Granny said, "no need for that kind of language!"

Bobbie burst out laughing. "That's rich coming after what you just said."

"Oh, stop exaggerating, darling," Granny said with a wounded expression. "I never swear."

CHAPTER 9

The days following Granny's discharge from hospital rolled by for Bobbie in a constant round of work, sleep, sit with Granny, work, sleep, sit with Granny until one evening at the end of shift Joy surprised Bobbie at the hospital. Joy offered to visit with Granny and give Bobbie some time to herself. Although exasperated by Joy's absence, Bobbie was heartened by her gesture.

"If she shows any shortness of breath, or anything indicating distress at all, call the hospital," Bobbie said to Joy. "There is a defibrillator in a black bag behind her sofa."

"Really?"

"You better believe it," Bobbie said. "I'm not letting Granny away without a fight."

"I'm glad you're on our side, big sis." Joy play-punched Bobbie's bicep. "I'll keep a good eye on her. Isn't Davitt getting home tonight?"

Bobbie hesitated, waited for the stinging commentary that Joy often deployed against Davitt. When nothing appeared forthcoming, she said, "Yes, he's due in this evening."

"Well then, kick back, have some fun."

"I feel like the last time I had fun, people were using chisels to write letters," Bobbie said, grimacing.

"That explains so-o-o much!" Joy grinned.

Bobbie could not help but return her sister's infectious grin. Things felt easier. Joy had stuck around and helped out with Granny more. The sisters' interactions were more amicable. Joy wasn't pushing Bobbie's buttons in her usual kid sister way, and Bobbie didn't feel the need to scold nor tiptoe across eggshells with Joy. Granny's newfound fitness was almost miraculous. Almost—if Bobbie could ignore Granny's bizarre outbursts. Perhaps Joy would have some insight about Granny's mood swings after spending some time with Granny.

The flashing icon of an incoming blink message appeared in her ONIV. *I'm home. You want to come over?*

"I have to go. Davitt's home." Bobbie told Joy, "Keep an eye on Granny, and I'll be back tomorrow."

"Don't do anything I wouldn't do." Joy called after a retreating Bobbie.

The journey to Davitt's apartment seemed to Bobbie to take longer than it should have as she fought to control her urge to push her hovercar above the speed limits imposed by RadarNet. Eventually, reaching the complex Davitt called home she hurried from her parking space, her ONIV announcing her arrival to his apartment's computer. Davitt met her at the door and pulled her into the bedroom before she'd gotten as far as the living area.

* * *

Lying together in the afterglow of reunion sex, Bobbie traced her finger along Davitt's jawline then propped herself on one elbow to kiss his mouth. A lilac tinge colored the skin in the hollows of his eyes.

"I'm glad you're back," she said, the realization a mild surprise.

Her fringe fell forward and skimmed his forehead like tendrils of some aquatic creature sensing its surroundings.

"I'm so sorry I wasn't here for you," he said, taking her hair back from her face, his dark blue eyes looking up into hers. "I had to make an impossible choice, you know, between letting you down or not making the presentation, and setting the research community back by at least months, if not years. I couldn't trust anyone to deliver the findings. No-one else has the same grasp of the research as I do." He kissed her on the tip of her nose. "You do understand though how important my works is, don't you?"

"I know."

"I wish you could have been there to see me. The timing was terrible."

"It's fine, really. I understand." She meant it. Watching her mother dying with him sitting there would have been too personal.

Davitt's brown curls, damp at his neck and temples, framed his broad forehead, high cheekbones, and square jaw. His lips were rosy pink against pale skin. Stubble scrubbed against her lips as she planted kisses from his mouth down the side of his neck and lingered at the hollow of his collarbone, making little circles, with her tongue, tasting salt.

"Mmm, that's good," Davitt said, his voice husky. "Are you ready for more?"

"Maybe later?" Bobbie snuggled down against him again, finding that place for her head between his shoulder and ribcage. "We fit like pieces of a jigsaw."

"Mmm." Davitt settled into the pillow.

Bobbie let herself doze a little, inhaling the musky tang of his sweat, relaxing for the first time since her mother died. Wanting to forget about death, she let sleep claim her. The rhythmical ebb and flow of his breathing gave her a sensation of swaying, drifting off. Bobbie wished she could hold on to this sense of wanting Davitt when he wasn't around. When she was with him, she longed to touch him, inhale him, taste him, but as soon as they parted, that desire evaporated. Out-of-sight, out-of-mind. Why couldn't she crave him, have him haunt her every waking thought, be upside down in love with him? Did her suppressed feelings for Hicks get in the way? Bobbie could only ignite a fleeting passion for Davitt. Nothing more. Strange that she yearned more for her dead sister than for this flesh-and-blood male in front of her. Thinking of Gracie conjured up memories of their childhood together.

When Bobbie and Gracie stood side by side, they didn't look at all like sisters, never mind fraternal twins. Bobbie stood taller, with a tangle of ginger hair that always fell into her eyes. But Gracie's height did not increase much after their fourth birthday. Bobbie could see over Gracie's head when she hugged her, and though she wasn't allowed to, she could pick Gracie up.

By the time the girls were seven, Bobbie knew that Gracie had Hutchinson–Gilford Progeria syndrome, the rapid-aging disease in children. The mist of death swirled about her feet, leaving Bobbie unsure where to tread.

"Be gentle with your big sister," Mum told her often. "She can't run around as much as you can."

Gracie learned to read and write first, helping Bobbie make wobbly letters on their tablet and later showing her how to arrange the letters to make words and put them into sentences. Gracie looked after Bobbie like a good older sister should, although only older by a matter of minutes.

By the time they were eight, Gracie was writing her own stories and plays. She cast Bobbie as the heroine because Bobbie had hair. Sometimes, Gracie would play the hag or the wicked witch, but when they performed for their parents, Mum would cry, and Dad would scold Bobbie, regardless of the fact those plays had been Gracie's idea.

Gracie comforted Bobbie. "They don't want me to be typecast." Bobbie hadn't known what typecast meant.

"But our Bobbie's no dummy," Bobbie heard Mum say one day to Granny through the kitchen window. Bobbie stood in the garden, pushing Gracie on the swing. Back in those days, there was enough room for houses with windows and single stories: a simple blanketing of humans over the land, not the beehive style apartment living of the near future.

"It's just, well, Gracie is so advanced she makes Bobbie look slower." Silence fell between the women.

Before Bobbie could protest, Gracie lifted her hand from where she grasped the chain of the swing and put a finger to her lips. Her protruding eyes slid toward the window, looking wise and all-knowing.

"It's not fair, Mum," their mother continued with a tone that triggered an alarm in Bobbie's heart. "Gracie could have been anything she wanted to be. Can you imagine her as an adult? So talented, so..."

The sob that escaped her mother rattled Bobbie to the core. Bobbie grabbed Gracie's hand and squeezed in beside her on the swing seat, putting her arm around her sister's back to support her. Gracie smelled like cut grass.

"Ach now, darling, don't be at it," said Granny. "God lends us his angels for a short while. Gracie's our little angel. He'll be wanting her back soon."

Bobbie felt more than heard Gracie giggle beside her.

"I'm no angel," Gracie said, grinning. "I'm one of the little people, a leprechaun! And I'm going to escape to Tír na nóg."

"To where?" Bobbie asked.

"The land of everlasting youth. Everyone is beautiful and young there, and when I go there, I'll look just like you," Gracie said. "But with black hair, like Dad."

"How do you know all this?"

"I read about it on the internet."

"Can I come?" Bobbie couldn't imagine being anywhere without Gracie.

"Yes, but you'll have to wait until when you're old. Like me." Gracie's fuchsia pink dress reflected off her skin, giving her bare, veined scalp an ethereal glow.

"But you're only nine. We're the same age."

"Yes, but I'm the one who's a fairy, remember? I'll watch over you from Tír na nóg. Time passes slower there than it does in Armagh, so it will only feel like ten minutes to me before you're there, too."

"Like in Narnia?" Bobbie said.

"Yes! Exactly like Narnia, except no lions and no witches."

"And no talking mice?" Bobbie wasn't too keen on mice.

"Nope!" Gracie snuggled in against Bobbie.

By the time death carried Gracie to Tír na nóg four years later, Bobbie had read scores of legends about the Land of the Forever Young. Alone in the bedroom, Bobbie had once shared with Gracie, she'd jolt awake after dreaming of her twin sister returning for her on a white horse, young and beautiful, her black hair billowing out behind her. Bobbie would reach for Gracie, but as their hands touched, Gracie's hair would turn white, her skin would wrinkle, her body crumple as she died all over again from old age.

* * *

Bobbie couldn't tell how long she'd slept when she woke up next to Davitt. Poor, exhausted Davitt hadn't moved. The intewalls projected real-time images from outdoor cameras as if they were windows. The sky glowed in mauve hues across green farmland tinged purple. It was about 9:00 p.m.—twilight. As she tried to sit up, Davitt's arm tightened around her.

"Where are you going?" he asked.

"I need a pee." Bobbie eased his arm away and sidled off the bed.

"Okay. But come straight back. I have a surprise for you in the living room. Don't go in there without me." He stretched and interlaced his fingers, placing his hands behind his head.

Bobbie went to the bathroom, wondering why he would need a whole room for a gift from India? Perhaps he hadn't brought anything from India. He'd said before he left for his speaking tour that their relationship needed to take the next step. When she'd frowned, he'd laughed and said hopefully, "A puppy, maybe?"

"No way," she'd told him. She couldn't keep robotic pets alive, never mind the hoops you had to jump through to get a permit for a real, live pet. A simple souvenir or a new outfit, or sleepwear would have sufficed, but she knew that Davitt, feeling guilty about missing being with her for her mother's passing, would over-compensate with the gift.

When she returned from the bathroom, the bed was empty. She slipped on her dress, blinking the sensorfabrik to select the color code 'burnt sunrise,' more like a red brown, which should have clashed with her hair but somehow did not.

"Can I come out now?" she called through the door.

"No, wait."

Two seconds later, the door opened a crack.

"Close your eyes," Davitt said.

Bobbie complied; her pulse quickened. Davitt's warm hand folded around hers. Holding her other hand out in front of her, she followed the beckoning tug.

"If I stub my toe or walk into something, you're a dead man!"

"Don't worry, I've got you." Davitt moved behind Bobbie, wrapping his arms around her, drawing her close, the warmth of his body against her back. His cheek slid in beside hers, warm and rough. "Okay, open your eyes."

"Wow!" Bobbie breathed as she gazed in wonderment at the transformed room. They were surrounded by cliffs, layers of red sandstone in a million hues of peach, terra cotta and rust, topped with an azure sky. The screens on the floor and ceiling had also been programmed with a hologram chip. High above them, an eagle soared, looking for prey.

The sound of running water filled the room as a holographic waterfall poured from the canyon wall and flowed along the side of the room. Not that the space they were in looked like a room anymore. Depth and perspective made the area feel massive. The only furniture that remained apart from the matter streamer was a table and chairs in the middle of the room with a white tablecloth, set up for a meal.

"It's just like the pictures my father had of the Grand Canyon," Bobbie said, barely louder than a whisper. The chip for the view-sim must have cost a fortune. No-one had been able to go near the Grand Canyon since the Melters had turned North America into a scorch zone. "It looks so real!" She twisted her head around to kiss him. "Thank you."

Davitt turned around to face her. He took both of her hands in his. "Isn't it wonderful? I knew you'd like it."

"I love it!" Bobbie meant it.

"I travel so much these days. I feel like I'm neglecting you. You need some special treatment." He pulled out a chair. "Now, let's eat. I'm starving. And I can tell you all about the conference. I'd say you could follow a fair bit of the science. It's mostly genetics... some nanotech, but I can steer you through that." He brought a couple of plates piled high with food over from the matter streamer and set them down on the table.

"Mmm, burritos!" Bobbie's appetite kicked in for the first time in days, and the food vanished from her plate.

She struggled to concentrate as Davitt recounted his trip.

"... everyone was on their feet clapping," Davitt was saying. "You should have seen Jinko's team. They were pissed off that we'd taken all the glory."

"Serves him right for stealing your matter streamer credits in the lunchroom." It constantly amazed Bobbie how two such intelligent men could behave like little boys.

Davitt waved a hand dismissively. "He can have them. After this, I'll have free credit!" Davitt sat back with a sigh. "I wish you'd been there."

"Next time, maybe," she mumbled. Tummy full, she sat back and stretched, stifling a yawn.

"Ah, next time will be awesome—this next project." He pulled his finger across his lips—zip. "But as soon as I'm at liberty to talk about it, well, believe me, this is the best yet. I can't wait to share the details with you."

"Me too." Bobbie was usually more able to feign interest in his work, allowing Davitt's enthusiasm to carry her over the mundane details, but tonight she was too exhausted. She stifled another yawn.

"Sweetie, do you mind if I check-in?" Davitt asked. "There are important developments at work. I need to keep an eye on things."

"Sure." Bobbie decided she should catch up with the world too and switched on her blinks. There was a missed call from Granny, and five from Joy. Bobbie's heart accelerated. She directed her ONIV to place a call. Joy answered straight away, and a blast of music filled Bobbie's head.

"What the...?" Bobbie said. The blink had selected Joy's number instead of Granny's.

Davitt looked over at her, probably disturbed by her loud voice as he worked. She rolled her eyes and shook her head. He stared off at a spot over her shoulder as he picked up his feed again.

Joy's laughter came through the vibro-implants.

"Bobbie, turn on your foureyes!" Joy shouted.

"Really? Is this important?" Bobbie hated using the live camera in someone else's ONIV. The lack of control of the keel and tilt always had the effect of making her feel light-headed.

"Yes!" Joy yelled. "Just do it!"

Bobbie switched her blink into foureyes mode, battling down the queasy sensation that accompanied the shift to seeing the world through someone else's eyes.

"Keep your eyes steady," she hissed to Joy.

"Oops!"

Joy steadied her gaze in one direction long enough for Bobbie's brain to catch up with what she was seeing.

"Where are you?" Bobbie asked as she took in the large open space filled shoulder to shoulder with people, most of them fit and seemingly in their fifties with a sprinkling of younger folks, though few seemed to be younger than twenty.

Pink and blue lights bounced off figures on a stage crammed with drums, guitars, and a keyboard. Music throbbed in the background, and the players bounced with the beat.

"I'm at the Highland Fling," Joy said, her voice louder than necessary for Bobbie to hear her.

"Well... Good for you." Bobbie could not keep the bitter edge of disappointment out of her voice. *One night was all I had asked. Just sit with Granny for one night while I take a break. But no, you had to go clubbing.*

If Joy had caught her sister's tone, then she chose to ignore it. "No, wait, wait, she's here somewhere." The image spun to the left, then the right of the stage, before centering on a six-foot-high platform closer but blurred.

Another wave of nausea lapped at Bobbie, but as the camera focused on the raised platform, she could see the back of a woman dancing, hands above her head punching the air to the beat, feet skipping along off-rhythm. The hairstyle seemed too old for the dancer, and the jeans she wore were at odds with the trendy style of the other patrons of the gig. The color of her blouse—a grayish, dusty pink—reminded Bobbie of Granny's 'ashes of roses' top.

Granny!

"What the hell, Joy?" Bobbie couldn't believe what she was seeing.

"Isn't she something?" Joy squealed.

"Stop her! Stop her now!" Bobbie yelled, her heart thudding in her chest.

"Oh, come on Bobbie. She's just having a bit of fun."

"No! D'you want her to kill herself?" Bobbie heard her own voice rise in panic.

"She's feeling great! She wanted to come here," Joy said. "But I do think she's getting a bit out of hand."

"Has she been drinking? Oh, my God! Is she high?" Bobbie couldn't control her own heart rate, and she was only watching. Granny was sure to have a heart attack.

"Just high on life, big sis!" Joy laughed, making Bobbie's blood boil.

"Jesus Christ! She's sick. We don't know what's wrong with her. She could drop any minute." *What was Joy thinking? What an idiot! And Granny... had she lost the plot completely?*

"Look, don't get mad at me. I know all that. That's why I had to call you. Will you come help?"

"Yes, yes, just get her down off there, call security," Bobbie said.

"It's the Highland Fling." Joy laughed once more. "There is no security!"

"Christ!" Bobbie had to get herself there.

A touch on her arm, Davitt's voice said, "What's wrong with Granny?"

Bobbie waved him away and swore as she watched Granny dance closer to the edge of the raised platform. Granny stumbled and stepped back but then righted herself and danced on.

"Granny! Get down!" Bobbie yelled. Davitt moved close beside her, but she ignored him.

"She can't hear you!" The laughter in Joy's voice raised Bobbie's hackles.

Granny rocked back. The crowd surged forward. Granny righted herself, and the crowd cheered, raising their hands in the air. Granny turned and punched the air raising another cheer as she proceeded to play an air guitar.

"Well, that's a tad embarrassing." Joy said, her voice soaked in mirth. "Oh, shit!" Her tone changed to alarm.

Bobbie gave a smothered yelp as Granny ran to the edge of the platform and threw herself headfirst into the crowd.

The image jostled. Bobbie and Joy shouted in unison, "Granny!"

Joy must have been running, the picture a blur of heads, backs, and arms.

"Can you see her? Can you see her? Joy? Answer me!"

"Oh, my God!" Joy's voice came through, laughing. "Granny's crowd surfing!"

CHAPTER 10

"Joy's crowd surfing?" Davitt asked.

"No, Granny's crowd surfing!" Bobbie jumped to her feet and immediately regretted it as a wave of nausea washed over her. "Turn this bloody thing off." Her ONIV was still in foureyes mode and blinding her to her actual surroundings.

"Fascinating..." He seemed intrigued, not shocked.

"Seriously? Fascinating?" Bobbie said, her eyes adjusting to the room around her as Joy disconnected. "Am I the only one who thinks that Granny's behavior is outrageous?"

"Sorry." Davitt's eyes focused on Bobbie. He'd probably been reading a blink and maintaining two conversations at once, as usual. At least now she had his full attention.

"I mean. No. Absolutely. Her behavior's unacceptable, I agree. But why would she do that?" he asked.

"God knows. I have to go get her." She scooted around the room picking up a jacket and her bag.

"I'll come," said Davitt.

"Really?" Bobbie felt grateful to him for his support. He'd just come back from the other side of the planet, having traveled all day, and now his body clock thought it was somewhere in the middle of tomorrow. "No, you're too tired. I'll get Hicks to come."

"Why do you need him?" Davitt said. A panel slid back, splitting the Grand Canyon in two to reveal a direct access door to the carport. Bobbie jumped. Davitt's use of complete mind-controlled tech, integrated with his ONIV and house system, came in handy, but doors opening, music coming on, scourbots swinging into action all by themselves, often took her by surprise. The remainder of the room's graphics shifted to off-white panels as the Grand Canyon disappeared around her.

"She's Hicks's patient. I don't have access to Granny's biometrics."

"I wasn't here for you when your mother passed. Please, I want to be here for you. I can catch forty winks on the trip over." He pushed in his chair. "And we'll swing by for Hicks on the way."

"If you think you're up to it." She couldn't help but smile. Was he jealous?

He shrugged on his jacket. Poor Davitt, sleep-deprived, and getting paranoid. She stood on her tiptoes and pecked his cheek.

* * *

Spotlights crisscrossed the night sky as Bobbie's car approached The Highland Fling. Bright lights bouncing off low-hanging clouds—the sight always sent a shiver down Bobbie's spine. It was a haunting reminder of the first Melter raids when the Earth's defenses had proven so pathetically low tech compared with their attackers. The tiny alien crafts had slipped past the human's radar, pummeling the cities below with devastating energy blasts. The defenders on the ground and in the air may as well of been Boy Scouts waving flashlights in the air, humanities best fighter aircraft had been swatted out of the sky by the Melters like annoying mosquitos. Their most advanced surface-to-air missiles had failed to lock onto the Melters craft and exploded uselessly in midair. In desperation, the military had resorted to tactics from nearly a century before; high powered spotlights would illuminate the night sky and anti-aircraft guns would blast away at anything that looked remotely suspicious. From their concealed positions within the clouds high above, the Melters had rained down fire on the defenders like angry gods. Bobbie and her family had watched the unfolding horror through the news reports and social media uploads. Even a teenager had known the fight was useless, that the human race was looking at extinction. Then, the politicians' and generals' long-promised wonder weapons had appeared as if by magic. Belus Corp had developed and rushed into production drones capable of detecting and destroying the Melter fleets as they entered the Earth's exosphere. The tide was turned and the Melter threat disappeared as quickly as it had arrived.

Warning. Proximity alert. The Mercedes guidance system in her ONIV overrode the hovercar's systems to slow it in the crowded sky. The change in speed woke Davitt from his snoring sleep and Bobbie from her memories.

"Looks pretty busy down there," Hicks said from the back seat.

People came from all over the world to this week-long outdoor party held on a Scottish hillside. They emptied out of their vehicles in excited huddles and joined the queues of people at the giant fake logs of the forest-themed entrance gate. The now empty cars then flew off by themselves to park in the lower-lying fields that had been outfitted with portable solar battery stations to be recharged.

Bobbie maneuvered her car toward the medical vehicle zone close by the gates, blinking her status as a doctor to the events parking control system. Davitt raised an eyebrow.

"Well, Granny could become a medical emergency at any minute," she said with a shrug.

"Okay, okay," Davitt said as the doors opened, and they jumped out.

"Let's just get Granny and go," Bobbie said as she bounced out of the car and set off toward the gates at a jog. Davitt and Hicks fell into stride beside her.

They'd be charged for the time spent inside the gates, their biosensors registering their presence, but she didn't care. They wouldn't take that long anyway. At the priority gate, Bobbie held her thumb to the reader, again her ONIV identified her and her companions as medical personnel. As the door slid back, they stepped through a wall of sound into the concert area.

"Being a doctor does have its perks," Davitt said in a loud voice as the music and crowd thrummed around them. Davitt's foot tapped. Hick's index finger bounced in time to the beat. Had Bobbie not been on a mission to retrieve Granny, perhaps she'd have been inclined to jig along to the music too.

"Bobbie's been telling me a bit about this new disease," Davitt shouted above the noise to Hicks. "I'm curious to see Granny. What do you think is causing her symptoms?"

"No idea." Hicks shrugged, "Your guess is as good as mine."

Bobbie sent a blink to Joy, updating her on their progress and asking for their location. Joy sent the directions straight to Bobbie's locator b-app. Bobbie's ONIV projected the outline of an arrow into her vision. Turning her head until the arrow turned a solid green, Bobbie walked that direction. If the arrow turned amber, or red–she was badly off course and would adjust her direction until the arrow went green again.

Bobbie followed the arrow through the swarming crowds until she spotted Joy's unmistakable blue-tipped-hair in the distance. She was sitting in a quiet area on a table with her back to them, her arm around another girl. *Where was Granny?* Panicking, Bobbie broke into a run.

"Joy!" she shouted above the drumming of the music.

Joy turned toward her. The girl with her did too—her eyes flashing, the bright orange pupils catching the dancing colors of the light show flickering around them.

Bobbie staggered to a halt. It was Granny.

Despite the weird effect of her orange eyes, Granny pulsed with energy. If not for her dated clothes, heavy denim jeans, and an old-fashioned smock top, Granny could easily have passed for fifty-something. Her straight back and good posture recalled a much younger woman though up-close her hair was white, not blonde as Bobbie had first thought. Unbelievable that the same woman had been hunched over weeping at her daughter's deathbed two weeks ago.

When Granny spotted them approaching, she stood and put her arms out to embrace Hicks.

"Now this is really a party! Doctor Hicks, how lovely to see you." Granny hugged him then turned to Davitt. "Darling, Davitt." She fluttered her eyelashes and presented her cheek for a kiss.

"I had a dream about you recently," Granny said to Davitt. "It seemed so real. You came into my bedroom."

Davitt flushed red. Bobbie felt uncomfortable for him.

"And you stuck something into me." She arched her eyebrow.

"Granny!" Bobbie said. Granny's humor had always had an edge but never smutty, certainly not this crude.

Granny gave Bobbie 'the look' and said in a cold voice, "My name is Gloria, please use it!"

Bobbie nearly choked.

Joy gave a nervous laugh and then shot a grimace in Bobbie's direction, her lips mouthing the words, "What the fuck?"

Before Bobbie could respond, Granny had turned back to Davitt, who stood blushing with a tight smile and linked herself to his arm.

"You pricked me with a needle. What did you think I was talking about?" Granny asked wide-eyed, looking around the group as if absorbing their reactions. She flashed her orange eyes at Davitt, saying, "He was dressed in a white coat. Perhaps he was playing doctor?" Granny turned to Hicks. "Maybe Doctor Hicks told him I had," she paused, letting her gaze sweep the length of her body, "acute angina. Perhaps he wanted to, you know…" She winked. "Check it out."

Joy's attempt to cover a laugh by putting a hand up over her mouth earned her a withering look from Bobbie.

Bobbie could have cheerfully throttled Joy, but she had to keep cool and handle Granny with calm directness. How could Granny be saying these things?

"Quite the dream," Davitt said, so red-faced that his eyelids were flushed.

Granny seemed like she was preening as she looked around at the little group. Bobbie couldn't help feeling that Granny measured the weight of her words as they landed.

"Seems like you had lots of fun tonight, Granny," Bobbie said, stepping in beside her. "I'd love an ice cream." *Maybe distraction would work.*

"My name's Gloria!" Granny's orange eyes blazed at Bobbie. She stepped away from Bobbie. "I don't want ice cream! I want a drink. A real drink."

"Me too, Gloria," Hicks said. "I have a bottle of Jameson back at my place."

"Now that's a great idea," Bobbie said, keeping her voice cheerful, distilling out the worry and hurt she felt. Hicks lived in the staff residential quarters in Subscraper One, above the Pelagic levels. If they could get Granny that far, they'd be off to a good start. "If your doctor says it's alright. How is she, Doc?" Bobbie asked Hicks.

"Her biometrics are fine. She's not in any physical distress." Hick's eyes lost focus as he scanned his blink feed.

Send them to me. Bobbie blinked to him.

"No," Hicks said aloud, as he glared at Bobbie, causing the rest of them to look puzzled. Bobbie felt her face redden.

"You know, these days simply everyone is trying to get into my... biometrics," Granny said, enunciating the last word.

"Don't worry," Hicks said, and Bobbie saw him fight a flicker of a smile, "I won't let her. Now tell me, Gloria, how do you feel?"

"Oh, this is ridiculous!" Granny said, dropping her sultry tone. "I've never felt better. I don't know why there's all this damn fuss."

"You know we worry because we love you, Gra-Gloria," Bobbie said as pleasantly as she could. "Let me give you a lift as far as the Buckets."

Granny seemed to deflate. "Alright," she said, "perhaps it would be a bit of a squash sleeping in Joy's car tonight."

Joy shrugged and ran her fingers through the ends of her hair, tugging at the fine tats that gathered there. "I like my car, it's... quaint."

"Quaint," Bobbie scoffed. "That heap should have been sent to the recycling yard years ago." Joy's live-in car, its design based on the old camper vans, had become her permanent home after she had failed repeatedly to pay her rent. Bobbie suspected all her available cash went on neuro gaming and recreational viruses.

Did Joy care where Granny slept tonight? Bobbie wondered. She caught Hicks's eye, and he gave her the faintest of nods. He was onside.

"I want to be sure you're okay, Gloria," Bobbie said.

"Give over, would you?" Granny snapped. "Just be happy that I'm getting fitter, feeling better."

"But the others died..."

"Well, I'd rather die fit and having fun, than live all withered up and ancient." Granny stood up. "But yes, I could do with a lift home now." Defeat slumped her shoulders. Was she in pain? Worry struck up an orchestra of nerves in the pit of Bobbie's stomach, but at least Granny had given up on the idea of drinking whiskey with Hicks, for now.

"I'll take you." Bobbie turned to Joy. "How long are you docked up here?"

"Until the Fling ends—two more days," Joy said, flipping her blue-tipped hair over her shoulders.

"And then?"

"Well," Joy smiled and tucked her fringe behind her ear. "I was hoping to dock at your place?"

"Fine," Bobbie said, irritated. "But no more leading Granny astray."

Granny and Joy exchanged a grin that sent a spike of fury through Bobbie. Joy never took anything seriously, and ultimately Bobbie would be left to pick up the pieces.

"Right, taxi's leaving," Hicks said. He extended a hand to Granny. "Madam?"

Granny accepted his hand and pulled herself to him.

Bobbie felt a twinge of envy. Was it because Hicks could handle Granny so well or because Granny was flirting with him? Confused, Bobbie sought out eye contact with Hicks and gave him a quick nod in thanks before he turned and led Granny back to the car.

Davitt fell in behind Hicks and Granny, and Bobbie matched his pace. Fatigue made her emotional and irrational. Was she jealous of Granny flirting with Davitt too? Of course, she wasn't. Granny was nearly a hundred years old!

The group left the event through the same entrance they had entered through and, as the door closed behind them, they were at last able to speak without shouting.

"How are the other patients sharing Gr-Gloria's symptoms doing?" Davitt asked.

"Two died yesterday in Poland," Bobbie said. If Granny overheard them, perhaps she'd exercise more caution.

"But no more here?" Davitt asked. "That's heartening, isn't it?"

"And five more of my neighbors have gotten better since I got this... this... rejuvenation." Granny walked the last few steps toward Bobbie's car and stopped. Hicks opened the door for her.

"And there's been another six showing the symptoms in the last forty-eight hours. That's a total of twelve who haven't died here!" Bobbie said, piecing together a new puzzle picture. Lightness crept into her heart for the first time in weeks, months. The disease had changed since its first onset. Granny and the other five had lasted longer than anyone other afflicted person and were improving every day. If the other six followed that symptomatic route, there would be twelve survivors.

"What's different about these new cases?" she said aloud as they settled into the car.

"The only thing I can think of is that the patients at the start were older," Hicks said. "And they presented the iris pigmentation symptoms at a later stage."

Bobbie's head spun as she tried to recall the details. Her ONIV screen didn't have enough room to display all the data she had on her patients. If only she could get Hicks alone in front of an intewall and do some brainstorming. Never mind that she couldn't share patient data in front of Granny and Davitt.

She set the destination for Belfast, Subscraper One, allowing the cars systems to control their flight then orientated her seat to face the rear catching sight of Davitt's face. Gray etched into the hollows circling Davitt's eyes, but his face was alert and interested.

"Davitt, are you feeling okay? You look exhausted," she said.

"Thanks, I'm fine."

She wanted to go over the data with Hicks, but she didn't want to inflict that on Davitt. She needed sleep too, but the questions buzzing around in her brain would not let her rest. Not yet.

"Let's catch a cat nap en route to the Buckets," Bobbie said to Hicks. "Davitt, you can take the car home and send it back for me."

"Oh, don't worry about me. I can sleep anywhere. My place is too out of the way. I'll snooze in the car while you guys are working," Davitt said, reclining his chair a little and settling down.

Granny was already purring snores. As they flew out over the restless North Sea, Bobbie's gaze lingered on Granny. In the dim lights, Granny looked as she had in the black and white wedding photo she kept in the old-fashioned frame in her house. A pretty trick of the light, Bobbie thought as the sleep she was convinced her buzzing brain would repel, snuck up and carried her off.

CHAPTER 11

Over the next couple of weeks, rejuvenation set in, and youth recaptured the twelve who now refused to be called patients. Granny's hair had grown at an astonishing rate – an inch of the bright golden copper tones she'd sported in her youth now showed at her roots. Of the five other women who had developed orange pigmentation in their irises, their new hair grew in a variety of black, brunette, and blonde, tipped with the pigmentless gray and white they'd lived with for decades.

The six of them decided to dye the ends to match the roots. Bobbie watched as the women piled into a hovertaxi gossiping and laughing like a group of excited schoolgirls and set out for the hair salon. Bobbie was curious how they'd look on their return. Granny's orange eyes and flawless skin still made Bobbie gawk. Juxtaposed to the gray ends on the hair, the whole look had been weird. Perhaps with the hair dyed to match the roots, they'd all look a little more natural, if that were at all possible with those glowing orange eyes. But they all seemed healthy, and Bobbie had kept a close watch of her patients' biometrics and there was no sign of the heart murmurs that had killed the first Rejuvenees.

As Bobbie waited for them to return, she visited with some of her other patients. The Day Room on Benthic 3 had a hushed atmosphere punctuated by the occasional raised voice from a lady arguing with the empty space beside her. Agitation seemed to swoop over the woman, like waves on a beach, making her shout out then recede as she forgot why she was angry before she settled down again. A couple of residents, their genders barely discernible as their features melted into wrinkles, framed with a smattering of wispy white hair, sat propped up in front of an intewall showing a film, framed in an image of the old flat-screen TV they'd watched in their heydays.

Bobbie walked over and took a seat beside Bradley Smiles, who looked more like staff these days than a resident – with the exception of his bright orange eyes.

"So, you decided not to join the ladies for a trip to the hairdressers then," Bobbie said as she checked his biometrics. She'd never get used to this syndrome, but she was growing accustomed to reading vitals from 100-year-old patients that made them seem like they were in their thirties.

"I'm just too delighted to have hair to cut off," he said, running his hand through his short blonde curls. He'd be quite handsome if it weren't for his orange eyes.

"Well, your biometrics are great. Remember…"

"…If I feel unwell at all, call you," Bradley said.

"Yes." Bobbie laughed. "Sorry for nagging."

"So, what time do you get off duty?" Bradley said, staring into her face.

"Pardon me?" Bobbie asked, thinking she'd misheard him.

"Fancy a bite to eat with me after you finish up here?" He put his hand on her thigh and squeezed.

Bobbie snapped into a standing position. "I don't think so." Warding off a dementia patient was one thing, but Bradley had never shown symptoms of dementia before rejuvenation. He had always been a perfect gentleman.

Bradley raised both hands and laughed.

Bobbie bit her lip, turned, and strode off to see her next patient, while adding a note to Bradley's patient files that his behavior was *uncharacteristic*.

Miley was next on her list. Miley hadn't rejuvenated, although her husband Justin had. Bobbie wondered how Miley felt as she watched her husband bounce back to the handsome man she had married. Would she feel even older and frailer by comparison? According to Bobbie's patient locator b-app, Miley was in her bedroom in the couple's section that she shared with Justin. There was no response when Bobbie knocked, but she could see from the b-app that Miley was inside. Concerned, Bobbie called up her ONIV and overrode the door lock. Entering, she quickly scanned the room for any sign of Miley.

"Miley, it's Doctor Chan. Are you okay?" When Miley didn't reply, Bobbie called up the patient locator app again. It indicated Miley was in the bedroom. Bobbie hurried across the small living room and pushed open the bedroom door. In one corner, a carebot supported what looked like a pile of clothes. As Bobbie moved closer, she saw to her horror that the pile of clothes was actually Miley, coiled up with her hand covering her head.

"Hello, Miley," Bobbie said in a clear voice as she approached. "What's wrong?"

Miley lifted her head but remained in a fetal position.

Bobbie scanned her patient's biometrics. Blood pressure higher than normal and pulse elevated. Miley stared up at her with scared eyes. They didn't have that vacant look Miley might have when her lucidity escaped her. Miley was in there.

"Here, let me settle you onto your seat better," Bobbie said, reaching out to touch Miley's shoulder. The woman flinched with a yelp. "Are you hurt?"

Miley sniffed and nodded.

"Please, let me examine you, Miley." Bobbie's knees cracked as she hunkered beside the seat, making herself lower than Miley.

Miley coiled further into herself, hiding her face behind her clenched fists. Bobbie's heart clenched at Miley's choking sobs.

"What happened? You can tell me." Bobbie reached up and took one hand. Purple bruises dotted from Miley's wrist up her arm, a pattern consistent with a large hand squeezing or pulling at Miley's arm. Gently Bobbie examined her other arm which had a similar pattern of bruising. Alarm vibrated within her, but she kept her expression calm.

"Who hurt you?" Bobbie asked, switching on the recorder b-app in her ONIV. This initial interview could prove to be crucial evidence for the police. If someone was attacking the patients, they needed to be apprehended.

Miley looked at her with red-rimmed eyes. Tears caught on the folds of her skin. Her lips quivered. "A man came into my room. He… he forced me to… he forced…" Tears streamed from Miley's eyes. She gulped then said, "He forced himself on me." Miley lifted the edge of her dress to above her knees, revealing a massive bruise on the inside of her thigh, black, radiating out to blue.

Bobbie struggled to keep her professional exterior, hiding her outrage. "What did he look like?"

"He was young, and he had a staring orange eye." Miley trembled.

"Only one orange eye?" Bobbie went cold inside. "Justin?"

"No, no, Justin is gone. He's not in there anymore. I can't find him." Miley's words sent a chill over Bobbie's scalp. Miley seemed lucid, but her words held a new confusion. There was only one patient on the Benthic levels with one eye. With Miley's dementia, any accusation of rape might not stick if Justin denied it. Bobbie struggled to believe that Miley's adoring husband would do such a thing.

Just then, the outer door to the couple's unit opened to giggling and laughing voices.

"I need to grab a change of clothes, and then we can go to your place," a man's voice said.

Miley pulled her dress down below her knees and curled up again, whimpering.

Bobbie went to the bedroom door to meet him, resisting the temptation to be judge and jury.

"Oh, hello, Doctor Chan," Justin said, smiling, his glass eye gray and his other one shining orange, giving his face a lopsided leer.

"Hello, Bobbie," said the glamorous forty-something redhead at his side. After a moment's hesitation, Bobbie matched the voice with the visual. Granny stood tall and with great poise. A mint green sensorfabrik V-neck dress displayed a flash of cleavage. The material flowed in at the waist, over a flat tummy and shapely hips. Granny's hair tumbled over her shoulders in loose bronze curls. Her skin glowed peachy and smooth, the only visible lines on her face the delicate crinkles attaching her smile to the edges of her eyes.

"Granny!" Bobbie said. She switched off her recorder, not wanting to involve Granny in what was shaping up to be a domestic elder abuse case.

"It's Gloria now. How dumb are you, Darling?" She hooked her arm into Justin's. "Don't worry, Justy, you won't need any clothes at my place."

"Wait, Gran... Gloria!" Bobbie had to warn her that Justin was violent, that he'd raped his wife. She moved out of the bedroom, closed the door behind her and stood facing Justin and Gloria in the small living room area. Justin seemed too big for the space, didn't seem to fit in there, surrounded by pictures on the intewalls of his wife and family. His shock of white hair had been cut, leaving a sheen of white tips on the ends of his newly grown brown hair. The once accordion-textured face that Bobbie had associated with a lifetime of smiles and kindness was now smooth. He stood tall, his limbs straight and supple, the skin covering them taut and wrinkle-free.

"How can I help you, Bobbie?" he said as if he were a shop assistant in an old movie.

"Miley says you attacked her." Bobbie watched Gloria's face. No reaction.

"Oh, you know Miley," Justin said, slipping his hands into his trouser pockets, relaxed and confident. "She gets confused. She's getting worse now, paranoid, you know?"

"She has bruises," Bobbie said. The rape was a police matter, but Bobbie wanted her grandmother to know what she was dealing with.

"So?" Justin shrugged his shoulders. "She fell over. She's 100 years old!" His booming laugh filled the room.

"Did you rape her?" Bobbie asked. Bile rose in her throat.

"Honey, look at me." He ran his hand down over his chest in a parody of a sexy pose. "Do I look like I need to have sex with old crumblies like her?"

"Rape is not about sex," Bobbie said, barely keeping her anger in check.

"Enough with the lecture, Bobbie," Gloria said, snapping her fingers. "We have better things to do." Gloria reached out and slapped Justin on the ass.

"Gra... Gloria," Bobbie said in a low voice, "Justin raped his wife. You really want to put yourself at risk?"

"Justin?" Gloria turned and looked at him, one hand on her hip, cinching in her tiny waist, exaggerating her curves.

"She's talking codswallop!" he said, a grin spread across his face.

Gloria gave Bobbie a shrug.

"Miley is a witness," Bobbie said. Rage pounded in her chest.

"As if anyone can rely on the evidence from an insignificant senile old woman," Justin said. He flashed Bobbie another broad smile that fell short of his mismatched eyes, both glassy cold, and cocked his head before he added, "Her testimony would never hold up in court."

He moved toward Gloria, gathered her up, and kissed her on the mouth, taking his time about it. Then he glared at Bobbie as she blocked the bedroom doorway. Bobbie considered holding her ground, but one look at his frosty face made her think twice. She stepped back as he shoved past her.

He would have happily knocked me over, Bobbie told herself as she followed him, moving around him to place herself between him and Miley. She'd never seen him use these bully-boy tactics before. The man before her wasn't Justin. Bobbie saw now what Miley had meant.

Justin is gone. He's not in there anymore.

Justin ignored Miley as she cowered in the corner and began filling a bag with items from drawers and cupboards.

Bobbie bent down beside Miley and put her arm around her. Bobbie could feel the old lady's frail frame shaking. Bobbie whispered in her ear, "You're okay, I'm here. I won't let anyone hurt you."

Miley's snuffling sobs made Bobbie's vision blur with angry tears. She held them back with effort.

"Hurry up, Justy," Gloria called from the other room. "I'm getting bored."

"I'm coming," Justin replied.

"Oh, you will be." Gloria gave a throaty laugh. Bobbie could hardly believe that the creature outside the door was Granny.

"You better believe it, Sunshine." Justin laughed.

"How can you do this to her?" Bobbie demanded. Rage spilled into every cell in her body. She clenched her teeth.

"Her?" Justin nodded at Miley. "I'm done with her. She's no use to anyone." Slamming the final drawer closed, he spun on his heel and, in a few strides, he'd left the room.

Bobbie knelt beside Miley. Her logical doctors mind trying in desperation to rationalize what she had just witnessed. Gloria and Justin's bodies may have become younger, but their minds seemed to have devolved into rotten imitations of the worse parts of them. Psychiatric disorders in the elderly were usually related to cerebral neurodegeneration. Dementia presented in about 10 percent of Bobbi's ultra-elderly patients. As for those over sixty-five, she saw depression in about 3 percent of her patients. Justin's behavior was explained by neither of these conditions. Paranoia was the third most common mental ailment. Her mind clicked through all those elderly people she'd treated who were convinced that someone was out to steal their money. Justin did not have paranoia.

His lack of remorse and shame at his obvious sexual entanglements with Granny showed poor judgment that bordered on antisocial behavior. Granny shared his lack of inhibitions, flaunting their affair, despite the fact that Miley and Granny had been friends for a very long time. Granny and Justin's symptoms pointed toward sociopathic behavior. Sociopaths were more spontaneous, more intense than other people, with a tendency to do bizarre, sometimes erratic things that most regular people wouldn't do because they were unbound by normal social contracts.

Bobbie felt sick at the thought that Granny, or any of the Rejuvenees, may have become sociopaths, especially since this syndrome seemed to bring them so many physical benefits. Perhaps she was jumping to conclusions –or was she in a state of shock?

Right now, she had more urgent matters to attend to. Miley sat, hands over her face, crying.

Bobbie hugged Miley, then sat back on her heels, and looked into the old woman's face. Cognizance had drained from Miley, leaving her eyes vacant and unfocused, her mouth slack, and her fingers twisting through one another. Bobbie's heart broke as she realized that Miley, too, had left the room.

CHAPTER 12

Bobbie was completing her review of the fresh data she was to present to the medical board that afternoon when a knock on her office door startled her. She opened the door to a sturdy woman with gray, short-back-and-sides hair.

"Hello?" Bobbie said, her voice lifted in a polite, inquiring tone as she moved out into the hallway with her guest. There wasn't time to invite her in for a chat.

"I'm looking for Doctor Chan."

"Well, you've found her," Bobbie said. "How can I help you?"

"I'm Detective Cross. You filed a report of alleged rape yesterday."

"Yes," Bobbie said. "Have you detained Justin McGregor yet?"

"I'd like a list of all the men who have access to the McGregors' living area," said Cross ignoring Bobbie's question.

Bobbie took a second to process what the detective had asked for. The request was absurd when the obvious perpetrator was Justin. Straightening up to her full height, she decided to assume the detective thought the same way as she did—that Miley's rape was an open and shut case. "Ah, to eliminate them from your inquiry. Because the victim was able to name her attacker..."

"I can't talk about the details of the case with you, Doctor Chan." Cross gave a tight little smile. "I hope you understand."

"Of course," Bobbie said. Was Justin's taunt that no-one would believe an old, insignificant senile woman true? The DNA would prove he was the rapist. She'd no doubt of that. "But can you at least tell me if the DNA results have been processed by the lab? As I'm sure you know, I am Mrs. McGregor's attending doctor."

"I can't speak to that, Doctor Chan, because it is part of the investigation," Cross said. Her thin smile dissolved. In a slow voice, she repeated her words as if Bobbie were a child, "I need the names of the men who had access to that apartment."

Bobbie's intuition screamed at her that Justin's threat was uncanny and possibly true. Heat rose to her cheeks.

"Justin, for all intents and purposes, bragged that he raped his wife." Bobbie reigned in her righteous indignation before adding, "Be aware the man you are dealing with is very slick and extremely dangerous."

"Like I said, Doctor Chan, I cannot discuss specific details of the case with you." Cross folded her arms and stared, her eyes grim, her jaw square.

Bobbie modulated her voice, "Okay, I understand. Sorry." She checked the time, knowing that the detective would notice as she unhooked her gaze to read from her ONIV. "Look, I'm in a hurry to get to an important meeting right now," a little white lie but true on a certain level. "Could we make an appointment for later this afternoon, and I'll get you those names, at say 5:00 p.m.?" Bobbie hoped to buy herself some time so she could figure out what was going on.

Cross's eyes glazed over as she checked her own ONIV, possibly for her schedule. Cross refocused, gave a curt nod. "Okay. I have other inquiries to make here, but I want that list at five p.m." Cross nodded at the closed door of Bobbie's office. "Meet you back here."

* * *

Joy surprised Bobbie by asking to meet her for a quick lunch in The Seaspray Café, a restaurant at the top of Subscraper One. The café used the rooftop gardens to supplement the matter-streamers, and their food tasted fresher than any found in the various staffrooms spread throughout the hospital. Bobbie was too curious to turn Joy down despite being up to her eyes reviewing case files for the Medical Board meeting that afternoon. Bobbie and Hicks had petitioned to move the meeting to an earlier date, but Slade had insisted on keeping it to three weeks.

Bobbie spotted her sister as soon as she entered the café. A surge of unfamiliar affection caught her off guard. Joy looked stunning, sitting staring out to sea. Bobbie saw in her the ideal marriage of their parents' features: their father's gentle almond eyes, their mother's peaches-and-cream skin. Joy had their father's hair with its blue-black sheen. Bobbie always admired the way Joy added her own flare by dying the tips of her flowing locks electric blue.

"We lucked out with the table today, especially on such short notice," Joy said as Bobbie sat down opposite her. Their table, right against the curved glass, gave them a 180° plus view of the ocean to the east of the subscraper, out toward the open sea.

Far off in the distance, light spilled through a hole in the cloud cover onto the Irish Sea below, illuminating a brilliant patch of aquamarine waves.

"Do you remember what Mum used to say?" Joy began.

"A spotlight from God," they said in unison.

They smiled; their eyes locked for a moment in acknowledgment of their mutual loss.

"She said God did that to remind you he was up there waiting, watching," Bobbie said.

"I always thought that was kinda creepy," Joy said. "Like he was stalking me. Perhaps it was my guilty conscience." Joy chuckled.

Bobbie wondered if her mother was up there too, waiting, watching—wherever *there* was. Loss sliced through her, and her appetite waned. She ordered a seafood salad, anyway, in the hope that the fresh greens might encourage her to eat.

"Thanks for suggesting lunch," Bobbie said after they'd blinked in their order. "What brings you out to the Buckets?"

"You did."

"Me?"

"Well, I wanted to apologize for that whole thing with Granny at the Highland Fling," Joy said.

Bobbie picked apart a bread roll. She'd heard Joy's apologies before.

"Granny said she was feeling great, that she wanted to live it up a little," Joy continued. "And she looked well, too. She'd been so sad during Mum's illness."

The memory pierced Bobbie, sharp as a sliver of glass.

Joy kept going, "Granny was so persuasive and, well, the situation was so bizarre."

"You got that right," Bobbie said.

"But then she just... just got out of hand." Joy looked so contrite that Bobbie felt like reaching out to touch her as her sister continued.

"And so, you called me to fix it?" Bobbie said, trying to blunt the edge in her voice.

"You're my big sister." Joy's hair fell in a black silken sheet over one eye. "It's what you do best." Joy tucked her hair behind her ear. "Please forgive me, Bobbie," she said.

Bobbie didn't know what to say. She wanted to trust her sister but feared there was another agenda. There was always another agenda with Joy. She looked down at her bread, now reduced to a pile of crumbs.

"And I wanted to say thank you for letting me dock at your place," Joy said. Bobbie looked up into her sister's beseeching face. Something about the dark, puppy-like eyes made her smile and puff a tiny laugh through her nose. Joy really was something.

"Look, I know you see me as the crazy sister, while you're the responsible one, but to be honest, I'm worried about Granny. I want to help." Joy poured water into two glasses from a pitcher on the table.

"Go on." *I could get to like this edition of Joy—if only I could trust her,* thought Bobbie.

"Is Granny actually getting younger?" Joy lifted her glass and gulped down water.

"Technically, no. Physically, she certainly appears to be. I'm waiting on the lab results, but the labs are taking an unusually long time. Staff shortages they claim," Bobbie said. "But that's ridiculous."

"How so?"

"Well, Granny's condition is a huge thing, Joy. If people can get *younger*, it will impact our whole society and how we live life. Belus Corp should be throwing all their resources into figuring out what is causing the ultra-elderly to rejuvenate."

A dark look passed over Joy's face. A server-bot rolled up to the table to deliver their food.

"Enjoy your meal," the server-bot said in a velvety voice before trundling away.

"Where do they get the voices for these things?" Joy asked, rolling her eyes skyward.

"God knows," Bobbie said, amused. Joy was hard to please. She always thought she could do better than the original designers.

"You were saying something about how Granny's thing could impact life as we know it." Joy pulled her plate closer and stabbed at the chucks of vegetables with her fork.

"I'm not exaggerating," Bobbie added, picking up her cutlery. "We need to figure out what's making Granny appear younger."

"You say *appear* younger?" Joy said, chewing.

"Well, she's still ninety-three though she is physiologically younger now," Bobbie clarified.

"For simplicity sakes, can we just say younger?" Joy asked.

"So far, it's been possible to slow down aging, for example, with calorie restriction in some species," said Bobbie. "Scientists have known for decades that restrictive dietary regimens prolong the lives of rodents and other mammals, but their effects in humans have not been well understood."

Joy swallowed before saying, "Is that why Belus Corp monitors what we consume?"

"No, the biomonitors are purely for health and functionality. Diseases like obesity, diabetes, and heart disease were a huge problem before the war; before Belus Corp took over. Now you don't see anyone overweight, like when I was a kid."

"I've seen pictures," Joy said. "It's hard to imagine that people would do that to themselves."

"Belus Corp would like nothing better than to keep our population young and healthy. The workforce stays stable, medical costs go down. But the best Belus Corp can hope to do is keep the population healthy and active for as long as possible. I don't think they aimed to prolong life. Caring for the ultra-elderly is simply too expensive and resource intensive. In Granny's case, we aren't talking about slowing down aging. We're talking about reversing aging... that's a different kettle of fish altogether."

"Do we know what causes aging?" Joy asked, shoving a forkful of pasta into her mouth.

"Not exactly," Bobbie said. "But we think it's to do with how cells multiply themselves. Each time they do, they incorporate little defects and do their job less well until the cell actually dies."

Joy nodded; her dark eyes connected with Bobbie's.

Bobbie went on, "Aging's really down to DNA replication. So, you know how in the nucleus of a cell, our genes are arranged along double-stranded molecules of DNA?"

"Yes, chromosomes."

"Right," Bobbie said. "Well, the ends of the chromosomes have sections called telomeres. They're kind of like the plastic tips on shoelaces that keep the chromosome's ends from fraying and getting damaged or interfering with the rest of the chromosome."

"Because that would cause mutations in the cell?"

"Exactly," Bobbie said. "So, each time a cell divides, the telomeres get shorter. Most human cells can divide about fifty times before the telomeres become too short, and the cell can't divide anymore. Then the cell becomes inactive or, in some cases, actually dies."

"So longer telomeres mean you age more slowly," Joy said.

"Right." With a sense of excitement, Bobbie realized that she'd never talked science before with her sister. Joy was extremely intelligent, gifted both musically and with electronics. Bobbie had never considered how much pleasure she'd derive geeking out with Joy over her own career interests, yet here sat Joy, bright-eyed and eager to learn from her big sister—the way Bobbie often sat and listened to Gracie. The parallel was both barbed and blissful. Joy wasn't Gracie. Could never fill that niche, but maybe she fitted into Bobbie's heart differently.

"Can't we make the telomeres longer?" Joy asked.

"Yeah, we can, with an enzyme called telomerase. In fact, some of our cells do exactly that naturally. White blood cells, sperm cells, they need to have telomere shortening switched off to make copies of themselves indefinitely. But if other types of cells stop dying and keep replicating, the balance is disrupted, the cells form tumors. There's a danger with cancer cells—they create telomerase, which prevents telomere shortening, allowing them to replicate without dying."

"So, messing about with the telomeres could lead to cancer?" Joy's plate was clean.

Bobbie hadn't made much headway into her salad. "Exactly," she said, taking a mouthful of lettuce. The great taste surprised her, crunchy and green, the lemon dressing zinging off her taste buds. She jabbed a piece of lobster meat with her fork and held it up.

"Actually, lobsters are said to be immortal, though that's not quite true. They continue to grow and eventually reach a size where molting requires energy levels they can't cope with. They die of exhaustion, but they don't age. They express telomerase through most of their tissues all during their lives—unlike humans where telomerase is generally absent after the embryonic stage of development." Bobbie looked at the succulent white meat on her fork and waved it in the air. "Mmm, I love lobster." She bit down on the sweet, salty flesh.

Joy waited while Bobbie chewed.

"But I don't think Granny's condition has anything to do with telomerase because you'd expect to see tumors growing, and we haven't seen that yet," Bobbie added.

"Yet? So, tumors could still happen?"

"Hells bells, Granny is looking like she did at forty. It seems anything can happen," Bobbie speared a prawn. "But the cause of her rejuvenation must have more to do with DNA. We believe that aging is accompanied by global and local changes in DNA methylation, histone modifications, and noncoding RNA expression brought about by intrinsic and environmental factors." Bobbie popped the prawn on her fork into her mouth.

"Wait, you've lost me," Joy said. "Back up."

"Simply put, as you age, your DNA is damaged," Bobbie began. "The code is affected, and the proteins that are coded for are either not made, or incorrectly made. What's different here is that aging seems to be actually reversing as if the DNA has been fixed. Granny has physically gone from a ninety-three-year-old to her forties, actually more like her thirties now." Bobbie stopped for a moment, remembering Granny prancing into Miley's room on Justin's arm. She suppressed a shudder and went on. "What we're observing in Granny is different than stopping aging or prolonging life. We are talking fountain of youth here. As far as we can tell, something has triggered the DNA in every cell in her body to switch on and run perfectly. Or nearly every cell," Bobbie added.

"But something's wrong, right?" Joy whispered as she leaned in so Bobbie could hear her.

"Absolutely—you spent time with Granny the other day. Look at her behavior at the fling." Bobbie didn't want to mention Granny's conduct with Justin. No need to involve Joy in that. "It's so unlike Granny."

"Gloria, you mean?" Joy raised an eyebrow.

"God! I don't know where to start." Bobbie felt relieved to admit her bewilderment to Joy. "I thought a virus..."

"Because that would work on every cell?" Joy added.

Bobbie admired her sister's quick uptake and assimilation of the facts. "Yes, but nothing is coming up in the toxicology reports. I need to have a look at the DNA and check to see if I can find a retrovirus. They're smaller, harder to detect, and they work by changing the host cell's DNA. But the lab keeps telling me they haven't had the resources to process that yet. Ridiculous! I've sent all our data to the medical board, the nanopharm companies, and gone so far as to blink a copy to Belus Corp head office in Zurich. I know that old people dying is not something they get excited about. But old people getting younger?" Bobbie set down the fork she'd been waving the air. "Sorry to get all worked up, but I don't understand why Belus Corp isn't more heavily involved."

"Unless they already are," Joy whispered so quietly that Bobbie wondered if she'd heard her right.

A warning alarm rang in Bobbie's head. Her enjoyment of their conversation slammed to a halt. Was Joy sliding back into that conspiracy theory phase she'd wallowed in throughout most of her teens?

The old anger surfaced in Bobbie, unwelcome as it was familiar. *Caution is the smart move here. Have I given Joy too much information to sensationalize over*? Her sister had always been over-dramatic. Like the time the fifteen-year-old Joy had refused to eat anything from a matter streamer. She and her buddies had developed a theory that Belus Corp was the front for a branch of Melters who had survived the war and were mind controlling Lisette Fox. They'd decided that matter streamers were how they were going to reach everyone else. Since fresh food was so expensive, Joy had eaten nothing but fish and seaweed for a month. A healthy enough diet that didn't trigger any biosensor alarms, but Bobbie did have a private snigger when Joy relented because she'd gotten bored with her diet, succumbing to a bacon sandwich straight from the matter streamer.

Bobbie suspected the teenagers had developed this group paranoia because, unlike hers, their teenage years had been so lacking in drama. Had they too lived through the reality of war, perhaps they'd have been less inclined to conjure up a fantasy war.

"Joy, I sincerely doubt that they have any idea about this syndrome. Otherwise, they'd have capitalized on it by now."

"Jeez, Bobbie, don't you think you put too much faith in our glorious leaders?"

"You have no idea what it was like before and during the war, Joy," Bobbie said, trying to keep her voice low and her tone steady. She looked at the other tables around them. No-one was paying them any attention, but Bobbie knew that Joy could get a stint at the PARC if she were overheard and reported. "Belus has continued to keep the Melters at bay too. Three sightings of Melter drones in Earth's orbit in the last year. What would happen if Belus wasn't so efficient?"

Joy folded her arms and shrugged.

"Look, I know you think this government is oppressive because you can't go out and eat and drink what you like, do drugs and party like people did before the war."

"We aren't free, we have no choice," Joy said. "We are so cosseted and looked after that we're missing out on life! Back then, there was democracy, freedom and fun!"

"Those days were not all fun, Joy. They were filled with war, hate, and corruption. People killed other people because they didn't like who they prayed to or the color of their skin... Jesus Christ, can you imagine that? And democracy–what a joke!" Bobbie gave a splintered laugh. "The people abused it or else ignored it. Politicians lied. Governments lied. The News lied. No-one knew who to trust. You're romanticizing it too much. Democracy!" Bobbie spat the word out. "Democracy turned into nothing more than a popularity contest. People are generally foolish, you know. They voted for dictators! Oh, yeah, that worked nicely for the banks and big corporations. They gathered up all the wealth and left the rest of the humans on the planet to starve. And where the fuck where they when the Melters attacked?"

"Sssh!" Joy put her hand over Bobbie's. "I know. I know."

Bobbie lowered her voice again, annoyed that she was the one who might be drawing attention to their conversation. She sucked air in through her nose and clutched Joy's hand.

"You don't know what it was like. How could you? You were just a baby. But I do know. I remember how Lisette Fox turned over her corporation for the good of the planet, and when the Unified Planet asked her to lead the government, we all rejoiced. She set up the truth summit that put an end to propaganda and false news. There has been nothing close to war among humans since."

"I know," Joy said. She sounded weary, bored almost. "They nip discord in the bud."

"Not just that. No-one starves, everyone is taken care of. Poverty doesn't exist. Yes, there are policies I question, but Belus Corp is helping us to stay healthy. Father always said, 'Your health is your wealth,' and he was right. If you knew what it is to live a life of ill health..." Bobbie stopped herself. She didn't want to throw Gracie's illness at Joy. If Gracie had lived, Joy wouldn't exist.

"I get it," Joy said. "Lisette is everyone's big sister." She held Bobbie's gaze before adding, "It's good to have a big sis, you know." Joy squeezed Bobbie's hand and gave it a little shake. "Even ones who boss you about."

Emotion washed over Bobbie. She'd had a big sister and lost her. Now she was the big sister. Maybe Joy loved her like she had loved Gracie. Bobbie was sorry she had kept Joy at bay. Letting her in would be hard. She wasn't sure she was ready to do that, at least not now in the middle of all this crazy stuff with Granny.

A blinking clockface appeared in the corner of Bobbie's ONIV. "Holy cow, I need to go! I have a meeting with the medical board in an hour."

"Is the meeting about Granny?"

"No and yes," Bobbie said as she blinked to call in the bill. Originally the meeting was about the DNR Law, but now that things had changed, she wanted to shift the agenda to investigating the rejuvenation and highlight Miley's rape case as part of the evidence to illustrate the dire impact of Justin's rejuvenation on his moral compass. She couldn't discuss that with Joy, of course.

The cafe's billing system informed her Joy had already paid for lunch. For the first time in what felt like forever, the gesture made her feel looked after, cherished—and from a source she had least expected.

"Thanks for lunch, Kiddo," Bobbie said. "I really enjoyed it. Let's do it again. Soon. My treat next time."

"Sure—maybe we'll go somewhere posh!"

They laughed as they embraced, so unlike the stiff, awkward greetings and goodbyes that had characterized the last few years. It was good to have her sister on her side.

"Sorry, I do have to rush," she said, awash with nerves at the thought of the medical board meeting. She didn't mind. A certain level of adrenalin helped her to work better.

"It's okay," Joy said, "I'll catch you later back at your place. You can tell me how the meeting went."

Bobbie smiled and gave her hand a quick squeeze. "Sure." Not that she would. The proceedings were confidential. Hicks could be her confidant on a professional level, but she wasn't about to tell Joy that and spoil their unexpected closeness.

CHAPTER 13

Bobbie exited the elevator and strode down the corridor toward the conference room past a carebot pushing a trolley stacked with empty bedpans. She trained her thoughts on the matters she wanted to discuss with the board but found her mind wandering off down different avenues. Justin still hadn't been detained. Fury ripped through her at the thought of him waltzing around with Granny. Despite Bobbie's repeated attempts to warn her, she seemed besotted with Justin the way a teenager would be with the guy she wasn't allowed to date. Meanwhile, his wife Miley, had been admitted into a hospital ward while she recovered from her injuries, but she would only be there for a couple of days before being returned to the rooms she shared with Justin.

Justin's behavior formed the backbone of Bobbie's presentation to the board. She needed to officially present the phenomenon of rejuvenation to the medical board, address any rumors that might be being reported in the media, and request more resources to allow her to investigate further. As far as Bobbie could see, rejuvenation would have disastrous consequences, both for the affected individual and for future populations.

Three weeks had passed since she'd tried in vain to save Aayushi's life. Granny now looked like a thirty-something and answered only to Gloria. Okay, so it was her name, but rejection stung Bobbie at the thought that her own grandmother would not answer to 'Granny' anymore. That was the least worrying thing. She tried to accept that Granny's behavior was a symptom, but the woman Bobbie had known was gone, replaced by a sassy younger Gloria.

Perhaps whatever was affecting Granny could one day treat children suffering from genetic diseases similar to the one that had stolen youth and life from Gracie. It seemed only right that she should now have the chance to help both the young and the old if they could study the disease and safely harness the side effects.

Bobbie wished Hicks were here, but he was in a meeting with the clinical psychologist who had spent yesterday afternoon and evening examining the twelve

Rejuvenees—the patients, like Granny, who'd been getting younger–attempting to determine possible patterns in their behavior and personality changes. Bobbie had seen this herself in Granny's outrageous, insulting talk and promiscuity, never mind the calculated cruelty of flaunting her relationship with Justin in front of Miley. Hicks would send the findings to her as soon as he could.

Bobbie had a list of examples to present to the board where other Rejuvenees had displayed irrational and risky behavior. Hopefully, she wouldn't need to dwell too long on Granny's shortcomings.

The conference room door swished open. Blue lights illuminated three of the ten seats indicating that an attendee's holographic image occupied that seat, one at the far end of the oval touch table and one on each side of it, as if in a huddle. As soon as Bobbie logged in, she would be able to see the holographic images and know who was present. She frowned. There should be six others. Who was missing?

Bobbie took an unlit seat and logged in via a blink. The other figures materialized, looking as real as if in the flesh. An excited buzz of conversation filled her ears. No-one seemed to notice Bobbie's arrival. She took a deep breath to settle her nerves as she viewed the attendees.

Doctor Jarret sat at the top of the table, a woman on his right whose name Bobbie couldn't remember. On his left, between him and Bobbie sat Doctor Coughlin, her old mentor.

Bobbie realized that Doctor Lichtenberg from Munich, the other woman from the last meeting, and Slade, the Director of the Medical Board were missing. Slade was the one Bobbie really needed to convince to provide the resources she needed to fully investigate rejuvenation.

"Apparently," the woman Bobbie didn't recognize said, "These patients aren't just getting better. They are getting younger. Think how elderly people getting younger will boost global productivity. No more resources wasted on the elderly."

Wasted? Bobbie winced.

"Doctor Avignon," Coughlin said.

Ah yes, Kiara Avignon, thought Bobbie, remembering her from the last board meeting.

"It may not be as simple as that," Coughlin continued. "What will a return to youth mean for population control? The Dependency Law? Remember, the Dependency Law is defined by a person's age, not their medical status. Will these Reju..." Coughlin seemed to struggle with the title these patients had been given, "Rejuvenees be able to have children? Or, if not and there are no new children, will human evolution be arrested?"

"Human evolution is so slow that we don't notice it from one generation to the next as it is," Bobbie said. "Evolution is dependent upon mutation and frequency of births. I think The Dependency Law, as it stands, will affect evolution regardless of rejuvenation."

They all turned to look at Bobbie. No one greeted her. Nerves made her stomach gurgle, and she hoped the audio pickup wouldn't transmit the sound.

"I agree with Doctor Chan," Avignon said. "Also, to answer your concerns, Doctor Coughlin, longevity allows more opportunity to develop biological mechanisms over time that will maintain health and repair physical flaws. Longer-lived individuals will nurture and pass on resources to the younger generation. Accumulated experiences increase efficiency, and the progress and advances of the community can foster specialization and innovations. So, all told, I believe that rejuvenation will benefit humankind."

"Are there any theories as to its origin?" Jarret asked.

"None thus far," Bobbie answered in a steady voice. "The labs have been slow getting our test results back."

"They are very busy and understaffed..." Jarret interrupted.

"I understand, but this is an unprecedented event. I believe that Belus Corp needs to put more resources into finding out what is happening." She scanned the holographic images trying to make eye contact with as many as possible.

Everyone nodded.

"There are some theories." Avignon flicked her brown hair off her shoulders with both hands. "Some are saying the symptoms we are seeing are caused by a virus."

"We haven't been able to detect viruses, bacteria, fungi, or protozoan in any of the initial blood samples," Bobbie said, feeling more confident.

"Perhaps a genetic switch has been turned on," Avignon said, "Like puberty, or menopause. Perhaps humans are only reaching the age where the gene code for getting younger gets triggered."

"I suppose thousands of years ago when humans died before women reached menopause, menopause was probably unheard of," Bobbie mused.

"Exactly." Avignon sounded excited. "There would be huge economic advantages to finding this theoretical genetic switch and flicking it on earlier in life, bypassing old age altogether."

"But let's consider the consequences of the Rejuvenees being able to reproduce," Jarret said.

"Would that be fair on young people who want their own children?" Coughlin asked. "And if the Rejuvenees can have children, will the population numbers increase significantly? Can society sustain that?"

"We already have laws in place to manage population increases," Avignon countered. "As far as I can see, we leave the Dependency Law in place. Why should any person feel that procreation is their right anyway? What's important is having a fit population, not a constantly renewing one. Rejuvenation is a fantastic opportunity for the human race. Fewer sick, fewer frail people, more workers! It's a no brainer. A blueprint for a brilliant future."

"Wait a minute," Bobbie said. "Let's not get carried away. Let's focus on the fact that we are talking about real living people, here and now. Rejuvenation is evolving, apparently in a positive way, but these patients also have some very disturbing... side-effects. We need to exercise caution."

"Nevertheless, we need to find the trigger," Avignon said. "We are looking at what could be the most valuable discovery medical science has seen in decades, centuries. Eternal youth! Imagine."

"So it seems," Bobbie said. "But regardless of what's causing our patients to appear more youthful, this rejuvenation phenomenon, we require significantly more documented study of the condition before we consider replicating the cause. If we can replicate it."

"Agreed," Coughlin said. "As of yesterday, worldwide, our twelve patients exhibiting the rejuvenation symptoms are the only ones who have survived without the heart failure issue that killed the other symptomatic patients. How do we know how far back they will continue to devolve? What if they become babies again? How will that affect the workload of the able-bodied?"

"Personality disorders have developed that weren't evident before the onset of the rejuvenation," Bobbie said, feeling nervous again. "That's why I am suggesting that we investigate rejuvenation thoroughly." She hadn't wanted to start into the main thrust of her argument until Slade arrived, but if she could get. Avignon and Coughlin on her side, their backing would support her argument.

"Personality disorders?" Avignon asked. "Doctor Chan, are you qualified to diagnose psychiatric conditions? Do you have a psychiatry qualification?"

English wasn't Avignon's first language, and from her tone, Bobbie knew she wasn't being rude, merely direct. Rather than take offense, Bobbie continued in a steady voice, "We have a psychologist assessing them now. I've been working closely with these patients for several years. Their behavior has changed alarmingly, and their personalities have altered drastically. This phenomenon is not as positive as it appears on the surface. The Rejuvenees have been exhibiting behavior that is distinctly out of character. Some of these symptoms are low key, such as Mr. Kranz bragging about his exploits during the war. When, in fact, he did not fight in the war."

"Perhaps he's delusional," Avignon said. "Elderly people get delusional all the time."

"Actually," Bobbie said, "Until the onset of rejuvenation, two weeks ago, Kranz showed no symptoms of dementia, nor was he delusional."

"Another Rejuvenee," Bobbie continued, "Suzana Tang, was caught trying to set fire to an orchard. She denies arson. Police are investigating it. And last week Rejuvenee Toby Hamm, a former veterinarian, was accused by another resident of torturing a seagull. He is, of course..."

"... denying it?" Coughlin interjected.

In the chair opposite Bobbie, Slade materialized, looking up and down the table, her black bob swishing like a little curtain. Slade clasped her hands in front of her chest and peered down the length of her long pointy nose at the people gathered. In a loud voice that seemed out of place, she boomed, "Good afternoon."

Irritation swooped down on Bobbie like a black crow attacking.

"Welcome, Doctor Slade," Jarret said. "Let me begin by introducing everyone. Doctor Slade is the Director of the Medical Board..."

"Yes, yes. Thank you," Slade flicked her hand as if swatting away a fly. Then she clasped her hands together and leaned forward. "We all met the last time. Let's get down to business. Time is fleeting. I was in a meeting with Ms. Fox. I got here as soon as I could."

"Certainly," Jarret cleared his throat. "Doctor Chan..."

All the faces swiveled toward Bobbie.

"... You called the last meeting three weeks ago to request that we make an exception for the DNR rule. You wanted to be allowed to resuscitate people over the age of 100 who have rejuvenation symptoms."

"Yes, Doctor Jarret, but—" Bobbie began, her heart rate rising.

"The point is moot," Slade interrupted. "The DNR rule stands. My people are taking over the rejuvenation project now."

"Your people?" Bobbie asked, first to recover from the room's stunned silence.

"Your non-disclosure agreements are being blinked to you now. You must blink-sign them before you leave the conference," Slade said, ignoring Bobbie's question.

"Wait," Bobbie said. "Where's the due process? Citizen Transparency?"

"This meeting is over, Doctor Chan," Slade said, her voice clipped.

"Now, Orinda, I suggest we at least listen to her concerns," Doctor Coughlin said.

Bobbie drew strength from his gravelly voice. She could depend on him to be fair.

"Thank you," Bobbie smiled at him. "Rejuvenation is not simply a case of discovering the fountain of youth. Yes, we need more research. Something is wrong with these people, these Rejuvenees." Bobbie paused then decided to push on. "I had to report Justin McGregor to the police for rape yesterday." Sweat popped on her forehead. Her palms felt clammy. She hated using Miley's rape to further her argument.

Slade closed her eyes and laid her hands on the table in front of her. "Doctor Chan, I am aware of the report you filed yesterday," she said. "The rape kit analysis from Miley

McGregor was given priority. The DNA did not match that which we have on record for Justin McGregor. He is not the perpetrator of the crime."

Bobbie felt the air sucked from her lungs.

"But Mrs. McGregor said–" Bobbie began.

"Miley McGregor is senile." Slade cut her off. "She gets confused. Someone has taken terrible advantage of the situation. The police will be investigating this case to find the real rapist." Slade lowered her head, peering out at Bobbie from under her precision-penciled eyebrows.

Detective Cross's request for details of all males who had access to the McGregor's rooms made sense to Bobbie now. But how could the rapist not have been Justin? Cold logic told Bobbie that DNA never lies. *Either he didn't rape Miley*, suspicion crept into Bobbies thoughts, *or someone tampered with the results*. Hard to believe he could do that by himself, but who would help him? Bobbie found it impossible to believe in Justin's innocence—she had been there when Miley named him. She had witnessed how he had denied it with such blasé. "Do I look like I need to have sex with old crumblies like her now?" Justin's words haunted Bobbie.

"So," Slade said. "I'm glad that we agree on how to proceed. More research is necessary, and as I have informed you, Belus Corp will now be spearheading this investigation. A specialist diagnostic team has been assigned to deal with this issue." Slade took the time to meet the eye of everyone present. "You will not discuss rejuvenation with anyone until the matter has been thoroughly investigated."

"Who will be on this team?" Bobbie asked. Perhaps this was why the other two Medical Board members had not shown up. They'd always seemed like Slade's puppets, quick to agree with her, and vote in her same direction.

"That is none of your concern," Slade said in a crisp tone.

"Can you at least tell us what facility the team will be working in?" Bobbie pressed on.

"Isn't one of these patients your grandmother?" Slade said.

"Yes. That's why you need me on the team. I have a good insight as to the way these twelve people have changed." Bobbie was desperate to be on that team, but Slade had hated her ever since she'd crossed her at the student rally against the DNR rule.

"Actually, I think you are too closely involved in the case," Slade said in a loud voice. "In fact, I think it is unprofessional that you are working with the Rejuvenees at all since you have a personal connection with one of them."

"Doctor Chan, is this correct?" Jarret asked, his dark eyes boring into hers.

"Yes, but she's not my patient. She's Doctor Hicks's patient," Bobbie said, frantic to be heard, but she knew it was no use. All the other doctors talked at once, arguing over one another.

"Order! Order, please," Jarret shouted above the pandemonium. They settled down, muttering and uneasy.

Bobbie swallowed the bile that had risen in her throat.

"I'm afraid that Doctor Slade is correct—if we go by the law governing medical trials, you cannot preside over your own relations in any research capacity. Objectivity is compromised." Jarret shook his head slowly as he looked at the doctors sitting around him.

Bobbie willed her limbs to stop shaking.

"Doctor Chan, you will turn over all your rejuvenation patients to the Specialist Diagnostic Team," Slade said. "All their notes are sealed and confidential. We will decide when and how the news of this phenomenon will be broadcast."

"But this condition has already been on the news," Bobbie protested.

"Yesterday's news." Slade pointed out. "The world will forget as soon as there is no more coverage. I trust you understand the repercussions to your career should this sensitive information leak before we have the full picture." Slade smiled. "That is all." Her image disappeared.

"Wait!" Bobbie cried out. She couldn't let the meeting end now.

"I think the message is clear," Jarret said. "I urge you all..." He directed his dark eyes toward Bobbie. Did she detect sympathy? "... to take Doctor Slade's advice, sign your non-disclosures, and forget about this project." His image disappeared.

The others signed out and vanished, one by one.

CHAPTER 14

Stunned, Bobbie sat alone in the empty conference room. A blink message seemingly hanging in thin air before her informed her the conference had been terminated and that as soon as she signed her non-disclosure agreement, she would be automatically signed out. Her ONIV filled with the text of the contract, and unless she signed, she'd not be able to see anything else. She searched for a 'postpone action' button, but there wasn't one. Switching off her ONIV would trigger an alert, and Slade would know she'd not signed the NDA.

A sheen of sweat broke out over her body. *No way around the NDA, I'll have to sign.* Clenching her teeth, she focused the floating target symbol on the 'Accept' button and pressed her thumb to her little finger, feeling the nub of the electrodes connect. A message appeared, 'You have agreed to enter into a confidential relationship concerning the disclosure of certain proprietary and confidential information. Should this confidential relationship be breached, your employment will be terminated, and admission to a Personality Augmentation and Rehabilitation Center may be enforced.'

A walk in the PARC! Her gallows humor twisted her mouth into a wry smile. A smile that faded as an image from her time as a young med student at the PARC flashed into her head. A young man, barely out of his teens. His blank gaze was not that disconcerting if Bobbie told herself he was merely taking part in a prolonged blink interaction, but the slack jaw and the elastic drool dangling from the bottom lip had chilled her. This man's personality had not been corrected, it had been eradicated, and because he had committed a crime, no-one seemed to care. At the time Bobbie had worried, the same could happen to Joy if she were sent to a PARC. Now, for the first time, Bobbie had cause to worry for herself.

Her vision cleared of text, leaving black specks floating in front of her eyes. She was hyperventilating, so she drew in a deep breath to prevent herself from passing out. She rested her forehead on the cool glass of the conference table, anger soaking into every thought she tried to form.

She wanted to rail against the injustice of the meeting, scream at Slade, and demand to talk to someone in government. Had Belus Corp received her blink? There was no confirmation that her message had been delivered. Did they know the ultra-elderly were getting younger and crazier every day? Did Lisette Fox know? Would the woman who had saved the human race from annihilation and who'd brought peace to the planet allow these affected citizens to remain at risk?

'The full picture...' Slade had said, a phrase she had used more than once while discussing rejuvenation.

Did Slade have a full picture? Fuller than the snippet Bobbie saw? Did the government have the full blueprint on rejuvenation?

Blueprint... DNA!

Bobbie sat bolt upright. The DNA sample in the rape kit had been compared with Justin's sample on record, which was probably taken during the war. Could rejuvenation have changed Justin's DNA somehow, and that's why his DNA on record didn't match? She had to get a sample of Justin's DNA now and convince Detective Cross to rerun the test. If Bobbie could somehow lead Cross to discovering a change in Justin's DNA, the detective might take the case to her superiors. If the police were to take a renewed interest in the case, it might highlight this rejuvenation syndrome to someone higher up the food chain at Belus Corp, sidestepping Slade. Bobbie was convinced that Lisette Fox would never stand for her citizens being treated like this no matter how old they were. Fox needed to be made aware of the situation. Slade was no doubt blocking the upward movement of medical information, but she may not have as much power on the legal side. Cross was the key. A surge of determination gave her the energy to rise from the conference table.

A lot of if's and maybe's, she thought. *But I'll be damned if I'm going to give into Slade without a fight.*

Hicks should have the psychologist's report by now. Sharing the contents of the report wouldn't break the NDA, but she had to get to him quickly... before Slade did. She had arranged to meet Cross at five, and she had a bit of detective work of her own to do before she met with her. Bobbie stopped before opening the door and concentrated on her next move. She blinked to Hicks. *Can you meet me at Granny's apartment?*

Not for another 45 mins. Break due then.

Bobbie brought up the time in her ONIV in response to Hicks' reply. 2:30 p.m. — enough time to get to the McGregor's apartment, meet Hicks at 3:15 p.m., check in with Granny, and get back in her office in time to meet with Cross by 5:00 p.m.

Perfect, see you at Granny's at 3 pm

Bobbie strode out of the conference room with renewed purpose. In the corridor outside she located an unlocked supply closet. Bobbie slipped inside and helped herself to a bundle of sterile sample bags, a couple of 100 ml sample pots, and a pair of disposable gloves.

Closing the supply closet's door noiselessly behind her as she left, Bobbie hurried to the elevator, heart pounding with a mixture of fear of being caught and hope that at last, she had found a way to best Slade. At the last moment she caught sight of the door leading to the emergency staircase and swerved in its direction. The stairs would not be faster than the elevator since Benthic 3 was eight floors down but there was less chance of meeting anyone on route and she didn't feel like answering any awkward questions. She took the stairs two at a time. LED light bulbs hung from the walls at intervals, throwing off shadows of Bobbie at different angles, like furtive, creeping creatures. The stagnant air of this under-used area seemed to awaken with the *thup, thup* of her rubber-soled shoes echoing off the concrete. Her shoes squealed as she swung around the landing. She arrived on Benthic 3 out of breath and dewy skinned, despite her sensorfabrik clothing.

Bobbie slipped through the door into the corridor and took a second to orient herself. Deep breaths did little to calm her racing pulse. The elevators were to her left. She set off past them down the hallway. The intewalls on both sides glowed with soft natural daylight. She approached the point where the corridor branched off to the left and right. Following it left, Bobbie entered a section of corridor with doors on her right, spaced twenty feet apart on the outer circumference. These were the doors to the residents' apartments, situated on the exterior of the columnar buildings of the Buckets. A door further down to her left led to the inner chambers of the building that housed the canteen, dayrooms, storage, and utility areas.

Bobbie walked down the corridor trying desperately to look as if she belonged there. Technically, she didn't need to avoid anyone. It was perfectly reasonable that she be here checking on Miley McGregor, who was, after all, her patient, but Bobbie was relieved that the hall was empty so she did not have to speak to anyone who might have asked awkward questions. When she reached the McGregors' apartment, she blinked on her patient locator and saw that Miley was still upstairs in the hospital ward, where she had been admitted after the rape had come to light.

Unfortunately, since Justin wasn't classed as a patient, his location did not automatically appear in her ONIV, so Bobbie had no idea if he was at home or not. Bobbie took in a deep breath and steeled herself as she reached the McGregors' apartment. Reaching out to the doorbell she noted the slight tremble in her hand. Get a grip, Bobbie, you need to seem completely at ease. Taking a breath, she reached out a now steady hand, rang the doorbell and stepped back.

Bobbie counted to ten in her head. The door before her remained closed. That made things easier. As Miley's doctor, Bobbie had access to the override code for the door to her apartment. If Justin was home then she was merely here collecting some of Miley's things, right? A reasonable explanation, yet a knot of fear tightened in her chest. Justin was no longer some frail old man. He could overpower her if he tried, but why would he try?

Stop over thinking it, Bobbie. Just get in, get the DNA, and get out.

Blinking the override code to the door lock, Bobbie pushed the door open.

"Hello. Anyone home?" she called. Receiving no reply, Bobbie quickly crossed the living area and went straight to the bedroom. The room smelled of musky perfume and the tinge of ammonia from incontinence. A laundry basket sat in the corner. Bobbie pulled on the disposable gloves, fumbling the fingers into the thumbs, and having to start over. *Calm down*, Bobbie chastised herself cursing the wasted seconds as she bent over the laundry basket and fished out a pair of men's underpants, holding them at arm's length in the tips of her forefinger and thumb. It was a start, but she needed more samples to give her a reliable cross-reference. She crammed the underpants into a sample bag and sealed it. Pivoting, she looked around the room for a second likely source of DNA. There! A comb rested on the top of a dresser.

Removing a few brown and gray hairs from the comb, she popped them in a jar and sealed it. She slid the jar back into the larger bag.

One more should do it, she thought, moving from the bedroom into the bathroom. Two vibro-toothbrushes, one pink and the other blue, sat side by side on a dual charger, stirring a moment of poignancy in Bobbie. These vibrating head toothbrushes had been replaced by USOCs, ultrasonic oral cleaners, but the Ultra-elderly hung on fiercely to their old gadgets. The simplicity of the once gender-significant colors, side by side, made Bobbie sad. Miley and Justin had once been a matching set, a perfect complement to one another...

A female voice in the living room made Bobbie freeze. The words were hard to make out since there were two doors, albeit ajar, and a bedroom between them. Bobbie lifted the blue toothbrush; confident it would be Justin's but then decided to take the pink one too. You never knew, maybe they had switched colors. Rehearsing her cover story in her head, she crept into the bedroom, pretending to look for some fresh clothes for Miley. As Bobbie lifted a tunic from the closet, her heart nearly jumped out her throat as she heard Justin's voice in the other room.

"Okay, Miley, time to take your medicine!" He sounded cheerful, but there was no response. Seconds clicked by as the sinister silence raised goosebumps on Bobbie's arms. Making sure that the sample bags were hidden within the folded tunic, she crept to the bedroom door to hear more clearly.

"Remember..." Miley's voice sounded breezy and playful, "My afternoon dose."

Bobbie stopped in her tracks. What the hell was Miley doing here? Miley would blow any reason Bobbie had for being here clean out of the water!

"Okay, one of these..." Miley paused. "Like this..."

Bobbie waited for Justin to interject, but Miley continued talking to herself.

"Now, one of these..." Another pause, this time longer.

Bobbie's heart thudded in her ears. Her mouth felt dry, and she wanted to clear her throat to ease a building tickle there, but she needed a new story before she revealed her presence. Oh, God, what if they came into the bedroom?

Then Bobbie heard a low electronic tone.

Justin spoke again in that same cheerful voice, "Okay, Miley, time to take your medicine!"

He was going to make her take an overdose, Bobbie thought with alarm, the perfect way for him to get rid of his senile old wife. Everyone would think she'd taken extra medication by mistake. *I need to stop him.* Frantically she scanned the room looking for a weapon. Propped behind the door was a metallic rod, with grippers on one end ¬–the kind of device older, less agile people like the McGregor's might have used to pick things up off the floor without having to bend down. *Not exactly Zorro*, she thought, grabbing the picker-upper anyway, hefting it above her head, and charging out into the living room yelling, "Leave her alone!"

The room was empty.

The intewall played a movie of Miley standing beside Justin—old Justin with his shock of white hair, his accordion-wrinkled face, split open with a wide smile. Miley was holding up the patches she had to take and demonstrating how to apply them. She finished and then hugged her husband. They stood looking at each other, laughing self-consciously as the sound muted out, and the screen went blank. The low tone sounded. Justin came back on, smiling. He bent forward and wagged a finger into the camera like an amateur actor in a school play. "Okay, Miley, time to take your medicine!" Humor danced in his one good eye that still matched the color of the fake one.

Bobbie nearly cried with relief. She checked the time - 3:02 p.m. Yes—Miley's med time was 3:00 p.m. The video alert must serve as Miley's reminder to take her medication when she was in the apartment alone.

Bobbie lowered her improvised weapon, her gaze lingering on the sight of Miley and Justin's smiling happy faces, tears welled, and before Bobbie could blink them back, one dripped down her face. She tugged off the disposable gloves and wiped her cheek, angry with herself. This was work. If she didn't cry delivering a bad prognosis or watching helpless while a patient died, she damn well wasn't going to cry watching Miley's happy memories play out.

Bobbie left the apartment, tucking the gloves into the tunic-wrapped bundle of samples she'd collected. Granny's apartment was further down the hall. If Justin were there, at least Bobbie would have Hicks with her. Bobbie wanted to talk to Granny about the psychologist's report. Although Gloria wasn't the Granny she knew and loved, Bobbie felt confident that her Granny was still in there somewhere—if only she could reach her.

Whatever had triggered the onset of Granny's reverse aging had also caused her personality disorder. If Bobbie could figure out what had caused the reverse aging, she might be able to help Granny overcome whatever was going awry with her brain functions and cure her while maintaining her youth. Unless, Bobbie thought with dread, it was a form of dementia. She remembered the heart-rending attempts of the patients' families to stay connected. The times she'd overheard sobbing sons and daughters appealing to parents for recognition, trying to jog one last memory, one last coherent conversation. Her heart sank, and she felt weary. What if she couldn't reach Granny? Where was the real Granny? Granny's soul? Bobbie wasn't sure she believed in souls, yet something, possibly the indoctrination of her parents' religious beliefs, kept tugging her back to the possibility.

As a medical student, Bobbie had been fortunate enough to attend lectures by Doctor Bahab Gruse, the doctor who had developed a cure for Alzheimer's. The media at the time had named it the Lazarus cure because it literally brought people back from a waking death. A brilliant scientist, her grace, and humanity impressed Bobbie, who never forgot her words, 'From the day we are born, we are destined to die. What we do in-between is live—let's make it matter.' At the time, Bobbie had thought of Gracie, but now she thought of Granny—she had to be in there. Sorrow splintered up from Bobbie's sternum into the base of her throat. She could not bear to lose Granny to this Gloria person. There had to be some way to reach her.

Bobbie found herself outside Granny's apartment without noticing getting there. Tucking the absconded goods under her arm, Bobbie ran her hands down the length of her tunic, feeling the sweat linger for a split second before the fabric adjusted back to normal. Her palms dry, she scooped her hair into a knot and tucked back the loose bits that dangled in her face. Just as she was about to send an announcement blink to 'knock,' Hicks strode around the corner in an easy gait toward her.

The worry and agitation Bobbie had felt earlier melted away. He gave her a relaxed smile as if they were meeting for lunch on a lazy day off.

"How'd the meeting go?" he asked. As he got closer, his expression changed, his eyes widened and then narrowed, like a little boy asking her not to give him away.

She raised an eyebrow as Hicks pulled her in close and gave her a friendly hug, his head close to her ear. "Surveillance cameras," he whispered.

She stiffened. Shit - there were security cameras everywhere. Claustrophobia bore down on her. The government could be watching them now. Hell, Joy could do that, had done versions of that. They lived in such an interconnected world, it was hard to be somewhere and not be digitally recorded. Most of the time, she didn't care because she knew no-one cared about her boring daily routine. *Oh God, had the cameras caught her going in and out of the McGregors' apartment?* The thought of the PARC constricted her chest. *No, you have an excuse. You were just getting some clothes for Miley. Nothing unusual about that.*

"The meeting went okay," Bobbie lied, taking a step back.

He tilted his head in concern.

She bit her lip then said in a shiny bright voice, "So how was your meeting with the psychologist?"

"O-kay, too," he said slowly, his cool gray eyes hooked into hers, making Bobbie feel that despite everything, she was in a safe place. Hicks had a knack of making her feel strong.

Bobbie curled her fingers to her thumb as if she were holding a pen and made a quick writing motion in the space between them, little more than a twitch. Their bodies would have blocked the hand signal from the security cameras that nestled between the ceiling and the walls at regular intervals throughout the hallway.

Hicks gave one quick nod, then with a too-jolly voice said, "So, let's say hi to your granny!"

He turned to face the door leaving Bobbie frozen in the same position as she processed her thoughts. Hicks must have been forced to sign too, and he also seemed to think that someone could be watching them. Wrestling her fear away, she turned to the door, standing side by side with Hicks. The 'knock' blink transmitted.

Nothing happened.

"Granny's not here," she said tonelessly. "Can you use your patient locator?"

"No, not since CDC discharged her, so I don't have access," he said. "I did get a message from the grandson of one of my other patients to say they hadn't been able to get in contact with his grandfather today. Maybe they've gone on some kind of outing?"

Bobbie couldn't gauge from his expression if he really believed that or not.

He kept his features blank. "But I do have access to Granny's apartment as her geriatrician."

"Okay. We could wait for her to come back or leave her a note." Bobbie didn't want to add that an old-fashioned paper note might be better than a blink that could be intercepted. She got the feeling that Hicks knew that already.

"That's weird," Hicks said, scratching his chin as he tried to open the door.

"What?"

"I keep getting the message that this resident no longer occupies this apartment." Hicks looked at Bobbie, wide-eyed. "Your granny's moved out."

"Oh, God," Bobbie whispered, her heart heavy with dread, "What the hell is she up to now?" She composed a blink to her grandmother. *I'm at your apartment. Where are you?*

As soon as she sent her message, the little eye icon flashed a reply. Bobbie, surprised at Granny's speedy response, opened Granny's blink. *They won't let me go. Hel...*

The truncated message sent goosebumps tingling up the back of Bobbie's scalp. She kept her voice mild and worry-free. "Granny replied," she told Hicks. "I'll forward you the blink."

But the blink was gone from her message list. Fear spiked through her. She scrolled back through her blink folders. Perhaps she'd accidentally filed the message in a different place. Using Granny's blink address, Bobbie searched again. Nothing. No past blinks that Bobbie had saved—no sweet messages from birthdays and special occasions, funny messages that only Granny could send, cute ones from when Granny had made daft mistakes when she first tried to send blinks. All gone.

CHAPTER 15

With great difficulty, Bobbie avoided looking in the direction of the security cameras. Who was spying? The same people who had deleted her blinks? Disease Control? Slade? Her heart pounded in her ears, but she leaned back against the wall of the corridor outside Granny's apartment and tried to look nonchalant.

"You know," she said, adopting what she hoped sounded like an innocent voice. "It's no surprise that Granny went on vacation, seeing as how well she's doing. We always took Gracie on an outing when she was feeling well too. Do you remember?"

"Yes," Hicks said. "Yes, in fact, I do." He smiled nodding following her lead in the show they were putting on for the benefit of their unidentified watchers.

"She loved watching the sunset from that one special place. We should do that again *soon*. We could both use a break." She forced a smile, hoping that Hicks could interpret her code. In their younger days Hicks, Gracie and Bobbie would sneak off to Seagahan Dam to watch the sun go down. Gracie had loved how the last rays of sunlight had reflected from the still water. As Gracie's illness had gotten progressively worse, their visits to the dam had become fewer and fewer until, following her death, the visits had stopped altogether.

"Great idea. Let's make that happen." Hicks mirrored her smile.

"Next opportunity then," Bobbie said. She needed a chance to talk to him about what had happened during her meeting with the medical board and find out what he'd gleaned from the psychologist. Bobbie had one more person she could glean some information from her mentor, Doctor Coughlin. She'd drop in on him before she returned to her office. As management, he'd surely know what was going on with the Rejuvenees.

"Wouldn't miss a good sunset for the world," Hicks said. "I gotta get back and finish my shift now." Then he added in a low voice, "Will you be okay?"

He put his hand on her shoulder and gave it a squeeze. Heat from his hand permeated through Bobbie's bones. Hicks had always been good at helping her straighten out her mental kinks.

"Sure." Bobbie smiled, warmed by his tenderness, but something about his concern frightened her. "Go, I'll be fine."

As Hicks strode down the corridor, a message blinked through on Bobbie's ONIV from Davitt. *I ump am in the Buckets. Can you break for a cuppa?*

Usually, the 'ump' thinko made Bobbie smile. It frustrated the hell out of Davitt that he couldn't fix his blink feed to run perfectly, and the devil in Bobbie usually found that funny, today, though, it only seemed to add to her aggravation.

She checked the time— 3:40 p.m. Enough time to pop in to see Doctor Coughlin, meet Cross at five, and then get to the dam to meet Hicks before the sunset at... she blink-searched sunset times... 6:52 p.m. Doable, if she was organized. *Bring a decaf to my office for a 10 min cuppa? Be there in 30 mins. S*he blinked as she made her way to Doctor Coughlin's office on the floor above hers.

* * *

Doctor Coughlin's voice answered her blink-knock on his office door with a sonorous, "Enter."

The door slid back, triggered by his command. He sat with his head lowered, a slight shine on his tanned pate where the pattern balding didn't cover the crown. Scratching his white beard, he lifted his head. His features darkened upon seeing her, making Bobbie's heart sink.

"Who would I talk to about arranging a visit to my grandmother?" Bobbie asked, hoping she sounded like she knew where Granny was and who'd taken her there.

"Doctor Chan," Doctor Coughlin's brown eyes darted from side to side as he stood up behind his large inte desk. "We cannot discuss where your grandmother is or why."

He knows where she is!

"Why ever not? I understand that she needs treatment." Bobbie paused but looked him in the eye. "That, we can't discuss, but she is my family. I only agreed to give up my patients, not my family." Bobbie worked to keep her voice level. "I want to know what the protocols are in situations such as these." Such as these... As far as she knew, there were no other situations such as these.

"Please trust them, Bobbie. I know how you must feel, but there is a team of scientists working on her condition." Coughlin chewed on his bottom lip and raised a shaking hand to smooth the patch of hair at the back of his head.

Seeing him tremble set off alarm bells in Bobbie's brain. W*hat is he scared of?*

The Rejuvenees had developed sociopathic tendencies and could be a danger to themselves and others. Belus Corp understandably would want to monitor the rejuvenation of these individuals and treat their psychoses, but why would they isolate them from their families? What would happen as the other families started to look for their relatives?

"I'd like to see my grandmother," Bobbie said, rattled. His fear was infectious.

"Not at present. It's simply not possible." Doctor Coughlin shut her down with a shake of his head. Scared dark eyes glared from beneath lowered bushy white eyebrows. He sighed, then in a defeated voice said, "You and I both signed an NDA–"

"I'm not talking about the non-disclosure agreement." Bobbie stepped closer to his desk. "I'm talking about my grandmother."

"Good grief!" Doctor Coughlin slammed his hand down on his desk, making Bobbie jump back with a yelp. Doctor Coughlin pleaded, "Listen to me - stop now while you can. You're not going to be any good to her lobotomized!"

Bobbie stood shocked. They all knew what a surgical treatment gone-wrong added up to. Coughlin was the first person she'd heard refer to the PARC's Personality Augmentation Procedure as a lobotomy.

"Just," his tone softened, "Do your job and leave this be." His eyes dampened. Bobbie could see that emotion had stopped his tongue as much as the NDA had.

With a flood of guilt, she realized that she had put him at risk. Bobbie assumed that she was under surveillance, by visiting Coughlin's office she had now brought him under that same suspicion. Slade had Granny. Coughlin's reaction to Bobbie's demand to see Granny only confirmed that, and it did not bode well if Slade was not allowing contact with relatives, not least because Granny had sent Bobbie a blink for help. The protocol surrounding Granny's treatment violated Belus Corp's standard procedures. Bobbie had never heard of Belus Corp sanctioning any such human rights infringements before. Slade and whoever else were behind it, would be hauled over the coals for this—a visit to the PARC for sure.

"I'm sorry," Bobbie said, turning toward the door on shaky legs. "You won't hear from me again on this matter, I can assure you." As she left, the door swished closed behind her.

Bobbie's hands trembled as she walked to the elevators forcing her to clasp them together in front of her to stop people noticing. She worked to pull herself together, to stop fraying at the edges. Fear colored her thoughts, fear for Granny, Hicks, herself, and poor old Doctor Coughlin, who had provided so many answers to her questions in the past. She knew he had the answers today, but his hands and tongue were tied. One thing was for sure, though—she could not take Doctor Coughlin's advice. She could not abandon Granny.

She rode the elevator in silence now acutely aware of the dark lens of the surveillance camera that captured her every action. When she reached her office, she tried to contact Granny again. No response. She tried calling up Justin's patient locator, but she was blocked from accessing any of his information. That wasn't a surprise. There was no answer from Bradley Smiles, another of the rejuvenated residents she tried to blink. If she tried them all, Slade would be alerted to the fact that Bobbie was following up on them.

Bobbie slouched in her seat. *What was the point? The Rejuvenees are gone.*

Again, the image of the surgical procedure that had gone wrong at PARC, the man with the slack jaw and viscous drool, brushed past her consciousness like a bad smell. *You're not going to be any good to Granny lobotomized.* If Slade thought she was trying to investigate the whereabouts of the Rejuvenees, Bobbie had no doubt that she would trump up some charges that would send her to the PARC. She felt like slamming the desk but instead lowered her head onto her hands and massaged her forehead with her fingertips. As her heart hammered against her chest, Bobbie pulled in deep breaths to slow down the pumping organ, aware that traitorous little biosensors were sending Belus Corp every contraction. If only she could take herself offline, the way Joy did when she played her neuro-games to avoid detection. If she had Joy's hacking skills, she'd be able to at least read Granny's blinks, the way Joy had read hers all those years ago. Maybe she could jump into Granny's eye cam-di and see where she was. Bobbie shook her head. She didn't have that skill set. That belonged to Joy. She recalled Joy's prideful boast when she'd challenged her at her mother's wake about gaming too much.

"Please! I do my own hacking."

Bobbie sat up straight. That's what she needed, the skill to hack into Granny's ONIV—if only she could learn a few of Joy's tricks.

* * *

Bobbie was pretending to work when Davitt arrived twenty minutes later. As she saved her work and cleared the screens on the interactive desk surface, Davitt pulled a chair up to the other side.

"Okay, if I set these here?" he asked, hovering a little plastic cup tray with two steaming mugs over the desk.

"It's fine," Bobbie said. "I've closed down the inte desk now. Mmm, that coffee smells so good." She reached over and placed her finger on the orange mug. "Decaf? Right?"

"Yup," Davitt said, sitting down. "I talked the admin in our lab into trying out this new matter streamer. It's supposed to be the best in the industry. Cost a pretty penny too, but hey, if their golden goose asks for something..." He turned his hands palm-up and shrugged.

"Nice." Bobbie lifted a cup.

"So, working on anything interesting?"

"Dude, I'm a geriatrician." She forced a smile, shrugging her shoulders.

"Some of your patients are doing some pretty unique things though, right?" Davitt said. "Your job's starting to compete with mine for exciting innovations."

Bobbie stiffened.

"You know I can't talk about my patients," she said, taking a sip of her coffee.

"Sorry, my bad." Davitt grinned as he stretched back in his chair and crossed one leg over the other, so his ankle rested on the other knee. "How's Granny?" he asked. "You can talk about your grandmother, can't you?"

"She's fine," Bobbie lied. How else could she answer his question? Where was the line that would land her in the PARC?

"We did have a rather interesting night with her at the Highland Fling. Isn't it fabulous how well she's doing? It's like a miracle, really. Don't you think so?" Davitt enthused.

Bobbie buried her face in her cup and chugged down another gulp of coffee. "Hmm," she murmured. Of course, he'd ask about Granny. It was only natural. This damned non-disclosure agreement was making her paranoid.

"Wouldn't you love to know what's causing her new condition?" Davitt leaned forward.

Should I tell him about what's going on with Granny? He might have an interesting perspective, but she couldn't... Her gut reaction told her no. Why add him to the list of people she had put at risk of Slade's wrath, too?

"I'm sure we'll figure it out." Bobbie avoided eye contact with him. She owed him her protection, especially since she couldn't commit to loving him. Perhaps that was the first stage of love, her need to keep him safe. Maybe over time, love would develop from that, grow stronger. Perhaps their relationship could become what they both wanted, given enough time and nurturing.

Davitt gave her a long look, then took a sip of his coffee, and smacked his lips. "Huh! Pretty good coffee, considering it's from a matter streamer. Nearly as good as the coffee I make."

"Yeah, their programs have been getting better and better," Bobbie said. "So, what brings you to the Buckets?"

"Just some work stuff," he said. "I was here, and I wanted to drop by and see you. We've hardly spent any time together since I got back from Switzerland."

"Switzerland? Don't you mean India?" Bobbie said, "When were you in Switzerland?"

"Oh, shit!" Davitt laughed. "India, yes. God, did I say Switzerland?"

"How do you mix up Switzerland and India?"

"Ladakh, the mountains, you know. It all looks like Switzerland."

She scrunched up her face. "There's a bit of a difference..."

He unfolded his leg, sat forward in his seat, and set his mug back on the desk. "Okay, you caught me out," he said, holding up his hands. "I wanted to surprise you. I had Switzerland on my mind because, well, you remember the trip we took there for our second anniversary?"

"Oh, I remember, alright." Bobbie arched an eyebrow and smiled. They'd spent a week there after a long separation due to a talking tour he'd had to attend. They hadn't left the hotel room. The mere memory was enough to shoot tingling sparks through her. Yes, given enough time, perhaps she could turn her affection, her lust for him, into love.

"I was going to take you there for a break, and I was researching places to stay." He reached across the table and enfolded her hand in his.

"That's nice," she said, drumming up some enthusiasm. "We might get to see the sights this time."

He laughed.

"Let's have dinner tonight and talk about it some more? I'll cook—real food–none of your old matter stream slop."

"I'm sorry," Bobbie said. "I have to work tonight." It wasn't a lie. There was all that admin to catch up on—and never enough time for him.

Davitt gave her a puppy-dog-eyes look. "What about later?"

Bobbie longed to rekindle that spark from Switzerland, but right now, she had to hide too much from Davitt. She needed some distance from him for his own safety. Time together could come later.

"I have to check on Granny later," she said. "She wasn't there when I called earlier."

His eyes narrowed fleetingly. Could he tell she was lying? His chocolate-colored eyes softened as he leaned closer to her and said, "Bobbie, I'm worried about us. I don't know where our relationship is going. We need to talk."

"Tomorrow night," she said. Unease squirmed in the pit of her stomach. Davitt wanted more from her than she was prepared to give. When she had Granny's condition under control, she'd make time for him. He deserved that much. Up until now, it had been easy to hold him at arm's length and not let him in, but if he wanted more, she would try to find more.

"Okay, dinner at my place tomorrow night," Davitt said, getting up and walking around the desk. She stood to hug him, but he put a hand on each of her shoulders, looked her up and down. "You're beautiful, you know?" He hugged her to him.

She inhaled his musky scent and searched again for the primal reaction she'd felt in Switzerland. Nothing.

As soon as Davitt left, some of Bobbie's tension left with him. She was expecting Detective Cross to arrive soon, but her office felt airless despite the air-conditioning, so Bobbie left the door to her office ajar. Her thoughts strayed back to Davitt. Had their relationship run its course? Sorrow competed with her aversion to hurting him. She should stop wasting his time, their time, but she'd miss parts of their relationship—the sex, if she were honest, and not much more than that.

A voice from the doorway interrupted her thoughts.

"Doctor Chan," Detective Cross said. "May I come in?"

"Please, sit down," Bobbie said.

Cross sat in the chair Davitt had vacated minutes beforehand. She leaned back in a confident pose, legs slightly apart, resting a hand on each knee.

Bobbie cleared her throat and said, "I have those names for you. I can blink them to you now." An icon in her ONIV indicated that Cross's blink-feed was receptive to the direct data transfer. Bobbie sent the information.

Cross's eyes lost focus as she scanned the list.

"Not a very long list," Cross said. "That makes things easier." She leaned forward, getting to her feet.

"One more thing." Bobbie stood too.

Cross arched her eyebrow, throwing her square set face askew.

"You need to test Justin McGregor directly." Bobbie's voice sounded steadier and more confident than she felt. One wrong word and she'd end up in the PARC. "Don't use the global database."

"Really?" Cross sat back down, cocked her head, and peered up at Bobbie. "Why not?"

"I have reason to believe that the data on record is inaccurate." Bobbie mirrored Cross by sitting again also, confident she had the detective's full attention.

"Inaccurate? You mean the data has been corrupted?" Cross asked, frowning.

"In a manner of speaking, yes," Bobbie's blood pumped in her ears.

"In a manner of speaking?" Cross said slowly.

"It's a medical matter. I can't say anymore."

Cross folded her arms.

"Please," Bobbie said. "Just help me out here." She put the bag of samples she'd collected from Justin's apartment on the desk between them. "If the DNA in here matches the DNA from the rape kit, I urge you to test Justin directly."

"Is this Mr. McGregor's toothbrush?"

"One of them is. I'm guessing the blue one."

"Did he give this toothbrush to you?" Cross asked.

"No."

"You know this evidence is not admissible in court," Cross said, narrowing her eyes.

"I know, but you can get a sample directly from Justin, which would be allowed as evidence. And you do have probable cause since the victim named him," Bobbie said. "Test these, and if there's a match, test Justin."

Cross unfolded her arms, reached forward, and picked up the bag saying, "I can't promise anything, and you know I can't discuss the case with you, regardless of the results." She tucked the sample bag into her briefcase.

"Thank you," Bobbie said. At least one tiny thing was working in her favor. While the detective hadn't agreed, Bobbie guessed that, at the very least, curiosity would get the better of Cross, especially if she had no other leads. Slade may have taken Justin, but she wouldn't be able to keep him from the police. Bobbie stood up to indicate the meeting was over, saying, "Well, we both have jobs to do. I appreciate your indulgence."

* * *

The water behind Seagahan Dam was as still as glass. The grassy banks along the edges of the reservoir reflected off the water in a blaze of green along with patches of blue sky and a churning mosaic of white and gray clouds.

Bobbie sat on the old limestone wall of the dam, one of the few things that had not changed since she was a child. Back then, the straight stretch of road running along the top of the dam had looked like such a long way. Now that same short third of a mile seemed like nothing. The seventy-acre reservoir was beautiful as ever. She leaned over the limestone wall and looked down into the u-shaped overspill. Her ears filled with the roar of the white water tumbling into a sinkhole fifty feet below. The water fed through the dam and into channels on the other side.

Bobbie always followed the same routine at the dam. After she'd been sufficiently mesmerized by the overspill, she crossed the road to the north side and watched the water run down the old limestone channels back to the Butterwater River. The countryside stretched before her for miles to where the horizon met the sky. Lazy drifts of mists hung heavy in the hollows of the fields, ready to coat the vegetation with dew once the sun set.

Gracie had loved to come up here on her good days. She liked seeing the gorse bushes that ran amok, the air heavy with the sweet coconut scent of their yellow blossoms that attracted a steady hum from happy bees.

When the Melters raised the planet's temperature, some places became too hot for human survival. In Ireland, though, the rain had warmed up, transforming the climatic zone from cold, temperate rainforest to warm, nearly tropical, rainforest, barely altering the chugging theater of clouds they'd always watched. The temperature change had seen the native plants die off. Even if they could have grown happily, the land was now needed for food. Fields of sweet potatoes and chickpeas gave way to rice fields in the lower-lying land that retained enough sogginess for that crop.

Just above the horizon in a thin sliver of blue sky, cotton-ball clouds appeared suspended from a celestial ceiling of cloud cover. Five miles north, the twin spires of the Scholar's Cathedral Skyscraper in Armagh perched across from its sister, The Markets Cathedral Complex, with its single tower—larger versions of the originals that had been seen from this vantage point for more than a century. Hovercars zipped across the landscape, trailed by a twinkle of lights like splashes of fairy dust.

The sun was low, about fifteen minutes away from setting. Light filtering through gaps in the clouds made the trees and hedgerows iridescent. A couple of anglers stood at the banks casting their lines with a *zip* and a *plop*. If Bobbie ignored the fishermen hovering on pads out over the water, she could almost take herself back in time, and feel Gracie beside her.

She sensed rather than heard Hicks approach.

"Great view," he said, lining up beside her, leaning both elbows on the wall.

"Yep, it's soothing," she answered, enjoying the warmth of his nearness. "And I can sure do with that now." The sweet sensation that Gracie was nearby, lingered.

In the west, a blazing orb of molten light slid from behind the clouds and breached the blue strip above the horizon. Bronze light flooded the countryside. The still waters of the reservoir glowed golden.

"Wow," Hicks said, lifting a lock of her orange hair from the end, catching the sun. "Your hair looks like flames."

Bobbie enjoyed the admiration she heard in his voice.

"ONIV off?" she said.

Hicks nodded. "So, you got a non-disclosure agreement too?"

"Yes." She drew in a breath then filled him in on how Slade had shut down the meeting.

"That's pretty extreme," Hicks said.

"How'd the meeting go with the psychologist?" she asked.

Hicks leaned on the wall, pitching forward onto his elbows and joined the tips of his fingers. "Grim. She said that they all showed delusional tendencies and manic behavior. Many of the patients seemed oblivious to the effect of their actions on others. Some of those actions involved extreme cruelty, but the interviewee attempted to spin the story to make it sound as if they had little other option." Hicks stopped, stared out over the green fields. "Bobbie," he turned toward her. "She said they all showed sociopathic behavior and suggested treatment… surgical treatment."

Bobbie fought back panic.

"Just when the psychologist told me that, I got a blink to stop what I was doing and read the incoming text," Hicks continued. "I think she got the same message. She went pale and seemed distracted and then left quickly. That's when I opened the bloody NDA. I wish I'd ignored the blink."

"So, you had to sign the non-disclosure?"

"There was no way to turn the damn thing off once I'd opened the document."

"Same here," Bobbie said. "At least you got to decide when to open it. Mine opened automatically during the meeting."

"They probably didn't want to risk blinding me during a procedure, but I wished I'd left the blink unopened until I spoke to you. If we hadn't signed the non-disclosure, we'd not have the threat of the PARC hanging over us." A shadow fell across his features.

"I know. I thought about turning off the ONIV without signing," Bobbie said.

"That's a dangerous move," Hicks said, frowning. "Even if you are not full mind-controlled tech, you could have short circuited your neural network by disengaging the ONIV without the proper shutdown procedure."

"I was more worried about it sending an alert to Belus Corp. Slade gave us no choice. But there's more. Justin's DNA on record didn't match the rape kit."

"Holy shit! How can that be? Who else could have raped her?" Hicks stood up and ran his fingers through his hair.

Bobbie explained her theory that Justin's DNA had changed since he'd rejuvenated and told him how she'd gone to get the DNA samples.

"Christ, Bobbie!" Hicks exclaimed when she told him she thought she'd heard Justin come into the apartment. "You need to be careful around him." He put his hand on her shoulder and turned her to face him.

"Well, it wasn't him," she said, sinking into his gaze. "It was Miley's medication reminder. I gave the samples to Detective Cross. She hasn't promised anything, but I'm guessing she'll test them."

"And if she doesn't?"

Bobbie shook her head. "I don't know. I'll cross that bridge when I come to it."

"Funny old turn of phrase that," Hicks muttered, breaking eye contact and looking at a hovercar soaring between distant hills.

Bobbie followed his gaze for a moment before gathering up the courage to continue outlining her idea. "But right now, I'm more concerned about Granny after getting that blink from her. I have this awful image of the Rejuvenees being tied to gurneys and hooked up to machines while white-coated scientists try to figure out what has caused them to rejuvenate."

"As if Granny would let them!"

"But that's the problem," Bobbie said. "What if she resists, fights them, especially now that she's stronger physically? They'll tie her down, sedate her. Hurt her. Or... or if they followed up the psychologist's report..." She stopped when she heard the panic rising in her voice.

"... Belus would surgically *improve* our patient's personalities?" Hicks finished for her.

"Jesus!" Her ribcage tightened.

"I made every excuse to do house calls with outpatients on the Benthic levels," Hicks said. "I didn't see a single one of the Rejuvenees all afternoon."

"Bloody hell," Bobbie said, feeling short of breath. "Be careful." Just how far-reaching was Slade's authority? Had all the Rejuvenees been sent to the PARC?

"Don't worry. I was smart about trying to connect with the residents. Most of the house-calls were routine," Hicks said. "No one has seen any of the Rejuvenees since yesterday afternoon."

"We need to know where Granny is and find a way to communicate with her."

"How do we do that without breaching the NDA?" Hicks asked.

"We already have, just by talking to each other. We need to go one step further." Bobbie inhaled deeply, now or never. "I need to ask Joy for help."

"What?" Hick searched her face.

"You heard me."

"You can't. If you involve Joy and something goes wrong, she could end up..." Hicks covered his mouth with his hand. Concerned gray eyes bored into hers. He pulled his hand down as if wiping away the idea... wiping away drool.

Hicks had always protected Joy, always stood up for her, and fought her battles. Bobbie had always suspected that Hicks held a torch for her little sister and his reaction now did everything to confirm that. Bobbie should have expected that. What she hadn't expected was the jealousy that ripped through her.

"And if something happens to Joy, the guilt will tear you apart. You'll never get past it," Hicks continued.

Was he warning or threatening me? Did he think I hadn't considered the consequences of Joy being caught?

"We need help with the tech end of things. Joy has the skill set that we need," Bobbie said, less convinced for a split second.

"I worry about what losing both of them would do to you," Hicks said, taking Bobbie's hands and holding them to his chest. "And," he added slowly, "Maybe she won't help us."

Hicks was fighting for the woman he loved. Bobbie could see that in his eyes. Joy didn't know how lucky she was.

Lucky, until I get her into deep shit...

"Have you any other suggestions?" Bobbie asked coldly, pulling her hands away from him.

"No," he said softly and swallowed hard.

"Then we go with asking Joy for help," Bobbie said, sounding stronger than she felt. Joy would not turn down the challenge. Talking her sister into doing something risky was going to be the easy part.

CHAPTER 16

By the following morning, Bobbie knew she had no alternative. She had called Joy and arranged to meet her for a picnic lunch in an isolated spot that was close enough to work that she could slip away unnoticed for a short while.

They sat together, cross-legged on the grass at the top of Slieve Donard, a rare nature reserve on the highest point of Mourne Island. Lower peaks nestled around them, covered in purple heather, yellow gorse blossom, and greenery from small palm trees that had sprung up with the change in the climate. The poor quality of the soil didn't support crops, so the gorse hadn't been cleared the way it had been from the more fertile agricultural land lower down. The air hung damp around them, laden with the sweet coconut fragrance of the gorse blossom, in keeping with the presence of the invasive palm trees. The smell reminded Bobbie of May-time hiking trips with her parents as a child, back when the Mournes were a mountain range connected to the land and not steep islands towering from the ocean.

Bobbie had let them finish eating before she'd told Joy that she wanted her to hack into Granny's ONIV. Joy had not disappointed Bobbie in her enthusiasm to do so.

"So, let me get this straight," Joy said with a grin. "You want me to hack into Granny's feed?"

"Yes," Bobbie said. "I need your help."

Joy smiled. Bobbie searched her face but found no trace of malice. She felt that at least a part of the enormity facing her had been lifted.

She had to find Granny as quickly as possible before Slade's team experimented on her or sent her for a walk in the PARC. The only person Bobbie could think of with the necessary tech skills was Joy.

If Bobbie could find Granny, she would need to figure out a way to test her and prove that rejuvenation was not all positive, to show that whatever was happening needed to be halted, and find a way bring back Granny's old personality. Then, Bobbie would have to get word to someone in the top tiers of government, someone above Slade, perhaps directly to Lisette Fox. She was the only person who could order the necessary resources to combat the spread of rejuvenation. Belus Corp needed to know the details of what was going on, but Bobbie was at a loss when it came to who in Belus Corp to trust. How would she be able to present this information to Lisette Fox? It's not like she could just walk in to Belus Corp HQ in Geneva and request an audience with the woman who was effectively ruler of the whole planet.

One thing at a time, Bobbie, one thing at a time.

"I want to help," Joy said. "In fact, I'm delighted to help."

Bobbie felt a rush of gratitude that clogged up her words.

Joy's brown eyes held on to the smile as her lips relaxed. Bobbie caught a glimpse of the woman her sister had grown up into, standing by Bobbie, supporting her, instead of the spoiled brat Bobbie had spent her life nagging.

"Thank you," Bobbie said once she got past the surprise rush of emotion. This was it. Once she told Joy about the NDA and that Granny was missing, there was no un-telling her. She might as well sign Joy into the PARC herself... if they got caught.

"First, let me bring you up to speed."

"Oh, goody! There's speed..." Joy chuckled. Bobbie doubted she'd be laughing at the end of her brief.

Bobbie began with the Medical Board meeting and how she'd been kicked off the case by Slade. Mirth slipped from Joy's face. A crease gouged the skin between her eyebrows when Bobbie told her that she and Hicks had to sign non-disclosure agreements and that they couldn't find Granny now. Joy listened with rapt attention to every word Bobbie spoke. She seemed to grow up right in front of Bobbie's eyes, saddening and heartening all at once.

"The psychologist's report stated that Granny and the others who had rejuvenated demonstrated sociopathic behavior," Bobbie continued.

"Sociopathic behavior? Like what?" Joy asked.

"Well, for example, one of them, Justin McGregor–"

"Oh, I know Justin, the guy with the glass eye?"

"Yes, that's the one," Bobbie said.

"He's a sweet old guy. What could he do that's sociopathic?" Joy asked.

"That sweet old guy raped his ultra-elderly wife, Miley."

"Oh, my God!" Joy clasped her hands to her chest.

"At least Miley named him as the rapist," Bobbie continued. "But the crime scene DNA didn't match the DNA they have on file for him. I took some samples from his room and gave them to Detective Cross, who's investigating the case."

"Christ almighty!" Joy shook her head, wide-eyed. "And these changes in Granny, wow! It's like they've been possessed, right? We need to find her, pronto." Joy rubbed her hands together. "So, what's the plan?

"To begin with, what I'm about to ask is really risky..." Bobbie's mouth went dry.

Joy held up her hand. "Stop. That doesn't matter to me. I'm in. All the way!"

Bobbie nodded then began, "My blinks to Granny don't work. Someone has hacked my blink register and taken out all the blinks with Granny's address. So, you'll have to figure out some way to connect with her."

"I'll have to hack her feed somehow..."

"So, basically, if we can't access her blinks, maybe we can *see* what Granny sees..." Bobbie suggested.

Joy finished her idea: "We might be able to identify who is holding her captive."

"And maybe, if we get a clue as to where she is..."

"Oh, sis, we have so much to catch up on," Joy said so softly that Bobbie thought she'd heard her wrong.

"What?" Bobbie asked.

"Later," Joy said and squeezed Bobbie's hand. "Let's focus on the task at hand."

Bobbie brushed her finger across her sister's cheek.

Joy absorbed the gesture, like a cat receiving a caress. "So," Joy smiled, igniting mischief in her eyes. "What shall we start with? Eavesdropping? A foureyes patch in?"

"You can do that?" Bobbie asked, shocked. "Granny doesn't have the foureyes b-app."

"No problem, I can download the blink-app to her ONIV. She won't notice. Let's call it a clandestine gift from her favorite granddaughter!"

Bobbie nudged her with her elbow but couldn't contain a laugh. "That's a fairly dubious title, all things considered!"

Joy reached to the nape of her neck and flicked back her hair. Bobbie watched the hair settle into a shiny sheet of blue-black.

"But seriously," Joy said. "Hacking into Granny's feed has some tricky elements."

"If it's too risky..." Bobbie's heart thudded sickeningly. "If you get caught..."

"I won't get caught." Joy's confidence bordered upon arrogance, which bothered more than comforted Bobbie.

"If you do get caught," Bobbie talked over Joy's objections, "You will be sent to the PARC, bypassing chemical treatments and electric shock therapy. You'll be taken straight to surgery and I've seen the outcome. Joy, it's basically a frontal lobotomy. If they don't kill you, that is." Her voice rose urgently. "The PARC is a butcher's shop!"

Joy held up her hand, "Okay, I get it. I won't get caught. I promise. But," she went on. "I'll need a bit of time to set up the hack so it can't be traced. Each foureyes hack can only be for 90 seconds. Then I need to break the connection and reconnect through a different route, so if they do notice the hack, it can't be traced back to me."

"What? Traced back to you?" Bobbie's voice sounded too high in her ears. "No, forget it, it's too risky!"

"Don't worry! I said it won't be traced back. Geez. Trust me, will ya?" Joy shook her head and hissed a sigh between her teeth. "I have a way of doing that, but my point is that sometimes we miss up to thirty seconds between segments. The interruptions won't prevent us from seeing enough of what she sees to help us piece together her location. Sure, we might miss a word here or there if we're lucky enough to hack into a conversation. Worse case, we'll miss the context of what's said." Joy's eyes stared off to the horizon. "So, what are we looking for?"

Bobbie guessed from Joy's thousand-yard stare that she wasn't taking in the low-hanging clouds in the distance. Tinged with mauve, they seemed to float above the slight chop of gray water. Bobbie picked blades of grass from beside her and flicked them away, then turned to Joy.

"Are you hacking in right now?" Bobbie asked her.

Joy heaved a sigh and smiled, her face brightening as if she'd adjusted a light within. "No. Just checking something else... Look, let me set the hack up for you. I'll record what I see and run the segments together. It'll be a little jumpy, but most of the footage will be mundane stuff," Joy continued, almost muttering to herself. "Might be a couple of days before I get back to you."

"Time is not on our side," Bobbie said, her brow puckering. "All this risk and it might yield nothing."

Joy reached forward and traced the skin between Bobbie's eyebrows as if smoothing out her frown. "Trust me. As soon as I have footage, I will send it to your foureyes with a secure patch. I'll warn you first," Joy grinned. "Given your foureyes nausea, we don't want you hurling on a patient!"

"Will we have a record of the footage?" Bobbie needed proof to offer Lisette Fox if she were able to reach the CEO of Belus Corp.

"Yes. I'll store a copy, and I'll tap into Granny's audio too. Don't want picture and no sound, right?" Joy's fingers jigged against her thumbs. Bobbie guessed that Joy had more than one implant in her fingers, judging by the flick of her thumb between different digits.

"Thanks, Joy," Bobbie said as she gathered up the remains of their picnic.

"No thanks needed," Joy said, resting her gaze on Bobbie. "She's my granny, too. But one last thing..." Joy took Bobbie's hand. "I need to go dark to cut into the feed. If you try to blink me too much, the activity could raise a flag." She gave Bobbie's hand a squeeze. "I know you hate when I don't answer blinks, but just this once, let me call you. Okay?"

"Okay," Bobbie said, wondering if she'd put Joy at risk of being discovered while she was playing neuro-games by blinking her too much in the past.

Lost in their own thoughts, they walked to the parking area.

Bobbie hugged her sister before climbing into her blue F-Class Mercedes, small and sleek beside the hulk of Joy's orange Volkswagen camper.

"Laters!" Joy called out through her driver's side window and slapped the side of her van before lifting off and zooming away, out over the ocean.

* * *

Bobbie had postponed dinner with Davitt, claiming that she was too tired. That had been a mistake, she realized. She spent the evening pacing around her apartment, obsessing about Joy getting caught and imagined dreadful scenarios of visiting Joy at the PARC and wiping drool from her face.

The following afternoon, Bobbie received a blink from Davitt. *I ump have to cancel dinner tonight. Sorry, honey. Something important came up at work.*

Thank God, she thought, then immediately vowed to give Davitt more attention in the future. Poor Davitt—always trying to prove his worth. She longed to confront the abandoned kid who peeked out from beneath that ego, a shield erected by a lonely boy whose mother had had to care full time, not just for her own elderly parents and grandparents, but for several in-laws as well.

Bobbie recognized that Davitt had suffered childhood emotional neglect, and that made him needy, but was she making things worse by not loving him enough?

Worry gnawed at her from all angles as she paced her apartment and waited for Joy to call. Eventually, Bobbie gave in to exhaustion and fell into a restless sleep where fuzzy-edged dreams woke her with a jolt before she slid back to sleep.

At four in the morning, Bobbie awoke with another start. This time her doorbell was buzzing in a continuous monotone.

"Coming!" she shouted to no effect. The units were soundproof. Bobbie wriggled out of her sleepsuit, pulled a long sheath dress over her head, and walked through her apartment as her dress unfolded down the length of her body. She smoothed her hand over her hips, checking she was covered up before she opened the door.

Joy stood on the doorstep, white-faced and eyes darting. As soon as the door slid back far enough, she squeezed into the apartment.

"Hi, Bobbie, give me a sec," she said in a rush. Her fingertips flicked against each other, and her eyes went vacant for a couple of seconds. "Okay, that should do it."

"Do what?" Bobbie asked, wondering if she was in the midst of a crazy dream.

"I've frozen the output from all your audio and visual sensors," Joy said. "We can speak freely here for a short time."

"Oh, God, what's happened?" Bobbie's flipped. Had Joy been caught trying to hack into Granny's ONIV? Were the police, or worse, Slade on their way here? Her mind raced over the precautions she had taken. She had only discussed Granny's condition in areas where connectivity was patchy or where background noise would distort the audio feed. Joy's news must be bad if she were willing to risk talking here.

"I got something!" Joy said, focusing her fear-filled gaze on Bobbie. "The footage is really disturbing. You don't want to see it... But, oh, my God you... you have to... just watch it." She pushed her hair back from her pale face. A few errant strands stuck to the sheen of sweat glistening on her forehead.

"What's wrong? Is Granny alright?" Bobbie placed her hand over her heart.

"Yes. She's fine. It's just... oh, God..." Joy shoved her hands through her hair again before sitting down. "I hacked into her blink feed last night. It wasn't easy. Her blinks are blocked, but I managed to set up a workaround that."

"Is she in a PARC? They block the inmate's blinks." *Please God, no!*

"No, I don't think so because I was able to get some footage, but only outside. That's how I first got the ping from Granny's ONIV. They were all sitting around in a yard outside, having breakfast." Joy bounced to her feet and paced the length of the room again, rubbing her arms as she talked, then she returned to the sofa and sat down.

"Where? Who?" Bobbie sat down beside her.

"Them," Joy said, "the others with orange eyes. Twelve of them. But there didn't seem to be anyone else. There was a yard—a flat concrete area bounded by high walls that I couldn't see past and so couldn't determine where they were. I kept the foureyes rolling all day though if she went inside, it went blank because of the blink block. After breakfast, they worked out in the yard."

"Granny worked out?"

"Yes, like they had exercises to do, push-ups and squats. Sets of them, and staff were watching with a portable intepanels set up, filled with data—too much for their ONIVs to view in one go. I think they were being timed and tested." Joy stood up again.

"So, they are being assessed," Bobbie said, heart pumping, her eyes following Joy pacing again. "This is probably just the beginning." Bobbie went on. "I hope we can get to her before the investigation gets too invasive."

"Granny, later she... she..."

"She what?"

"Something happened... you need to see," Joy said, sitting back down beside Bobbie. "It's easiest if I hook you in. I can't describe it."

What could be that bad?

"Sit still, will you?" Bobbie snapped at Joy. "Foureye viewing is nauseating enough without you flitting about." Joy could really milk a situation. Bobbie was tired of her sister ramping up the tension when there was already so much stress and worry.

"Okay, I'm patching you in." Joy sat down.

Bobbie braced herself. The view before her eyes turned black with red and yellow blurry patches floating around at random. "It's not working," Bobbie whispered.

"You don't have to whisper—she can't hear us," Joy said. "Oh, it's working, alright. She has her eyes closed. You're looking at her retina ghosts."

Bobbie heard a deep resonating hum, broken with a whoosh of air and repeated.

"She's moaning," Bobbie said. "Is she hurt? Is she okay?" Bobbie's chest squeezed with fear. She clutched Joy's hand.

"Oh, God!" Granny's voice came through Bobbie's audio with tinny reverberations. "Yes! Don't stop! Yes! Yes!" Granny groaned.

"She's not hurt," Joy said. "She's shagging!"

"Yes!" They could hear Granny cry out. "Oh, God, Yesssss!"

"No! Gross. Turn it off!" But Joy had all the controls. If Bobbie closed her eyes, she'd still have to listen to Granny's orgasm. "Joy, turn it off, now!"

"No. There's more. Sex is not the worst bit," Joy said. "At least it's the natural bit!"

"There's nothing natural about being in your Granny's head when she's having sex!"

"Stop being so prudish! You're the doctor. How do you think you got made?"

Granny's cries turned to a low guttural groan.

"How long does she go on for?" Bobbie squirmed. "Seriously, I don't need to see and hear them... copulating!" Was Joy enjoying Bobbie's reaction? Bobbie couldn't see Joy's face, but her sister's voice seemed odd—as if trying not to cry... or laugh. With Joy, either was possible. Bobbie brushed aside the familiar sense of frustration with her sister.

"Wait, wait! She's opening her eyes," Joy said. "The footage jumps a few seconds here."

The image in Bobbie's eyes shifted to bright light. A face came into focus, floppy brown hair over a bright orange eye and an eye patch.

"Justin!" Bobbie said.

"That's Justin?" Joy said. "Does she know he's a rapist?"

Bobbie could hardly recognize the younger Justin. Sweat glistened on his smooth skin, the accordion wrinkles reabsorbed by his rejuvenating body. His aquiline nose, high cheekbones, and long chin held on the echoes of the old man enough to allow Bobbie to identify him. No amount of rejuvenation could replace the eye he'd lost in the 2030 climate riots. His face grimaced. His head bobbed as he delivered his last few thrusts.

"This is bad," Bobbie said, her irritation with Joy morphing into anger she wasn't sure how to direct. "Forget hacking! I should never have asked you to hack into her blink system. It's Granny's business who she..."

"No, sis. Them shagging is nothing. It gets much worse." Joy said with a feint quiver of laughter.

A rush of frustration made Bobbie click the electrode together in her fingers, trying to override Joy's hack into Bobbie's blink. No luck. Bobbie had no control. She felt a wild surge of panic.

"Turn it off, Joy. Please," Bobbie begged. The screen blinked dark. Bobbie thought Joy had turned it off, but the foureyes spluttered back on. Another jump. Bobbie felt her stomach twist with the familiar nausea she suffered while viewing foureyes.

"foureyes is not a pretty practice anytime," Joy muttered. "And I didn't have time to edit."

"When you've spied on me, was I... did you see...?" Bobbie asked her sister, mad at her now.

"No! I was a kid back then. And no, I didn't catch you doing anything, actually." Joy's voice was disdainful. "You're the ultimate goody two shoes. Spying on you was boring!" she added with a twist of venom.

Boring, huh?

Justin's face slid to the periphery of vision and disappeared. Granny looked up at a patchy blue sky. The picture pixilated and froze. The sky materialized again.

The view changed and swung vertically, making Bobbie's stomach lift. The patchy blue sky met a blue line of ocean at the horizon. They were somewhere high overlooking the sea. The sun hung low casting a golden sheen on the water.

In the foreground, Bobbie noticed a raised bed containing tomato plants and a trellis for beans.

"Is she on top of the Buckets?" Joy asked.

"No, she's in gardens all right, but most buildings have rooftop gardens, so that doesn't narrow down the location," Bobbie said, modulating her tone to neutral to mitigate the spat that threatened to brew between them. "And she's on the west coast. See how the sun was over the ocean. If she were at the Buckets at sunset, the sun would be setting over land."

The picture swung sideways, making Bobbie's head light. A round, stone structure came into view, possibly a couple of hundred yards away.

Bobbie sat up. "Wait! That little stone tower in the background, did you see it?"

"Yeah," Joy said. "So, she's on the ground, high ground."

"Beside the ocean... judging by the position of the sun over the water, and since it's evening, it must be west coast..."

"Cliffs, maybe?" Joy asked.

"That's it! The Cliffs of Moher," Bobbie said. "That's where I've seen that little stone tower before."

"Yes, O'Brien's Tower," Joy said.

"That's it! There's a medical research center there. Jesus! That's where they're holding them. What the hell are they doing to them?"

Bobbie fought back her queasiness as the image flashed with clothing, hands, sea, and sky. Then her foureyes went blank again.

"We know where they are now," Bobbie said gratitude, flushing out the annoyance she'd felt for Joy moments before. "Thank you."

"No, no, there's more. You need to see what Granny does. I'm sorry. I wouldn't put you through watching her have sex if there wasn't a reason," Joy murmured. "Just a short glitch. If I'd had time to edit, I suppose I could have started the footage here, but you need context. I think Granny's getting dressed again."

Bobbie hoped Justin was too.

"You know, Justin," Granny was saying as her eyes scanned for him. The picture swooped, taking Bobbie's stomach along for the ride.

Please be dressed, thought Bobbie, *please be dressed!*

Thankfully, Justin was, but he seemed to be reaching for Granny again.

"We have seen enough," Bobbie hissed, not wanting to go through another tryst, but then the distance to Justin's face stretched. Granny must have stepped back.

"No, wait," Joy said. "Be patient."

Bobbie felt Joy's hand on her arm.

"This is the last time we're doing that," Granny said to Justin.

He frowned and shook his head. "No. I don't want that."

"Well, Justin, that's too bad."

"Is it because of Miley?" Justin said. "You know she's just a doting old fart. She's nothing to me."

"No, it's not Miley. It's you." Bobbie heard an edge to Granny's voice she didn't recognize. "Look at you." Granny looked Justin up and down, then her eyes rested on his face. "You're just a one-eyed cripple. I can do far better than you!"

Justin's eye narrowed to a slit. His lips pressed into a thin line.

Bobbie yelled, "Granny, look out!" as he stepped toward her.

Granny couldn't hear her. Bobbie watched Justin clench his fingers, knuckles whitening. His fist flashed out toward her. Bobbie flinched. For a few moments, Bobbie saw a jumble of sky and clouds, then the image focused on Granny's hand gripping the edge of a raised bed.

"You bastard!" Granny shrieked. Her eyes stopped on a gardening fork; its prongs buried deep in the soil. Granny grabbed the handle, pulled the fork from the soil, and thrust the metal prongs toward Justin.

Bobbie, sure that Granny would stop short, gasped in horror as the four prongs of the fork embedded in Justin's body, right below the ribcage. His one orange eye bulged. A bubbly *Ouff!* escaped his lips. Blood oozed from his mouth and dribbled down his chin, dripping onto his chest. His hands found the shaft of the fork, but Granny kept driving him back.

"A. Real. Man. Never. Hits. A. Woman!" Granny punched out a word each time she thrust forward a step.

Bobbie gasped and wrapped her arms around her torso as she watched, aghast.

Blood seeped out where the prongs pierced Justin's body, dampening his sensorfabrik tunic with the same rust color that now flowed from his mouth. The material held on to the moisture, so it didn't drip on the ground. Justin, his one good eye frozen in shock, stumbled backward. Bubbles of blood frothed at his nose and mouth. He tried to speak, but the words got tangled.

"Ugh," Granny said, "Messy, messy, tut, tut!"

A waist-high wall came into view behind him. Granny pushed him until he bent back over the wall. A little fountain of blood spurted up from his mouth as he struggled to breathe. Granny pushed once more. Justin's feet lifted. He loosened his grip on the handle of the gardening fork. His head hung back; his hands dangled limply. *Was he still alive?* Granny gave a big heave, swung the fork handle out toward the sea, grabbed his flailing feet, and tipped his whole body over the wall.

Horrified, Bobbie gripped Joy's hand. This couldn't be real. He'd get up again... It was a prank or an error, something...

The feed stuttered then refocused as the viewpoint swung out over the wall. The body tumbled down, smashing off the cliff face like a rag doll. Arms and legs akimbo, he fell down, down, down to the waves, some twenty meters below. The body floated briefly away from the land and then disappeared, swallowed up by the restless ocean.

The feed went fuzzy again, then Bobbie could see the garden. The ground tilted, then disappeared, replaced by O'Brien's tower. The image changed again to a concrete and glass building further inland. There was no-one around. Bobbie's stomach tipped as Granny looked down at her hands. The absorbent sensorfabrik was as effective at soaking up blood as sweat.

"Clean as a whistle," Granny said in a metallic-edged voice. Her palms made a soft clapping sound as she brushed off her hands. "Now, that's better!"

Bobbie sat stupefied, unable to comprehend what she'd seen. When the image snapped off, she found herself staring at a white-faced Joy.

"Jesus Christ," Bobbie said. Her heart pounded in her ears like she'd woken from a bad dream. Had she witnessed her grandmother kill a man in cold blood? A chill crept over Bobbie's scalp. Her Granny would never kill another living thing, never mind her friend. Gloria was someone else, something else committing cold-blooded murder. Not Granny… not her Granny. But where was Granny? Was there any of her left to salvage?

CHAPTER 17

Joy started to cry and reached for Bobbie. They folded into each other, weeping. When they pulled apart, they sat on the edge of the couch in stunned silence, enveloped in numbing horror.

"Oh, God, what if any of the research center staff saw Granny with Justin?" said Bobbie. Panic rang in her tone.

"I hacked the center's server and wiped the surveillance footage throughout the facility during the time frame that they were in the garden. The gap will show up as a glitch," Joy said. She settled back into the couch. "The gardens look like they'd be far enough away from the buildings so that a security camera wouldn't pick them up anyway."

"Maybe that's why they chose that spot—seclusion?" Bobbie said, twisting in her seat to face her.

"Yeah, maybe even sociopaths like to keep their sex lives private," Joy said.

"But, oh, God, what if someone finds this recording?" Bobbie didn't want to admit that she was trying to protect a murderer.

"Don't worry. The data file is secure," Joy said. "I can lock the footage away, and no-one will ever find it."

"We need to show Hicks and make some decisions." Bobbie heard the quiver in her own voice. "And we need to find a way to get to Granny and stop her from hurting anyone else. Maybe I can find a way to reverse her psychosis, get her back."

"What if we can't? What if Granny's gone for good trapped inside that beast that calls itself Gloria?" Joy asked quietly.

Bobbie was horrified at what her grandmother had become yet terrified of losing her completely. She shook her head, tears spilling down her face. "We have to try," she said hoarsely. "We can't give up on her. That wasn't Granny. That was... that was–"

"Gloria?" Joy said.

Bobbie nodded. She couldn't bear to call that creature, Granny.

"Let's meet tomorrow at the dam after work and show Hicks," Bobbie said. "Do you want to stay here tonight? I can make up the spare room." Guilty that she'd been sharp with Joy earlier, Bobbie wasn't sure how to make amends.

"That would be really nice. Thank you. But I'll sleep in my van."

Sadness enveloped Bobbie. Had Joy detected her annoyance earlier? Had she hurt her sister's feeling, and all Joy had been doing was helping—and at great risk? Mute, Bobbie nodded.

Joy touched Bobbie's hand and said quietly, "But it will be nice to know you're close by."

* * *

Bobbie, Hicks, and Joy sat on the wall of Seagahan Dam with their backs to the reservoir. The water toppled down the overspill offering continuous background noise. Joy seemed sure that their conversation wouldn't be overheard. Hicks sat between the sisters, looking queasy, watching the footage of Gloria and Justin. Joy had edited out the sex scene. Little muscles flexed in his jawline. He pressed his lips together. His face screwed in on itself until Hicks jerked back, his eyes widened, and his mouth opened in a startled shout.

"Shit!" he cried, "Did she really just do that? Oh, my God! I… she… it's…"

Joy put a hand on his forearm. He covered her fingers with his massive hand. Bobbie felt a stab of jealousy.

"Something has taken over her mind," Hicks said. "Her whole body actually. How strong do you need to be to stick a garden fork through the middle of someone?"

"I thought exactly the same thing!" Joy jumped down from the wall and faced them. "Like that mind control fungus that takes over the ants' brains. Something has taken over her brain, her whole body actually, giving her that strength. What else can it be?"

"We've ruled out infections from unicellular sources, viruses, bacteria, fungi," Hicks said. "So, it can't be a mind control fungus."

"But what if," Joy lowered her voice. "What if she's possessed by another life form? Possibly something not from this planet?"

Bobbie whistled through her teeth. "That's unlikely," she said, hoping Joy wasn't going to bring up her conspiracy theories again.

"Unlikely?" Joy snorted. "As unlikely as, say, Granny getting the body of a thirty-year-old and the mind of a psycho-killer? As unlikely as creatures from outer space attacking us with energy weapons and totally fucking up the whole planet? Creatures, I might add, that we've never actually seen since we blasted them to whatever hell they originated from?"

"Joy..." Hicks stood up and took a step toward her with a hand outstretched, but she stepped back.

"No." Joy shook her head vehemently. "No more unlikely than an extraterrestrial life form infiltrating vulnerable humans, rejuvenating their bodies and taking over their minds. What if there's more of them? What if the plan is to make an army of these creatures? Every elderly person becoming the body for E fucking T with orange eyes. What then?"

What Joy said wasn't impossible, Bobbie had to concede. *How the hell would we fight something like that?*

"Joy, maybe you're not wrong," Bobbie began.

Hicks started to interrupt, but Bobbie held up a hand. "To figure out whatever is causing her rejuvenation and sociopathic behavior," she said. "We need to take a methodical approach. Like any disease..." She looked at Joy, "... or an invading army... or whatever. We need to first identify what we are dealing with and look for its weaknesses. And we need to alert the authorities."

"What if Lisette Fox and Belus Corp are in on it!" Joy hissed. "Slade doesn't seem in too much of a hurry to warn people. Maybe the Melters control them both?"

Bobbie glanced at Hicks as chills chased over her skin. Her thoughts had wandered in the direction of a secret Melter attack back when they'd first seen the symptoms of rejuvenation appear. He shook his head. She decided he was right.

"Oh, give over, Joy." Inhaling deeply to quell her surge of aggravation, Bobbie continued, "Lisette Fox defeated the Melters. Our armies were defeated. If it weren't for her, we'd probably be extinct now or enslaved to the Melters. Why would she be on their side? Or on the side of anything that wasn't human? I thought you'd gotten over all that stupid conspiracy stuff you raved about as a kid. It was far from cute back then, and it's downright dangerous now!"

"No! You can't say that to me now, not with what has happened to Granny. Whatever is happening is not natural. Something or someone is changing her!" Joy bordered on hysteria.

"Look, the pair of you, calm down!" Hicks stepped between the sisters. "Right now, we need a simple plan. What's our next step?"

Joy shrugged sullenly.

"We need to rescue Gloria from the research center," Bobbie said, jumping down from her place on the wall. "We can figure out exactly what's going on with her biologically once we have her, but we need to nab her before she's arrested for killing Justin."

"That will only take a day or two," Joy said, her sulk evaporated. "There are backups for the surveillance footage I wiped, and I can't get to those. I need to do that manually."

"We can't march up to the front door and ask for Granny." Bobbie's stomach flip-flopped as she formed her next thought. "We're going to have to break in." She focused on Joy. "Can you get us in?"

Did I really just say that? Me, the goody-two-shoes doctor?

But Bobbie realized that desperate measures were called for now that she'd watched Granny murder her lover with a garden fork without blinking an eye.

"The door locks can be overridden," Joy said. "But that hack will take me a bit of time. Breaking locks is not easy, and the research center's security staff will be on the lookout for more security breaches now if they've noticed the video surveillance glitch. But I'll figure it out. I'll crash their entire system if I have to."

"Assuming we get in," Hicks said. "What then? What if she doesn't want to leave? Granny is a woman who knows her own mind."

"She doesn't have her own mind right now," Bobbie said. "Anyway, she blinked for help. But then why didn't she run away?"

"Perhaps, she doesn't want to leave now," Hicks suggested. "She may be confused."

"Christ, I hope she's confused. This is not the grandmother I knew." Joy placed her elbows on the wall and dropped her head into her hands.

Sympathy for Joy turned the tide on Bobbie's annoyance with her, but it was Hicks's hand that patted Joy's shoulder as he murmured, "It's tough on you guys. I know."

"We can sedate Granny if needs be." Bobbie shoved her flash of envy into the dark recesses.

"Agreed," Hicks moved beside Joy and placed his hands on the top of the dam wall. "Okay. We start with Granny, with what we can do."

Joy said, "Do any of the other Rejuvenees have relatives worried about them?"

"One family did contact me. I don't want to involve them if we don't have to. Other than that... well..." He shrugged. "There wasn't a line of folk battering down the doors to visit at the best of times."

"A lot of the ultra-elderly lost everyone in the war," Bobbie said. The Armagh skyline silhouetted against the sky in the distance. Bobbie remembered one of the last conversations they'd had before Granny had morphed into Gloria. She'd loved seeing the Cathedral spires towering over her hometown. Bobbie wanted to bring Granny back so she could look at them every day.

"If Granny hadn't been there, maybe we wouldn't have noticed; maybe no-one would have noticed," Joy said, her voice tender. "They messed with the wrong old doll!"

"So, if we go and get Gloria, we need somewhere safe to take her, somewhere 'off the grid' so to speak." Bobbie looked at Joy. "Just to be on the safe side, okay?" Where would she look for such a place? Her whole adult life had been spent in populations with complete connectivity, street cams, security cameras, and lots of surveillance she was certainly unaware of. For all she knew, the government could patch into her ONIV the way Joy had to Granny. The same government she'd trusted to keep her safe. Now she, the boring one, the law-abiding citizen, was contemplating kidnapping her own grandmother and worse, aiding and abetting a murderer.

Joy stepped closer to Bobbie and Hicks.

"Only Granny? None of the others?" Joy asked, her eyes searching their faces.

Bobbie and Hicks nodded.

"Just Granny," Bobbie said. "To begin with..."

"I might have an idea, but I need to check something out first–" Joy looked behind her. "Oh, crap!" Joy spun around. "Somebody's coming!"

Along the wall of the dam, a hunched figure hobbled along the road toward them. Bobbie resisted an urge to laugh at her sister's concern. The figure approaching at a snail's pace was a very elderly man. All they had to do was calmly walk away.

"Let's go," Bobbie said. "We can take my car."

"Wait!" Hicks said, squinting in the direction of the old man who was gaining on them, albeit slowly. "That's Jimmy."

"Who?" Joy asked, irritation prickling her voice.

"Old Jimmy? Granny's friend?" Bobbie recognized the white mustache and the broad-shouldered old tweed jacket he insisted on wearing over his sensorfabrik tunic. "Don't you remember him from Mum's wake and funeral? He was there with Granny. He's a very nice man," Bobbie added with genuine affection.

"Nope, don't remember him," Joy said.

They turned to walk away.

"Doctor Chan! Doctor Hicks! Wait... please, wait," Jimmy called after them.

Hicks groaned.

The three of them turned back toward the old man.

"Hi, Jimmy," Bobbie said brightly. "Didn't recognize you there."

His leathery old face creased into a smile, and he stopped walking to lean against the wall. He wheezed and lifted his right hand in a salute to indicate that he'd speak when he caught his breath.

"Where's your carebot?" Bobbie said, walking up to his side.

Hicks and Joy stood back a little to give the old man some space. Bobbie took his wrist gently in her fingertips. His pulse fluttered but steadied as he rested. Sweat beaded on his forehead. One drop broke free and raced for his jawline. He pulled out an old cotton kerchief and dabbed at his face.

"In the car, charging," Jimmy wheezed. "Too much hassle to unload... didn't think I'd be walking... just came... case your granny might turn up here." His voice sounded stronger, but as he continued, it rang with an urgent undertow. "You know how she loved to come up here. Doctor Chan, she's missing. I can't get in contact with her. The hovercar dropped me here. I wasn't planning on walking." Jimmy took in another gulp of air. "Just gonna stand here a while, blink the carebot to come get me when I was done. Then I saw you..."

Bobbie patted the back of his hand gently, confident that his heartbeat was strong and happy to see his color coming back.

"Do you know where she is?" Jimmy asked in a way that stung Bobbie's heart.

Bobbie looked sideways at Hicks and caught the microscopic shift of his eyes telling her to say nothing. Not that she needed telling, but she took comfort from the fact that Hicks seemed as paranoid as she was.

Jimmy must have spotted their unspoken exchange. "It's serious, isn't it?" He slammed his weathered old hand, palm down, on the wall with a smack. "I knew it! They are experimenting on them."

"Who?" Bobbie said, dying to know if and how Jimmy knew about Slade.

"Gloria told me that–before she got younger, you know—" He glanced at them and dabbed his face again with the kerchief. "She said she didn't know if it were dreams or for real, but that someone vaguely familiar was coming into her room at night and giving her injections."

"Injections?" Hicks asked. "Are you sure that's what she said?"

"Yes," Jimmy said, nodding vigorously. "Injections with a needle."

"She must have been dreaming," Hicks said. "Very few medical procedures require the use of needle injections."

Injections—no more outlandish than mind-controlling aliens. Could someone have used a hypodermic needle on Granny?

"When did she tell you the injections happened?" Bobbie asked. "You're sure it was before she changed?"

"Yes, a couple of weeks ago, at least," Jimmy answered, nodding. "She said she always woke up feeling hung-over and groggy and unable to remember her dream clearly."

"How many times did she dream this? Over what period?" Bobbie's mind was ablaze with questions.

"A few times," Jimmy said. "Maybe once a week for a month and then she stopped confiding in me. She got young again, you see."

"Hicks, did you see any changes in her charts before she rejuvenated?" Bobbie asked, searching for a definitive moment. "Before her eyes turned orange?"

"We saw health improvements," Hicks said. "You did too, in Aayushi Dhawan."

Bobbie waved her hand like she was swatting the idea away. "Did she have any marks on her arms? Bruises?" she asked.

"No," Hicks said. "None that we noticed."

"Might have been better if she had," Jimmy added. "Maybe she'd have been more convinced it wasn't a dream. She was afraid she was losing her mind, poor thing. I told her to tell you." Jimmy nodded at Bobbie.

"She never mentioned strange dreams to me," Bobbie said, bewildered. "What about you, Joy?"

"Nope, she said nada to me," Joy said, frowning. "Maybe she was afraid that you would make a big deal out of it or something?"

"And she didn't think to mention weird events when she started getting younger?" Bobbie said, angry at her grandmother's stoicism.

Jimmy put his hand on her shoulder. His mustache twitched, and his eyes softened as he said, "Your mother was dying. She didn't want to worry either of you. We shared a lot, your grandmother and I." His eyes drifted off to the horizon. Bobbie knew he was not reading a blink. He was thinking of Granny. He'd been Grandpa's closest friend. Granny and Jimmy had shared a lifetime, grieving for Grandpa and Jimmy's own sons—all lost in the Melter War—later, Jimmy's wife and now Granny's daughter.

"At least, she talked to me about a lot of things, until she started to get younger. Then she got sort of," he hesitated and looked at Bobbie and Joy, "No offence girls, but the only word I can think of is *nasty*." He hung his head.

"That's one way of putting it alright," Hicks said, looking grim.

Bobbie knew he was thinking about the footage of Granny and Justin.

"I understand." Bobbie patted Jimmy's shoulder, warding off a tide of her own emotion.

Jimmy's face hardened. "I don't know what they're doing to her, but I want the old Gloria back. I imagine you do too," he said, "I know you kids are up to something, meeting up here on the QT so no-one... absolutely no-one can overhear you. I want to help."

Say nothing and stay offline. Bobbie displayed no reaction to Joy's blink, instead she said. "Hey, we're taking in the view. Like you said, this is kind of a family thing. Stop worrying about Granny, Jimmy. She's not missing, she volunteered for some tests. She'll probably be back before you know it."

"I'm old, but I ain't half-witted... yet," Jimmy said, his eyes blazing. "If they are experimenting on her, giving her injections against her will, we have to stop it. How else would a ninety... ninety... hell, I dunno, she never would tell me her real age, but she sure as hell isn't as young as she now looks. Dammit, the way she looks, what else could it be?"

Bobbie didn't know how to answer. Could these injections have caused her rejuvenation? What was injected? And by whom? Hick's tests detected nothing in her blood. Silence soaked into the humid air around them.

"Look, Belus Corp does a lot of good," Jimmy said. "I know it. But I don't trust 'em. They're not as warm and fuzzy as they pretend to be. I built research centers back in the day, and you'd be amazed what they wanted in some of those facilities. Underground mazes, lock-up cells. What's keeping them from throwing Gloria in one of those?"

The thought of Granny in a cell jogged Bobbie's heartbeat. But the footage Joy had recovered showed Granny and her cohorts allowed to roam freely. Was Jimmy trying to scare her? But he had helped build these places. He could be a useful guide if he knew his way around a research center. Could Bobbie justify letting Jimmy get involved? Was it fair to let him risk as much as she was prepared to risk? One look at the man's pleading eyes answered that question. Yes, if he wanted to.

Bobbie looked at Hicks, but he was watching Joy, whose gaze had drifted off, fingertips flickering against each other. Was she blinking someone? A bit rich after her telling them to stay offline.

Joy surprised her by speaking. "So, Jimmy." Joy moved to face him square on and stood with her hands on her hips, looking to Bobbie like a five-year-old trying to stand her ground. "I can't imagine Belus Corp would want you talking about cells in research facilities."

"Tough crap! I'm too old for them to lock me up." Jimmy's white mustache twitched.

"They could send you to the PARC." Joy cocked her head to the side.

"I'm not afraid of Belus Corp." Jimmy leaned back against the wall and folded his arms.

"And you worked for them?" Joy asked.

Jimmy narrowed his eyes. "I worked for lots of people. I was a contractor. Like I told you, I built things." He pulled himself up to his full height.

"How did you get started in that?" Joy asked, her eyes never leaving his face, her fingers moving, thumb tips to fingertips, tapping all the while.

"Started out as a bricklayer in my teens helping my uncle. Went to college and studied civil engineering and computer science, worked for Belus Corp since the war ended until I had to retire."

"What year was that? Why did you retire?" Joy asked.

"2044 Retired at eighty-five," Jimmy said quietly. "Old age slowed me up some, but I can help you guys find Granny. Once I have my carebot, I'll be grand."

Joy's eyes had tuned out, and she didn't appear to be listening.

"No," Hicks said. "It's too dangerous!"

"Hah, dangerous! Don't make me laugh." Jimmy barked out a laugh that held no mirth or fun. "I didn't get to be a ninety-four—or is it five? Hell, I'm so old I've lost count anyway, I didn't get to be this old and not squeeze my way through some danger and survive! I fought the Melters, I think I can handle a bunch of scientists and bureaucrats. Besides, I always wanted to be James Bond." He grinned and winked. "You know, go out with a bang."

"We don't want to be responsible for anything happening to you," Hicks said.

"Look," Jimmy said, anger snapping in his eyes. "Don't brush me off just because I'm old."

"It's not that…" Hicks began, but Bobbie knew it was.

"She's been gone two days now," Jimmy interrupted him.

Two days, thought Bobbie, only two days? She felt as if she'd been rattling around in this mental clangor of anxiety for weeks.

"I've cared about Gloria a lot longer than any of you. If you don't want me involved, I'll investigate my own way. I know a good lawyer I can talk to about getting her home."

Silence hung over them again. If Jimmy talked to an attorney, could he bring a lot of trouble upon himself? Never mind that he would also be exposing them to danger.

"Wait, Jimmy, can you give us a second to chat about your offer?" Bobbie asked, in saccharine tones, smiling at him as if they were talking about something as benign as buying his car.

"Sure." Jimmy held out his open palms. "Take your time."

Bobbie, Hicks, and Joy walked to the far end of the dam until they were out of earshot.

"We can't have Jimmy asking questions and making waves. Word will get back to Slade and we want the authorities to think no-one's paying attention," Bobbie began.

"We have two choices," Joy interrupted. She twisted with a blue-tipped lock of her hair between the fingers of her left hand. "We could take him with us."

"Or?" Hicks asked.

Joy closed her brown-black eyes for a moment, then re-opened them. "We kill him," she said tonelessly.

"Jesus Christ!" Hicks said as Bobbie hissed, "What?"

Had she misheard Joy? Was Joy suggesting they kill Jimmy?

"You can't be serious?" Bobbie said.

"You're right," Joy said, obviously enjoying their reaction. "But those are the only two sensible options we have."

"We could ask him to not tell anyone," Hicks said, but the expression on his face suggested he didn't have much faith in that.

"Then he'll have something to blackmail us with," Bobbie said, her heart sinking.

"Screw it," Joy said. "Let's take him with us, for the sake of a quiet life. He checks out. Trust me."

"What?" Hicks said. "I've seen his chart, and believe me, he's in no condition to be playing James Bond."

"We could use him," Bobbie said slowly.

"What are you on about?" Hicks asked.

Bobbie sighed. "He used to work at Belus Corp. He knows the research facilities. We need him."

He raised his hands in surrender.

Bobbie looked at Joy. "Would you have killed him?"

"Good, God, no! I just always wanted to say that. It's so *gangsta*!" Joy blew on her pointed finger and laughed but sobered up quickly. "Seriously, if this old guy knows his way around the facility, that would be useful."

Bobbie walked back to Jimmy, aware of Hicks close on her heels.

"You're in," Bobbie said as she approached him. She flung her ginger locks over her shoulder with a toss of her head, then scooched up close to Jimmy's face. "But please don't act the hero. Understood?"

"Yes, Boss!" Jimmy punched the air with a feeble fist and laughed. Hope shone from his eyes such that Bobbie could see the boy's heart in the man's face. "We can be..." His lungs tripped on a wheeze that caused him to cough until he brought up a lump of phlegm, which he spat out over the dam wall. He pulled in a clear breath and exhaled, saying, "We can be the Fearless Four!"

"God help us!" Hicks said, shaking his head.

Despite her trepidation, Bobbie could not resist a little smile. Jimmy sure had balls. Joy stood alone but seemed to be nodding her head as if in blink-conversation. Bobbie fought down her impatience. What could be so damn important? Who the hell would Joy be talking to or blinking with at a time like this?

When Joy turned back, her face was solemn. The light humor that always seemed to dance across her features had vanished. *What now?*

"I need you all to promise not to tell anyone what I am about to tell you," Joy said.

"Joy, we don't need any more drama," Hicks said in a measured tone.

She snapped her gaze onto Hicks. "People's lives depend on your discretion." A chill rippled through Bobbie. "Some of us have been... finished..." she continued, "I need to know you can keep what I'm going to tell you quiet."

"Some of us? What? Finished? What are you on about?" Bobbie asked, her insides twisting.

"Can you keep a secret?" Joy hissed through gritted teeth.

"God almighty, Joy, of course," Bobbie said. "Especially now things have changed, but..." She stole a look sideways at Jimmy. Hicks was trustworthy—but Jimmy?

"I need your verbal agreement to keep what I am about to tell you confidential," Joy said. "Consider it a formality. I trust you to keep your word once we have it."

We?

"You have my word," Hicks said.

"Mine too," Jimmy said. "Tell us, love."

Bobbie looked from Joy to Jimmy and back to Joy.

"Bobbie, I'm waiting for you. I need your word." Emotions seemed to battle behind Joy's eyes.

The expression on her sister's face sharpened Bobbie's curiosity.

"You have my word," Bobbie said tenderly.

"This will probably come as a shock," Joy said.

Bobbie wondered what could be left to shock her.

CHAPTER 18

"I know a place to take Granny," said Joy, "but only Granny. We can't accommodate the other Rejuvenees, not yet."

Mist dampened the world around them, enough to lend a slight chill to exposed skin.

"Okay," Bobbie sighed, suddenly impatient.

"We take her to California." Joy leaned in close enough for Bobbie to smell the lemony twist of her perfume.

"Oh, be serious, Joy, we aren't heading off on some road trip holo-flick," Hicks said stepping back.

"How can we go anywhere in North America? The whole continent is a scorch zone," Bobbie said, standing up straight on both feet. "Except for Alaska and Canada, I suppose, but those are too densely populated."

"There's a place in the Sierra Nevada Mountains of California," Joy said, holding a hand up as Jimmy cleared his throat to speak. "The temperatures have been dropping there faster than expected. The re-solidified granite rocks are radiating the heat faster than the soil, and then there's the thinner air at that altitude not holding on to the heat. Belus Corp hasn't noticed because we've interfered with their sensors in that region."

"We?" Hicks and Bobbie said in unison.

Joy waved her hands and shook her head. "I'm getting to that. One thing at a time, okay?"

Bobbie wondered who this kid was in front of her, taking over and talking about hiding places from Belus Corp.

Jimmy nodded and frowned.

"Go on," Hicks said, stepping back into the formation of the huddle.

"So, we grab Granny and hole up in Yosemite–" Joy began.

"Yosemite?" Hicks and Bobbie exclaimed.

"Jesus, stereo, you two!" Joy said, suppressing a self-satisfied grin.

Jimmy leaned against the wall, silent, arms folded.

"Yosemite," Joy said while standing opposite Jimmy. She rested one hand on Bobbie's arm and the other on Hicks's elbow, as if to steady both and continued, "The valley suffered a direct hit during the Melter War. The intense heat caused weird formations, weirder than anything geological that you've ever seen. That mountain they used to call Half Dome melted. We call it Candle Dome now. A lot of the granite turned to a type of molten glass and flowed, kind of like lava, cooling on the outside first, forming tunnels, and caves. Working with that stuff is hell on your fingernails if you forget to wear your gloves." Joy glanced at Bobbie.

Then the truth dawned on Bobbie, "Oh, my God, you let me think..."

"I'm sorry, but we couldn't tell you," Joy said, squeezing her Bobbie's arm.

"Who's we?" Bobbie asked.

"Some who escaped Finishing at the PARC..."

"No," Bobbie interrupted, and shrugged away Joy's hand. "Final Intervention Nulling Intellectual Scope Humanely. Is that what you are referring to?"

"So, you have heard of it?" Joy folded her arms.

"Yes, but it is never employed. It's a myth. The PARC has made mistakes but has never set out to wipe someone's intellect on purpose." Bobbie stopped. She swallowed a bitter taste from her mouth as she realized it was no myth.

"You've got a lot to learn, big sis," Joy said with a steely confidence that scared Bobbie. "But the rest of us are a group who don't want to be forced to live in this society. We don't want to be constantly monitored and told to toe the line for the common good."

Once or twice after the Melter War, the idea of independence from Belus Corp had been floated by various rebellious fringe factions. The local populations, faced with the prospect of rebuilding from scratch without help, ignored the rebels whose ideas lost traction. The rebel groups faded away, never to be heard from again. To strike out on your own after Belus Corp had taken everyone through the war and provided care and support was considered by polite society to be a selfish notion. Some considered it treasonous. Bobbie had avoided people who talked of such things, and now, here was her own sister telling her... what? That she was a rebel, part of a splinter faction?

"But–" Bobbie began.

"It's not that we don't want to help society," Joy went on as if she'd been able to read Bobbie's mind. Maybe she had. Nothing would surprise Bobbie right now.

Joy continued with evangelistic excitement. "There are rules in *Belus Land* that we cannot live by. The Dependency Law is outrageous. We want to choose how we reproduce and when. The planet can support a larger population better now than it ever could. We need children. We need to rebuild the population after the Melters took so many of us."

Bobbie nodded. This was one area they agreed upon.

"Let's lay judgment aside," Hicks said. "Tell us what you've got, and how can we move forward in our plan."

Bobbie said nothing. Something about Joy's attitude reminded her of that rascal in Gracie that had been the yin to Bobbie's sensible yang. That indiscernible thing that had made Bobbie complete but had been stripped away when she'd lost Gracie, to live alone in a boring world full of rules and regulations. Those very rules and regulations had gotten them through a war that had ended all wars but had left Bobbie wooden and unbending in her approach to life. She was now realizing that if she didn't flex a little, she'd snap in two and be no good to anyone.

"Have you any lab facilities?" Bobbie asked.

"Not a lot, only some basic equipment we've managed to scrounge up."

"Or steal?" Hicks said.

Joy ignored him. "That's where you come in, Jimmy."

The old man pursed his lips, saying nothing. Bobbie marveled at his silence, at how he seemed to absorb all the information without commentary.

"So, you were interviewing him back there," Bobbie said.

Joy nodded and gave a contrite little grimace.

"I wondered why all the questions," Bobbie said. She halted and peered at Joy. "Are there members of your group watching us through your foureyes now?"

"Yep, give 'em a wave." Joy smiled. "One of the group already knows Jimmy, and the council has been considering recruiting him for a while. You will be surprised at who some of the founders are." Her smile faded. She added hastily, "But we'll get to that later. We are happy to have a man with your expertise." Joy turned to Bobbie and took her hand. "And, of course, two doctors on board will really help the group in general."

On board? What the hell did that mean? Would she have to ditch her old life? Leave the hospital and scratch out an existence with these dissidents? One thing at a time, she told herself.

"How many of you are there?" Hicks asked.

"About fifty."

Jimmy sagged a little against the wall. He looked tired.

"And John, the guy you brought to Mum's wake," Bobbie said. "Is he one of them?"

"Yes," Joy said.

"How do you survive? What do people eat there?" Jimmy asked.

"We've some gardens started, simple farms. No matter streamers. We're aiming to be self- sufficient eventually, but until then, I bring them additional supplies." Joy smiled.

"That's where you were when I thought you were playing neuro-games... when Mum died?" Bobbie's heart constricted. She'd been so judgmental.

Joy nodded and lowered her head, letting her hair fall forward.

"But how can you fly over the scorch zone?" Hicks asked.

"We head out over Greenland, over Baffin Bay, follow the sea passage across the remote North Canadian Islands to the Beaufort Sea. We stop in Nome, Alaska, refuel there, stock up..."

"... and then fly down over the Pacific and in from the coast?" Bobbie cut in as the pieces fell into place.

"Yup!" Joy said. "It's a hot 160 miles from the Pacific coast, but if you go fast enough, you get to the cool patch before the engines overheat and fail."

"Unbelievable," Bobbie murmured.

"Oh, believe it, sis." Joy rocked back on her heels and folded her arms, nodding and looking very proud of herself.

"Were you planning ongoing off-grid too?" Bobbie asked, fighting down a rush of unwelcome emotion that burned her chest.

"Bobbie, I wasn't going to abandon you," Joy said gently. "Besides, I have stuff to do here."

No-one asked what stuff. Bobbie didn't want to know right now. She swallowed, her throat so dry, it hurt. "Okay, but if we do this thing, if we go get Granny, how can we return to work? The people in charge of this conspiracy, Slade, or whoever it is, are going to know I'm responsible. I have to go off-grid too. But Hicks, you don't. You can't give up your life. What about your parents?"

Hicks curled his fingers around his chin in a gesture that Bobbie knew well. He always did that when he was thinking hard. She might be able to walk away from her job, her life—but leave Hicks?

"What about Davitt?" Joy asked.

Guilt flushed through Bobbie.

"Perhaps I can come back for him? When the dust settles?" Bobbie asked.

Joy hesitated, chewing on her lip. "We'd have to see how it plays out, Bobbie."

"I need a chance to explain–" *Explain what? That I'd chosen an aging relative over him and my leaving him was not his fault?*

"Do you love him?" Hicks asked without meeting her eyes.

"It's complicated." Bobbie stared at Hicks.

"Always is." Hicks's calm gray eyes found hers, his expression guarded. He broke eye contact and looked at Joy instead. Was he trying to tell her he loved her sister, thirteen years his junior? Was he still clueless that that was more complicated for Bobbie than Hicks realized?

Losing Davitt would sting but going without Hicks was going to be bad.

She pulled all her strength together and said to Hicks, "Go back to the hospital. They need you. Joy and I can handle finding and rescuing Granny, with Jimmy's backup, of course."

Jimmy nodded sagely. Bobbie couldn't trust herself to say anything else for now. The thought of going off-grid to join Joy's group terrified her. She felt like she was balanced on the edge of a precipice. Jump, and she'd never recapture that humdrum life she had so carefully crafted.

Hicks had always been the point at the center of her compass, the place of origin where everything she knew led back to. Bobbie's compass needle had spun off its pivot. Everything was back to front, like the ghost images from staring at a picture on an intewall too long before looking at a pale screen. Now Joy was the one who knew what was happening—was taking charge—and she, Bobbie, was the kid, grappling to catch up and make sense of the planet.

A hand warmed her shoulder. Hicks had a hand on Joy's shoulder too. Tears streamed down Joy's face. She had always cried with abandon. Bobbie wished she could do that too, but if she started, she'd end up howling at the moon.

"You two are as much my family as my parents. You are my life. If you go off-grid and leave me here..." Hicks paused with a tortured look. "There's nothing for me here without you guys. Christ almighty!" He looked at Bobbie. "You're my best friend. I can't bail now when you need me most."

She tried to speak, but the words choked her up. Joy flung her arms around his neck, sobbing, "Oh, Ryan. Thank you. Thank you."

He rocked her and whispered, "It's okay." His eyes met Bobbie's over Joy's head.

Bobbie watched them embrace. If their love kept her best friend close to her, then she could find it in her heart to be happy for them. His friendship was as crucial to her as oxygen. Losing him after a failed romantic relationship or after an unreciprocated declaration of her feelings would be more painful. He was part of her, and she'd take whatever he could offer.

"Joy, you managed to go back and forth. Can we do that? Not for work, of course, but could Hicks visit his folks?" Bobbie said.

"I can mask his biometrics. We'll have to do that anyway for all three of you and Granny when we get her," Joy said.

"Hicks," Bobbie had to ask once more. "Are you sure?"

His steady gray eyes locked into hers, like a docking station for her soul.

"Absolutely, wouldn't miss it for the world."

So be it.

"Joy," Bobbie said, thinking out loud, "Do you think there's any way we can get our hands on the medical staff from the research centers findings? That would give us a jump start."

"I'll see what I can do. Jimmy, can you help me pull up schematics?" Joy's fingers began tapping together, her gaze distant.

"I wondered how long we'd go without a revolution," Jimmy said, at last, pushing off the wall and taking a few steps toward the parking area. "I'm so glad I didn't miss it." He smiled at Joy, his mustache tucking up at the corners. "I kept the *back door* open for just such an occasion. Machine code is still how machines talk, right?"

"Sure is!" Joy grinned and fell into step beside him.

"Cool bananas—I'm practically fluent!" Jimmy clapped his hands together once then rubbed the palms together.

"You coded too?" Hicks sounded surprised. He and Bobbie walked beside Joy at Jimmy's snail-pace.

"Sure did," Jimmy said. "Computers were a hobby for the likes of us engineering nerds. All the degrees had '… and Computer Science' tagged on, even Animal Husbandry." Jimmy snorted a laugh and wagged a finger in the air. "You'll be glad you brought me along."

* * *

Bobbie blinked her *knock* and stood at the door of Detective Cross's apartment. The intepanels lining the hall glowed half-heartedly, casting a dim gray light, fading to darkness where the motion sensors did not trigger them. She looked at Hicks who stood silently beside her and shrugged.

"She told me to come right away," Bobbie said. "I said I'd be right here."

While the four of them had been solidifying their plans to leave that night to rescue Granny, Bobbie had gotten a blink from Cross, indicating she had information about Justin's DNA. Bobbie had considered telling Cross everything about the kidnapping of the Rejuvenees but had yet to figure a way to do that without breaking the NDA Slade had forced her to sign.

Well if we all skip to the scorch zone that's not really going to matter now is it?

Bobbie and Hicks waited for Cross to answer her door.

"Did she answer your blink?" Hicks asked as the seconds stretched into a minute.

Bobbie shook her head. A bad feeling fermented in the pit of her stomach.

Joy had stayed in the hovervan having dropped Bobbie and Hicks at the dock for the external door to Cross's apart. The plan was for Joy to bring Jimmy to his place to pick up some supplies and for Bobbie to summon her hovercar to pick her and Hicks up from Cross's apartment. They wouldn't be on their own though—Joy was patched into Bobbie's eye cam-di through the foureyes b-app. Joy could also speak directly to Bobbie and Hicks, which made them both jump when she said, "I can hack the door open if you like."

"I think we should," Bobbie said, her skin stiff with goosebumps. "Something's wrong."

The door in front of them slid back. Bobbie slunk in looking all around her so Joy could see as much as possible.

Bobbie called out, "Hello?" making Hicks jump and fling her a shriveling look.

"Detective Cross, are you here?" Hicks called.

The silence simmered. Bobbie looked at Hicks. He shrugged.

They moved down a hallway that had two closed doors to their left. A door on the right was ajar and opened into a bathroom that housed a toilet and washbasin. Motion-activated intepanels flickered on, casting a pale-yellow glow. The light behind them stayed on but faded in intensity. The end of the hall led into a living room big enough for a love seat and a large desk in the corner, positioned out from the wall so the person sitting at it could look out over the room.

For a split second, Bobbie thought no-one was in the room. Just as she was about to investigate the closed doors in the hallway, her eyes picked out a hand on the floor, sticking out from behind the desk.

"Oh, no," Bobbie whispered. A prickling sensation crept over her scalp. The chair was back against the wall. She moved further into the room with Hicks on her heels.

Joy inhaled in a sharp hiss in Bobbie's ear as they both saw the detective lying on her side.

"Oh, no! It's Cross," Bobbie said, recognizing the stocky figure on the floor, with the gray crewcut. Rivulets of blood trickled from Cross's ears and nose. Her lips were pressed together in a grimace, her jaws clamped closed. Bobbie knew the detective was dead by the vacant bloodshot eyes that stared past them as if perpetually reading blinks. The right eye protruded from the socket.

"Taser," Hicks pointed at the rectangular device in her left hand.

"She popped the medulla biosensor alright," Bobbie said, pointing to a large purple blemish under the skin at the back of Cross's neck. "Don't touch anything until I get a recording." Bobbie scanned the room again, the muscles from her neck to her shoulders as taut as steel cables. The doors in the hall stayed closed, but what if someone were in there, waiting for them? Past those doors was the only way out. Bobbie's eyes flicked back to the Taser.

"What the hell?" Joy asked.

"We've seen this MO before," Hicks said softly. "The elderly uses this technique to commit suicide when they don't qualify for Elective Passing. Typically, when one of their descendants gets pregnant and they want to make way for the new baby. This method of suicide is fast and painless and leaves little mess."

"Jesus Christ," Joy said. "But how can a Taser kill? Aren't they only supposed to subdue someone?"

"Supposed to," Hicks agreed. "The standard police Taser settings are set to incapacitate, but with some adjustments, a Taser can deliver enough charge to explode the circuit in the biosensor in the medulla oblongata resulting in instant death."

"We should get out of here quick," Bobbie whispered, "Joy, can you save this footage?" Bobbie inspected the burn wound on Cross's upper left arm, where the Taser had been applied. She zeroed in on the bruising at the base of the detective's neck where a purple stain oozed out beneath the skin from under the gray crewcut, then at the eyes, nose and ears, and finally at the Taser still clenched in the dead woman's left hand.

"Absolutely but, well, holy shit!" Joy said. "Why would the cop want to kill herself?"

"She didn't," Bobbie said. "Her death was no suicide."

CHAPTER 19

Bobbie reached down and pried the Taser from Cross's clawed fingers.

"Wait! What are you doing?" Hicks said. "We can't disturb a crime scene."

"Someone killed her," Bobbie said, looking down the hall past the closed doors to which led to their only exit. "They could be still around. I want a weapon." She thumbed the setting to sting, stepped back from the body and faced Hicks. "We should go."

The display, set into the desk's surface, was closed down, without Cross's passwords. There was no way to access her computer to look for the DNA report. Slowly, they backed away from the body. Bobbie glanced anxiously over her shoulder at the closed doors, wishing she had opened them as they'd passed by. Her palms dampened with sweat as she held the Taser ready, just in case. Having never so much as slapped anyone in her life, she did not feel equipped to confront a killer, Taser, or no Taser.

"Joy, could someone else have sent that message asking me to come here and made it look like Cross sent it?" Bobbie asked, her mind clicking through possibilities. Was someone trying to frame her for the detective's death? Was this Slade?

"It's a possibility," Joy cut in on audio. "Can you tell when Cross died?"

"Hard to tell the time of death. That hemorrhaging at the base of her skull took at least an hour to develop—depending on where the medulla biosensor was placed and oriented," Hicks said.

"So, anywhere between one and three hours. Hmmm, I got her message..." Bobbie checked her blink. "An hour before we found the body."

"If someone is framing you, why try to make the death look like a suicide?" Hicks asked in a low voice. His eyes rested on the closed doors. Bobbie guessed he didn't want to spook her. Too late for that. Hicks went to step between her and the closed doors, but Bobbie held up the Taser, mimed a shush with her lips, and made a rolling motion with hand - keep going, let them think we aren't aware they may be in there - if indeed they were.

"To cover their own asses, in case I didn't take the bait?" Bobbie said, talking in what she hoped was a normal voice. "Regardless—we need to get out of here now."

They scurried down the hall, pressed against the wall opposite the closed doors. Bobbie clenched the Taser ready to spring should either of the doors open as they skittered past. If the doors opened, what could they do, doctors against trained killers? Even untrained killers would be more than a match for them. Never in her worst nightmares had Bobbie faced a more terrifying moment. Once they moved past the doors, which mercifully remained closed, they strode down the corridor just short of breaking into a run. Bobbie could breathe freely once they'd left the apartment, but her nerves jangled as they wound their way out of the warren of corridors in the apartment complex.

"Can we check surveillance?" Hicks asked Joy.

"On it," Joy's voice said in Bobbie's ear.

"And can you leave the door exactly as you found it, Joy? Taking the Taser will blow a hole in the suicide theory if that's what the murderer intended and hoped to get away with."

"How can you be so sure it was murder?" Joy asked.

"She had the Taser in her left hand," Bobbie said, spotting the exit door to the apartment block that led to the dock Joy had dropped them off at earlier, and nudged Hicks toward it.

"So?" Hicks asked.

Bobbie shoved the exit door to the building, and Hicks reached over her head to hold the door for her as they left the building. The damp evening air smelled of decaying leaves. "Hang on… I blinked my car to come and pick us it, it should be here any second. Ah, there it is."

The drone of an engine grew louder. The car slowed and stopped at the dock. They tumbled in as fast as they could. Using her ONIV, Bobbie directed the self-drive to take off.

"My place is too risky. We should get out of Armagh." Bobbie settled back in her seat. "Joy, let's meet at Jimmy's apartment in the Buckets. At least we know the building well, more witnesses, less chance of whoever killed Cross having a go at us there. And I want to pick up some supplies, maybe something to sedate Gloria. Joy, where are you?"

The car lifted into the air with a whine of engines powering them away. They left the City of Armagh behind, its Cathedral spires puncturing the low hanging cloud that reflected the city lights.

"I'm leaving your place now," Joy said. "I grabbed some things for you, a change of clothes, your rain gear, and hiking stuff. I also stocked up from your matter streamer storage."

"Good job. And Jimmy?"

"Heading for his place too," Joy said.

"Right, see you guys there, but stay tuned, okay?" Bobbie looked out her window at the other traffic flitting about the evening sky to see if she might spot Joy. They weren't too far apart, but Bobbie couldn't see her van as they plunged into the mist.

"So how do you know Cross didn't commit suicide?" Joy prompted.

"The Taser was in her left hand when it was fired," Bobbie explained. "Since that type of shock makes the muscles contract, she wouldn't have been able to let go of the weapon. The burn marks were on her upper left arm. It's pretty hard to touch that spot on your arm with something in the same hand."

"It's like trying to scratch your left elbow with your left hand," Hick added.

"Cross was already holding her Taser, so she must have felt threatened," Bobbie said.

"Or been forced to hold it." Hicks frowned.

"Possibly." Bobbie nodded.

"We'll never know." Joy sighed. "I checked. The security camera footage from the corridor outside Cross's apartment is deleted for that timestamp."

Hicks gave Bobbie a grim look.

"And we'll never know what she saw in that DNA report." Bobbie felt bleak. Nothing was working out for them. She'd never intended to involve Cross. *All I wanted was a fair trial to prove that Justin had raped Miley. But now did justice matter? Justin and Cross were dead.*

"I'll see if I can lift something from her computer," Joy's voice chimed in.

"Brilliant," Bobbie said with enthusiasm she didn't feel. She glanced across at the cars navigation system. "We'll arrive at Jimmy's in a few minutes."

"Bobbie, is there anything else you want from your place?" Joy asked. "You know, keepsakes, anything of sentimental value? It's just..."

Joy didn't finish. Bobbie knew she would never be back in her apartment. Ever.

How do you pick out the most important items in your life at the drop of a hat and flee?

"Just get out, Joy and we'll see you at Jimmy's."

* * *

As soon as Bobbie and Hicks arrived at Jimmy's apartment Joy pulled her to one side saying, "Jimmy needs to rest. I need to recharge the back battery in the hovervan and one of you needs to grab medical supplies." Joy pointed at Bobbie. "Which one of you is supposed to be on duty now."

Bobbie opened her mouth to protest that she'd never leave the hospital when she was on duty, then realized she would be leaving forever—without notice—once they found Granny.

Hicks answered, "I'm on duty in an hour but being early won't raise suspicions. I'll go."

"I'm not on duty until the morning. And I think Slade has me under surveillance of what happened to Cross is anything to go by," Bobbie said. "I'll stay here with Jimmy. But please, be quick and stay safe."

Bobbie and Jimmy waited in his dimly lit apartment at the bottom of Subscraper One. Bobbie stared out into the gloomy ocean. Once darkness had fallen, phosphorescence twinkled and sparked in random patterns.

Jimmy snored woolly purrs beside her. She wished she could calm her mind enough to doze off, but she couldn't feel safe until they were all together and on the way to the west coast of Ireland. Apparently, Jimmy planned to work the night through on some techie stuff from Joy's van once they set out, so Bobbie was glad he could rest now.

Perhaps, thought Bobbie, *she and Joy should have met Hicks somewhere else?* Somewhere more isolated than Seagahan Dam as Jimmy had easily found them. Who else might figure out they were working on Granny's case and where to find them? Maybe they should have gone to the top of Slieve Donard in the Mourne Mountains, like the time she'd met Joy and asked her to hack into Granny's foureyes. It was more isolated and farther away, but they'd had to come to the hospital for supplies, to steal supplies really, but no point in thinking about that now. Bobbie was an outlaw now… an outlaw! *How the hell had that happened?*

Regret about Davitt condensed and dripped through her. He'd be so confused about why she'd left him with no explanation. *Might he come looking for me?* Thankfully, Bobbie hadn't heard from him all day—some crisis at work he'd blinked yesterday, or perhaps the day before? She figured he must have his hands full. Good job. His distraction bought her some time before he reported her missing, alerting the authorities and no doubt Slade that she was up to something.

Two people had already died. So many more lives had changed completely. How would Granny ever come to terms with killing her old friend if she got her mind back? No, not if, when Bobbie corrected herself. How would Miley get over the treatment she'd suffered at Justin's hands? And poor Detective Cross—just doing her job, and now she was dead. If Bobbie hadn't interfered in the case and gathered the DNA from Justin's apartment and insisted that Cross test the samples, perhaps Cross would be alive. Now Hicks, Joy and Jimmy were all at risk because Bobbie had insisted on finding Granny and trying to cure her. What if she failed and all this was for nothing?

Bobbie could turn herself in and exonerate the others, explain how they'd found Cross dead. She'd have to confess to breaking the NDA, but they probably wouldn't subject her to correctional surgery straight off. Not if she was contrite enough and promised to change and take whatever therapy they offered. Maybe Bobbie could save the others, and maybe, just maybe, the authorities could fix granny and the Rejuvenees.

Bobbie stood up and strode to the glass wall. The growing darkness emboldened her reflection. Her red hair caught the light from the room, glowing back at her from the ocean like a mermaid ghost.

Outside, a large cod burst out of the blackness catching the light from the window. Bobbie looked through her reflection as the fish swam to the glass. Before it hit the window, the fish turned and swam away, swallowed up by the vast ocean, scattering ripples of phosphorescence. *Big fish eat little fish*, Bobbie thought, haunted by the image of Cross lying on the floor, her dead eyes vacant and staring. Had Slade and her lackeys killed Cross to hide Justin's DNA? Perhaps some other case had gotten the detective killed. Maybe her death was not Bobbie's fault. Slade had always been a bully. How far a stretch was murder for someone ruthless like that? In her bones, Bobbie felt that Slade was behind Cross's murder and had taken Granny and the others away.

I won't be a little fish!

Just then, the door opened, and Joy arrived in a flurry of black hair and fabric.

"I tried to find the report that Cross had on the DNA. Nada," Joy said, shaking her head.

"So, she didn't have the report, or it didn't tell you anything?" Bobbie asked.

"Nothing," Joy said. "Nothing at all. Every blink, every file all gone. As if Cross had never existed. Her biometric records are wiped. Whoever is behind this is thorough and high up."

A rod of ice slid down Bobbie's spine. *Was Slade this influential?*

"Ready to go?" Joy asked.

"Yes," Bobbie said. "Just waiting on Hicks."

"Found him, sent him to the van." Joy looked at the snoring Jimmy and tapped her fingers together.

The carebot Jimmy napped on moved toward the door. Jimmy jolted awake and made some guttural snorting noises as his body caught up.

"Hey!" Jimmy cried. "Bloody 'ell, I wish you wouldn't do that. Don't cut into my shit, girl, ya don't wanna start a hacking war with me."

Joy's dress changed from black to a muddy gray. She looked down at herself and held her hands up. "Cool bananas, old-timer, I'm impressed. You'll have to show me how you did that."

"Still working on how to turn sensorfabrik transparent," he said with a wink and rolled out the door past them.

"Dirty old bugger!" Joy said, following him out the door.

Bobbie left the apartment and blinked the door closed behind her, its swish a soft whisper of farewell. She'd miss visiting the Benthic residents, their eccentricities concentrated by time into quirks and characteristics that made her work more challenging and precious.

Bobbie and Jimmy followed Joy to the elevators and out into the carport. The entry hatches and windows interspersed along the walls yawned like cavernous mouths into the black abyss of the night. Harsh bright lighting cast a glare on the concrete interiors, throwing every crack and ripple into stark contrast. Bobbie usually parked in staff parking a floor above this one, but the layout was identical. Pedestrians accessed the parking area from corridors that fed from elevators in the center of the building past utility areas, fanning out like the spokes of a wheel. Each floor was divided into four sections so that the inside of each parking lot was a massive arc that stretched over one-quarter of the cross-section of the subscraper. Joy pointed at her van parked all the way over by the stairwell, so far away that Jimmy had to squint to see it.

"Send your car home," Joy said to Bobbie as they traversed the lot, taking a shortcut through one of the rows of vehicles lined up against charging stations. "The more normal and routine we look the longer it will be before they start looking for you." Joy stopped as she angled her body to squeeze between a unihover and a sedan version of Bobbie's Mercedes. Jimmy followed on his carebot.

"Does that thing have hover capabilities?" Joy asked, nodding at Jimmy's carebot.

"Of course, it has, but I ain't wasting the energy in a parking area—hover mode sucks the battery clean dry," Jimmy answered. "Go on. I'll go around."

Bobbie stayed with Jimmy, and Joy waited for them at the van. From the outside, Joy's hovervan looked like classic vintage-hippy. Bobbie expected the interior to be equally shabby. She knew Joy lived in the van and expected an old mattress on the floor amid a jumble of clothes and electronics, like the pigsty Joy's bedroom had always been at home.

The interior of the van looked more like office space than living space. A matter streamer and a recycler at the front end, the only evidence of food consumption on board. Joy stepped in, ducked her head at the doorway, and straightened up once inside. The vehicle was taller than Bobbie had thought—longer, larger than the old VWs she remembered from her childhood. Intepanels lined the inside. The floor glowed with soft gray lighting. *Why hadn't I ever gotten into Joy's van before?* Bobbie felt ashamed of herself. Hoping she'd not left her relationship with Joy founder too long, she vowed to do better.

"Joy, the van is amazing," Bobbie said. She took in the four adjustable chairs covered in sensorfabrik coded with an animation—bubbles, tinged with pink and mauve, flowed over the seats and popped when they met seams. The chairs, set up in a social configuration in a circle facing one another, similar to the ones she had in her own car, took up the front half of the van while a desk and counter space ran halfway along the side toward the back.

"You haven't seen the best of it yet." When Joy pressed a button, the intepanels displayed spidery red lines creeping across maps of the West Coast of Ireland.

"Plotting routes?" Jimmy's voice carried an edge of sarcasm. "My carebot can do that!"

"Gimme a sec," Joy said. As a section of the floor slid back, a lumpy gray fabric, six-foot square, emerged. The fabric sparked into life with bubble animations. "That area converts to a bed. Room enough for two. I'm afraid the other two will have to sleep in the chairs. They do recline a bit, but... well, it's the best I can offer." Joy waved her hand as if she were a sales rep showing off a product. The bed retracted.

"I'll take a seat," Jimmy said, shifting from his carebot to the chair and turning it around to face the dash. "I need to work - get us into the system."

"That panel," Joy continued, pointing at the back wall, "hides the ablutions station!" She grinned.

"So, you didn't need to hook up at my place?" Bobbie asked settling into the seat behind Jimmy. His reflection in the windscreen glass smiled at her. Bobbie could tell he was in his element.

Joy looked sheepish, "Actually, I was recycling for the California crew. Might as well get the credits for the matter streamer's input cargo. I couldn't tell you. But no, I didn't need to use the sani-disposals really, nor the shower. I have all mod cons all here."

She turned to Jimmy. "You might like this." She pressed a section on the intescreen in front of him. An image of an old-fashioned computer terminal appeared in front of him, complete with a vintage black screen and green text.

"Linux," Jimmy breathed as if saying the name of a long-lost lover.

Joy nodded, her eyes sparkling, "Yup. It's still the best way to talk to the machine."

"Cool bananas!" Jimmy maneuvered his chair in front of the intescreen keypad and began tapping. "Let's see if I can find Gloria." A dozen windows opened up around his main screen, filled with lines of code. "Cliffs of Moher, you said, right?"

"That's right," Bobbie said.

"That would be the Lislorcan Facility," Jimmy said and closed down all but four windows. "Gotta scan quickly. Once I can get in, I only have 45 seconds in each feed before we have to switch frequencies."

"When we get closer, you can access the facility's system locally," Joy said taking the seat beside him and turning it side on to Bobbie's seat. "Now where the hell is Hicks?" Joy murmured as if talking to herself. Her fingers flicked. Her eyes zoned out. "Oh, shit!" she spat, making Bobbie jump.

"What?" Adrenalin spiked through Bobbie.

"He's talking to someone, and it doesn't look friendly," Joy said. "Gimme a sec." She tapped at the panels on the countertop. "There we go."

A screen opened up on the wall of the van, showing Hicks from an elevated angle. A ceiling camera Bobbie guessed. Though she couldn't see her face, Bobbie recognized the black bob of the woman who stood between him and the door of the lab.

"Slade!" Bobbie cried. "What's she doing here?"

"You know that woman?" Joy asked.

"She's the chair of the medical board, the one who took Granny and the rest of our patients and made us sign the non-disclosure agreement." Bobbie leaned forward in her seat to get a better view. "She's probably the one who ordered Cross killed! My guess is that Slade knew Justin's DNA didn't match the database. Tell him to get out of there, Joy."

"I can't get through," Joy said. "His blink feed is blocked, and so is his eye cam-di. Dammit. Slade's people must be doing that."

"Shit! They must know we're here," Bobbie said. "It's just a matter of time until they find us."

They watched Hicks shaking his head while holding a gray, polyexoskel medical case to his chest. Slade stepped closer to him, pointing at the case. Her body language oozed anger.

"What the hell are they talking about?" Joy said. "Agh! I wish I had audio." She flicked her fingers and punched commands into the panels in front of her, but nothing happened. "Dammit!"

"Slade's a devious bitch. I bet you she's trying to get him to tell her what we're planning," Bobbie said. "Hopefully, she doesn't know that he's stealing from the hospital, but if she figures it out, she'll have no qualms about raising the alarm. Our blinks are blocked, but hers won't be. We need to get him out of there,"

"I got this," Jimmy said. "Our blinks might be blocked, but there are other systems they probably won't be monitoring."

He typed in some commands and then clicked his fingers and thumbs together as if pounding out Morse Code. Bobbie watched the screen feeling like she would scream from frustration. She couldn't do a thing to help Hicks, who was gesturing with one hand and holding the case in the other. He tried to step around Slade, but she stayed between him and the door.

"For Christ's sake, just push her out of the way!" Bobbie said. Hicks towered above Slade. Shoving her aside would be easy for him if he wasn't so damn chivalrous.

"So far, the hallways are empty," Joy said as more security feeds popped up on the wall. "Thank God it's so late at night. Easy to see the approaches."

"He knows we're at the van, and he knows which bay we're in," Jimmy said. "He'll come straight here once he gets away from her, but he can't lift a hand to her, or security will have a legal cause to detain him."

"I don't think they're too worried about legal cause," Joy said.

"Let's not burn bridges where we don't need to," Jimmy said. "Ah, now, we're in business."

A carebot appeared at the door of the room where Hicks and Slade stood, then moved into the space behind Slade and nudged her. Another carebot materialized alongside her, corralling her against the wall, it gave Hicks enough room to skirt out past Slade.

With one hand up, as if to apologize, Slade pushed the machines, but they were too heavy for her to move. Realizing she was trapped; Slade thumped her fist down on one.

"The machine's probably citing Protocol 57 at her," Bobbie said. All three of them scrunched in closer to the screen.

"I think she may have broken that protocol, if my lip reading's up to speed," Joy said with a snort.

Bobbie watched with black satisfaction as Slade told the carebots where to go, resulting in a barrage of flashing lights from the offended machines.

"Nice one, Jimmy!" Joy bumped fists with him.

In a second feed, Hicks sprinted to the stairwell. *Smart,* thought Bobbie, *an elevator could trap you too easily.*

"Oh, shit," Joy said. "Look! The eastside corridor."

Two large men armed with guns strode down the hall. Guns! Bobbie hadn't seen a real one since the war. According to Belus Corp, society did not need them. She didn't know what kind of weapons they were or what they shot. Bullets, lasers, high-frequency audio pulses, it didn't matter—all had one goal; to maim or kill humans.

By now, the men were on the other side of the building, less than a half-mile away. In a few minutes, they'd reach the carport and be within shooting distance.

"Go!" Bobbie yelled. "Now!"

"We can't leave Hicks," Joy said, her face ashen.

"We won't, trust me," Bobbie said. "They'll come through that door." She pointed through the front windshield at an entrance in the recesses of the carport. "Hicks is coming out of that staircase at about the same time." The stairwell, on the other side of the huge concrete space, was opposite a six-feet-square opening in the carport exterior walls that let the air in and fumes out. "How good's your manual driving?"

"Oh, pretty proficient!" Joy said, tapping out some commands. The side flap folded down, encapsulating them. The van lifted off and maneuvered toward the black square of the main exit.

It was almost midnight, and they were the only traffic, but Bobbie held her breath until they were clear of the main exit. Away from the harsh artificial lighting, their eyes adjusted. A gibbous moon hung in the sky, for the moment unobscured by clouds, casting a silver sheen over the water below. They headed left, toward the block of light pouring out of the side of the building through the vent, and hovered.

"Hang on," Joy said. With a push of a button, the side of the van slid open. Wind tore at them through the opening.

Heartbeat racing, Bobbie watched the door of the stairwell through the vent. The screen in the van showed her the position of the armed men. Any second now, the men would reach the entrance to the carport. The housing of the stairwell stood between them and Hicks's exit door. They wouldn't see Hicks at first, but they would spot the van hovering outside the vent opening. Hicks would have to run into their line of sight, their line of fire, to get to the van.

Hurry Hicks, hurry!

Fear-fueled impatience gnawed at her. The wind caught and tipped the van, giving her a glimpse of steel-gray waves nipped into white tips and skittering off in all directions twenty feet below. Bobbie broke into a sweat.

"There he is!" Joy said, sounding the horn.

Hicks sprinted to the edge of the vent, head moving as he appeared to judge the distance from where he stood to the van.

"Jump!" Bobbie yelled above the wind.

"What the fuck?" he roared back.

"They're coming!" Bobbie shouted. Two men burst through the entrance at the rear of the carport, about a hundred yards away. They looked around the carport, spotted Bobbie in the van, and broke into a run.

"Can you get closer, Joy?" Panic sent Bobbie's heart into overdrive.

The gap between the van and the vent closed to about six feet.

"Go lower," Bobbie said to Joy. "Let gravity help him." She hoped it didn't help him too much. A fall from this high into the water wouldn't kill him but fishing him out would cause a delay long enough for men with guns to shoot.

The running men raised their weapons. Muzzles flashed. A series of high-pitched whizzes echoed around the building. Hicks flinched and ducked.

Bobbie screamed, "Jump!"

Hicks flung the case into the van. It whacked off Bobbie's armrest and clattered to the floor. Another round of shots split the surrounding air. Hicks stepped up, using one foot to launch himself, and dove through the vent. His upper body sprawled on the floor of the van, his legs dangling over the water. He began sliding backward. Bobbie grabbed his hands and heaved. Hicks wriggled and kicked his way into the van, as more shots sounded. The side door closed, and Joy applied power to the engines racing the van away from the subscraper. For a second, Bobbie and Hicks lay there, his weight pressing down on her, his nose nearly touching hers, his breathing heavy and warm on her face. She panted, struggling to control her breathing.

"Maybe I should have taken swim lessons," he said, rolling off her.

"You can't swim?" Bobbie said, sitting up and smoothing down her tunic, her heart still hammering. "How did I not know that?"

"Subject never came up," Hicks said. "Until jumping from a subscraper into a hovervan twenty feet above the ocean made it relevant."

Despite Hicks's banter, Bobbie noticed a tremor in his hands. Hers shook too.

"Who were those guys?" Hicks asked.

"We don't know, but I'm guessing they're connected to Slade. What's the story there?"

"She wanted to know if we knew where Granny was. She's accusing you of kidnapping her and the others," Hicks said. "Seems like she's not responsible for taking them."

"So, if she's not," Bobbie said with a mixture of fear and confusion, "Who the hell is?"

"Never mind that," Joy cried, as the van dipped to the left before righting itself. "We've been hit. Hicks, you might regret not learning how to swim!"

CHAPTER 20

Joy's fingers flew over panels. "Strap in," she said, without looking up. "We still have some upward thrust. I can probably make it as far as Cave Hill. But it's gonna be a hard landing."

Bobbie grappled along the edges of her chair, not sure where the seatbelt was. Self-drivers were so safe, it rendered them almost obsolete. Her searching fingers found her seatbelt, and she strapped in. As Hicks fumbled with his, he swore under his breath. If they hit the water, she'd have to grab him and help him stay afloat. The thought petrified her, and judging by his pallor, terrified Hicks too.

Bobbie's stomach lurched as the hovervan plummeted and then pulled up only to drop once more before steadying out.

In the front seat, Jimmy poured over the readouts on the panels. Bobbie felt helpless. She'd succumbed to the magic of technology without questioning how it performed, whereas Joy made the digital world bend to her will. They were in Joy's hands now as she pummeled commands into the van's control systems.

"Set down in thirty seconds," Joy shouted. "Brace!"

Bobbie clung to her armrests as the van landed with a jarring thud.

They'd made it.

Bobbie was about to undo her seatbelt when the van angled to the right with a metallic crunch, flinging her against the restraints as the van tipped sideways. She felt pressure in her head.

Hicks swore through clenched teeth. A kaleidoscope of distant lights, clouds, and blackness slid past the windscreen.

They were upside down.

The shoulder strap dug into Bobbie's neck. The vehicle creaked. Tinny rattles and thuds told of small loose objects landing in new places. She slid askew in her seat, twisted by the battle between gravity and the seatbelt. Then they were sideways again. More pings as unfastened debris ricocheted around the inside of the cabin. Hair fell in a tumble around her face. Clutching the armrests didn't help, but she hung on anyway, afraid to move. Outside the window, the world hung on its side. Momentum carried the van all the way over to rest the right way up again. She shook her face free of her hair.

Bobbie remembered to breathe. She looked out the window. Despite the roll, the headlamps shone, lighting up a slope—thankfully with a gentle gradient—otherwise, they'd have kept turning over all the way back to the ocean. Joy had put them down on a flattened section of Cave Hill, the first dry land rising from the sea a couple of miles from the Buckets and the gunmen. By some miracle, they'd landed in one piece. Relief didn't counteract Bobbie's adrenaline.

Joy flicked off the headlamps. The outside world disappeared, replaced by the black reflective rectangle of the windshield.

Dim overhead lights glowed inside the cabin. The hard-metallic case Hicks had taken from the hospital had slid along the walls and ceiling with the roll but hadn't hit anyone nor seemed to have damaged any of the controls.

"Is everyone okay?" Bobbie asked.

"Yes," Joy said, looking around with wide eyes.

"That was some landing, girl!" Jimmy said. He unbuckled his seatbelt and tweaked the corners of his mustache with steady fingertips.

Bobbie looked over at Hicks. His eyes were scrunched shut, and his jaw muscles flexed.

"You okay?" she asked, releasing her seatbelt.

Hick's face was gray. He held up his right hand, covered in blood. "They nicked my side."

It took Bobbie a moment to realize what he was saying.

Hicks had been shot!

Bobbie sprang from her chair. Blood, already drying to a crispy rust thanks to the sensorfabrik, had wicked all the way up to his armpit and into his trousers as far down as his knee. She lifted his shirt.

Hicks hissed through clenched teeth. A flap of skin gaped outwards from his side. Blood oozed.

Bobbie could see that the underlying tissue looked intact, his organs safe below the abdominal wall. The rush of adrenalin during his dive into the van must have masked the pain—until now.

"It's a straight through and through," Bobbie told Hicks, in doctor mode, steady and reassuring. "I can clean the wound. Did you bring wound glue in the case?"

Hicks grunted, "Yeh."

"You'll be fine," Bobbie said. "You know how fast this stuff heals, but you're going into shock."

"No, no," Hicks stammered. "I'll be okay in a minute." He tried to wave her away as she took his pulse.

Hicks flinched and then surrendered. His pulse was thready. His skin felt clammy to touch. Every muscle in his body seemed to be trembling. His teeth chattered.

"We've got some synthetic blood in the case. That will tide you over. You'll be good as new in a few hours." Bobbie wondered if they had that much time before the gunmen caught up with them. Her hands worked to open the case and find the supplies she needed. "I need to keep him warm. We should put him into the bed."

Joy turned from the control panel. "Okay. I need to disguise the van so they can't find us. I'd imagine it won't take them long to get mobile. Can you manage for a minute more?"

"Sure." Bobbie felt sick at the thought of the gunmen catching up. Her head spun. Granny's abduction, Cross's murder, their fleeing from the men at the hospital, all seemed like a bad dream. But the slick blood on her hands made the danger real. Bobbie reverted to doctor mode, *deal with what's in front of you and worry about the rest later.* Sterilizing the wound with the portable sani-aid her fingers found the wound glue.

"This will sting," she said, squeezing glue into the wound.

Hicks hissed as she pieced the edges of skin back together. Sweat beaded on his forehead and upper lip.

Bobbie suppressed a desire to hug him.

Joy pulled up the bed and helped Bobbie settle him in before turning her attention back to the damaged vehicles systems. Bobbie applied a patch impregnated with pain relief which would be absorbed into his skin.

"The pain meds will help you sleep." Of course, Hicks already knew that, but as a doctor, Bobbie had her script.

Hicks's eyes closed, and his pulse steadied. Color rose in his cheeks, driving the grayness away. When his breathing deepened, Bobbie lifted his shirt again to check the wound. Neat and clean, it had stopped bleeding.

"Is he okay?" Jimmy asked. He and Joy had kept working at the controls, pouring over the van's engine schematics, working their magic as Bobbie had been working her own.

"He'll be nearly as good as new when he wakes up," Bobbie said. "The wound glue should bond in the next half an hour or so. The injury will be tender, but he'll be able to move about."

"Nice work, Doc," Jimmy said. "We can't afford to be a man down."

"And what about the van?" Bobbie asked.

"There's damage to the engine management system. That's why we lost power," Joy said. "But the roll shouldn't have done much other than dent a few of the outside panels. At least that's how it was the last time."

"The last time?" Bobbie wasn't sure she wanted to know.

Joy shrugged. "The van's not great at landing on uneven surfaces in a hurry."

"Ah-ha!" Jimmy put his finger on the on-screen schematics. "Conduits damaged. Right there."

"Can you fix it?" Bobbie asked.

"You betcha," Jimmy said, getting up slowly, lacing his fingers together and stretching his arms out in front of him. "I take it you have insulation tape and pliers in your tool kit, Joy?"

"Sure," Joy said, looking over his shoulder. "Wow." She whistled. "Lucky! The shot missed the circuit boards. Better get that bandaged up too." Joy directed a smile at Hicks and caught Bobbie's eye.

Bobbie held her gaze, letting her expression soften as she nodded slowly.

Joy and Jimmy went outside to find the broken conduit. Lucky, Joy had said.

Lucky?

Bobbie realized that she agreed. Sure, they were the first people to have been shot at since the war, at least the first she'd heard of. They'd almost crashed into the Irish Sea in the dead of night. Hicks was injured. The van was broken, but they were lucky they'd gotten away at all.

From their position near the top of Cave Hill, the closest island to the subscrapers, Bobbie could see the lights of the three buildings that made up the Buckets about two miles offshore, a shamrock of winking lights. The structures seemed closer in the way that light and sound at night play tricks on the senses. Bobbie felt a tug of fondness for the place where she'd worked for the past ten years. Would she ever see the Buckets again? Or Cave Hill? The mountain whose outline resembled the profile of a man's face, as familiar to her as a person, a face she'd seen every day as she had traveled back and forth from work. Her mother had loved to take them hiking on Cave Hill.

The lights blurred. Bobbie wiped her eyes. As her vision cleared, she saw flashes of red, like sparks traveling through the night sky—vehicles of all kinds zipping from one place to another, the world busy with its own agenda. Joy had masked the electronic emissions from the van, but they would have to be gone by first light, or they'd be visible to the eye.

Hicks snored burred buzzes from the bed. Bobbie sat in the chair nearest to him. The soft panel lights flickered, and bubble animations cast gently edged shadows across the ceiling. Bobbie was on the brink of drifting off when a flush of anxiety jerked her awake. Time was slipping away from them. An hour had passed. She listened to Joy and Jimmy outside unscrewing panels and chatting as they worked.

Someone dropped something that clanged its way through machine parts against a backdrop of expletives. A little while later, Bobbie heard them give a subdued cheer, and she hoped they had fixed whatever wire they'd needed to. Then: more clanging and metal scraping and swearing.

Hurry, Bobbie urged them on silently. They had to reach Granny. Get her away from those who seemed intent on using her.

Bobbie gazed over at Hicks. His features relaxed in sleep, handsome and peaceful. She needed to let Hicks rest enough to make some inroads to recovery. If nothing else, they needed his help and expertise. She needed more than that from him, but if he loved Joy... He'd always be in Bobbie's life and for that, she was grateful.

The front cab door opened. Joy climbed in, turned around, and held out a hand for Jimmy. He clambered in panting, his wispy white hair disheveled, but he glowed with success. His mustache twitched, and he rubbed his nose, smearing a black mark across his face.

Joy and Jimmy settled into the front seats and poured over the intepanels on the dashboard.

"Good as new." Whistling through his teeth, Jimmy typed in some commands, and the engine powered up, rattling and clunking. The soft glowing intepanels lights intensified then flickered. They came back on but not to their full brightness. Some display sections didn't come on. Bobbie threw a worried glance in Joy's direction.

"It's only superficial damage," Joy said. "Technically, we don't need half of this control panel—it's a self-drive car.

"You betcha." Jimmy chuckled. "If we leave now, we can be at the cliffs of Moher in half an hour."

The van lifted with a jerky stutter that made Bobbie grab for her seat belt.

"We're good," Joy said. Their momentum smoothed out. "Ordinarily, it would take me about twenty minutes to fly to the west coast from here but I want to take it a little more slowly this time, fly lower to keep out of traffic streams, less chance of being seen by any surveillance systems."

"So how long d'you reckon," Bobbie asked.

"An hour tops." Joy gave Bobbie a smile. "It will be grand. We'll get Granny and be on our way within a couple of hours."

A rustling from the bed made them all turn their heads. Slowly, Hicks sat up, looking disheveled. Dried blood crackled the sensorfabrik into a myriad of creases all down his right side.

"How d'you feel?" Bobbie asked.

Gingerly he poked the site of the wound. "Not bad." He smiled. "Not bad at all, I just–"

"Really don't want to swim?" Joy interrupted.

"Yeah." He chuffed a little laugh and winced. "Something like that. So, what's the plan?"

"Are you up to a little hiking?" Bobbie asked.

"I think I can manage." Hicks worked his shoulders in circles, stretching out the kinks in his neck.

"We can't just drive up to the research facility's front door," Bobbie said. "We need to get dropped off about a mile away and walk-in. Jimmy, you stay with the van. Are you going through Granny's ONIV archives?"

"Yep," Jimmy said, "Looking for any regular communications about her condition. If I spot anything suspicious, I'll forward the blinks to you."

"Thanks," Bobbie said, stretching forward and giving his shoulder a squeeze. "Can you keep in touch with us all the way? Let us know if she's still sleeping?"

"Only up to the gate. Once you are inside the compound, our blinks will be blocked." Jimmy's carebot trundled to him from where he'd stowed it in the back. Jimmy unfastened a small side panel in the carebot and pulled out four plastic cuboids attached to thin black cabling with little bulbs on each end.

"Oh, Jesus!" Joy snorted. "Look at all that wire. What the hell are these? Old man's toys?"

Jimmy gave her the squint-eye. "Technology from the last century, my dear. And it will work when we can't use your fancy-pants modern stuff. Behold walkie-talkies."

"Cool," Joy murmured as Jimmy handed her one of the little bulbs.

"Stick that in your ear," he instructed. "Don't let the cable come out of here..." He pointed at where the wire plugged into the device. "... or you'll hear this sound..." He pulled the other end out of the walkie-talkie, and a loud crackle of static burst out of the device. After he'd shown them how to select a frequency and push the button to talk, he let them practice talking to each other for a few minutes.

When two or more of them spoke at the same time, they missed words and phrases. Their voices were scratchy and broken, not anywhere as clear as using their ONIV embedded devices but workable.

"Now listen," Jimmy interrupted them. "The modern communication technology won't be able to demodulate the old-school walkie-talkie analog signal."

Bobbie looked at him blankly.

"They won't intercept what you are saying," he rephrased. "However," he peered into their faces with a grave expression, "They will detect your presence, and they will realize something is going on..."

"Could we set up a distraction?" Bobbie asked.

"Yes. Or, a decoy." Jimmy nodded. "Here's the thing. They don't need regular guards on patrol because all the surfaces of the complex are coated in that new nano-paint, paint with tiny sensors that detect electrical impulses as well as heat signatures. The nano-paint relays the information back to an artificial intelligence monitor that will send out real live humans to investigate."

"So, can we mask our body heat?" Hicks asked.

"Maybe, but we can't stop your biosensors from emitting their signals." Joy held up her hands as if she were conducting an orchestra. "There's no way to avoid announcing our presence, but now, time for some of Joy's toys."

A bin folded out from the wall, behind Hicks's head. Joy stretched past him and pulled out a round silver ball about the size of a baseball. Holding it up in her hand, the ball cracked open around its equator and split into two halves, joined together by a thin rod, like a dumbbell. After a series of clicks, a propeller emerged and began to spin with a buzz, faster and faster until the propeller was invisible. The device lifted off and hovered at eye level. A blue ray of light appeared from the center rod and expanded down. Pulses of violet traveled from the orb to the floor of the van and bounced back up to the little device, like a visual echo.

"This little birdie emulates the heat signature and the bioelectric of a human," Joy said. "I have six of them. We can set them off outside the gate, draw out the human security, and slip inside when they go to investigate." She handed them to Bobbie. They were lighter than they looked.

"But, can't they equally come investigate us?" Bobbie asked.

"Funny thing is that AI machines don't like reading us humans," Joy explained. "Our biometrics fluctuate, the heat sensors waver, but these birdies sing strong and true. When making a choice as to what to prioritize, AI loves to zero in on these little guys and leave us alone, for the most part."

"For the most part..." Bobbie repeated. "So, you've used them before?"

"Oh, yes," Joy said, appearing pleased with herself.

All those times, Bobbie had imagined that Joy was lost in her addiction to neuro-games when really Joy was sneaking around Belus Corp's facilities and God knows what other dangerous activities. Bobbie stared at Joy, taking in the confident, smart woman in front of her with newfound pride.

"Did you ever play neuro-games?" Bobbie asked in a quiet voice.

Joy grinned. "Nope, never touch the stuff." She kept her eyes on the panels in front of her.

The relief felt weird to Bobbie, replaced as it was by the knowledge that Joy and she now had bigger fish to fry. *Eat or be eaten...*

Bobbie touched Joy's shoulder and said on an exhale, "You're amazing."

Joy turned. Her eyes locked with Bobbie's and crinkled into a smile.

"Okay," Jimmy said, breaking into the moment the sisters shared. "Comms set up, distraction of AI in place—That solves two problems. Hopefully, the analog presence from the walkie-talkies will be attributed to your birdies, and they will help with our nano-paint problem by providing the necessary distraction. Once we land, I'll be able to link into the on-site network. That will show us the layout. I'll be able to copy them into this." He held up a hand-sized electronic device.

"What is that?" Bobbie asked.

"More antique technology, m'dear," Jimmy smiled. "It's a Personal Digital Assistant. Take it with you. The device is self-contained and will act as a backup if the walkie-talkies hit a dead spot. Because it's offline, the on-site systems won't detect the PDA as you follow the map of the facility. You're going to have to do more than follow the green arrow once you're inside."

"Old fashioned map reading," Hicks said. "We can do that."

"Good," Jimmy continued. "If I find anything in Granny's ONIV feed before you get to the facility, I'll let you know. Once you're inside, we should keep offline."

Bobbie flipped the PDA over in her hands. She turned it on, and a blue screen glowed.

"I'll set the PDA up, so it opens straight into the map." Jimmy took the handheld device and hooked it up to a cable coming from the dash of the van. "We're nearly there."

"I wonder what time they get up." Bobbie checked the time—4:00 a.m. "The sun will be up in one hour thirty. We need to hurry."

"It's rough terrain, bog land interspersed with rocks, but it's pretty flat," Jimmy said.

A map appeared on the screen. The PDA in his hands began blinking and beeping as Jimmy transferred data.

Bobbie left her seat, stood by the intescreen, pointed to the map, and said, "We'll land here and hike a mile to here. Joy will send out the birdies to lure security out, then we sneak in. Jimmy will hack into the facility's security system, watch us on the cameras and override the gates and any locked doors we come across. Should take us thirty minutes tops."

Joy nodded, saying, "Remember, we need to keep the plan flexible."

Nausea rose in Bobbie at the idea of anything going not to plan. So many things could go wrong...

Jimmy highlighted an area on the map. "The compound is a maze. I'll direct you on the walkie-talkie as best I can. These are the sleeping quarters. According to the data I'm getting from her blink, Granny is right here." He pointed at a room. The number 1049 appeared on the screen. "Sedate her. Take her out this door. Across the courtyard, there's another door like the one you'll enter through. All the doors are locked and have video surveillance, so no guards. According to the security logs I've been able to tap into so far, only thirty people are inside—the twelve Rejuvenees and eighteen others - scientists, caretakers, and half a dozen guards. No-one is moving around right now. My guess is they are all sleeping and either not expecting visitors, or confident that the AI security will warn them of anything unusual. You should be able to get out the way you go in. If not, go to this point..." He indicated a place on the roof. "And call me on the walkie-talkie, or fire this."

He handed Bobbie a large orange gun and a handful of metallic cylinders.

"What-what is this," she stammered, hefting the weapon.

"A flare gun and reloads," Hicks said, back in his seat thanks to the pain meds and replacement synthetic blood.

Of course, Bobbie remembered. All the vehicles were required by law to carry flare guns and spare flares in the emergency compartment in case they crash-landed in a remote area. She was so tense she wasn't thinking straight.

"Won't that alert the guards?" Bobbie asked.

"Yes, but by then, they'll be outside chasing Joy's birdies. I'll be able to fly over and pick you up before they get to you on the roof," Jimmy said.

"Our first option is to use the walkie-talkies and call you? Save all the drama," Bobbie said, sitting back in her seat.

"Precisely!" Joy and Jimmy said together.

"But we always want a Plan B," Jimmy added.

"Remember, we don't know who we're dealing with," Bobbie said. "Slade might have been bluffing about not knowing anything about who took Granny and the others, but those gunmen were no bluff. I don't trust a word she says."

"If worst comes to worst, we have the Taser," Bobbie said. "So, we go straight to Granny before anyone wakes up, sedate her, and carry her out between the three of us. We'll deal with her indignation later."

"We'll be setting down shortly," Joy said, swinging her chair around to face out the windscreen. "Get your shit together, team."

"It's pretty miserable out there," Jimmy said, lining up beside Joy. "Patchy fog and intermittent rain. Visibility will be challenging. Be careful - the bog is riddled with holes from back when they cut the peat for turf. Those bog holes can be hard to spot. They're deep and full of water."

A hatch rolled back in the side panel beside where Bobbie sat and revealed a cargo area. Bobbie extracted her red pack. She pulled her boots and socks out, replacing them with the flare gun, the PDA, and the six birdies. Once organized, she checked on Hicks. Still wearing his bloody clothes, he walked in tight circles around the area where the bed had been, delicately raising and lowering his right arm. He seemed to be quite mobile, his color was good, and he was chatting and laughing with Jimmy. He'd survive, Bobbie decided.

The engine noise increased for a moment and the van rocked slightly then touched down with a gentle bump and the engines spun down until they stopped completely.

"Much better landing this time," Hicks said when the van stopped.

The side hatch opened. Mist swirled around the van. Visibility wasn't much more than three or four feet. In the lower right of Bobbie's field of vision, her ONIV projected a bright green arrow pointing the way.

"See ya later," Jimmy said as they descended.

Bobbie turned around to wave at Jimmy. The arrow turned red and flashed until she turned back again.

They left the van. Fog swallowed them up completely.

Joy, Hicks, and Bobbie each had a head torch and a compass. Bobbie had insisted on using the compass as a backup though they would navigate through their map-b-app. They set off at a slower pace than Bobbie liked, but Hicks grunted with pain when they tried to pick up the pace.

"I was thinking," began Joy. "You should put the Taser on a higher setting than sting, at least on immobilize–"

"Oh, shit!" Bobbie stopped dead in her tracks. "I left the damn Taser in the van. I was just about to get it out of the drawer, and I got sidetracked. Give me two minutes to run back and get it. Keep going, I'll catch up."

She'd blinked ahead so when she arrived, out of breath after running the short distance over the rough terrain back to the van, Jimmy stood with the hatch open, the light from the van like a welcoming hearth.

"There's always something left behind," he said, passing her the Taser.

"Thanks." Bobbie stuffed the Taser into the red pack and zippered up the pack again. She turned toward the compound and wasn't surprised she'd lost sight of the others in the gloom. The arrow glowed in her feed. She sprinted in the direction indicated. Soon the lights from two head torches penetrated the fog. Her arrow changed to yellow. Strange, they must have veered off course. She pitched straight for them. The sooner she got to them, the sooner they'd all be on course again.

She ran, jumping over rocks as they appeared in the light of her head torch. A larger rock materialized. She sprang off it. Too late. A smooth black oval of water yawned open below her. Before she could stop, she had plunged into water, so deep it closed in over her head.

CHAPTER 21

Water filled Bobbie's mouth as she tried to scream, and her head went underwater. She thrashed her legs and arms, slowing her downward momentum. Her booted feet still hadn't touched bottom. Bobbie thrust for the surface, and after long moments her head broke the surface. Coughing out dank water, she sucked in air. Her jacketed arms pummeled the dark water. Her sodden trousers stuck to her legs as heavy as lead. Her lungs ached.

Bobbie stretched her neck, trying to keep her head above the water, waving her arms in circles and kicking with her legs. Light from her head torch bounced off black glistening mud banks that rose straight up three feet, all around her. She'd fallen into a bog hole.

I'm going to drown!

Performing a trick she'd acquired while learning to swim, Bobbie flipped her body over to lie on her back and allowed the water to lap at her tightly pressed lips. She called this move 'floating with composure.'

Calm down... think!

Water sloshed into her eyes. With ears submerged, the thud of her heartbeat reverberated in her head. Bobbie forced herself to calm down by listening to the rhythmic whoosh of her breathing. She dragged earthy, dank air through her nostrils.

Something soft bobbed against her head—the rucksack, tugging where the straps looped under her arms. A pocket of air trapped within the bag's waterproof fibers made it buoyant. Bobbie twisted her arms out of the straps and pulled the rucksack to her chest. Wrapping both arms around the bag, she stopped kicking. Slowly, she began to sink.

Bobbie gathered a lungful of air and screamed.

"Help!"

Silence answered. Whatever sound the soft muddy banks didn't absorb, the fog did. Even if Hicks and Joy could hear her, they might not get to her before the combination of heavy, water-filled clothing and exhaustion claimed her. What if the guards from the research center heard her?

Get caught or drown... some choice.

Bobbie kicked out with one leg, and toe of her boot stuck in the soft muddy wall. She swung her other leg and dug that toe in level with the first leg's knee. She plunged her hands into the walls of squidgy mud, malleable like a potter's clay. Her fingers strained, but her legs took a moment of much-needed rest. The rucksack now bobbed freely on the dark water's surface. The beam of light from her head torch lit the bog walls around her as she turned her head.

The walls were close to her on all sides. Perhaps two meters in diameter, the hole was a cylinder cut into the bog where peat had been harvested—the vertical walls, slick with wet muck. The water that filled the bog hole wasn't cold in the near tropical climate that had become the norm for Ireland after the Melter War's damage to the planets environment, but it was colder than her body temperature, and Bobbie knew it wouldn't be long before her muscles began to shake as her body felt the loss of heat.

Now that all her efforts were no longer focused on staying above water, she could compose a blink. *I've fallen in a bog hole. Near the van. Light working.* To send the blink, she'd have to take her hand off the wall to connect the electrodes. *Dammit! I wish I'd gone with the complete mind-controlled b-app*, she thought.

Pulling her right hand from the mud, she jabbed her thumb and little finger together before sticking her hand back into the muddy wall further up.

The message didn't send. Bobbie swore as she noticed the GPS arrow in her ONIV was gone—no connectivity. Her rescue was all up to her—if Bobbie could somehow claw her way up the face of the mud-wall, she would be out. She pushed down on her higher foot and wrenched the lower one out. Pulling her body up with her hands, she kicked her free foot into the mud. The foot slipped out. Bobbie tumbled back into the water, taking a few wet clods of black mud with her. For a few frantic seconds, she didn't know which way was up. Her bag seemed to be below her. Her arms flayed against the bag as they smacked off the sides of the bog hole.

Her head broke the surface. Clawing at the banks, lung squeezing coughs alternated with gulping down air. Bobbie spat out mouthfuls of her hair and swiped clingy wet strands back from her face.

Keeping her head back and her nostrils high, she clung to the rucksack and bobbed. The wall above was scored where her hands had scrabbled to gain ground. As she lay on her back, Bobbie noticed the wall was lower across from where she'd fallen in.

Swimming on her back across to the lower part of the wall she maneuvered her body into a kind of upright position and kicked her leg out. This time her anchor foot held. She placed the free foot higher up. Stretching her left hand as far up the wall as she could,

Bobbie punched her fingers into the walls. Pain ripped at her fingernails as they caught on the dryer mud closer to the top. She gritted her teeth and pushed on in with less than a foot to go till she reached the top and pulled herself up, repositioning her feet.

Extending her right hand, Bobbie realized she'd reached the top. She laid her forearm along the ground and grasped at thick stems of heather. Bobbie's foot slipped out, but her left hand, already scrabbling for the top, grabbed at naked roots. Both feet swung free. Her arms bore her full weight. For a second, as the tendons in her shoulders screamed at her, Bobbie thought she'd have to let go and start again. Instead, she summoned up the last of her strength and kicked her feet while hauling with her arms, pulling her sodden body up over the lip of the bog hole.

Trembling, Bobbie lay on her belly with her feet dangling over the edge. Then she crawled forward and struggled to stand. The direction arrow flashed orange in her visual display. The bog hole was now a benign-looking cavity, about two-and-a-half feet down. Illuminated by the head torch, a flash of red showed in the black water below her.

The rucksack! Shit!

They needed Joy's birdies, the walkie-talkies, and the PDA to get past security and navigate the research center, not to mention the flare gun and the damn Taser. If Bobbie hadn't forgotten that in the first place, she wouldn't have fallen down the damn hole.

Cursing her own stupidity, Bobbie inched forward on her belly until she hung over the hole she'd fought so hard to escape. Pressure throbbed in her head from hanging upside down. Black spots floated in her vision. Reaching out as far as she dared her fingers rasped her nails along the rucksacks material but gained nothing more than a stinging pain in her fingertips. A terrifying inch forward brought her close enough to grasp the bag. She swung it up in one sodden arc to land on the bank. Wriggling back, Bobbie lay once more by the side of the bog hole, panting and waiting for her head to stop thumping.

The green arrow came back on when Bobbie sat up—connected again. No point sending the blink now she was out. It would hold them back further if Hicks and Joy tried to come find her. Shivering, Bobbie stood and forced herself to move, hoping that her activity would warm her. Bobbie's sensorfabrik tunic and leggings were already drying out stiff and scratchy against her skin. Mud covered her from head to toe.

This time Bobbie didn't run, but she pushed herself to hurry, watching the ground warily with every step. Water sloshed in her shoes, and gritty pebbles lodged painfully between her toes. Bobbie checked the time. Her fall and self-rescue had only taken ten minutes, but Bobbie felt like she'd been down that hole for hours. After a short while, she saw lights bounce and bob in the distance. It didn't take her long to catch up. Bobbie came up behind Hicks and Joy, panting, and tapped Joy on the shoulder.

Joy turned around and shrieked.

Bobby jumped.

"It's me!" Bobbie cried, realizing how she must look.

"What happened?" Hicks said.

As Bobbie told them, Hicks turned ghost white. Of course, Bobbie's brush with drowning would terrify Hicks. The bog hole was bad enough for someone who could swim.

"Oh, God, Bobbie," Hicks said. He lifted his arm as if to hug her, but then placed his hand on Bobbie's shoulder. Its warmth spread across her back.

"Look at the state of you," Joy said, her eyes popping. "I thought we were being attacked by the swamp monster. Are you okay?"

"Yes, just a bit stiff," Bobbie said.

"You're hurt?" Hicks said, his voice thick with concern.

"No, no, the clothes are stiff." Bobbie bent her arms, and clods of mud fell away. "Minor cuts on the fingers."

"Let me–"

"No, no, I'm fine." Bobbie pulled away from him. "Look, we gotta make tracks," she said, starting a brisk walk. "We have to get there, grab Granny, and get away before the whole compound wakes up."

"What about the equipment?" Joy asked with alarm.

"The rucksack's waterproof," Bobbie said. "Are the birdies very delicate?"

"We'll find out," Joy responded darkly.

"There's about a quarter of a mile left," Hicks said. "Five minutes tops if we hurry. We should check in with Jimmy before we close down the blinks."

"Sure, but don't mention my swim," Bobbie said. "No need to worry him." She peered through the swirling mist, hoping to see lights.

"Nice work," Joy said and stopped walking. "Have a look. Jimmy's managed to isolate a blink feed between Gloria and someone with the handle 'Agewiz.' Wait!"

Bobbie and Hicks stopped too and turned to face her.

"Joy, we have to keep moving," Bobbie said.

"I know." Joy stepped forward, but her focus was lost in the blink. "Oh, my God, check out what Jimmy's sending us on ONIV. It's a series of communications between Agewiz and Granny actually discussing Granny's condition. Agewiz refers to 'Rejuvenation,' and apparently, Gloria is his best test subject."

"Test subject?" Bobbie said, indignant. Granny had never consented to be a test subject. These supposed test-trials had killed at least twelve other patients and possibly more. "When I get that bastard..." Bobbie said through clenched teeth as she selected the blink feed from her ONIV display.

"There's tons of data here," Hicks said and began moving as Joy caught up with them. "Plenty to work on when we get set up."

Bobbie kept walking as she opened the blink feed exchange that Jimmy had sent. Ordered by oldest date first, the blinks began after Gloria had fully rejuvenated. A long list scrolled past Bobbie's eyes, the text blurring until she got to the end. The most recent one was from the man who'd code-named himself Agewiz. *I ump couldn't get in touch with her but will let you know when I ump do.*

Bobbie's chest clenched as the words trickled across her vision, popping out against the gloom of the fog. She reread them, and then again before scrolling back through the blinks. There was a consistent pattern—*ump* after every *I.*

"Joy." Bobbie's voice wobbled. "What are the odds of two people having the same thinko?"

Joy shrugged. "Well, there is a 1 in 3 million chance that two people have the same thinko, and since there are three and a half billion people on the planet, that means that there are..." She paused. "... 1,166 people walking around on the entire planet with this particular thinko. Why?"

"I know someone with this thinko... this exact one." Bobbie's words almost broke up as she spoke.

"Who?" Joy said. "Tell us!"

Bobbie's lips quivered. "1,166 people—that's a lot of people, right?"

"No," Hicks said. "She said it's 1 in 3 million. That's, like, three times more unlikely than 1 in a million."

"You've seen this thinko before?" Joy said, taking Bobbie's hand as they walked. "Who is it?"

Bobbie's mouth dried up, pasting her tongue to the roof of her mouth as she struggled to whisper, "Davitt."

There was a long silence, then Joy said in a rush, "Maybe it's not him. 1,166 people is still a lot of people–"

Gutted, Bobbie murmured, "Agewiz can't be Davitt. He wouldn't, he couldn't. Experimenting on my grandmother? Christ almighty! Who would do that?"

Then she remembered his enthusiasm for his current project.

Wait till you see what I'm working on next, he had said, my research is really going to change lives, more than anyone realizes...

Bobbie felt sick.

"Maybe," Joy said thinly. "Someone is trying to make us think Davitt is Agewiz, you know. To hide their true identity and fling us off the trail."

"But they'd have to know about his thinko," Bobbie said. She stopped talking as she sidestepped around a boggy looking patch of ground and then trotted a couple of steps to catch up with Joy.

"That's easy," Joy said. "My guess is that we've all been under surveillance. That's actually my default assumption, so in my case, I have a false account they can follow—belongs to a dumbass from my class way back in school. She has no clue, with the added advantage of making me look dumb to anyone reading her blinks. You always want to be underestimated when it comes to intelligence." Joy smirked. "Let's see what else the messages say."

Bobbie unsuccessfully tried her ONIV. "Nothing," she said. "We must be close enough to the compound to be blink blocked."

"Look!" Hicks pointed ahead.

The swirling mists had thinned, unveiling a massive concrete wall fifty yards ahead. The top stood twenty feet tall, outlined by bluish-white light from within. The endless wall spanned Bobbie's vision and disappeared into the fog.

She pulled the PDA out of the pack and turned the equipment on. For a heart-stopping second, nothing happened. Was the ancient device damaged? Then the screen winked on with a blue background. A little hourglass emptied and filled mid-screen. There was good reason as to why she hadn't seen one of these in years - opening a view of the facility map took forever, but eventually Bobbie was able to study the plan.

"The facility looks bigger than on the maps," Bobbie said in a hushed voice, handing the PDA to Hicks.

"The compound is 25 thousand square yards—about four and a half acres, and the building fills most of that area," Hicks said. He turned the PDA around. "There's a gate down that way. We just follow the wall."

"Let's not get too close to the wall. We don't to encounter the nano-paint detector sooner than is necessary." Joy said.

"Wait, the walkie-talkies!" Bobbie handed them out. They switched them on to a rustling and static popping. Jimmy's unexpected voice in her earpiece made her jump.

"This is the Oul Fella, can you read me?"

She pressed the button, "Yes, we can."

No reply. Bobbie went to speak again, but Joy put her hand on her arm and spoke into her walkie-talkie. Bobbie heard Joy's voice in two places at once. "This is Dark Shadow here. Oul Fella, come in. Do you read me? Over."

Joy turned to Hicks and Bobbie. "You have to say over, so he knows it's his turn to speak."

Jimmy's voice burst into her ear. "Nice handle. Should have sorted that at base. Reading you loud and clear. Over."

"We'll let you know when we are inside. Over," Joy said.

"Copy that. I'll keep backing up Gloria's blink feed for you to look at later. In the meantime, I'm standing by to give you directions. Over."

"Thanks. Over." Joy looked toward the east. "We should hurry."

Bobbie followed her gaze. The clouds obliterated any chance of seeing the sunrise, but the gray did appear a shade lighter. The fog seemed to be lifting. The wall was more visible now. She set off in the direction of the gate according to the PDA, her feet squelching with every step. Inside the complex, she might have to take off her boots. The skin on the back of her right heel stung. A piece of a twig had wedged itself in there.

"Hicks, can you manage the sedative for Gloria?" Bobbie looked down at her swollen fingers.

"Sure," Hicks said. "I am, or at least, was, her doctor." He gave Bobbie a wry smile.

"There'll probably be a carebot we can commandeer to carry her," Bobbie said. "Or we can carry her if we have to—she's light."

As they approached a path, Joy said, "I'll bet that goes to the gate. Let's hide over here." She nodded toward an outcrop of rock.

Dirt trapped in Bobbie's clothes irritated her skin in the folds of her knees, crotch, armpits, and elbows as she folded her body up to crouch with Hicks and Joy behind the rocks.

In the distance, Bobbie could make out where the path reached the wall at the gate; a seven-foot by three-foot rectangle, a shade darker than the gray wall. If she hadn't known to look for the entrance, Bobbie might have missed the opening. A patch of mist wafted in carried on a gentle breeze. Bobbie gave a grim smile, this flat expanse of bog land with a smattering of rocks didn't provide them much cover. She was grateful for any help she could get.

Joy lifted three birdies from the mud-coated bag and held them up one at a time. Her fingertips tapped against their smooth shells one after the other before she laid them on the ground in front of her. After a moment two birdies took off. One remained motionless.

"Shit!" Joy pulled another out of the bag, tapped the shell and lay the drone on the ground, a second later the little machine obediently lifted into the air and took off after its comrades. Lifting the rucksack, Joy settled the weight between her shoulder blades and watched the birdies' flight path.

Bobbie said nothing, glad to be rid of her load which had ground into her shoulders and rubbed her skin raw.

The birdies flew toward the compound. Then, three blue lights moved in the distance. The gray rectangle of a door shifted. Blue-white light spilled out into the gloomy predawn. Silhouettes of three figures filled the frame. Dark, featureless men paced out from the compound, scanning in all directions before placing their next step.

One man slunk toward their rocky outcrop. Bobbie's hand tightened around the Taser. The puddle of light didn't reach the rocks. He edged toward them. The backlighting obscured his face. Then his head snapped around toward his buddies. They must have called him, but the sound hadn't carried to her. He took a long look toward the area where Bobbie, Joy, and Hicks crouched.

Bobbie froze as she peeked out around the rock, afraid he'd sense the movement of her withdrawing head.

Relief left her trembling as he turned and ran after the birdies with the others.

"Jesus Christ! I thought he was on to us," Hicks said, straightening up and flexing his limbs.

"The AI must have picked us up, but the birdies fooled it," Joy said. "The AI will ignore us for a little while, thinking we're a glitch, but not for long."

"Minutes, hours, days... what are we talking?" Bobbie asked.

Joy shrugged, "Maybe half an hour. If we're lucky."

"Let's get in, grab Gloria, and get your granny back to normal," Hicks said.

Bobbie nodded her agreement. Maybe an hour from now, they'd be back in the van and on their way. One more push to the finish line.

"Jimmy, you there?" Bobbie said into the walkie-talkie.

"Oul Fella," Joy hissed.

"Go ahead," Jimmy's voice said in her earpiece.

"We're approaching the gate in the compound wall. Over," Bobbie said, feeling awkward about the *over* bit.

"I have opened the gate. Slip on in. I'll see you on cameras when you get inside. Over," Jimmy said.

"Nice," Joy said.

They reached the gate and stepped inside. The research facility buildings were made from some kind of white composite material that gave off a sheen but no reflection. Something photovoltaic, Bobbie guessed. Could the opacity change? The thought of those walls being one-way glass, that someone may be inside looking out at them, turned her insides to water. *Well, too late to worry about that now,* she thought. They headed down a path that led to a black metallic door, halfway down the building.

Bobbie checked the map on the PDA. The building was massive and seemed to be a maze on the inside. There were several exits around the building, but only one on the same side as the gate. That at least meant she was able to orient the map.

Get Gloria. Get out. Get Granny back to normal.

Bobbie beckoned to Hicks and Joy to follow her.

"Oul Fella?" Bobbie whispered. "Can you see us?" There weren't any obvious cameras. "Ah, over?"

"Yes, what the hell happened to you?" Jimmy's voice nestled among a series of crackles and whistles in her ear. He must be able to see them now through the facility's cameras. She dreaded to think what she looked like caked in bog mud.

"Long story. All's well now," Bobbie whispered, wiping mud from her forehead. "We're approaching the exterior door nearest the gate. Can you get us in?"

"Hang tight."

They waited. Nothing happened.

"Oul Fella?" Bobbie whispered into the walkie-talkie.

A barrage of hisses fizzled in her ear.

"Shit!" Joy said. "We need to move. Try to get better coverage and an easier way to open the door, maybe."

Bobbie placed her finger on her lips. Hicks went first, hugging the outside of the building. Bobbie pointed at his back. Joy nodded and moved off. Bobbie followed, clasping the Taser in her hand. She'd increased the strength from 'Sting' to 'Deter' but refused the temptation to change the setting to 'Immobilize.' Her body clenched with fear at the thought of using the Taser.

They turned the corner of the building and, in a few minutes, came to another door. Larger this time, more like a gate, with vertical slats. An engine started up, startling them. The gate began to move.

"Good man, Jimmy," Joy whispered.

"Too easy," Hicks said, grinning.

The gate swung open. Two men in security uniforms stood in the entrance. Both parties stared, frozen in stunned silence for a few seconds. Bobbie heart thumped so hard she thought the organ would burst from her chest as she broke the spell, stepping between the men and Joy, and screamed to Joy, "Run!"

CHAPTER 22

Bobbie's yell jerked the two guards to life. As the first guard stepped toward them, Hicks charged forward, head down. His shoulder barreled into the guard's chest. "Oof!" the guard grunted as he fell backward. Hicks piled on top of the falling man. The guard smacked his head with a wet sounding thwack off the metallic corner of a piece of machinery before hitting the ground. He lay on his back, eyes staring vacant, Hicks on top of him.

The other guard raced forward and grabbed Bobbie's arm, but his grip slid off the slick mud. She wrenched free, bringing the Taser up into the aim and pulled the trigger. Two probes shot out and embedded in the man's chest. His back arched, and all his limbs went rigid. His eyes popped wide open, his face a gargoyle grimace. As his jaw dropped open, his eyes rolled back, and he slumped to the floor.

Bobbie's hands shook so much, she fumbled the Taser, but she recovered enough to avoid dropping the weapon. Hicks had gotten back to his feet and was bending over the guy he'd tackled, feeling his neck.

"Is he dead?" Bobbie managed to say.

"He's got a pulse, but he has an ugly head wound," Hick said. "Your guy?"

Bobbie kneeled on one knee as she felt for the carotid. "He's alive." *Thank God.* She didn't want to add murder to her growing list of crimes.

Hicks straightened up and looked at the two men lying on the floor.

"Holy crap! We did that." He flexed his hand and rubbed his knuckles.

As Bobbie tried to unhook the spent cartridge from the front of the Taser, she fumbled and dropped the weapon. She looked down at her hands, commanding them to stop trembling, her doctor's logical brain telling her the involuntary shaking was simply post adrenaline shock. Flexing her fingers, she bent to retrieve the weapon when she spotted a loaded Taser on the guard's belt and snatched that stun gun from his holster.

"We must have surprised them," she said, scanning his belt for spare cartridges and finding none. *No point in taking the spent Taser*, she thought kicking the gun away to lie under machinery that now trailed blood down its side.

"Hope they'd no time to blink for help," Hicks said.

"Didn't Jimmy say the facility was blink-blocked?"

"Yes, but they're bound to have some kind of internal comms." Looping an arm under the guard's shoulder, Hicks lifted the man's upper torso from the concrete floor with some effort. He nodded at an area between the machinery and the wall. "Help me drag them over there. We should hide them in case anyone else comes. At least Joy got away."

"Hopefully, she'll be able to connect with Jimmy." Bobbie tried to tell herself she was moving sacks of wet sand—large, heavy, ungainly sacks of wet sand. Hicks found a plastic tarp and covered the two unconscious men.

Bobbie looked around the cavernous area–a warehouse. The ceiling, far above them, appeared to have a hinged roof. Vehicles could be loaded right into this area from the rooftop hoverport. A line of machines stood idle against one wall. They looked like larger versions of carebots, used for loading and unloading containers.

"J-J-Oul Fella? Dark Shadow?" Hicks spoke into his walkie-talkie, but Bobbie only heard a crackle in her earpiece.

The shaking in Bobbie's limbs was subsiding as the adrenalin left her system. She checked the map on her PDA and found the loading bay. Along the far wall, she picked out a door the map showed connecting to an outside atrium. Once they got across that, they could take a corridor to the stairwell. From there, they could make their way to Granny's floor.

Get Gloria. Get out. Get Granny back to normal. The words became a mantra to divert Bobbie's mind from the fear that screamed at her to turn around and run.

"Let's go." Bobbie moved farther into the loading bay, pointing at the door. "That way."

"I wonder where Joy went." Hicks strode toward the door. "She sure made herself scarce."

"Joy will go to the roof. She knows that's where we'll take Granny," Bobbie said.

"Let's hope Jimmy doesn't doze off," Hicks said as they reached a door with a keypad lock.

"Any ideas?" Hicks asked.

Bobbie looked around. Cameras hung on the wall above the door. Maybe Jimmy could see them.

"Let's try the door." Bobbie reached forward and jiggled the handle.

The door swung open. Was Jimmy watching? Or did the door open because the guards had come through here recently? She'd give anything to hear Jimmy or Joy's voice in her earpiece right now.

Once through the door, they found themselves in a covered patio area with tables and chairs arranged like an outdoor cafe. Some tables had yellow and orange gerbera daisies growing in pots and the odd cup or plate as if left behind by careless teenagers. Hicks nudged Bobbie and pointed at a sliding panel section in the wall across the patio. Nothing indicated that Jimmy had been able to open this door yet. As they approached, Bobbie expected the panel to slide open. Surely Jimmy would see them, but the door stayed shut. Hicks looked around at her, his forehead wrinkled in concern.

Bobbie tried the walkie-talkie again, "Oul Fella? Can you read me?"

Nothing.

"Maybe he can't see us," Hicks whispered.

Bobbie looked around for the camera that covered this area. Above the door, a piece of cloth hung over the camera. Jimmy couldn't see them to open the door.

On closer inspection, Bobbie realized the fabric was a pair of panties. *Had these people rejuvenated so much that they were teenagers?* Perhaps Gloria had snuck out to the gardens by the cliffs with Justin and, to avoid detection, they'd covered the cameras with panties; perhaps they were pranking each other. Either way, this scene was disturbingly bizarre. No-one, not even the facilities staff, had bothered to remove the undies.

Bobbie grabbed a chair and set it down slowly, soundlessly below the camera. Hicks saw what she was doing and put a hand up, indicating she stop. He walked to the wall and stretched up, recoiling instantly, clutching his injured side. Bobbie moved toward him, but he shooed her off, put his head down and his thumb up. He'd be okay in a minute.

Bobbie climbed up on the chair and removed the panties, holding them between finger and thumb and dropped them, leaving them where they fell in a bundle along the wall. She wiped her hand on her tunic as she climbed down.

Hicks straightened up. Bobbie nodded to his side. He nodded back and mouthed, "I'm okay." They waited off to one side for the door to open. Nothing happened. Bobbie's mind raced. What would they do if the door didn't open? After a few long moments, a pneumatic hiss sounded. The door slid back.

Bobbie gave a thumbs-up hoping Jimmy would see her *thank-you* on the camera.

"Look," Bobbie whispered, shoving the map beneath Hicks's nose. "According to this, Granny's room is two floors above us at the end of this corridor. The stairs are over there. Let's go."

Through the door, two steps down the hallway, the intewalls on their right side winked on, providing soft white light. Behind them, the door swooshed closed. Straight ahead, floor to ceiling windows lined the left side of the hallway. Bobbie looked through the window into an airy space topped with an expanse of white ceiling.

Bobbie looked down. Her gut clenched.

Three stories below them about a dozen people milled around in a laboratory. She pulled Hicks back, dropping down and flattening herself against the floor. Not ideal cover but better than nothing. They lay there, banking on the premise that if they could not see the laboratory floor, then the people down there were at the wrong angle to see them.

"Shit!" she hissed. "We'll be exposed."

They were on the ground floor. Jimmy had told them that there were five underground levels within the main building, but he obviously had not known about this transparent wall. The corridor seemed to stretch to infinity ahead of them. If someone came along the corridor, how would they explain lying on the floor? They peeked over the edge of the corridor floor and looked down through the glass wall.

The lab had three rows of four stations, each with a narrow bed that ran perpendicular to a counter, like an array of "L" shapes from this bird's-eye view. Each counter had a gray two-foot-cubed box, dangling thin clear tubes. Young-looking people sat on some of the beds: three men and four women. Almost as if choreographed, they lay back at the same time, their faces upturned. None had Granny's flaming red hair. They all wore the same gray sensorfabrik tunic and pants, like a uniform. The three men stood at the end of a row, chatting. Bobbie wondered if these were her old patients, but could not see their faces, her view from that angle catching the crowns of their heads.

One had the small frame and caramel skin tones of Ester Banks, who had grown up in Singapore before the war. She had been visiting Belfast when the Melters struck. With nowhere to return when her beloved Singapore had been obliterated by floods and tidal waves, Ester had stayed in Ireland. Bobbie had enjoyed listening to her reminisce about her exotic homeland.

Perhaps she was too far away, but something about their faces niggled Bobbie. They all seemed similar somehow. They reminded Bobbie of the times she'd seen Gracie alongside other children who had the same genetic disease, Progeria. They'd shared distinctive features—narrow faces, recessed jaws, and pinched noses—yet each child bore a unique quality to distinguish them as individuals.

A door opened at the far end of the lab. Six more people and a carebot entered. These people were dressed in different colors and styles. They split up into pairs, and each pair strode to one of the women and began working with tubes from the gray boxes beside the beds. Bobbie couldn't make out what they were doing.

A hiss in her earpiece made Bobbie jump back from the window.

"Big sis, you there?" Joy's voice sounded distant and thin but clear.

"We're in," Bobbie spoke quietly into the walkie-talkie in her hand. "Are you okay?"

"Yes," Joy continued. "I've found a spot where I can hear Jimmy. He says he's not reading you. I'll have to stay here and relay. Can you manage without me?"

"Yes," Bobbie said, relieved that Joy was safe and that they could all communicate.

"There's a problem," Hicks said. "Can Jimmy see us? Can he see the glass wall?"

"Hold on..."

Bobbie could hear Joy talking to Jimmy but not his answers.

"Okay, he sees your problem." Joy's voice was interlaced with fizzles. "You can't go down that way. Most of the corridors have glass walls. Dammit! Hang on..."

Her voice burbled in the background as she conversed with Jimmy again.

"There's a utility hatch right opposite you. Jimmy's working on opening it. The duct leads to a conduit that goes to the stairwell. You'll need to crawl along the duct all the way to the end. You can push out the panel from the inside when you get there. The duct is cramped but big enough."

The intewall clicked. One side of an intepanel popped out about six inches up from the floor.

"I see the hatch," Bobbie said.

"When you get in the duct, we'll not be able to talk to you," Joy said. "Hopefully, we'll connect on the other side."

"Understood," Bobbie said, sounding braver than she felt.

Bobbie and Hicks scuttled over to the wall on their bellies.

Hicks swung the panel open on its hinges, revealing a cuboidal metal duct about two feet wide and three feet high that disappeared into blackness. The maintenance duct walls were lined with bunched cabling that enabled the tech for the building.

"Head torches on," Bobbie said as she crawled up into the hatch.

"I'll go first," Hicks said, his voice brittle.

"No," she said, refusing to budge. "I'm smaller. I can't see past you. I'll go first."

"You're not claustrophobic, are you?" Hicks said.

"No," she said, wondering why he'd asked then pushing the thought aside. "I want to see where I'm going. Come on, hurry."

Bobbie scrambled further into the duct and crawled forward on hands and knees. Her sensorfabrik leggings, stiff with mud, weren't stretching as they should. The tender skin behind her knees pinched. Her waistband chaffed. At least being on her knees gave her relief from the blisters on her feet caused by the grit in her shoes.

Hicks clambered in behind her. Bobbie inched forward and heard the air compress with a hiss as he pulled the panel closed behind him. The murky light offered up by their waning head torches all they had to help them navigate through the vent-like tunnel.

"Now, I know why you wanted to go first," Hicks whispered.

Tension splintered his forced chuckle.

"What?"

"I have a great view of your muddy butt." He sounded falsely bright like his words were strung along a too-taut wire.

Bobbie needed Hicks to be his usual steady self, but she understood how unnerved he must be feeling. They were doctors, for God's sake, not even high-adrenaline emergency doctors, at that. Geriatricians did not expect to encounter much excitement in their line of work, so yes, breaking into research facilities and crawling through utility ducts had them out of their depths.

They crept along the duct trying to be quiet, unsure how the sound would travel beyond this enclosed space. Bobbie had assumed they would run parallel to the corridor, but soon the metal floor began to tilt up so that the effort to gain ground became more difficult. Every so often, she slid back into Hicks. Eventually, the floor flattened out again. The duct turned a right angle and ran for another six feet before ending in a hatch.

"Why is the duct smaller?" Hicks asked. He sounded out of breath.

"It's not," she said, looking over her shoulder. The right angle on the tunnel meant that the area they were now squeezed into felt like a box.

The light from Hicks's head torch bounced around the cramped space as he swung his head around, examining the inside of the hatch. "No airflow?" He panted.

Bobbie pushed against the corner of the panel, expecting a door to pop open, but nothing happened.

"Open the damn hatch," Hicks hissed, his voice edged with unfamiliar harshness. "Now!"

Oh, God. He's claustrophobic. "It won't budge," Bobbie whispered. Hicks shoved against her, struggling up beside her toward the hatch. She flattened herself against the side and moved her head so that her torch could pick out the edge of the panel. "Ow!"

He dug an elbow into her stomach as he wriggled his arm over her head to push against the panel. "It... has... to... open." Hicks punctuated each word with a gasp. He wedged in beside her, up against the hatch.

Pressed against her, Bobbie felt Hicks's body tense as he pushed the panel door again. Her torchlight glinted in the sheen of sweat that coated his face, now level with hers, ten inches away.

His chest heaved with his rapid panting.

"I can't breathe." He pounded at the hatch with one hand, the other clawed at the neck of his tunic. "I can't breathe."

"Shhhhhh!" Bobbie whispered as loud as she dared. "You're okay." She smoothed her hands from his shoulders, down his arms, stilling his trembling hands and held them, tracing circles with her thumbs and making little shushing sounds.

He squeezed his eyes shut.

"There's plenty of air in here. It's okay," Bobbie soothed.

Hicks gripped her already delicate hands until they hurt.

"This is as big as our treehouse, and we used to sit there all day. Remember?" Bobbie said.

He shook his head, groaning.

"Listen to my voice," Bobbie crooned in hushed tones. "I'm right here. You're going to be okay."

Fear rippled through her. If he lost all control and started thrashing about in this confined space, Hicks could hurt them both, or get them caught. He was frozen, for now, panting, sweating, his hands curled into fists.

"You're having a panic attack," she said. "Are you claustrophobic?"

He nodded, his face scrunched up, holding his eyes shut.

She'd never known that about him, just as she'd never known he couldn't swim, though they'd been best friends since childhood. He was claustrophobic, yet he'd climbed into this metal tube with her. He'd let her go first. She wished she'd let him go first when he'd asked her. Love and compassion welled up in Bobbie for this man she had known all her life.

"Take a deep breath," Bobbie said as if talking to a child. "In through your nose, out through your mouth. There's space and lots of oxygen around us."

Hicks's body trembled as he drew air in. His nostrils flared. He opened his eyes wide, his gaze swung in frantic arcs not focusing on Bobbie. If he passed out now, she might have a panic attack of her own.

Bobbie leaned into him, pressing her forehead against his.

"Look at me," she commanded in as loud a whisper as she dared. "Focus on me! I'm here with you. We'll be alright. There is plenty of air."

Hicks's eyes dived into hers, his forehead, hot against her skin and his breathing steadied.

"You're going to be okay," Bobbie reassured him. "It's–"

There was a loud click, and the hatch popped open.

Hicks tore his hands from Bobbie's and pushed the little door all the way out. He grabbed the edges of the hatchway and pulled, spilling both of them out and down a drop of about three feet. Hicks landed with a soft thud on his back. Bobbie fell on top of him, squashing a swift expulsion of air from his lungs. She scrambled to her feet, glancing in all directions.

They were on a flat, gray, concrete winder where the stairs pivoted to follow the lines of the dimly lit stairwell. Had they gone up a full story?

Hicks lay for a moment, repeatedly heaving a lung full of air.

"Are you okay?" Bobbie asked.

"Jesus, Bobbie, I'm so sorry." Shame weighed down Hicks's brows.

"It's okay," Bobbie said. "I didn't know."

Hicks flushed red. "Bad experience as a kid. I've never told anyone before."

"Why not?" she asked.

"Because I was somewhere I wasn't supposed to be and then later because I didn't want to look like a coward," he said, standing up and shaking himself down. He took his walkie-talkie off his waistband, stared at the little lump of black plastic, and absentmindedly turned the device over in his hands.

"A coward is not the person who's afraid. It takes courage to do the things you are afraid of." Bobbie wanted to know more, but there wasn't time. "Besides, a coward doesn't jump from subscrapers into hovering vehicles." She smiled and bumped his shoulder playfully. "Or tackle security guards, now do they?"

Hicks's face relaxed a little.

"We need to move." Bobbie nodded at the walkie-talkie in his hands.

"Dark Shadow, can you hear me?" Hicks said into his walkie-talkie, and Bobbie heard his voice, a tinny echo in her own earpiece.

"Yes!" Joy sounded elated.

"Can Oul Fella see us now?" Bobbie asked.

"Yes. Nearly there guys," Joy's voice said in her ear. "Only one more flight of stairs. Hurry. Oul Fella says keep your Taser handy... it's just that... oh, never mind, just go."

Bobbie and Hicks took the stairs two at a time. They found the entrance to the corridor they were looking for. Entering the corridor, Bobbie saw that the first door on the left had the number 1020, the door opposite, 1021. *Fourteen rooms down, and we'll find Granny.* They trod with light, quick footsteps and as they reached room 1049, the door slid open.

The room was heavy with the musky scent of sex and a smell familiar to Bobbie that she could not pin down. The intepanels didn't come on. Bobbie turned on her head torch. By its light, she picked out Gloria's red tresses spilled across the pillow. In her peripheral vision, she saw Hicks raise a finger to his mouth. Gloria was not alone in the bed. A dark mass poked out from beneath the covers beside Gloria, the crown of a man's head. Would they have time to sedate two people before they woke up? Bobbie would have to Taser the sleeping man. She pointed at Hicks then at Gloria's side of the bed. Hicks gave a thumbs up and moved into place. Bobbie showed Hicks the Taser and then pointed at the lumpy form beside Gloria. Hicks nodded, message received and understood.

Suddenly Gloria sat up. "What's going on?" she asked in a loud voice, raising her hand to block the lights from Bobbie's head torch.

Bobbie and Hicks froze.

Then Gloria flung back the covers, revealing herself and the other naked body in the bed.

Bobbie realized why she had recognized the smell—the fragrance was her favorite aftershave. The man in the bed beside Granny was Davitt.

CHAPTER 23

"What the fuck is going on here?" Gloria asked, scooping a scrap of fabric from the floor before pulling the dress over her head, all without leaving the bed.

The intewalls ignited, illuminating a small room with a single bed. Judging by the clothes strewn on the floor and the bed linen tangled around their naked bodies, Davitt and Gloria had made the best of the confined space.

Rage, confusion, disgust roiled hot in Bobbie's gut. Her ragged fingernails sang with pain as she clenched her fists, the ache a welcome distraction to the fury building inside her. She'd been right about the thinko. Davitt had been involved from the start. What else had he lied about? For how long? He was so proud of his work, so fucking vain.

And their original plan to take Granny away—well, that was kaput. They now had Davitt to deal with. *Just Taser the fucker*, her brain shouted at her. She pictured him convulsing in agony at her feet. Hicks studied her with worried eyes as if gauging her reaction.

"Bobbie, I can explain," Davitt said, pulling the bedding around him, his eyes darting between her and Gloria.

"Oh, shut up, Davitt," Gloria said with a wave of her hand. "There's nothing to explain. You were an adequate lay. She can have you back. If she'll take you." Her words were chips of pain lodging in Bobbie's heart. Davit had slept with Granny and Granny, no, Gloria had let him; perhaps encouraged him. Gloria looked up at Hicks and purred. "And what brings you here, Doctor Hicks? Have they patched you in on this gig too?"

This gig?

Hicks looked around worriedly, and Bobbie realized he was listening for the sound of running feet. If Davitt had sent an alert using total thought control, guards would be on their way. Bobbie looked at the pathetic figure still lying in the bed trying to cover himself up. Could he also be here against his will? Had Slade coerced him into taking part in whatever was going on here? So, fucking what? Bobbie was convinced he was Agewiz, the mystery man behind the blinks to Granny and the development of Rejuvenation.

Bobbie wouldn't Taser Davitt—not yet. Maybe they could use him to their advantage. If she fed his ego enough, he'd boast about what he was involved in here and the more information they had the better chance they had of bringing Granny back. *Of course, he'd boast—it's what Davitt did best.*

"I'm with Gloria," Bobbie said, her voice loud, pretending she was talking to her ONIV. Inside her pocket, she pressed the button on the walkie-talkie, hoping Joy could hear her. Bobbie slid the Taser up her sleeve with her other hand, keeping the fact she was armed a secret. "Yes, Doctor, we'll be reporting back shortly." Bobbie continued the bluff. After a few seconds, she heard a high-pitched beep in her earpiece and realized she was still holding down the button on the walkie talkie. Crap! Had she pressed the button too long? What did that do? What had Jimmy told them? Turn the radio off? Change channels?

Please let Joy have heard me.

Bobbie's hair concealed the thin cable going to her earpiece, but she could see the black wire trailing up the back of Hicks's head. Hopefully, neither Granny nor Davitt would recognize this ancient technology.

Gloria slid out of bed and pranced around the room, finding her panties on the floor, and wriggled into them. Davitt sat in the bed looking lost at sea, avoiding eye-contact.

"Smart move, Big Sis," Joy's voice sounded in her earpiece. "You are on voice activation mode. Oul Fella can hear you, too."

Bobbie needed to hurry things up, guards could arrive any minute. But how to do that without causing suspicion with Davitt? She needed to convince him she was here under Slade's orders. If that bastard could lie to her, she was damn well capable of lying right back. Bobbie faced Davitt, her stomach doing flip flops, and said, "They put us on the research team."

"That's wonderful. I told them they should. Look, Bobbie, I made a mistake. It was just ..." Davitt said from the bed, the covers pulled over his nakedness, as he raised his eyes to hers, beseeching her.

Bobbie held up one hand and shook her head. With one finger, she tapped the outside of her eye, the universal symbol for, 'Don't interrupt me, I'm blinking.'

Davitt crunched his dark eyebrows together, his confusion deepening into alarm.

Joy's voice continued in her ear, "Get the basic information from Davitt on Granny's condition. Oul Fella is monitoring a perimeter out to thirty miles and is reporting no suspicious vehicle activity. The entire facility is still blink blocked—Davitt can't have called for help!"

"A mistake?" Gloria swiveled toward the bed, hands on her hips, and said in a mock whine, "'Bobbie's too busy for me' and 'She doesn't understand my needs!' What about, 'Oh, Gloria, you're so beautiful now!'"

"Leave it, Gloria!" Davitt glared at her.

"Well, don't you think Bobbie should hear all the ins and outs..." Gloria smiled languidly. "... and ins and outs and ins and outs..."

Bobbie and Joy were on the same page. With no guards about to interrupt them they had time to get the information they needed. Bobbie looked at Hicks, who would have heard Joy as well, and raised an eyebrow.

"She's right," Hicks said. Bobbie hoped he referred to what Joy was saying in their earpieces and not Granny's revelations.

"You dirty boy!" Gloria admonished in fake modesty.

Positioning herself between Hicks and Gloria, Bobbie addressed Davitt directly, "You're to give us an update on your progress."

Bobbie turned her head and faced the woman who now looked more like her sister than her grandmother and said, "And then Gloria is coming with us."

Gloria laughed, tossing back her head, and clapping her hands. "Now, why would I do that?" She walked behind Hicks and trailed a finger from his shoulder down his arm to his elbow.

Hicks stood solid as stone.

Loathing for the woman swelled in Bobbie, she almost tasted the bitterness. Bobbie reminded herself that this was Granny, Granny was not of sound mind, regardless of how sound her body seemed to be. She swallowed hard and cleared her palate.

"What sort of deal can you offer me? Can you offer the same - *perks* as Davitt?" Gloria leered at Davitt in a way that made Bobbie queasy with fury.

"Jesus, Gloria, stop." Davitt turned his back to them, pulling the sheets around his naked body.

"Oh, get over yourself. I was talking about those fun little cocktails we get." Gloria's smile tugged at the corner of her mouth. As she folded her arms, Granny's hands fidgeted against the crook of her elbow. "I mean, look at you! Bobbie, is it any wonder he went looking elsewhere?" Gloria slid up beside her and held Bobbie's hand up level with her face. "You really could use a good wash, blow-dry, and manicure."

Bobbie's fingers were caked in mud, her nails ragged and bleeding. She caught sight of herself and Hicks in the mirror across the small room. They were a sorry looking crew, Hicks covered down one side in rust-colored dried blood and Bobbie slathered in bog.

Stay calm, ignore the trash talk. "We are here to help you," Bobbie said.

"Help me?" Gloria laughed and dropped Bobbie's hand. "What makes you think I need help?" She looked down at Davitt, who had crept to the edge of the bed, face aflame. He reached down, found his pants, and fumbled under the covers to dress.

Gloria tutted. "So modest all of a sudden." She gave a little girlish laugh. "It's not like we haven't seen the family jewels before—well, maybe not Hicks." She shrugged. "But who knows?"

Bobbie was aware that the clock was ticking, but she suppressed the urge to turn and run. She felt Hicks's agitation as he shifted his weight from foot to foot. He was probably counting the seconds tick by, too. She had always admired his skill for staying silent and letting things unfold. His trust in her gave her strength.

"That's interesting. You sent me a blink," Bobbie said. "You said you wanted to leave and that they wouldn't let you."

"True," Gloria cooed. She sat back down on the bed and stretched her legs out, pointing her bare toes. "That was before I realized it was so…" She looked sideways at Davitt and lifted one corner of her mouth in a sly smile. "… Cozy." Reaching out, she caressed Davitt's bare shoulder.

He snatched his body away as if he'd been scalded and shot up out of bed. Standing before them bare-chested, he said, "Bobbie, please, can we discuss this later?"

"Gloria's right," Bobbie said, her throat tight. "There's nothing to discuss. At least not about us… We're done." Despite her anger, a weight rolled off her back. Her spine straightened. "Slade will be very interested to hear about your tryst with a research subject, though." Bobbie looked him up and down slowly, enjoying how the color drained from his face. "However, you are required to bring me up to speed on the research."

"I-I, I can't. You-you don't have clearance," Davitt stammered. He tipped his head to one side like a confused puppy. "Do you?"

Joy's voice spoke in her ear, "Remember, Davitt is blink blocked. Davitt cannot, I repeat, cannot, blink Slade. Over."

So, Davitt had no authority here, thought Bobbie. *He is nothing more than a puppet after all.*

Davitt's tunic lay near his feet. Bobbie stooped down, grasped the garment, and tossed the shirt to him in one smooth movement.

"Of course, I do," Bobbie lied smoothly, surprising herself. "Slade sent me. How else do you think we knew where they were keeping Gloria? And just what do you think she'd make of you banging the subjects? I don't think she'd be best pleased, do you?"

Davitt pulled on his tunic. "But what happened to you? The mud–"

"Oh, what a pain in the ass that was!" Bobbie waved her hand as if a bug was irritating her. "Damn hovercar nav-system went down, and we got stuck in the bog."

"The nav-system went down? Really?" Davitt asked.

"What?" Hicks drawled as he stifled a yawn. "You think I want to be here? That I chose to come without clearance? Hell, how would I find this place if I didn't have Slade's directive? What do you think? That we just broke into this highly secure research facility?" Hicks's fixed smile turned a little waxy beneath his steady gray eyes.

"Besides," Bobbie spat with true venom, "You're the one who has the explaining to do!" Bobbie flicked her eyes from Davitt to Gloria and back, gratified to see shame flush his cheeks again.

"Now, Bobbie," Hicks said, smiling apologetically at Davitt, all boys together. "Let's keep it professional. Whad'ya say, Davitt?"

Davitt ruffled his hands through his dark curls as if trying to arrange them, along with his thoughts, into some order. The coils of hair sprung back to their original positions again as soon as he placed his hands on his hips. "It all sounds bizarre."

"What part of all this isn't strange?" Hicks asked, sounding casual, conversational. "Come on, we're wasting time here." Hicks turned to Bobbie. "I want to get into a fresh tunic. We can tell Slade he wouldn't co-operate, and she can deal with him."

Bobbie forced herself to appear composed despite her heart pounding against her chest. This bluff could backfire.

Gloria walked to a small closet, pulled open the door, found a tunic, and handed Hicks the garment she had just fished out.

"You and Davitt are about the same size, right?" Her eyes rested on Bobbie's, and although Bobbie knew this creature was not her Granny, a fragment of pain sliced through her as she acknowledged that not only had Davitt cheated on her prior to last night, but this woman wanted to rub Bobbie's nose in his philandering.

"Thanks." Hicks accepted the tunic. "Bathroom? May I?" Hicks pointed at a door.

"If you must," Gloria answered. "Damn shame, he's so modest."

"We could blink Slade and let her know where we found you, Davitt," Bobbie said, wondering if she should mention Disease Control, see if Davitt reacted. No, she decided. Keep it simple... or as simple as possible under the circumstances.

Davitt's eyes narrowed again. "Blink? We can't blink from here."

"Maybe you can't." Bobbie faked a laugh, her heart thudding as she played her joker. "Evidently, we've got a higher clearance grade than you. We have Slade in our ear. I guess she really doesn't trust you. And with good reason—she had her suspicions about you and your liaisons. Do you want me to bring her up to speed with all the juicy details?"

"Bobbie, please let me explain." Davitt took a step toward her.

"Explain to Slade. We've wasted enough time here and to be honest Davitt-" Bobbie narrowed her eyes. "I don't care."

"Okay, okay. Please don't." Davitt stopped, hung his head. The muscles in his jaw fluttered.

She had him! *Now all we need to do is get past the guards and the rest of Davitt's staff before someone calls our bluff.*

"So." Hicks returned, rubbing his hands together, ready for business. "Can we move this along now?" Hicks turned to Gloria, "Be a dear, perhaps you can give Bobbie something to wear too. She's such a mess."

Gloria threw a camel-colored sheath dress at Bobbie. "This old thing should do."

Bobbie caught the dress in one hand and headed into the bathroom. The room was small, a toilet, a sink recessed in the wall, and a shower in the corner. Bobbie had enough room to wriggle out of her own muddy tunic and pants, and into the shift dress, relieved to be wearing something soft against her rubbed-raw skin.

Bobbie washed her hands, awakening the throbbing where the water hit the exposed beds of the broken nails. She splashed water over her face, clearing patches of dried mud. Tiny twigs and clots of dirt fell from her hair as she shook her head over the sink. She quickly braided her hair to the side, wincing as the hairs snagged her tender fingernails. For a second, Bobbie met her reflection—gray smudges nestled beneath red-rimmed eyes. Her light ginger eyelashes made her eyelids look bald. Her golden-copper hair was darkened with mud but in bright contrast with her pale skin. Blood welled up in beads along a thin scratch above her temple that she hadn't felt before. Her pulse pounded in her head. Hurry, hurry. Bobbie patted dry with a tissue and went back to the bedroom.

"Quite the fashion statement." Gloria's eyes flitted to Bobbie's muddy boots peeking out a couple of inches below the hem of the long, flowing dress.

"Let me escort you," Hicks said to Gloria and held out his left arm, bent at the elbow. Bobbie felt like thumping him, but she knew the charm offensive was as effective as any under these circumstances.

"Straight to the lab. My favorite part of the day." Gloria took Hicks's arm and followed Davitt. Hicks's puzzled gaze connected with Bobbie's. Granny liked the lab?

Davitt led them to the elevator. Bobbie's stomach plunged with the lift as they rode to the lowest level. They were now, by her reckoning, below sea level, the waves crashing against the Cliffs of Moher above their heads, less than a mile to the west. The elevator doors opened into the laboratory that they'd looked down on through the glass windows.

Ten beds were occupied with prone people attached with tubes to metal boxes on the countertops beside the beds. Bobbie recognized her former patients though they looked years younger. Like Karen Kane, her now youthful face a ghost to the memory of the one that used to sell Bobbie ice-cream when she was a little girl. The Rejuvenees had a uniform look about them that rattled Bobbie—same clothes, yes—but more disquieting than that—something in their facial structures seemed homogeneous.

Research staff milled about, monitoring the gray boxes, and talking in muted tones over intepanels on the countertops beside the beds. They cast sidelong glances at Bobbie and Hicks, but swiftly looked away when they saw the scowl on Davitt's face. Some staff Bobbie vaguely recognized, a woman walked past, and Bobbie wracked her brain to remember her name… Jenna… Jenna something. She'd tutored her as students on the Pelagic wards. They walked on passing whirring, buzzing, and purring machinery which blended with the burble of conversation, providing a hypnotic soundtrack, punctuated by sharp beeps and pings, and the occasional squeak of plastic-soled shoes.

Gloria raced to an empty station and lay down on the bed. Apart from her red hair, she had taken on the same the same features as the other Rejuvenees. Her forehead wider, hairline lower, and younger countenance. The Granny that Bobbie new was indiscernible in this face which was far from the appearance of Granny as a young woman. What the hell could do that?

"Hurry up and get me connected!" Gloria snapped. "It's my turn. I know the schedule!"

A member of staff attached tubes to a plastic port on the inside of her elbow.

"Intravenous?" Bobbie asked Davitt.

"For now," he answered. "We're following an older protocol, more invasive, but intravenous is the only way to introduce the vector." His dark eyebrows pinched together as he looked at the last empty bed. "Cooper."

The staff member nearest to him swung around to face Davitt.

"Still no sign of Subject 9?" Davitt asked.

Cooper shook his head. "Sorry, no."

Subject 9? Christ! Was he talking about Justin?

Bobbie kept her face empty, masking the tide of rage seething within her. Were all the Rejuvenees now just numbers to Davitt? The gruesome image of Justin's eye-popping wide open as Granny had embedded the garden fork in his abdomen flashed into Bobbie's head and she glanced toward Granny. The woman lay calmly on her bed, seemingly oblivious to the conversation.

"So, what happens at each station?" Bobbie asked, trying not to sound rushed. She was dying to take Davitt and shake the information out of him. What did you do to Granny? Instead, she took a deep breath and let him continue with his explanation.

"We are administering correctional therapy upgrades now," Davitt said.

Correctional therapy? Like in the PARC? Bobbie's heart beat hard, like someone pounds a door.

"Upgrades? To combat the side effects such as cardiac failure?" Hicks asked.

Davitt sucked in a sharp breath and glanced sideways at the person on the bed nearest them. "Something like that," he stammered.

"Be precise Davitt, I haven't got all day." Bobbie wasn't sure how much she could pretend to know. She hadn't heard from Joy in a while. And what if the guards she and Hicks had dealt with earlier were discovered? Worry sliced into Bobbie's thoughts. There was no way for them to know if trouble was on the way. She caught Hicks's cool gray eyes. He raised one brow a fraction, just enough for her to notice.

"So, Slade briefed me, but take it from the top for Doctor Hicks," Bobbie said, walking Davitt and Hicks away from her former patients and toward the sidewall of the lab.

"Basically, our nanobots are programmed with a genetic blueprint of a cell in prime working condition. Initially, they are manufactured in these machines, then injected into the subject," Davitt began, nodding at the machines on the counters. He touched the intewall nearest him. A screen appeared with an animated diagram of the DNA double helix folding into a chromosome.

The sneaky bastard used nanobots, thought Bobbie. *We were looking for a retrovirus not anything as small as a nanobot. That's why nothing showed up on the tests for pathogens.*

"These nano-machines or nanobots work on the molecular level. They follow the blueprint we've given them and replicate themselves in the host body so that there are enough to patrol and support the DNA in each cell, ensuring that each cell is functioning perfectly. It's like nano-housekeeping and maintenance. My work here will change humanity for the better—imagine never getting old." Davitt finished with a smile, puffed up and proud of his spiel. Bobbie's bet was cashing in. Davitt spoke with great pride in his work. *What a conceited fool,* she thought. *How did I never see it before? Perhaps I did notice but had never found it as offensive as right now.*

"So, the nanotech provides scaffolding for the DNA," Hicks said, rubbing his chin. "How far back do they regress? Babies?"

"Oh, no, not that far," Davitt replied. "The nanobots keep them at their peak; in normal human years between eighteen and thirty-five. I've designed it, so there are no errors as the DNA copies itself. In Phase Two, we'll introduce the nanobots earlier in the human life cycle, allowing the nanobots to read the individual's DNA and tailor-make themselves based on that blueprint. Our test subjects were too old, so for Phase One, we used donor DNA for the blueprint."

That's why they all looked the same!

Bobbie allowed her eyes to run over the Rejuvenees lying on the beds. Each of the women had a little brown mole nestled in the hollow of her cheekbone. *I wonder who supplied the genes for the blueprint? It wasn't someone chosen for their beauty. The forehead is too low and broad and the cheekbones too high and narrow.*

Bobbie reached for that compartment in her brain that functioned as the objective scientist as her gaze settled on Granny, no, Gloria.

Granny's genes were supported by nanobots, and in places rebuilt to a new blueprint carried by those molecular-sized machines. Did this mean that over time each affected person became a clone of the donor? Perhaps Davitt had used a blend of DNA—the men had that same forehead and cheekbone structure, but no mole. They needed different genes. One of the rejuvenated men had risen from his bed and was walking toward the far exit. As he passed close to Bobbie, she spotted a little nick in the bottom of his pinna as if a mouse had taken a little bite out of his earlobe. That feature was familiar. She turned to face Davitt, the same little piece of missing earlobe jumping out at her. Unsolicited, emotion slammed Bobbie's thought process with white-hot anger. Sweat dampened the small of her back. Self-control wrestled with her desire to tear her nails down Davitt's face.

"Who's the donor?" Bobbie asked, through clenched teeth already knowing the answer. Davitt had used his genes for the males!

"That's classified, I'm not cleared for that information," Davitt said, rubbing his hand across his mouth.

Liar! No surprise there. Perhaps Davitt was, as he'd claimed, trying to bring about a cure for aging and help the human race, but at what cost to these innocent people whose bodies he'd hijacked? Would they, given time, become something else, someone else? Perhaps a clone of Davitt? And what of the female with the mole on her face?

Hicks must have seen the anger building up in her as he quickly intervened. "Can they reproduce?"

"In theory, yes, but we don't know how or if the nanobots will interact with the growing embryo. So, we don't know yet," Davitt said.

"What about the side effects? The orange eyes? The behavior modifications?" Bobbie asked, keeping her voice mild and conversational, despite her urgency and her rage.

If not for the horrifying side effects, and the deception and coercion of the subjects, Bobbie could be excited about the nanobot application to reverse the aging process. A cure for aging, a cure for Progeria, perhaps, too. Could this technology be salvaged for more benign uses? Could scientists forego using a donor DNA and utilize the DNA of the person on whom the nanobots would work? Did the unethical approach to the development and testing leave too a sour a stench for Bobbie at this stage?

"The eye-color was a surprise. It may be a mutation from the donor's gene code, an interesting anomaly but not damaging to the subject." Davitt indicated the Rejuvenees lying behind him at the treatment stations with a wave of his hand. "We haven't corrected it because the feature is a useful marker and will help us to identify test subjects from the wild population during integration."

"Integration?" Hicks lowered his voice to a harsh whisper. "You can't integrate sociopaths!"

Davitt sighed and scratched the crown of his head. "We now know that the transport of the nanobots across the blood-brain barrier and how they function within the gray matter of the brain are not as we first projected. Why?" Davitt shrugged. "We aren't sure.

Also, as the bodies rejuvenate, hormonal fluctuations increase in huge surges, similar to the way they do during puberty. The hormonal instability might be overloading an already fragile brain chemistry. We are trying to balance that chemistry now. The subjects are receiving regular but small doses of Central-Nervous-System depressors–"

"You're drugging them with narcotics?" Bobbie said.

Davitt nodded; lips pressed together.

"They're addicted now?" she asked, aghast.

"Yes, the subjects have developed a dependency on the drug."

"Jesus, Davitt! Their brain chemistry is already compromised! You just said so."

Davitt held up a hand. "Let me finish, please."

"Go on," Bobbie spat through clenched teeth.

Davitt lowered his voice. "We needed something to keep them coming back for more. Otherwise, they would have left the facility. The other option would be to lock them into cells. Surely you wouldn't want that?"

He's turned Granny into a junkie.

The Rejuvenees were being held in a chemical cage rather than a physical one. Rage threatened to go supernova in Bobbie's chest. How would detoxing Gloria play into her plans to get Granny back? Bobbie had read about detox, but since the war, recreational intravenous drug use had been eliminated. Government-regulated recreational viruses had taken over to prevent dependency. Yet here, Granny was an addict.

Keep professional. Hurry up. If Bobbie protested too much now, Davitt might get suspicious and blow their cover.

"We are constantly re-engineering the nanobot's circuitry and coding," Davitt said smoothly. "We'll be conducting trials with these updates soon."

Davitt pulled up another diagram. Bobbie recognized the stylized depiction of a bacteriophage, a virus that infects and replicates within a bacterium. The shape of the protein head that housed the DNA, atop the sheath, the corridor through which the DNA is injected into the bacterium, and its base plate, pins and tail fibers, always reminded Bobbie of the pictures she'd seen of the lunar landing modules of the last century.

Viruses. Bobbie's guts tightened with dread. She cast her eye over the eleven Rejuvenees lounging contentedly on the hospital beds, addicts getting their daily fix. These people had been Bobbie's patients, their aches and pains she'd medicated, their concerns and fears she'd assuaged, now little more than conscripted test subjects partaking of a new unethical science.

"Instead of delivering DNA the way a virus usually does, we are working on an airborne virus that will deliver nanobots so we can distribute them without using needles. The nanobots cannot get into the body without an introductory vector—such as needles or a virus. That way, we can issue upgrades without using nanobotmanufacturing machines." Davitt cast his hand over the array of gray boxes at the test stations. "I've engineered the virus so that it is temperature and UV sensitive that way we can kill it off easily with heat and sunlight," Davitt added. "We are working on perfecting the anti-virus to go with the virus at the same time. We can't risk releasing the virus as a vector for the nanobots to the general population until we know we can control it."

"Release the virus to the general population? Without their consent?" Hicks said. "You can't go infecting everyone with this disease."

"Rejuvenation is not a disease," Davitt said. "My research has begun a new era for humanity. In the same way that we gained control over bacterial infections with the advent of antibiotics, now we'll be able to eradicate aging. Keep the population young, healthy, and productive."

"And insane," Hicks hissed and cast a glance over at Gloria. "Not really healthy or productive."

"They were all ultra-elderly," Davitt said. "They were expendable."

"Pardon me?" Bobbie could hardly breathe.

"Look at what I turned them into." Davitt waved his arm over the Rejuvenees like an amateur actor in a school play. "They're all fit and healthy now. Once addicted, we can manage them. They can do the dirty jobs that people don't want to do. These guys will do anything to get a fix."

"Are you fucking kidding me? That's human trafficking! Slavery!" Hicks squared up to Davitt.

Davitt raised a hand as if taming a wild horse. "When I perfect the tech and eliminate the psychosis bug - think of the profits! Eternal youth—for everyone!"

"And what about these people? The lives you've already wrecked?" Hicks said.

"Except," Davitt said, "They've already lived their lives. We've looked after them for years, carried them, been stuck without children and lives of our own. It's our turn now." Davitt stepped back.

Hicks clenched his fists and stepped forward.

Bobbie rested a hand on Hicks's arm. Punching Davitt would almost certainly bring guards and she needed one more piece of information before they made their escape. "Where is the Rejuvenation virus and its antidote now?"

"Em, well..." Davitt's dark eyes looked away. He ran his hands through his mop of black curls. "We are working on the antidote in a smaller lab, upstairs. I already have a sample of the virus ready to go. Then, when we have a larger sample size, we'll really be able to pick out trends and determine the nature of the... the..." Davitt searched for a word, then shook his head and settled on, "... glitch."

"Glitch?" Bobbie raised her hands to her forehead and pressed, feeling like her head might explode. *Does this man's ego have no bounds? Sociopathic behavior was a glitch?*

"Yes." Davitt dropped his chin. "A glitch, that's all the side-effect is."

"And while you experiment, how many of these people," Bobbie reined herself in and chipped the edge off her tone. "How many might die?"

"Bobbie, old people dying is not the problem," Davitt said in a low voice. "Old people living too long is. No more of the diseases that afflict the elderly, free from the aches and pains of old age. You're a geriatrician, you don't need me to spell it out."

Bobbie saw with gut-crumbling horror that he believed what he said. He'd often told her that his own mother had spent most of her life looking after his elderly grandparents. He'd felt abandoned as a child because of this. Bobbie had always assumed that was why Davitt needed to brag about his achievements, had thirsted for so much praise. Was this his answer? Some kind of twisted revenge, perhaps? Eradicate the elderly by whatever means necessary? Speechless, Bobbie shook her head.

"What's wrong, Bobbie? Afraid you'll be out of a job?" Davitt huffed out a little laugh.

"Perhaps I'll retrain as a psychiatrist. Sounds like there'll be lots of work for shrinks," Bobbie snapped back.

"Don't worry, we'll perfect how the nanobots interact in brain tissue. Iron out the glitches," Davitt said, energized. "Then we can administer nanobots to the entire population."

The entire population?

"Please, excuse me, doctor," one of the staff called to Davitt. "Can you come over here, please?"

All eyes turned toward the man who had interrupted.

"Sorry to interrupt, doctor," he spluttered, cleared his throat, and cast his eyes down at the counter beside him. "There's a message—your eyes only."

Davitt hurried to a nearby empty workstation. Bobbie's scalp prickled as she watched him open the screen.

Hicks stepped closer to Bobbie and whispered, "I have the sedative."

Bobbie nodded and stepped out of his way so he could get closer to Granny. Bobbie observed Davitt. Something in the message obviously shocked him because he paused, looked at her, and pulled the shutters down over his face.

"You bitch," Davitt said coldly. His hands rolled into fists. His eyes shot daggers at Bobbie.

Oh shit! Terror paralyzed every muscle in her body.

Bobbie followed his eyes up to the corridor overlooking the lab that she and Hicks had stumbled upon earlier. Slade glared at her and behind her stood six men in combat gear, armed with evil looking guns. Slade's mouth moved as she continued to stare down into the lad and the armed men raced toward the elevators.

CHAPTER 24

Slade marched along the windowed corridor toward the elevator lobby. Her gaze bore down on Bobbie. Just before she reached the end of the glass, two stories above, Slade shook her head slowly. Then she disappeared as her entourage moved into the lobby that housed the lift.

"Get Granny!" Bobbie shouted. Hicks sprung toward Gloria on the bed. No sound came from the walkie-talkie earpiece. Was the radio on her belt still transmitting? Could Joy hear them? Chances were they were on their own.

Bobbie pulled the concealed Taser from her sleeve and aimed the stun gun at Davitt. Two male staff members went to step forward to help their boss.

"Stop!" Bobbie yelled, making a point of thrusting the Taser in Davitt's direction so the men realized who was going to get Tasered if they took another step.

The men froze and looked to Davitt.

"We're all going to the correction center," Davitt said, panic making his voice rise. "Slade will think I helped you. Dammit, Bobbie! You have to tell them."

"Tell who what?" Bobbie's voice exploded from her, louder than she'd intended. The game was up. Who was *them*? Did he know? Prickles of fear goose bumped her scalp. She had no regrets about landing Davitt in a shitload of trouble.

"You should be happy I cured aging," Davitt spat. "Think of Gracie - wouldn't you have wanted a cure for her?"

"Shut up and move!" Bobbie said through clenched teeth. How dare Davitt mention Gracie? Bobbie pointed the Taser at Davitt and rushed at him, making him jump backward. "You know nothing about her."

A pulse throbbed in Bobbie's head. Out of the corner of her eye, Bobbie saw Hicks administer the sedative jet to Gloria, unhook her from her IV, and lift her like a rag doll into his arms.

Bobbie scanned the room for a way out. There was one set of doors on the opposite side of the lab.

"That way!" Bobbie pointed, praying the doors led outside and not to a maze of internal corridors.

"You're coming with us," Hicks said to Davitt, moving beside Bobbie. "He knows how the virus delivers the nanobots." Hicks's eyes darkened. "With a little persuasion, he'll tell us."

Davitt swallowed hard and shook his head. "You wouldn't dare."

Hicks, cradling a sleeping Gloria, nodded at his hand. "Take that," he said to Bobbie. "I only used half the sedative. She's already full of drugs. Use it on him if you need to."

Bobbie took the jet from Hicks as he shoved his way past a stunned looking female Rejuvenee who'd stood up from the bed in a nearby station.

"The jet applicator surface is contaminated with nanobots now," Bobbie said, stepping around the woman, holding the Taser steadily at Davitt. "Administering the sedative would force nanobots into your bloodstream. What would that do to you? Or have you only tested the effects of nanobots on the vulnerable, ultra-elderly?"

Davitt's eyes narrowed. "Fuck you!" He screamed as he bounded to one side and pushed the hapless Rejuvenee into the line of fire. Sensing that she had lost control of the situation Bobbie backed toward the escape door waving the Taser in front of her, head swiveling from side to side as she attempted to keep the staff and Rejuvenees in sight. She spotted Davitt beside an open cupboard, loading micro-vials onto a plastic vial-tray. His hands fumbled. A couple of vials slipped between Davitt's fingers, dropping to the floor, but didn't break.

"Shit!" Davitt swung toward the nearest member of staff. "Get over here, you idiot, and help me. I'm not leaving my work behind for you or some other plebe to take the credit!"

A woman in her mid-twenties sprang into action. Her dark blond hair swung forward as she reached for the vial on the floor.

"Careful!" Davitt barked. "You break the vial; the virus is airborne. Do you want to be contaminated?" He snatched the little tube from her and inserted the phial into the tray holding the rest of the vials. Hugging the tray Davitt ran to the elevators.

"That's the virus?" Bobbie said, horrified. She needed those vials! She couldn't leave them here to be released on more victims. But could she reach Davitt, grab the vials and escape with Hicks and Granny?

The mechanical whirring of the elevators vibrated in the quiet of the room making her decision for her. Slade would be here any second. There was simply no time.

"Let's go!" Bobbie cried to Hicks.

Hicks ran. Bobbie followed, running awkwardly backward, keeping the Taser and the sedative jet pointed at the confused looking staff. Some Rejuvenees between Bobbie and the doors sat up, giving her their bleary attention. Would the drug Davitt had given them keep them groggy long enough for Bobbie and Hicks to escape? Would they care? Their vacant orange stares chilled Bobbie.

Hicks fumbled for the door handle, his arms full of Gloria. He banged her feet off the wall, she moaned and wriggled in Hicks's arms, turning her head and mumbling.

"She's waking up!" Hicks hissed. "Hurry."

Bobbie sprang to Hicks's side, stuck the Taser under her arm, and yanked the door open.

Their escape route had led to a storeroom. They had nowhere to go.

The staff and a couple of groggy Rejuvenees closed on them, a sinister, calm mob. Beside Bobbie, Gloria kicked and bucked against Hicks until he set her on her feet. Gloria staggered. Hicks steadied her as she leaned into his body, giggling girlishly, ratcheting Bobbie's nerves up another notch.

The lump in Bobbie's throat threatened to suffocate her, but she forced herself to turn and face the advancing Rejuvenees.

"Slade is using you." Bobbie scanned the group.

The Rejuvenees stared at Bobbie. Their orange eyes glowed as if in a trance. Their limbs looked strong and toned, belying their age. Firm skin radiated vitality. Their movements seemed synchronized as they closed in, making a semi-circle around Bobbie and Hicks, drawing in like a trawler's net. Bobbie stepped closer to Hicks and Granny.

"Slade doesn't care about you. You are just lab rats to her. I do care." Bobbie's voice wobbled, but she kept going.

"Yeah, but you didn't make us young again. Dit ya?" A voluptuous brunette slurred. She staggered, then caught her balance again.

Bobbie's brain raced to identify the woman's face, but her voice, rather than her features triggered the recognition; Suzana Tang, Bobbie's patient.

"No, Suzana, but this state might not last," Bobbie said gently, but urgency tugged at her. "I remember your pain. How arthritis in your knees and hips kept you awake in agony. I dressed your bed sores. I know how badly you suffered."

Suzana's orange eyes swam in a drug-induced fog as she struggled to focus on Bobbie. Was that a spark of comprehension?

Bobbie pushed on. "It must be wonderful to be young and fit again. They –" She waved the Taser at the staff behind Suzana. "They have killed scores of people to get to this stage. Remember Aayushi? They didn't care about her, and they don't care about you. If anything goes wrong, they'll let you die and start again."

Orange eyes around her darkened with frowns. Some of them murmured. They sounded disgruntled. Bobbie seized the moment. "We've been your doctors for years. You know we've cared for you. Help us now. Stand with us. Don't let Slade and her men take us away."

"Let me work with you to solve the issues that these guys are ignoring, drugging you to avoid dealing with," Bobbie said, glancing at Davitt, waiting on the lifts to arrive.

Suzana shook her head. A few others stepped back, definitely not volunteering to come forward.

Bobbie turned to one of the staff that she had recognized earlier. "Jenna, did you sign up for exploiting our ultra-elderly? We shared notes in pre-med. You wanted to help humanity. Rejuvenation is not helping anyone except whoever is behind developing the treatment. Do you know who you are working for? Do any of you?" Bobbie cast her eyes around the staff. Many of them avoided eye contact.

Jenna smoothed the front of her uniform. Her hands shook.

Bobbie refocused on her former patients. "You saw those armed men. You know our world rejects violence—on the principles of one unified, transparent government. Peaceful solutions to problems, dialogue, humanity for humanity, a united species."

Animosity flickered in the orange eyes.

Bobbie tried again. "Lisette Fox promotes peace and security. She abolished such violence. What you are doing here is wrong. Slade is wrong."

The sound of the elevator motor whirred again. Slade was on her way. Terror plunged through Bobbie's veins. Her heart sped up… hurry… hurry.

"Stand with us," Bobbie urged. "Let us help you. You'll never be more than expendable to Slade."

The eleven Rejuvenees closed in tighter, their expressionless quietude terrifying.

The staff hung back, exchanging worried looks.

They're scared!

"You don't know what you're talking about," Davitt spat at her from where he cowered behind his staff. "We made them young! All you did was help them die." His eyes held wild desperation. He swung his head toward the lifts then back to face her. His knuckles whitened as he pulled the box of vials into his chest. "When I give Slade these and turn you in, she'll know whose side I'm on."

The second elevator began to move.

Bobbie turned to Granny, desperation raw in her voice. "Rejuvenation is turning you into something you don't want to be. I know this is not you, not the woman who raised my mother."

Granny grinned and folded her arms, leaning back against Hicks in a fluid motion.

"Granny, you're in there," Bobbie pleaded. "The woman who held Gracie's hand as she slipped away..."

Something in Gloria's face ignited – a flutter of one eyebrow – a glimmer of her grandmother.

"I want to help you. I love you." Bobbie stepped toward her.

Granny shifted against Hicks, rubbing her hands along her upper arms, looking young and ancient in the same moment.

An elevator pinged. They were out of time.

"I'm not going to the PARC, Bobbie," Hicks said through gritted teeth, his gray eyes steely. His hands balled into fists. "They'll not take me alive."

Bobbie had as good as killed him. She moved to Hicks's side and turned to face the elevators, her mind a clatter of misery and regret. A mad panic froze her to the spot as the doors slid open with a hiss.

Joy bounded out of the elevator in a blaze of black clothes and blue-black hair.

Giddy with relief, Bobbie saw that the second elevator had stopped between floors. Slade and her henchmen were trapped.

"Freeze!" Joy yelled. Brandishing the flare gun in her right hand, she swung the weapon in an arc and deployed a birdie with the other hand. "This–" Joy nodded at the birdie hovering into position above the Rejuvenees head, "–is a bomb." The blue light on the birdie's shell flickered to life, followed by the pulsing violet rays Bobbie had seen before.

"Now it's armed." Joy's dark eyes glinted with enjoyment.

Davitt scurried behind the nearest counter, eyes wide with fear.

"If any of you move – boom!" Joy splayed the fingers on her left hand and extended her arm.

The ring of Rejuvenees in front of Bobbie parted like a biblical ocean as she strode toward Davitt. "Move," she demanded. "We're taking you with us." Bobbie needed Davitt's expertise and the virus filled vials he still clutched.

"No chance." Davitt backed away.

Bobbie passed the sedative jet to Hicks. "Finish it," she said, nodding at Gloria.

Hicks took the jet in one hand and grabbed Gloria's arm with his other. Bobbie heard the hiss of the jet. Gloria slumped as Hicks caught her.

Bobbie swiveled back to face Davitt and discovered that he had tried to make a run for his freedom while she had been talking to Hicks, only for the Rejuvenees to block his escape route.

"You're not getting me blown up," one of them spat. Others muttered an angry reverberation.

Bobbie stepped up to Davitt.

"Into the elevator, or I'll Taser you," Bobbie hissed through clenched teeth. "I'll pop your medulla sensor right now."

"Then, I'll drop this." Davitt nodded at the tray of virus vials he held. "And you'll all be infected."

"Yes, but you'd be dead. If I leave without you, you'll release the virus anyway. I have nothing to lose here." Bobbie paused and let that sit a second with him. "Oh, and I'll take those," Bobbie said, lifting the tray of virus vials from Davitt's hands.

Davitt's face twisted. "You bitch!" He stepped ahead of her toward the elevator and a grinning Joy.

Hicks rushed toward the elevator carrying Gloria.

Bobbie's legs felt like damp noodles, but she forced herself to hurry, waving the Taser at Davitt, who swore but did as he was told.

Joy jumped into the lift. As the door closed, she clicked her fingers. The Birdie swooped into the elevator a fraction of a second before the lift doors closed.

"Shit!" Davitt pounded the panel. "The bomb! Stop the elevator." But the elevator kept going.

Joy snickered.

Davitt turned toward her, nostrils flaring, his black eyes as fierce with rage as Joy's were dancing with mirth.

Joy raised the flare gun. "In this confined space, you'll make a huge mess." Joy shrugged and smirked. "But I'm not cleaning it up."

"You need me," Davitt hissed.

"I'm not so sure," Joy said. "My big sis is pretty smart, and I have access to all your data now."

Bobbie couldn't tell if this was another of Joy's bluffs.

"That's true,' Bobbie said, lifting the Taser. The steadiness of her hand surprised her. Emboldened, she aimed the Taser at Davitt and said, "But detonating a bomb in his brain would be neater. So, behave yourself, Davitt."

Davitt sunk back into the corner. "You won't get away with this. Slade has her men everywhere."

"Ha! Last I saw, Jimmy had them all stuck in the other elevator," Joy said, grinning. "And they'll remain there until we get clear away. Jimmy's in control of the entire facilities systems now and watching all of us."

The elevator rose to the top floor. Hicks exited first, carrying Gloria. Davitt followed with Bobbie and Joy training their weapons on him. Every one of Bobbie's senses was popping. Colors seemed more vivid. She could smell Davitt's sweat; a muskiness tainted rancid by his fear. The cable and pulleys in the elevator shaft hummed and clanked as the elevator descended again. A metallic taste lingered on Bobbie's tongue. She swallowed but her mouth was to dry.

Joy nodded at a gray door to their right. "Through there."

Joy kept the flare gun trained on Davitt while Bobbie pulled open the door and led them up a narrow flight of metallic stairs. Daylight flooded in. The clunk of their footsteps grew more rapid as they saw the sky through the door above.

A tall figure appeared silhouetted in the doorway. Bobbie gasped and took aim with the Taser.

"Shoot me with that thing and you can get your own ride out of here," Jimmy said, with a chuckle.

Bobbie squinted in the morning sun as she stepped onto the rooftop. The van sat on the other side of a hatch covered with big gray doors, attached with giant hinges to the roof. The edges of the closed doors met in the middle.

Hicks scrambled around the hatch toward the van and lifted Granny into its open side-door. Bobbie noticed a fresh rose of blood had blossomed at the wound in his side. Hicks had made carrying Granny look so effortless, but he must be in pain.

Joy prodded Davitt with the flare gun. "Move it, asshole," she said, looking over her shoulder.

Davitt got into the van, scowling.

"Tie him up," Bobbie said, nodding at Davitt.

Joy kept her flare gun trained on Davitt while Hicks duct-taped his hands together.

Bobbie kept a tight hold on the vials containing the virus with her left hand and shoved the Taser into her right-hand pocket before helping Jimmy into the driver's seat. When the man was settled, she jogged around the front of the van to climb in the other side when she felt a sharp punch to the back of her left arm closely followed by an ear-splitting pop.

Her fingers spasmed, and the tray flew into the air. White-hot pain exploded up her left arm, blazed into her shoulder, and consumed her upper body. Silver and black spots floated in her field of vision. Her right hand went to the site of the agony and she barely withstood the searing pain. Her breath caught, while sticky wetness covered her fingers. Bobbie stared at the red liquid, rubbed her fingers and thumb together and tested the fluid's viscosity.

Numb with shock her brain took a second to register the facts; she'd been shot! Bobbie looked around scanning the rooftop. Her chest heaved as she fought the pain which threatened her vision with grey patches and flickering stars, and she emitted a guttural animal sound through clenched teeth.

Movement! A figure skulked by the entrance to the stairway.

Gripped by pain and terror, Bobbie could only watch as Joy swung her flare gun around toward the figure and pulled the trigger. With a loud *whoosh* and a trail of acrid smoke like the trail of a comet, a bright green star flew, straight as an arrow, until the splash of green impacted square on the man who'd shot Bobbie. The flare ignited in a fireball that engulfed the man's chest and head. He managed a short, ear piercing scream before he fell back, flailing, into the stairwell.

"Move!" Hicks yelled.

Bobbie half climbed, half fell through the van's open door, her greying vision registering two of the virus vials lying broken on the floor beside her before unconsciousness claimed her.

CHAPTER 25

Pain pulsed from Bobbie's upper left arm, immobilizing her where she lay slouched against the bed in the van. Her eyes blinked rapidly as they cleared away the stars that floated in them. Looking down, she saw blood drip from her elbow, a rusty odor rose from the syrupy puddle forming beside the broken glass and spilled virus.

Bobbie had just released the virus Davitt had produced to carry the rejuvenation nanobots to an unsuspecting population.

Bobbie clamped her right hand over her wound, a clean in-and-out. Blood wasn't spurting, so the arteries were intact. The bone seemed okay too, but the pain drove up into her shoulder and neck, blasting into her head. The lack of reaction from the other occupants of the van, indicated that she had only passed out for a few seconds.

For a second, the world stopped as if taking a breath, and then chaos exploded around her.

Hicks grabbed a blanket from the bed and threw the covering over the broken vials.

Granny lay sedated, oblivious to the whirlwind around her.

Davitt, his hands tied before him, shouldered his way into the tiny toilet at the back. The door slammed behind him, the shower gushed, and he banged against walls and door, trying to wash off any trace of the virus.

Joy hung out the side door of the van, the flare gun aimed at the blazing stairwell. Black smoke billowed up and tugged at an angle by the breeze. Orange, blue, and green flames licked the door frame, tongues tasting, greedy for more sustenance. Joy launched herself toward the inferno, popping out the spent flare cartridge and slipping in a fresh one.

"Leave it," Jimmy yelled. "Get back here. Come on. Hurry!"

A shrieking wail rang out from the inferno, stopping Joy in her tracks. She looked back at Bobbie in the van, Joy's face a mask of horror. This was no game. Real people were hurt, were screaming.

The smell of the man's burning flesh curdled Bobbie's stomach. She sensed movement behind her and turned to see Hicks reaching for the blanket he had flung over the broken shards of glass and splashes of viral loaded fluid. Bobbie was bound to be exposed.

"Stop!" Bobbie said as Hicks mopped up the mess. "Let me. I've already been exposed." As Bobbie sat forward, the pain made her head swim. She retched, but her empty stomach produced nothing.

"I've got this," Hicks insisted. "Sit still."

Bobbie dragged in deep breaths to clear her head as black spots shimmered in her vision.

Hicks scooped up splintered glassware, fluids, and the unbroken vials, bundling everything deep within the blanket. Then he pushed out three intact vials and wiped them down with a dry corner of the blanket.

"Put down the windows and turn on the blower, Jimmy," Hicks shouted to the front seat. "Blast this shit out of here." Hicks pulled open a drawer, stowing the surviving vials with delicate care as if they contained nitroglycerine.

The engines of the van revved louder, the air-conditioning fans started, and the windows slid down.

"Let's go!" Jimmy shouted above the noise.

Joy backed toward the van, keeping a wary eye on the burning stairwell.

"Just a sec." Carrying the bundle, Hicks jumped out of the van, sprinted past Joy, and tossed everything into the flames. Smart. Davitt had said the virus was heat sensitive. Hicks stood for a second, as flames engulfed the blanket, broken vials, and virus.

A security guard burst from the flames and ran toward Hicks.

"Outta the way!" Joy screamed.

Hicks flung himself off to one side.

Joy fired at the man. A ball of flames ignited the ground before him and engulfed him in fire. Howling, the man flailed, stumbled, and fell. The rooftop surface ignited, the blaze cutting Hicks off from a direct route back to the van.

Joy threw up where she stood then backed toward the van, wiping her mouth.

The weapon shook in her hands as she broke the flare gun, ejected the cartridge and, with trembling fingers, reloaded. With an obvious effort she raised the gun and pointed it at the roof access.

Bobbie crawled to the doorway. She watched, helpless, as Hicks scanned the rooftop and took off running around the perimeter, rather than trying to come straight across the middle of the hatch. The flimsy cover over the opening might not hold his weight, and Bobbie was glad he wasn't trying to find out. His route would take Hicks precious minutes longer to get back to the van, but the way up onto the roof was now a raging inferno, there was no way any more security guards or Slade's men were using that route.

A sound, another motor starting, made Bobbie look up. The sky was clear below high clouds. Black smoke from the fire chugged off into the distance. The research center was in a remote part of Ireland, but might someone see the plume? Bobbie scanned the rooftop as she heard what sounded like gears clanking. The rooftop hatch shifted, the mouth of the jaws cracking.

"Joy, get back here! They're opening the hatch!" Bobbie screamed.

Hicks was all the way around on the far side of the roof.

"I've locked down the perimeter doors of the facility," Jimmy shouted. "But they must have a manual override for this hatch on the inside. It's their only way out. They've been sending for back up, but I've been blocking that. Stop that hatch from opening!"

Joy ran, skirting around the flames to the destroyed stairwell and lifted a foot-long piece of metal pipework that had once been a handrail. She sprinted to a raised metal box, no more than a couple of cubic feet big, sitting alongside the hatch. Prizing the lid open, Joy jammed the pipe into the gears within the box. A shower of sparks made her spring away, shielding her eyes.

"Hurry!" Bobbie yelled.

Hicks picked up speed on the far side of the hatch.

The motorized sound whirred at a higher pitch, but the movement of the hatch doors ceased.

Bobbie screamed in fresh pain as Gloria shoved her to one side and bounced her injured arm off the van's doorframe. Gloria dived out of the van and darted toward the pipe Joy had jammed into the gear box. Joy saw her approach and stepped in front of the sparking, clanging gears. Gloria swung a punch. A moment too late, Joy ducked. The blow glanced off Joy's forehead and sent her flying across the rooftop where she landed on the flat of her back with a loud grunt.

Gloria pulled but the pipe was wedged in tight. Joy staggered to her feet and grabbed Gloria's arm. Gloria shook her off and then turned and sprang on top of her like a cat pouncing on prey.

Oh, God, Bobbie realized with horror, Granny was attacking her own granddaughter. How could Granny hurt Joy?

"Hicks!" Bobbie screamed and pointed. But Hicks was still too far away. Bobbie had to help Joy. Adrenaline didn't cover the pain as Bobbie gritted her teeth and stood up. She gulped back nausea and shook her head to clear the dizziness.

Gloria wrapped both hands around Joy's throat.

Jesus Christ, she's trying to kill her.

Bobbie forced her limbs into motion.

Pinned underneath Gloria, Joy struggled and kicked. By the time Bobbie stumbled over, Joy's eyes bulged from a face turning mauve.

Bobbie tried to pull Gloria off, but the pain in her arm left her one-handed. Even with the sedative, albeit wearing off, Gloria had uncanny strength and shook Bobbie free without letting go of Joy.

With eyes rolling, Joy clawed at Gloria's arms. Joy's tongue stuck out as she made a guttural gurgling, desperate to suck in air.

Bobbie felt for the Taser, still in her pocket. The setting was on low, but she hesitated. What if she delivered too large a shock to both Gloria and Joy, one that would pop both of their medulla sensors?

The shock didn't kill the security guard - just do it!

Bobbie aimed the Taser at Gloria's back and fired.

The Taser discharged. A blue-white flash arced between the jaws of the Taser and connected with Gloria's shoulder blade. Her back arched, all her muscles contracting in one brief seizure. Dropping Joy, Gloria collapsed.

Joy gasped for air, but her lungs struggled to inflate, and she coughed.

Bobbie rushed to her sister. Joy was breathing—coughing and choking—but she'd live. Bobbie turned her attention to Gloria, ready to shock her again if needed.

Gloria lay on her back with her eyes closed. The eyelids flickered, hiding the cruel glare that had threatened Joy minutes before. Granny's eyes fluttered fully open, and Bobbie's jaw dropped as she realized what was missing—the orange color. Granny's soft blue eyes, wet with tears, looked up at her. Relief washed over Bobbie as she kneeled beside Granny. Had the Taser shock somehow stopped rejuvenation?

"Granny?" Bobbie said, taking her hand. But the texture of Granny's hand felt odd, cold, and squishy as if the skin was no longer connected to the flesh beneath, and the bones inside were disconnected from each other. Bobbie forced herself to hold on and not let go. Granny's eyes were blue again, her expression tender, her countenance sagging as the muscles beneath the skin relaxed. Wrinkles formed again at the sides of her eyes, lines bearing witness to her years.

"Granny, can you hear me?" Bobbie asked, ignoring the throbbing pain radiating from her wounded arm. Behind Bobbie, Joy had stopped coughing, and had moved to stand by Bobbie's shoulder.

"Oh, Darlings, I'm sorry," Granny whispered, her words swallowed by a sob. She clutched both of Bobbie's hands.

Bobbie yelped as a searing pain flashed up her arm. Something had changed in Granny. Hope fortified Bobbie as effectively as any analgesic. Granny's voice had lost the harsh edge that Gloria had spoken with. Bobbie sensed the gentle demeanor of Granny nudging Gloria away. The silken strength of the graceful old lady, who had borne her years with dignity, replaced the cruelty of the brazen impostor Gloria had become.

"You're back," Bobbie cried.

"I'm so sorry." Granny's voice was so soft that Bobbie struggled to hear her.

"None of this was your fault," Bobbie whispered.

As Bobbie watched, Granny's face changed. The youthful tightness of Granny's skin seemed to ripple. At first, Bobbie thought that she was winking, but realized that the muscles all over Granny's body were spasming in minute twitches, rolling over the muscles like clusters of little waves.

The seizure lasted a few seconds. Bobbie tried in vain to find Granny's pulse. When the contractions stopped, the skin and underlying muscle seemed spongy and limp. Granny's skin tone dulled to a lack-luster beige-gray, the color of porridge. Her jaw line sagged. Dark circles formed around her eyes as they sunk into deepening sockets. Tiny threads of capillaries brightened and pulsed red in patches on Granny's skin then faded as bruises bloomed in their place. Her skin crinkled like crepe paper.

Beside her, Bobbie felt Joy's body shudder, as Joy sobbed. Hicks appeared on the other side of Granny, across from Bobbie, pale and out of breath.

Bobbie watched, stricken, as Gloria aged into her beloved Granny in a matter of moments.

"Oh, Bobbie, love," Granny said. Her eyes focused and brightened a fraction as she stared at her granddaughter. Granny coughed. A spot of blood dribbled down her chin. Blood oozed from her nose and ears.

Bobbie wiped away the blood with the hem of her dress and caressed the papery skin at the side of Granny's cheek, crooning, "It's okay. You're going to be okay."

Hicks lifted Gloria's arm, trying to find her pulse. His eyes met Bobbie's. An almost imperceptible shake of his head, coupled with a wrinkling between his brows, a gesture Bobbie knew well. Hicks's look when his patients had no hope.

He's wrong, he has to be.

"Hang on," Bobbie begged, her vision blurred with tears. She scooped Granny up into her arms, her own physical discomfort nothing compared to the pain in her heart. Granny felt like a bag of loose sticks, her bones, tendons, muscles, all seemed disconnected. Bobbie tried to pick her up but fell forward onto her knees with Granny on her lap.

Granny wheezed, her face contorting with pain and decay. Bobbie cradled her grandmother's head and listened to the rasp of her breathing.

"What's going on out there?" Jimmy shouted from the driver's seat. "Let's go, let's go!"

"Let me." Hicks lifted Granny gently from Bobbie's lap. Granny groaned as Hicks stood up, and her body settled into his arms, her bones pulling against loosening tendons and muscles.

Joy sobbed and trembled.

Bobbie used her good arm to pull Joy along to the van, her own body quivering. The fire from the stairwell had spread and flames were steadily advancing across the rooftop and billowing black, acrid smoke filled the air.

"Come on, Joy. Time to go."

"Go, Jimmy!" Bobbie shouted as Joy helped her clamber up and close the side door.

Granny yelped as Hicks laid her on the bed.

The van took off. Bobbie's stomach rose in her throat as the van shot into the air, gaining speed.

Hicks staggered to the back of the van and hammered the shower-room door.

"Davitt, get out here now!" Hicks roared. He found a case and rummaged through the medical supplies.

Bobbie and Joy kneeled, one on each side of the bed, and held Granny's hands. Her forehead glistened with sweat and a crack in the skin at the corner of her mouth beaded up with blood.

"My girls," Granny whispered. "I'm so proud of you, but it's time for me to go."

"No," Bobbie cried. "I can't lose you now. Hold on, please."

"Death is not a failure, my darling." Granny's eyes softened in a smile. "Dying is natural. What's not natural is my being young again." Granny tried to laugh. Her eyes closed slowly. She panted as if she'd been running, and now had to catch her breath.

Bobbie looked up at Hicks. He shook his head. His gray eyes glittered.

Jimmy arrived at the foot of the bed. "We're out of range, and I've turned on self-drive along with all the masking programs. They can't follow us. I'm heading north northwest."

"That's perfect, Jimmy. Thank you," Joy murmured without taking her eyes off Granny.

Jimmy followed her gaze. "Oh, my God—what happened?"

"We aren't sure," Bobbie answered. "But, she's back." Emotion welled and Bobbie could say no more.

"Davitt, now!" Hicks yelled, making Bobbie jump, and sending shards of agony through her arm.

"He might be able to help." Hicks put his shoulder to the door and pushed hard. The bathroom door splintered at the latch and gave inwards. Hicks corrected his balance and shot a hand into the tiny bathroom, pulling Davitt out by the hair.

"Okay, okay!" Davitt wriggled out of Hicks's hands and stood dripping wet. His eyes popped open as he took in Granny lying on the bed. "Oh, shit! What did you do?" He gazed around them in disbelief. "How did you reverse the nanobots?"

"I didn't mean to." Bobby sobbed. Tears blurred her vision. She tried to compose herself, but her chin wobbled as she blurted out, "I used the Taser."

"Oh, shit! The electric charge has fried the nanobots," Davitt said. "They can't support her cells."

"I thought the setting was on low," Bobbie cried.

"It was on low," Joy said. "Or I'd have felt the shock, and I didn't. Granny's hands were... You... You saved my life."

"You did the right thing," Granny muttered. "You girls need to stick together. Be strong for each other."

Bobbie had Granny back once more.

During rejuvenation, Bobbie had seen Granny surrender who she was and live without faith or compassion. For Granny, that was a fate worse than death. Granny's blue eyes, the windows to her soul, locked onto Bobbie's, and shone like the sun on the ocean. Granny had lived a good life, full of meaning and love—until rejuvenation. Now Bobbie understood why Granny had always said death was the next stage in the journey, a step Granny said she would embrace when the right time came. Bobbie had fought death all her life through Gracie, her Dad, her career—and lost every time. Painful and wearying as losing was, death was not the worst thing life had to offer.

The knots in Bobbie's chest loosened. Yes, there were worse things than dying. Granny would prefer to die than live as Gloria, a counterfeit, soulless, imposter.

Bobbie gathered up her inner strength, determined to make this moment count. She had to let Granny go. Granny had been right about life and death all along. *That was the tragedy of life*, Bobbie thought, *we age from the moment we are born*. Death might be the enemy, but Bobbie could now accept mortality as a noble and natural foe.

"We will be strong for each other," Bobbie said to Granny, echoing her mother's last words. She looked across the bed at Joy. "Together, we can get through anything. Isn't that so, little sister?"

"Yes," Joy said, as a tear rolled down her face.

Granny coughed, deep and rumbling. She dragged in air, gurgling then exhaled in a rattle.

"It's okay to let go, Granny," Bobbie said. "I love you."

Tears flooded from Bobbie's eyes as Granny's drifted closed—once brilliant blue eyes that would never again light up upon greeting her, sparkle in humor, smile in kindness, nor ever cry again.

Air hissed from Granny's parted lips.

Then nothing.
Bobbie felt for a pulse.
Granny was gone.

CHAPTER 26

Grief rose within Bobbie, so potent it threatened to suffocate her. Frozen by anger, loss, and fatigue, Bobbie could have sat in that void forever, lost to life. What mattered anymore? How would she live in an exiled commune of Joy's in California, doing her best to tend to patients without the proper equipment and access to medicine?

At the foot of the bed, Jimmy lowered himself to his knees like an old, rusty machine. He sniffed loudly, crossed himself, and bowed his head.

This whole exercise had been a cataclysmic failure. Bobbie wasn't surprised by that. She was a geriatrician, damn it! She'd never experienced the world's evil underbelly up-close. For Bobbie, the Melters War had happened somewhere else, other countries destroyed, other cities drowned. Her grandfather and father sacrificed, yet Bobbie had always been safe. She'd even escaped the disease that had stolen her twin sister.

What had Bobbie been thinking, trying to rescue Granny? Her luck had run out, and she'd accomplished nothing at all.

Davitt lurched to the chair behind the driver's seat, wriggling his tied wrists, exhaling disgruntled sounds. He disgusted Bobbie—Rejuvenation, Granny's death, their exile—all because of him.

At least they had some vials of the virus. Perhaps they could stop or perhaps slow down the spread of this horror. Would they have the facilities to develop the vaccine? Could they figure out a way to eradicate it? Was that even the right thing to do? Some people wanted to be young again, no matter the cost. Did Bobbie care enough right now? Fatigue drained her. She hurt in too many places and in too many ways.

On the other side of Granny's body, Joy sobbed and rolled forward, so her forehead touched her grandmother's. Joy's youthful skin made Granny's look like melted candle wax. Joy's life stretched out in front of Bobbie. She didn't want her sister to live like a fugitive, forever running, hiding, always in danger. Joy deserved to be loved, that's all she'd ever asked of Bobbie. But from the moment Bobbie had seen Joy, squawking and squirming in their mother's arms, Bobbie had held Joy at arm's length in a vain effort to protect herself from loss. After the sorrow of Gracie's death, Bobbie thought she'd been smart to keep her heart tucked away from anyone and anything that might hurt her. Joy was Gracie's sister, too, and Gracie would have loved this crazy kid who was so much like her. Now Bobbie would give Joy all her love and...

Hicks...

Bobbie loved Hicks. With everything she had, she loved him. He and Joy were the two people Bobbie had left in the world, the two she loved most. Their happiness was the most important thing in her life. Hicks was in love with Joy, Bobbie was sure of that. Why else would he be willing to give up his life and go on the run with her? Bobbie could get over her envy. And who better than for the sister she loved?

As if reading Bobbie's mind, Hicks put his hand on Joy's shoulder. Joy patted it, sniffing loudly, as she tilted her head back to look up at Hicks. Bruising on Joy's neck was developing like a chain of sadistic hickeys.

"You okay?" Hicks asked.

Joy nodded, returning her gaze to Granny.

"Bobbie, I need to take a look at your wound." Hicks carried the first aid kit around to Bobbie's side of the bed and set it down. The ridiculous context of the first aid kit beside her dead Grandmother sent a tremor of hysteria through Bobbie. She clamped down on the sob or giggle, Bobbie wasn't sure which, but if she let go now, she'd never stop whatever erupted.

A shake of her head, a bleary glaze settled over her movements. Bobbie wobbled. Hicks pulled her to his shoulder. She rested there, the heat from his body warmed her, comforted her. Hicks familiar scent heightened with the tang of his sweat, sharp now, yet not unpleasant brought flashes of days spent studying on the rooftop of the Buckets, overlooking the Irish Sea, gray and restless.

"I'm giving you some pain killers, okay?" Hicks said.

Bobbie murmured, "Okay," but didn't care. She stared out through the window. Seagulls swooped between the clouds and the water. Bobbie floated with their flight. "This will put you to sleep. I need to stitch you up." Hicks's breath tickled her ear.

"Okay..." Bobbie drifted off in muted tones of gray, with the gulls, dipping and soaring, as a vast silence settled.

* * *

Pain peeled away the edges of Bobbie's slumber. Her arm throbbed beneath a bandage. Stiff-backed, she longed to turn over on her side and curl up, but the reclined chair she lay on didn't flatten out enough. Her neck ached. While she'd slept, her head had flopped to the right. Bobbie opened her eyes. Night made the black windows reflect the lights from the controls. Lying still, her vision adjusted to the van's dim lavender glow.

A chorus of regular breathing told Bobbie everyone was sleeping. Jimmy lay in the chair next to her, eyes closed, snoring. Joy's hair hung over the driver's seat in front of him, her head back, resting against the chair. Beside Joy and in front of Bobbie, Hicks lay on the front passenger seat, his legs stretched out, his feet nearly touching Joy's.

Muscles down the left side of Bobbie's neck sang out as she twisted to face forward. Hicks's head bobbed and lolled in a battle between sleep and consciousness. He was too tall for these chairs. Why didn't he lie on the bed?

Anguish bloomed violently in Bobbie's chest as she remembered that Granny lay dead on the bed.

Where was Davitt?

Bobbie sat up in a panic. She felt a stab from her wound.

Davitt lay in a loose fetal position, fast asleep on the floor behind her, his hands tied together and attached to the leg of Jimmy's seat. It took all Bobbie's restraint to not kick him in the groin.

On the bed, a sheet covered Granny's body, the folds and ridges outlining all that was left of her now.

Bobbie looked out the window. A pink blush seeped into the eastern sky. They should be heading south by now, over the Pacific Ocean.

A rustle from Joy's chair pulled Bobbie's attention back into the van.

Joy flung her arms above her head, stretching all the way down to her toes, emitting a creaking groan that triggered a shuffle in the other sleepers.

Joy looked over her shoulder, a soft smile warming her features, "Hey big sis, feeling any better?"

"Yeah, thanks. Hicks did a great job patching me up," Bobbie said.

In front of her, Hicks rubbed his face with both hands, snuffling and exhaling.

"Any idea how much longer before we arrive?" Bobbie asked.

"Just a sec." Joy bent forward, studying the screen on the panel in front of her.

"God, you're a noisy lot!" Jimmy protested, sucking in on his lips as he rejoined them from the Land of Nod. "An oul fella like me needs his rest, you know."

"I thought you oldies only slept three hours a night," Joy quipped. "We'll be reaching San Francisco Bay soon, where we'll stop to let the engines cool down, then on to Yosemite. We sedated Davitt while you were sleeping, Bobbie, but he'll probably come around soon. Just a precaution—we don't want him to know where we're going." Joy swung around to face Bobbie. "I have to warn you, the last hour of the journey gets really warm in here."

"We'll manage," Jimmy said.

Joy turned to face him. Her smile skidded into a grimace as she jumped back. "Oh, Sweet Jesus!"

"Nope, just Jimmy," Jimmy said, raising his hands in a shrug of innocence before adjusting his chair to the upright position.

"What is it?" Bobbie asked, panic sour in her mouth.

"Seriously… you…" Joy started to say. She stopped and pointed at Jimmy.

"What?" Jimmy said, concerned. "What is it?"

He turned his head and looked straight at Bobbie, his gray eyebrows pulled together above a pair of orange irises.

Bobbie felt as if she'd been punched in the chest. She tried to speak but couldn't. Black spots floated like malignant snowflakes in her vision. Bobbie pulled in a lungful of air to fight the threat of passing out.

Hicks took the old man's hand, touched his fingers to the pale wrist, and said in a calm voice, "Jimmy, the virus has delivered the nanobots to your system. Do you feel any different?"

"What?" Jimmy pulled his arm away and flattened himself against this chair. His face quivered. Bobbie's heart flew to this old gentleman who had helped her and risked so much for them. Jimmy swung his chair around and peered at the darkened windows, but the faint reflection wasn't clear enough to show him the changes to his face and eyes.

"Show me!" he demanded.

Joy stared into his face for a couple of seconds as she linked her ONIV to the van's systems. Jimmy's face appeared on the dash screen. He crumpled over the image, covering his face and muttering, "No, no, no!"

"Try to stay calm." Hicks rose from his seat and stood by Jimmy resting a hand on the bony shoulder. He reached again for Jimmy's wrist with his other hand.

Bobbie, too weak to move, spoke from her seat, "He's right, Jimmy. We need to keep your heart rate steady. Joy, wake Davitt. Slap him if you have too, the harder the better."

"With pleasure." Joy jumped up.

Bobbie's mind raced through the various possibilities. Aayushi's heart had seized when she'd been exposed to the nanobots. But then Granny's had not. Perhaps Jimmy had contracted the same version as Granny. Bobbie hoped Davitt would have some answers for them.

"We'll take care of you, Jimmy." Bobbie tried to sound reassuring. "What facilities will we have where we're going, Joy?" Bobbie asked, seeking solace in turning her mind to work and away from the grief of losing Granny that threatened to overcome her.

"There is a hospital," Joy said. "But it's primitive. We can order more supplies from the next raid." Joy stopped and looked at her hands in her lap. "Well, *raid* is a strong word. Some of us go back to the Belus Corp world and procure items that we can't make or grow. But it's tricky, especially if the items are specialized or expensive." She stopped and looked up at Bobbie and Hicks, then over at Jimmy. "That's not the problem."

"I'm the problem," Jimmy muttered.

"We're all the problem," Bobbie corrected. "We've all been exposed to the virus. We need someplace to quarantine before we go on to the colony, or we could infect more people..."

"What the–" Davitt croaked as he struggled with his bound wrists.

"Get up, shithead," Joy nudged him with her foot. "Jimmy's got the nanobots."

"No way! It worked." Davitt stopped fighting his restraints and looked up at Joy, his eyes wide, the expression on his face approaching wonder. He looked pleased. "They didn't think I could do it!"

Bobbie pushed down an urge to stomp on his face. "They? Who?"

"Look, I don't know. I got my instructions from an anonymous source," Davitt said and lay still.

"Slade? What did she have to do with it?" Bobbie asked.

"Look, I don't know, alright? I just did the science."

"Well, you'll have to do better than that now, fucker," Joy said. "Jimmy's our friend, and you better fix this."

"The only thing that destroys the nanobots is an electric shock," Davitt mumbled then shot a dark look at Bobbie. "But you already know that."

His dig hit home. Bobbie was frozen between self-loathing and hatred for Davitt.

Jimmy stood up. "Behave yourself, Davitt. I might just be turning into a psychopath, and if I do, you'll be my first victim. That's a promise."

"Really, I don't know how to stop the nanobots." Davitt scuttled back from Jimmy.

"We could zap you now with the Taser if you like," Hicks said. "Before the nanobots take hold or change the DNA too much."

Jimmy jumped back from them. "No, we don't know how that will go. It could blow the biosensor in my brain!"

Everyone looked at Bobbie.

"He's right. I'm not sure if the settings on the Taser are accurate," she said, thinking of how Detective Cross had died. She did not want to chance it with Jimmy.

"Could you remove the biosensor?" Jimmy's bushy white eyebrows raised.

"That would require brain surgery, Jimmy, and neither of us have that expertise," Hicks said.

Jimmy's face fell. His eyes watered.

Silence fell on the group. Bobbie could hear the hum of the engines and the swoosh of the wind against the outside of the van. No-one made eye contact.

"I know you're all 'fraid I'm going to go ape shit like Gloria did. And I might do," Jimmy said, pulling Bobbie from the quagmire of her thoughts. His Adam's apple bobbed as he swallowed. "But," he continued, "first sign of me going crazy, you have my permission now and as a sane man, or as sane as I can be..." He snorted a damp laugh. "... to... to send me for Elective Passing... basically."

No one made eye contact.

"Look, I'll get younger right?" Jimmy directed his question to Davitt.

Davitt nodded slack jawed.

"You've tweaked the program since the first round?" Jimmy asked.

"Yes, but we haven't tested it yet." Davitt struggled into a sitting position as far as his bonds would allow. "The virus has an incubation period of up to a week. After that, we won't be contagious. But you will have the nanobots."

"I'll be the test," Jimmy said. "Soon as my wits go AWOL, you can zap me with the Taser. Agreed?"

Bobbie shook her head.

Joy chewed her lips and stared at the floor.

"Agreed," Hicks said. He shook Jimmy's hand.

"Good. Glad that's sorted. Now, let's sedate this shit again." Jimmy nodded back at Davitt on the floor. "So, we don't have to listen to him. We can grill him when we get to where we are going."

"Wait, wait!" Davit pleaded, but without a word, Hicks administered another jet and Davitt slumped to the floor.

"Now, Joy," said Jimmy, "where the hell are we, and where are we going next?"

Joy raised her head, her dark eyes glittering. She leaned over the control panel. "We're nearly at the mouth of San Francisco Bay," Joy said. "We'll stay over the water of the bay southeast until we reach San Jose, before we cut straight across through to the Sierra Nevada's." Joy stood up straight and looked at all of them. "It's going to get very hot, unbearably hot before it gets cooler because we have to cross a section of Scorch Zone land. If the van stops at all in the Central Valley, we'll fry. There's a peak coming up, Mount Hamilton, where we'll stop and let the van's engines cool before the last leg."

"Can we quarantine there?" Bobbie asked.

"No, Belus Corp patrols the coast checking the heat levels of the Central Valley from here. The next patrol is due in two days." She absently kicked the unconscious Davitt with the toe of her shoe. "Shithead here reckons we are contagious for seven days so Mount Hamilton is out."

Joy flung a glance toward Jimmy then said in a lower tone, "Why do you think Jimmy got infected and not us? You were the closest to the virus, but you seem okay."

That was something Bobbie had been wondering herself and thought that maybe she had come up with an answer. "Elderly people don't have as robust an immune system. I'm hoping our immune systems will have fought off the virus so it can't release the nanobots into our system." Bobbie didn't add that she hoped it would provide them with a starting point for developing a vaccine too. No point in raising what may be a false hope.

"So, if this'd been a Corona Virus like COVID-32 or the common cold, chances are Jimmy would be the only one sneezing?" Joy said.

"Something like that. But we still need to quarantine all of us. Just in case. At least until I get some kind of blood test set up to detect the virus, and flag up the nanobots, now we know what we are looking for." Bobbie looked out through the window.

The first rays of the rising sun stretched across the ocean, painting the tips of the waves with gold. A pod of dolphins burst out of the sea fifty feet below Bobbie's side window, their joyful leaps lifting Bobbie's spirits for a brief moment. The dolphins plunged beneath the glassy blue surface, shiny gray sickles carving through the water in unison. As they disappeared from view, Bobbie cast her eyes out the window on the far side of the vehicle, hoping to catch sight of them as they surfaced again.

Joy leaned forward to look out the window, blocking Bobbie's view. The automatic guidance system kept the van traveling at a steady speed along its southbound course off the west coast of what used to be California, leaving the dolphins behind.

Joy shifted back from the window and turned to face Bobbie.

"Did you see them?" Joy asked, reaching for her sister's hand.

The tender gesture disarmed Bobbie, and her answer caught in her throat. Bobbie nodded. In a world consumed by rising oceans, dolphins were a symbol of hope, and right now, she needed all the hope she could muster.

"I know of a place near Yosemite where we can quarantine. I think I can get us there okay," Joy said.

"You think?" Bobbie didn't enjoy the flutter in her stomach.

"It's fine. Sorry, poor choice of words. I can get us there." Joy's gaze wandered over Bobbie's shoulder to the bed. "We could bury Granny at sea. Before we head inland."

"No," Hicks said quietly. "We need to do an autopsy. Find out exactly what effect the Taser shock had. Especially now..." He nodded toward Jimmy.

The old man waved a dismissive hand at him and nodded his agreement. Bobbie looked away from the still form lying shrouded on the bed and murmured her consent.

Bobbie felt the van tilt before settling back onto level flight. They had changed course and were now heading due east. Bright morning light flooded the vehicle and silhouetted a series of high peaks ahead of them. Before them, the mouth of the bay gaped open, punctuated by the twisted metal fragments of what remained of the Golden Gate Bridge like a rusted retainer in a forgotten mouth.

"Mount Hamilton is coming up. We'll be landing shortly," Joy said.

"Wouldn't it be better to wait for nightfall to cross if the heat inland is that bad?" Jimmy asked.

"No, we need to be able to see the dust devils," Joy answered. "They won't show up on the nav-sys in time to let the self-drive avoid them. I need to drive the next section. Early morning is the best and we are already eating into the clock, but we need to stop to cool the engines."

Joy circled Mount Hamilton once, allowing Bobbie to get a good view of their landing sight. Ruined buildings no more than piles of blackened bricks, charred beams, and mangled metal lay scattered over the summit.

"That used to be Lick Observatory before the Melters blast to the valley incinerated most of it," Joy said.

One little patch of land was clear enough for them to land. The doors of the van opened, and dry air pushed in. Bobbie stepped down onto the crumbling hardtop that, by the evenly spaced out faded painted lines, she guessed had once been a parking area. Hicks helped Jimmy down. Already Bobbie could discern more fluidity in the old man's movements, or did she? If Jimmy didn't have the telltale orange eyes, would they know he was infected?

Immediately, Bobbie missed the smell of the sea, the dry air parching her nostrils, devoid of scent. They stood on bare, rocky peaks that flowed into rounded sandy hills. To the west, the hills hugged a vast inlet of water. To the east, they rolled off into dunes that rippled away into the distance like waves on a sea of sand. The horizon to the west was obscured by a band of fog and to the east by a beige haze that blended into pale blue.

"How can it stay so dry with all that fog out there?" Bobbie asked.

Joy shrugged. "The weather patterns are weird here. The heat from the land keeps the fog in place, I guess. It's so dry in the central valley that the dust never settles. You can't walk there. If you could bear the heat—which is unlikely, your lungs would fill with dust and you would choke to death."

"And we have to cross that," Bobbie said softly.

"I can do it." Joy nodded, staring off to the east. "Not least, because I have you with me."

"Both of us together," Bobbie said as fresh tears gathered. "That's what Mum was trying to tell me before she died. Together, Joy and you, together, you can do anything."

"And she's right." Joy pulled Bobbie into an embrace that stung her injured arm but comforted her aching heart.

"Yes, together we'll find a vaccine for the virus and stop Slade, and whoever is behind her," Bobbie said, believing her words because she had no other choice. She needed a purpose to carry on.

Together Bobbie and Joy, along with Hicks and Jimmy, would start a new life in Yosemite. They would figure out a way to cure Jimmy and defeat Rejuvenation.

As long as they had each other, they had hope.

THE END

ABOUT THE AUTHOR

BYDDI LEE, A NATIVE OF ARMAGH, County Armagh, Northern Ireland, wrote Rejuvenation, a speculative fiction trilogy, after having published flash fiction, short stories and her novel, *March To November*.

Byddi co-founded and manages Flash Fiction Armagh which was shortlisted as Best Regular Spoken Word Night in the Saboteur Awards[1]. She co-edits *The Bramley – An Anthology of Flash Fiction Armagh* with two other members of the Armagh Theatre Group. Byddi wrote *IMPACT – Armagh's Train Disaster* which was staged for the anniversary of the tragedy in June 2019 in the Abbey Lane Theatre in Armagh.

In October 2019, Byddi received an Arts Council for Northern Ireland (ACNI) grant for her writing.

---

1 Sabotage Reviews provides dynamic commentary and reviews with focus on independent, small-budget literature; poetry pamphlets, short stories and live performance.

WORKS BY THE AUTHOR

NOVELS

THE REJUVENATION TRILOGY
Rejuvenation, book 1
Rejuvenation, book 2
Rejuvenation, book 3

March To November

PLAYS
IMPACT – Armagh's Train Disaster

Printed in Great Britain
by Amazon

78584716R00144